also by Ron Hutchinson

Rat in the Skull – a stage play

Ron Hutchinson

CONNIE

Methuen . London

A Methuen Paperback

First published in Great Britain in 1985
as a Methuen Paperback original
by Methuen London Ltd
11 New Fetter Lane, London EC4P 4EE

Reprinted 1985

Printed in Great Britain by
Hazell Watson & Viney Limited,
Member of the BPCC Group,
Aylesbury, Bucks

British Library Cataloguing in Publication Data
Hutchinson, Ron
Connie.
I. Title
823'.914[F] PR6058.U8/
ISBN 0-413-58170-5

This publication is based on
the television serial Connie
produced by
Central Independent Television plc.

One

– Connie's back.

Bea was the first to be told. Which was only right, because Bea was the Queen Bee of the House of Bea. Which was what the business was known as by those who found 'Hector Bea and Madam Bea, Fashion Knitwear, Baby Bea Infant's and Children's Wear' too much of a mouthful.

And the person who told her was Hector. Which was only right, too, because he was the 'Hector' in 'Hector Bea'. And presently her fifth husband. Or was it the fourth? It would be too much to say that sometimes even The Founder had to think twice about what number she was now on. But even some of the girls who had been with her for years had to check on their fingers, when asked.

Hector was certain that Connie was back. Impossible as it had to be. There was no mistaking the woman, and particularly no mistaking That Look. The Connie That Look. Even though he'd only seen her from two hundred yards. With them both in motion. He on the Travelator headed towards European Departures, she on the Travelator headed towards ditto Arrivals.

Bea didn't believe it.

– She can't be back. And what the hell are you doing phoning from the airport? You flew out to Paris last night. You phoned me from there.

Hector realised, with a sudden flush and a disturbance in his stomach, that he'd boobed. Understandable, considering the amount of bourbon still circulating around his insides. Understandable, considering the presence on his arm of the girl he'd drunk it with. In the bar, then in the lift, then under the shower, and finally in bed. Understandable. But, after six years with Bea, he should still have known better than to phone unless he was completely on the ball.

– I phoned last night pretending I'd already got to Paris. Even as he said it, he winced at how weak it sounded. – Charles de Gaulle was fogbound. Plane turned back. Didn't want you to worry.

Bea's reply was mercifully drowned by an arriving wide-body reversing thrust. And when he asked her to repeat it, somebody started breaking up concrete at her end.

– Forget it. For now. We can sort that out when you get back. With a full order book.

He decided to duck a reply.

– What's the racket? It sounds like somebody breaking up the floor of the factory.

– It is somebody breaking up the floor of the factory. Remember the knitting frame we haven't kept up the payments on? That you said don't worry about, because they'd never bother to dig it out of the concrete you set it in? Guess what? They're digging it out of the concrete.

Hector winced again. This more than ever seemed a bad time to break the news that Connie was headed homewards. But he was sure.

– We had a deal. She's in Greece, permanently retired from business. The fashion business, or any other business. Now sober up, get some selling done, and think of the pack of lies you're going to tell me about last night.

– It was her. It was That Look.

Bea waited for another burst of drilling on the floor below to finish.

– We had a deal. And you had too much to drink last night. Get on that silver bird, and find a way to save this firm.

Hector gave up. He'd done his best to pass on the warning. What Bea did with it was up to her. He rang off, swinging all his attention back to the girl who'd come to see him off. Whose name, in the light of day, he couldn't quite be sure of. But not before a post-script from Bea. That could only have come from Bea. And to him.

– Despite it all, I'm just as crazy about you, you sexual hooligan, you.

As Hector said his farewells to the girl he'd never see again—could it be Marylin, could it be Marcella?—Dev, on the ninth floor of the School of Textiles and Fashion building, was saying his hellos. To a girl called Janet. In very Dev style. With the door locked, the Venetian blinds shut. The rest of the building cleared for the canteen coffee break.

– Theory of Fashion, Worksheet Twelve, the Sexual Challenge.

Janet touched her lower lip with her tongue, and watched her tutor circle her. Hardly once did he need to refer to the stapled papers in his hands.

– The history of fashion shows that in most societies previous to our own, women have been forced to dress down, to reduce the provocative in the sweet disorder of their dress. Traditionally and rightly the woman has been seen as lacking moral fibre and sexual discipline—be she the well-rounded wife at her sensual peak in her mid to late thirties, or the wicked young slip of a thing in her first awkward but passionate encounters.

He did have a way with words. You had to give him that.

– Clothing as mere covering, used not only to lower the appetite of the male, but the female wearer, too. So that the kiss of silk on thigh, say –

And that way of looking at a girl.

– The voluptuous tumble of lace at a budding breast, say –

And that creamy, lightest of milk chocolate skins did something more.

As Dev paused, within touching distance, two things happened. The girl moved her hand from her throat to her navel, brushing every pink-pearl button of her blouse free, and the phone rang.

Leaving Dev with an interesting choice.

Much as he'd like to see what else the girl could do, his two half days a week at the faculty weren't secure. In fact, he was hanging on to them by the skin of his almost too-white teeth. Ignoring administrative details like answering his phone when it rang could cause problems.

– Damn.

One consolation, as he went for the phone, was that when she pouted, Janet pouted prettily. What wasn't so welcome was seeing that she could do up that lacey blouse again, as quickly as she had tugged it open.

– Connie's back?

He didn't believe it, either. Even though he was getting the news from her step-mother, who should have known.

– What are you after, Bea? He tried to stay the girl's fingers on the blouse, but got a back-hander, and a bigger pout for his pains. – I know you. I know that under that carefully nurtured image of yourself as a crafty old cow whose motto is 'If I can do any harm to anyone as I pass by I shall do it now, for I may not pass this way again' is a crafty old cow whose motto is exactly that.

She couldn't be back. Hadn't the family made a deal?

– Hector says she's back, and she's got That Look on her face.

Dev considered making a few quick points as to the reliability of Hector's testimony to anything, then thought better of it. Instead, he asked why Bea had chosen to wreck his day with the news?

– You were close. After she and Arnie broke up, it was you and her.

– But that was eight years ago. She's been in Greece since then, without a postcard.

He convinced her, in the finish, that he'd nothing to do with it. Almost convinced her that Hector could have made a mistake. That his own daughter could have changed so much in eight years beach-combing that he'd not have recognised her if she'd pushed up against him in the flight lounge. Let alone been travelating in the opposite direction entirely.

Dev's quick tongue, and almost as fast thinking made Bea see sense. Once, that Connie wasn't back. Twice, that if she was, the very last person who would have had anything to do with her return was him. Rather than face Connie again, he'd choose to be rubbed over lightly with a hungry tiger, would Dev.

By the time he hung up, the ninth floor was filling with a clatter of students again, and Janet was gone. Only the shut blind and the faintest remembrance of her cheap, but not unpleasant scent was left. Near miss. He owed Bea one, for wrecking it with Janet. And Connie yet another one, if it really could be her.

Near miss. If not yet the whole day, then the morning coffee break ruined.

Whose day could he now ruin with that same news, he pondered, as he slipped the catch off the door lock. Like one of the sexually transmitted diseases, this news was something you hardly wanted to keep to yourself.

David Jamieson, in line for the European Number Two slot for Siggins Bowser and Comer, could have confirmed that Connie was back. Save for the fact that he didn't know it was her who had hijacked his car and driver at the Arrivals Gate. All he knew, as he pounded down the concrete deck of the airport multi-storey, was that the car one hundred yards ahead had been sent for him. And that the driver, busily making interesting conversation with the blonde, was making it with the wrong passenger.

Undignified as it was for a Siggins Bowser and Comer euro-exec to chase after limos, this SBC euro-exec was quite prepared to throw his briefcase after it as well, if that was how to make it stop. You didn't get to have a shot at the European Number Two slot without drive and initiative. As well as the ability to cope with the unexpected that hit you as soon as you'd stepped off the Zurich shuttle.

– We're being followed.

Despite all his passenger's efforts at distraction, the driver of the limo's reflexive check in the rear-view mirror as he came up to the barrier arm clocked Jamieson.

– Madman. Airports are full of them. Put your foot down, Connie commanded. But without much conviction. It had been a little too easy. The quick scan of the drivers at the Arrivals Gate, holding up their name boards. Holding her breath as she approached the one whose eyes lingered longest on her skimpy cotton dress, and what was outlined behind it. Confidently slapping her one leather flight-bag at him and striding with long sun-tanned legs towards the car park exit.

Too easy. Too much like clockwork. And anything in Connie's life to now that had gone like that sooner or later had bits fly off it.

– My car, I think. Jamieson, once he saw it was indeed a woman in the rear seat of the stopped car, kept it dignified. Almost gentlemanly. – There's been a mistake, driver.

– There's been no mistake, driver. Connie sighed, slumping in the leather squab. It had been a long night and morning. And she had so very nearly got away with the car. – It's his car. I grabbed it.

She caught Jamieson's look as he sucked the breath back into his lungs after his successful chase. A sudden defiance that had a lot to do with being at the very finish of her reserves of fight made her punch at him.

– Well what would you do if you got back home with only ten drachmas in your pocket?

– I'd phone a friend. Jamieson came back, surprised into a response.

– I've been away eight years. The address book would be out of date, even if I'd kept it.

– I'd phone family. He punched again, despite his own better instincts.

– Admitting I'd only got ten drachmas?

– The Social Security?

– Do I look as if I would?

SBC's hot tip for the European Number Two slot decided to call off the fight at this point. They were being looked at, and the matter was simple. This was his car and driver, and he wanted it. He wouldn't make a fuss with the airport police, or anybody else. He'd take his car, and leave her.

– I'm going to have to ask you to remove your things from my car.

– He's going to have to ask me to remove my things from his car. Echoed Connie, keeping a straight face for the driver, as she reached in for her bag. Pompous prick, she thought. Very British. Two things she'd have to get used to, now she was back. Prickishness and Britishness. How often the two went together.

– Your hand –

He'd reached forward to help her with the bag, and stopped at the sight of her bruised knuckles.

– All right, so I'm back with ten drachmas, and a damaged hand. She went on the offensive again. – I suppose you want to know all about how I got it? You think you've got a right to True Confessions just because I stole your rotten car? And something else. You want to turn that jacket in for one with two vents. One vent makes your bum stick out.

That was no way to get a lift to town.

She knew that even as she blew it. But she didn't care. Not any more. She was tired. Tireder than she had ever been in her life. And straight off the plane, with ten drachmas to her name, she had to cope with prickish Britishness, or British prickishness, whichever the smoothie in the expensive suit was handing out to her.

No way to get a lift to town.

But she got it.

– I'm not sure why I'm doing this. Jamieson didn't look up from the papers he'd taken out of his calf-hide briefcase, as the car slid into the mid-morning traffic.

He'd no way of knowing that he'd just made a decision that would change his life. Even if he had, he'd have denied making a decision at all. The blonde in the car, half wearing and half not wearing an unseasonably summery dress, had handed him a challenge, and he'd called her bluff. She'd dared him to take the risk of giving her a lift to town, knowing that someone in a pinstripe with one vent wouldn't have the courage. And he'd showed he had.

But that wasn't a decision.

That was counter-punching.

She didn't answer. And it wasn't really a question that needed one. It was more an invitation to talk. To explain what she was doing at the airport on a drizzly English midland morning in a dress almost thin enough to see through. But the woman on the back seat with him didn't pick up the offer. She was giving nothing back for the favour of the ride.

He turned back to his papers, preparing himself for the presentation he was due to make in Nuneaton that afternoon, ignoring her as best he could. That little dress, and the sun-tanned legs drawn up beside his to avoid the transmission hump in the car, made ignoring her difficult.

And Connie . . .? Her thoughts as the car ground through the obstacle course of traffic lights and road jams? Each gear-change taking her further away from the airport, and where and who she'd been for the past eight years?

Connie was thinking of colour. She'd always been strong on colour. But she'd forgotten how grey and brick-red England was. Brick-red and brick-grey and brick-yellow. They were mucking up the Med, God knew—but breathing here was going to be like sucking Sunday gravy with the lumps in, into your lungs. Could she work here, let alone start making money again, real money, like she'd had before she left—here, so near the North Pole, in a country whose annual rainfall must equal that of Tierra del Fuego?

She was scared.

She sat beside the man she'd already labelled The Cashmere Kid, from his expensive, but conservatively-cut suit, and thought of colour, and was scared. And would have put her tired head on his cashmere shoulder, and told him everything, and asked him what to do. Because weren't you supposed to find a fella every time you were scared and didn't know what to do? And your hand hurt? And you only had ten useless drachmas in all the world? And the fella would tell you what to do to put it right.

But she was Connie. And she was on her own.

And for better or more likely worse, she was back.

– She can't be.

Nesta, her step-sister, chosen to have her day ruined by Dev, had been half way through a job interview when the news came.

Basically, she'd been looking for a creep. He'd have a fancy title and expensive exec motor to go with his expense account, but at the end of the day he'd be Nesta's nark. Employed to keep a beady on her shops. The ones that had previously belonged to Connie.

Nesta enjoyed job interviews. Now that she was on the dishing-it-out side of the antique leather-topped desk in the office-cum-flat she worked from, back of her city centre flagship shop. She'd been enjoying this one more than most, before the phone call from Dev slipped past the switchboard. Who had been told to hold all incoming calls, because when The Boss did an interview, she did it from soup to nuts.

– Before you get through the shop door you'd check the display, and give them hell if so much as one light bulb was missing from it. Inside you'd check the back of the rails and fittings, as well as looking for the obvious.

The job prospect pursed his lips and crossed his legs, the better to express concentration and approbation.

– You'd keep a straight face and your hand on your halfpenny if the Manageress started making eyes at you when you asked for the books. You'd phone me every night to report in, even if it took you to past midnight to get clear. And you'd still be on the road at half six the next morning, to bring fear and despondency into the lives of those in the next shop on your list.

The prospect nodded again. He'd spent fifteen years in cosmetics repping before deciding to make the sideways move into fashion retailing. He knew every trick and villainy that staff got up to.

– That's the job description. What do you think of it?

He was saved from having to lie. Or state what he felt, which was that Nesta had outlined less a job description than standing orders for a punishment battalion. The phone rang.

Dev's call had interrupted Nesta's flow, just as she was starting to get into her stride. She'd already decided against the prospect, but there was nothing in her Fashion Trades Weekly desk diary for the next hour, and why not keep him dangling? He was only a fella after all.

– Well, well, well. Nesta was never one to struggle hard against the honest expression of distaste. – Listen to who's just crawled out of one of the cracks around the toilet bowl of life.

She listened further.

Then bit.

– She can't be back. She's on the beach, being shafted by the wop.

She regretted biting straight away. Biting meant telling the opposition they'd got through to you. They'd read you right, and knew how to fish you. Nesta didn't like that, and chalked one up against Dev. Not a big one. Not one as big as she had down against Connie, say, if she had gone back on the agreement and returned to the UK. But one against him nonetheless.

Dev knew better than to linger making pleasantries after dropping the news. Especially to the fastest tongue in the East. And he'd just caught sight of Janet loitering moodily at the far end of the Design School corridor. Moodily and with intent. That morning he'd only been able to take her through the opening paragraphs on the sexual component in the history of fashion. With a free afternoon ahead of him, wasn't it his duty to lead her to the practical?

– Where were we?

Nesta had slammed the phone back so hard the girl on the switchboard decided to risk further disapproval, and take an early lunch. Inside the office, with its litter of advertising display material, samples, and new lines, the prospect kick-started his brain for the next barrage. Then he thought better of it. Was it really worth the salary she was offering, plus the fiddles? To have this female flame-thrower run his life until she decided to fire him?

– I'd just turned the job down.

She was too quick for him.

– You hadn't been offered it. I said two things to myself the minute you walked through that door. The first was he's not getting the job. What I need is some right old bitch of a rag-trade queen, and you're not that –

– No.

– Which leads me to numero two –

– Being?

– I bet he does a great horizontal samba.

The prospect checked his watch. It seemed pretty final he was now an ex-prospect, and with a full afternoon ahead to kill, until the next train back to London. A pity to waste it. Criminal not to take advantage of expanding his professional contacts, when he was looking for a toe-hold in fashion.

– Odd, that. He looked thoughtful. – There was me thinking the same about you sat there.

Nesta nodded, and the ex-prospect nodded back. Perfect understanding between two old traders in the skin trade.

– I live above the shop. She nodded towards the spiral staircase in the far corner of the room, its treads littered with more advertising gloss and rag. – Like to check if either of us was right?

She got another nod of perfect understanding back, as he got out of the uncomfortable chair she kept specially for interviews.

– There is one thing you can do for me, though.

He paused, expectant. You never know where these afternoon adventures in quiet provincial towns might lead you. Some of the oddest, and most hair-raising of his sexual memoirs would have been penned around chance offers like this.

– After, I want you to borrow a light cement mixer and run my step-sister down with it. And keep reversing until her heels stop kicking.

And though she smiled as she wrapped her knuckle into his black leather trouser belt, he felt it was only half a gag.

Two

Arnie was on the stall when his call came. Working like three men to sell one pair of denims.

– Inside leg thirty-four, was it, Chief? We haven't got a thirty-four in the cord, but then, you don't get the wear, do you? The shrewd buy, the denim. Thirty-two waist? Lucky sod, I don't like to think how long it is since I could get inside a thirty-two waist—especially if the bird was wearing them at the time, eh? Straights, flares, boot-length? Fourteen, sixteen or eighteen inch bottoms? Pre-shrunk, stone-washed or heavy duty?

And so on. The Barrow King going through his routine, half his mind on the sale, the other half worrying about the usual. Juggling money between different accounts, to keep one step ahead of the tax and Vatman. In his head. But that's where most of Arnie's money had been for the past couple of years.

He shouldered his way through the crowded market pub to the phone. He ought to buy drinks on the house for this. A phone call from his ex-wife's step-sister? Rarer than a week when the takings of his stall covered his expenses.

– Congratulations, Arnie.

It was her all right. A little out of breath, as if she'd just taken some horizontal exercise, but that was Nesta for you. What she missed in looks, she made up for in enthusiasm.

– You might have given us all some warning, though. You're still family, in a way.

– Don't understand a word, kimo savvy, Arnie replied, surveying the pub for his girl. – Have you been on the sweet sherry again?

– You're good for a pair of silver plated candlesticks, tell her. But don't bother to ask me to the wedding. I find these re-marrying of divorcees way over the top.

Arnie struggled to catch up.

– What can I say, Nesta, except keep taking the tablets? He really had no idea what she was on about.

– It's a fairy-tale ending to one of the all-time love affairs and bust-ups. For everyone except that piece of jail-bait you've shacked up with. The one you found on the lay-by.

Arnie got the message at the same moment as the piece of jail-bait, Babs, caused a moment's silence in the bar just by walking into it.

– You're saying to me that Connie's back? He tried to smile at Babs, making her way towards him, but his face seemed to be made of rubber.

– Not saying it, Arnie, no. I'm screeching it at the top of my lungs. She's back, and don't tell me you didn't know.

This time it was Nesta who had the phone slam down on her.

– Kyprianou? asked Babs, naming the supplier giving them the most hassle this particular month.

Arnie started to shake his head, then nodded. Why worry her, or risk upsetting the delicate balance of his relationship with the younger girl? Time enough for that when the implications of Connie's return, and the reasons for it, were clear.

For now, he needed four single malt scotches, fast. Malt scotch because he liked it. In four single measures because he liked it so much he'd promised the girl not to drink doubles any more.

– Some things haven't changed in eight years. Like fake French food served by fake French waiters.

Connie surveyed the executive restaurant with a professional eye. She had after all run a taverna for the past eight years. That was what she'd bought with the money Nesta had paid her for what was left of her business. The chain of shops which she'd built up on her own in the good years. The late sixties and early seventies.

Because of complications in Greek property law, it had been her boyfriend Georgiou who was the legal owner. But that was no matter. She'd bought it for him, and willingly. The choice had been between a share in a wind-surfing school, the pedalo concession on the nearest topless beach, or the taverna. Connie had plumped for the taverna, and after initial disagreement, Georgiou swung round. With Connie and his female relatives, down to his grandmother, actually running the business, his work-load consisted of lounging in the front, talking to his cronies. And the topless wind-surfers and pedal-pushers were always there in the evening.

Jamieson applied himself to the menu, as Connie debated the nationalities of the waiters. A little too loudly, for him. In the end she decided none of them were French or Swiss, and the home towns of most of them were either Liverpool or Birmingham.

He felt like repeating what he'd said in the car. That he didn't know exactly what he was doing here, having lunch with her, when he should have been on his way to his presentation. In the same way that he didn't know why he'd given her a lift in the first place.

More counter-punching? He really would have to stop thinking he had an obligation to engage in some sort of contest with his lunch guest.

– What do you do?

Her question to him, once the ordering was out of the way, was matter of fact. A request for information, not a conversational device. He'd never met a woman who less needed the conventional props.

He told her. She didn't seem too impressed that he was an efficiency consultant for one of the most important firms in the field. That he spent most of his life in planes, limousines, or four star hotel suites. That he was spoken of as the next Number Two in the European Division.

– So you don't actually do anything yourself? You just watch other people doing things, and smart-arse them?

He was learning. He didn't bite back straight away with a denial. Yes, that was one way of looking at it. Yes, that could be a way to put it.

What did she do?

– I hijack important people's cars at airports.

– And before that?

– I used to be in fashion. She caught his look at her skimpy dress. – I'm wearing this because I had to leave in a hurry.

– Ill health?

– You could say that.

When she smiled he found himself smiling too. Though he didn't know what at.

– I found my bloke on my taverna table with two topless windsurfers. Count 'em. Not just one. Two. So I tuned them up a little –

He looked down at her hand stiffly holding her knife.

– And ran like hell. They don't have the same attitude to female emancipation out there.

They ate for a moment, the smile shared between them. He didn't know whether to believe her or not, but it could explain the way she was dressed, the ten drachmas, the tiredness she managed to shake off for minutes at a time. When he could see what a vibrant person this could be to have beside you. In the car. Or opposite you. In a restaurant. Or alongside you. In bed.

He snapped his thoughts away from that, and reminded himself about the upcoming presentation. The girl was getting lunch out of him, and nothing else. As if someone who seemed so taken up by herself, and her reactions to coming back, would be asking for anything else.

– Give me a job.

Again she asked directly, without suggesting she had to pay in light conversation for her meal.

– What are you good at?

– I told you. Fashion. Knitwear. I ran my own chain. Then I had it robbed off me by my own step-sister.

– Like in all the best fairy stories.

– You could say.

They ate on.

– I'm not sure if I could fit you in. He tried to keep the bantering note. – Not even SBC could afford to keep you on the off chance we might need a car stolen at an airport. You've been away. There's just not the money around these days.

Again she surveyed the restaurant. Wall to wall overpaid and overweight pinstripes were putting ten pound notes down their throats. Here and there opposite companions who didn't look as if they were being taken out in case of sudden dictation.

– Business as usual, she caught the waiter's ferreting eye. – The rich get richer, and the poor get it in the neck. The economy's sinking, but things are getting better all the time for smoothies like you and this lot, who can defy the laws of financial gravity by hanging on to the firm's magic plastic.

– Smoothies like me and their free loading companions.

He'd been stung. But so had she.

– I'm a working girl, pal. I'll pay you back every mouthful. I'm back, and I'm hungry, and that's bad news for anyone who ever did me down. And something else—never wear checks with stripes, unless you're looking for a job in the circus.

The waiter hovered over them.

– Be a love, me old scouse. She said, again far too loudly for Jamieson's liking. – Fetch us a bottle of brown sauce for this steak you've had the nerve to serve me.

Nesta grabbed a burger for lunch, on her way across town to see Bea. Driving the Porsche with one hand, as she threaded her way out of the shopping centre into the factory belt. The rat-run of Victorian houses and fire-traps which were responsible for the city's unbroken prosperity going back to the turn of the century and beyond. It had always been possible for someone to set up a knitting frame in his back shed, and confidently expect, by working night and day, to own two in a year's time. And after that four, and after that a factory full of them.

That was the lure and promise of the knitwear business. And generations of small businesses had started in these mazey back-streets, and gone on to bigger and glitzier things.

The House of Bea wasn't among them. At some point things had stopped happening for Hector and Bea. You could tell it by the untidy yard and car park. The shuttered old building in the centre of it, which had been closed up for years now. The blistered paint-work, and spoiling brickwork, which had needed pointing for months and years. Knitwear people tend not to spend money on inessentials like obsessive maintenance of the physical plant. But there are certain things which have to be done every year or so, even if it's a matter of a tin of paint. That these had been neglected for so long showed how deeply the physical as well as commercial rot had set into the fabric of The House of Bea.

If further proof were needed, as Nesta came through the double doors into the machine room, the final gouging-up of the cement floor under the dunned machine was taking place.

– Why? echoed her mother, brushing Turkish cigarette ash from the black which she always wore. Black jersey, today. Simple, but expensive, in contrast to the cheap acrylics coming off the frames around them at so many hundred per hour.

– Why am I having that frame out? Because the girls have been asking for a sauna, and for the sake of good staff relations me and Hector thought what the hell, give them one. Why do you think it's coming out? We haven't kept the payments up, what else could it be?

– And you have to handle that while Hector fannies off to Paris?

Bea jumped to his defence, despite her row on the phone with him.

– He's been in the business as long as I have. He has contacts in

Paris.

– Who never take his calls any more.

Bea knew what was coming. The final appeal, yet again, for her to sell up, and get out of the business while she could still raise money on it. Before the inevitable happened, and a lifetime's work ended in the bankruptcy court. She swung the subject back to Connie.

A new angle on the Connie question had occurred to Nesta, however, as she watched the crane being backed in to remove the machine. Could it be that Hector and Bea had fixed for Connie to return? To apply the drive attack and know-how she'd used in building up the chain to save the House of Bea?

Bea denied it. And when Bea denied something, it stayed denied. Bea denied so hard that somebody less like Bea herself than Nesta would have curled at the edges and burst into flames. – Besides, she ended, almost as black in the face as what she was wearing – there's no proof she is back. Your dad's been on the duty frees, most like.

– So drunk he misrecognised his own daughter? And That Look?

That shut Bea up, as she stumped back up the wooden staircase to the main office. You couldn't argue with that. Connie you could mistake. That Look, never.

– Take warning. Nesta, always one for pushing the knife into the hilt, stopped her as she was about to crash the office door shut after her. – Take warning, mother dear. If it is her, whatever she wants, you come down on my side. Screw Hector, screw the business. You're in with me. The prodigal returned, never. The evil step-sister, all the way.

– I shouldn't be here. Jamieson wondered if he should fold his trousers neatly over the bed-head. Or if that would strike the domestic, the wimpish note. He compromised by laying them not too untidily on the bedside chair. And he meant what he said. He should not have been there. He couldn't have told Connie what he was doing there. Unless it would be enough to blame it on the two bottles of Beaune, and the one of Muscadet. And the long slow lunch, which had got better and better. And the fact that they had found, to his surprise, that they could talk to each other.

– I should not be here. He said more firmly, determined to make a stand. And again he meant it. For he should not have stopped her in mid yawn, and suggested what she needed more than another bottle of Beaune was a deep pillow and soft hotel sheets. And that he knew of somewhere nearby where SBC lodged their staff on their provincial sweeps. And that it was only round the corner, and he could afford another twenty minutes of his time to see her safely there.

– I really should not be here. He insisted a final time, and then stopped as she came out of the bathroom, hair down, face blotched with water after her shower. But the kick inside told him there was nowhere else he'd rather be, or should be, this afternoon. Especially not headed towards Nuneaton for the presentation.

Leroy, the van-boy at the factory, had to move smartish to get out of Nesta's way as she slalommed out of the yard. Then he had to move smartish again as Arnie's van turned into it. Arnie had things to say to Bea, as well. Like Nesta, he'd jumped to the conclusion that Connie's money was being sought to rescue the crumbling knitwear plant.

– You got her back. You got her back to put her money in this industrial slum here.

Bea denied it. She was getting a lot of practice in denying things today.

– I got her back? You got her back. She was on the offensive. – You got her back because you've never got over her.

Arnie's turn to look disbelieving. Arnie's turn to start denying. At the end of it nothing had been settled, except the need for a family conference if the alarm Hector had started turned out to be for real. On his way out to Babs, waiting in the van, as she waited so much and so often for him, he spotted a box of seconds. Managed to knock a fiver per dozen off the price Bea suggested, though her heart wasn't really in it. So something had been gained from his flying visit. Buying, that was what Arnie liked doing best. Selling, the other side of being a successful businessman, he wasn't so good at.

– I shouldn't be here. Connie pulled the hotel curtains across the afternoon light. She meant it as much as Jamieson did. Physically she needed a straight twenty-four hours' sleep. Emotionally she needed a straight lifetime with no more complications with men. Especially not with Cashmere Kids, like the man she found herself in the hotel suite with.

Right now she should have been having a late afternoon meal, on the roof of the villa, shaded by vines. On her plate would be grilled barbouni, the Greek name sounding much more music than the English mullet. With a simple peasant salada. Glistening with the olive oil they pressed in the next village, which still arrived on the back of a donkey. And, best of all, the honest sharpness of the lemon from her own tree. A real lemon, big and coarse and bruised, and never having known a supermarket shelf.

– I should not be here, she murmured, moving away from her dress to the sheets. – I should be walking down the hill, towards the village, past the olive trees, and the dogs too tired even to bark. I shouldn't be getting in bed with you. I should be opening the taverna, and hoping not to find my fella in it across two Danish birds.

– I should not be here.

But she was, and as she nuzzled against his welcome chest, and felt his heavy arm around her, she knew, just then, in that moment, she would rather not be anywhere else than in an afternoon bed, with a man whose first name she didn't even know.

Dev didn't head straight for the factory that afternoon. Janet proved as keen as he guessed she'd be on the practical. And bearding Bea in her little kingdom, in the mood she was in, was a long way second best. Besides, of them all, he had least to fear from a returned Connie.

Arnie had after all been responsible for the bust-up of the marriage and her business. After years of putting up with standing round in white slacks, looking more like fancy man than husband, he'd started to live a little. Living a little meant wrapping dream motors around tree-trunks, and drinking his way alphabetically across the shelves in every bar and club in town. Then had come the women. Who at times also seemed to be approached alphabetically.

Nesta had stepped in here, Dev knew. Because Connie had told him. Nesta, who'd been brought into the business by Connie as her number two, had got ambitious. Seen that she could take the shops on herself. Run them as well as her step-sister, and better, because she was a single lady and likely to remain so. And consequently unlikely to have Connie's problem of saving her marriage at the same time as the business, which was running into the first choppy waters of the mid-seventies.

Hector had arrived at this point. Hector, who'd put Bea's money into the chain, and sat on the board, Connie's puppet. Turning out to be a puppet who danced to Nesta's tugs, when it was clear that Connie just wasn't taking care of business anymore. All her time and sweat, and tears too, were taken up trying to slap some life back into Arnie and the marriage. So Hector had cut her throat. Voted her out of her own business, and voted Nesta into the driver's seat. The founder of the chain had got the usual five figure pay-off, and signed all away with relief, at the time. But there had always been the feeling among the other actors in the commercial drama, that she'd enter stage left again at some point. And mean no good for any of them.

Except for Dev, of course.

He'd felt the chill when he first got the news, but that was only reflex. It's never altogether welcome to have old flames pop back up after eight years. For one thing, it reminds you that you're eight years further on. For another, who can tell what complications they intend for you? And Connie usually meant complications on complications.

But what did he have to fear?

Hadn't he picked Connie up, after she'd lost the business and her husband? Hadn't he been on hand to massage her ego, and everything connected with it by nerve or tissue, back to health?

The affair had been brief, clawing, and therapeutic. They'd gone into it knowing that she was on the rebound and that Dev was snapping her up only because of that. It ended sharply and cleanly when he walked out on her. They were adults, and they'd been adults then, so where was the problem? What did Dev of all of them have to worry about?

Nothing, he knew.

Except that it was Connie they were dealing with.

He rolled over, dismissing her, giving his attention completely again to the almost too-eager student beside him.

Honest, uncomplicated lust, he thought. Why complicate it with love, which was what had so nearly happened back then, with Connie.

That afternoon Connie was all for simple uncomplicated lust, and her companion too, it seemed. The day was advanced to a Midlands evening, the presentation long since concluded without the benefit of Jamieson's hard-worked-on contribution, and even the driver had been sent off. The trace of perspiration on the down of the woman's upper lip, matched exactly that on his. They had met, rowed, made up, eaten, and made love. And in twenty minutes, or an hour, or next morning, when she awoke, that would be that. She would head on to where she was headed, and he would put together again the temporarily broken connections of his business career, and his marriage.

Except that when she slowly awoke, as he watched the evening slide into night, he put his finger to her lips, and warned her to say nothing until he had finished.

– I'm not an impulsive, irrational man. It sounded a wimpish, prickish start, he knew. But you had to start somewhere. – Never in my life can I remember taking a decision that didn't fit in with my life or career goal. Get this straight, he urged, as if she'd started to argue. – Everything is going rather well for me. Hunky dory. The Cashmere Kid is doing very nicely, thank you, even if it mostly is on the firm's magic plastic.

He wasn't bored with his wife or his job. The prospect of spending the next two or three decades with them was one he could face. This wasn't the identikit bleating of the comfortably-off executive wallowing in the luxury of a mid-life crisis. So far as he knew, nothing had been leading up to this.

– So I don't know why I'm going to ask you what I'm just about to ask you. Which is to drop everything you've planned for your return. And jump out of the window with me.

– Jump out of the window? She was still a little groggy from the afternoon, mentally stiff from the flight, as well as relaxed as a cat from its aftermath.

– For once I'm saying stuff the wall planner. I'm heading off and out. And I want to do it with you, because you seem to know how to live untidily, and I need to learn. I'm offering you three months, six, a year. However long it takes for me to come back to my senses, or, more likely, for you to get bored with me. You name where. Back to Greece, the States, anywhere. Let's just get the hell out now, tonight, or first thing in the morning. With no phone calls to explain to anyone. No backward looks. Let's just grab each other the way we grabbed each other this afternoon and jump out of the window. Whatever floor we're on.

– The fifteenth. Connie wriggled away from him, and sat on the edge of the bed. The Beaune was still making her sluggish, and she shook her head fiercely enough to hurt, to clear it. It was his turn to listen, because this was important.

– When you started, I thought here goes, another line being shot. Then I realised you meant it. I thought, oh God, it's happening again, I've done it again. Here's another fella sees me as the answer to his problems. And the answer is to take a flying leap out of the window. With me.

She put her fingers against his lips, feeling with surprise their smoothness. After eight years with Georgiou she'd almost forgotten what a shaved face felt like.

– I told you the third time I made you make love to me this afternoon I was bad news for you. You said you knew. I have to be trouble for someone who wears towelling socks and a gilt tie clip. Go home. She pushed hard against his lips, feeling the teeth underneath the flesh. Not so unnaturally white as Georgiou's, but good enough. Expert enough. Eager enough.

– Go home. She said again. – Go back to your very important job, and your very important company wife, and forget all about me. Forget what you just offered.

He shook himself free.

– I'll never get this chance again, in all my life. Here, now, in this hotel, it's all come together. Let's jump out of the window. Who's to stop us?

– Me. She had to put a stop to this. – Me, pal. Because I've been there. I've done it a dozen.

– But not with me.

He was telling her he was so different? And even if he was, could a girl afford to take three or six or twelve months out of her own life, to help him?

– I've a living to make. People to carve. I want to be sat in that fake French restaurant putting tenners down my throat, signing credit card slips for totals that look like telephone numbers. The rich are getting richer, and I'm not intending getting it in the back of the neck with the other poor sods. Not again.

– Things are different, he urged, feeling the moment go, the chance dissolve, even as he argued for it. – You made your money in the seventies, in the sixties. These are the eighties. Times are harder. People are uglier.

She wasn't having it.

– I say it's the Klondike out there. I say there's a business I know, which is fashion, and there's still money to be made in it. I say there's a firm that can give me a start, even though it'll choke the people who own it, to see me back.

She was at the window, the curtains pulled back.

C.—2

– And don't tell me there's sharks in the water, because if there are, they'd best look out. Because Connie's back, and she's getting in among them, with stainless steel teeth.

She turned to him, naked against the glass, and the city lights outside it, and he knew he was from now on hooked through the lip, and shackled arm and foot to this woman. Whatever the price he had to pay. Whatever the business and personal disasters.

– I'm having some of that. She said. – My spoon's going in the gravy, my snout's going in the trough. And nothing in trousers, or out of them, is going to get in my way ever again.

Three

She called on Arnie first.

Not the day after she arrived back, not the day after that. That wouldn't have had the Connie mark. That would have said she needed family and friends. That she was back to ask for favours, with ten drachmas to her name.

Leaving the hello-I'm-backs for a day or two meant that those family and friends ran around the town like blue-arsed flies, looking for her. Hoping hard not to find her. But knowing that Hector was sticking to his story.

Arnie had been playing one of his games with Babs, when Connie showed. The game where he walked into the back of the van as she was trying on new jeans. The game where he said – Take them off, tart. Take them all off. And Babs asked him what he was playing at, and he said – It's my stall, and my gear, and I know you tarts who come down here looking for a bit of rough. Thinking you can have anyone on the barrows for a quid. So here's a quid, tart. This pound note says I'm having you, now. In here. In the middle of the market. So take everything off.

Just one of the games that Arnie and Babs played. Games that always ended the same way. Except today, when he moved towards her, and Connie rapped on the van door.

– Why did you buy the canvas loons, Arnie? Was it a moment of nostalgia for the sixties? And you're never going to shift that gross of anoraks with the fun-fur collar. Not unless you get a bus-load of colour-blind Eskimos with a sense of humour in.

Connie surveyed the stall, with a critical eye. Out of the corner of it she watched Babs leave the van, flustered. Arnie was tucking a shirt-flap into his cords.

– So this is how you ended up? Running a barrow?

– I like the barrows. I like selling. Arnie, too, watched Babs walk quickly across to the market bar, getting out of the way. He knew she'd clocked who Connie was the moment the van door opened.

That meant facing up to things, over a few drinks, once he found out what Connie wanted.

– The new love life? Connie indicated the closing pub door, through which Babs had gone, again causing that sudden hush.

– The best thing that ever happened to me.

– Second only to me?

– I was a kept man when I was with you. I was your toy dog.

– But who else could have put up with you wrapping so many dream motors round tree trunks? And screwing everything that wiggled towards you?

As he reached for breath to carry on the row it was plain she'd come to see him for, she switched. She wasn't back for a row, she told him with a straight face. She was back to look him up, for old times sake. Look him up, walk out on him and forget him. A bonus was seeing the new love in his life, the person in her place. But she'd no wish to bust that up. Her feelings for him and what they'd had together had been baked out of her in eight years of blissful beachcombing.

– You don't want anything?

– Nothing you've got, Arnie. Certainly not an anorak that would give a reindeer fits.

Bea was next.

Wary, was Bea. Expecting the visit. Eyes narrowed to spot exactly what it was her step-daughter was back for.

– I just want to look a few people up. Connie's tanned face was as innocent of guile as a child's. But then, Bea reflected, she knew quite a few children who were right scheming little bastards. – I think of the factory a lot. They were walking between the frames, towards the interlockers, bent over their machines, each one aware to the fraction of a new pence how much the piece-work rate on the current piece of work was getting them. – To a lot of people it would be a doss-house for making rubbish gear. Another sweet disarming smile. – To me, it's a sort of home. I love the smell of oil and new-dyed fabric. The noise of the frames. I even like the faint smell of dry rot in the woodwork. I'm a Midlands girl, after all. Eight years in paradise beside the Med with my dream bloke can't change that. I miss here. I miss the busy little factories tucked down side streets you wouldn't give a second look at. But you and I, and Midlands girls know there's money being made down them, night, twilight shift, and day.

Bea muttered her reflective denial that there was any money to be made anywhere in the fashion business, as Connie lingered by the production sheets pinned up on the cork board. It occurred to Bea, as her finger ran down the figures, that she'd also, accidentally as it were, leafed through the order sheets on the desk upstairs. Could it be that her step-daughter's visit was in the nature of spying out the land? Casing the joint?

She dismissed the thought as soon as it arose. The way Connie was dressed, she was riding high. What would she want with any part of the crumbling House of Bea? If she'd known that the dress was the only one Connie now possessed, apart from the cotton print, her suspicions would have been doubled. And doubled again, if she had any way of knowing that Jamieson had been the not-too-reluctant provider of the plastic credit that had paid for it. Strictly as a loan, as Connie had insisted.

Connie didn't want anything from Bea, or the factory. Nor even from Hector, who had decided to lie low. Hector had received a drubbing over his fake Parisian phone call. He didn't want another, over the business of which way he'd swung the vote eight years back.

All she wanted was to look up the old faces in the old places, before heading off again. And when she left Bea it was with a compliment.

– Black suits you. I mean it. And when I've as many miles on the clock as you have, lover, I hope I've got the figure of a racing snake too.

Nesta kept her waiting. Kicking her heels in the shop, as she pretended to finish off some important letters. But really taking a slow coffee and extra large slice of Black Forest gateau, as she tried to work out the angles. In the end she decided that attack was going to be the best policy, whatever Connie's approach was.

– I know what you want. Nesta went for her, almost before she creased the leather of the chair. – You want half the shops. You want me to take everything I've worked for in the eight years you've been soaking up the ultra-violets, and split it down the middle. Because you still think I stole your shops off you. It isn't going to happen. Take warning. I'm even more the gutter fighter I was back then. When I was the gutterfighter you taught me to be, when you took me on as your Number Two. There's nothing for you in this town, or in this business. Go back now. How much is a one-way ticket?

Connie sat there.

Nesta had fired off all her rockets, set off all her landmines under her. And Connie just sat there. Then very softly she said –

– There's so much pain in your eyes. So much pain and hurt and anger. I don't want to add to it.

And left.

She went to ground again, for two more days. While family and friends did their impersonations of blue-arsed flies. While tempers got shorter, and suggestions wilder. Only Dev, who hadn't had a visit, and who deliberately kept away from the factory, came near to guessing what she was up to. Instead of crediting her with a grand design, of which the waiting game was only a part, he thought she was playing it by ear. Hoping for something to turn up to get her out of whatever hole she was in. For only Dev was prepared to think the unthinkable—that whatever she'd had going for her in Greece had come to a grinding stop.

The waiting game paid off. Flipping through the papers in Jamieson's briefcase as she waited for him to finish a phone call, explaining yet again why he was delayed on his way from Zurich, she found what she was looking for. A very glossy brochure for a very glossy business.

– Private medical clinic. Very big money, these days. Jamieson explained, firmly replacing the confidential papers in his file. – I've been advising one of the major firms on their organisation and methods.

– Whatever happened to the National Health Service? asked Connie, proving she had indeed been away for eight years. Without taking the English papers.

As Jamieson explained what had happened to socialised medicine, and what a honey pot the private clinics were turning out to be, Connie switched off. If he'd known, he'd have been able to name the look on her face as That Look. The Connie That Look. Which she got when she ran out of anything save determination. Or when an exceptionally good idea had struck her, to go with it.

Which was why Dev broke into the next daily family conference with the clinic card. Before he could break the news of her whereabouts he had to run the usual barrage from Arnie.

– This is family. If we let you in, who's to stop any Tom, Dick or Hare Krishna?

It had been eight years, and Arnie's legal and moral rights in Connie had long since been terminated when Dev and Connie had happened. But it was still a nagging pain in Arnie's side.

Dev ignored it. He knew he'd got something by the morning mail which would break up their coffee morning.

– Why you? Why did she send it to you? Nesta wanted to know, after the party had indeed broken up, and Hector had nearly killed Leroy yet again with a racing start out of the yard.

– Just think of all those sour faces when I brought out the card that explains why she's back. Dev smiled. He'd enjoyed holding the moment, and the sensation after it. – Very Connie?

Nesta agreed.

Very, very Connie.

The lunch order to the clinic kitchens had been sent in and was on its way to Connie's private room when Hector arrived. He'd had no time to stop for flowers on the drive to where the last of the executive ranch-style homes met the green belt. A discreet and expensive kiosk, in one corner of the discreet and expensive foyer, sold him orchids and Belgian chocolates.

The tray arrived at the same time as he did at the private room, and told him as definitely as the quality fittings in the corridors that this was not a run-down corner of the public health service.

He ticked off salmon mousse, jambon à la crème, brie, and a Calvados sorbet, as well as a heady brew of real coffee, as he waited for the okay to enter.

Connie, switching off the video which was showing a mildly pornographic movie, courtesy of the clinic video library, didn't look as if the meal would give her any trouble. Didn't look, in fact, as if she should be in a clinic bed at all. Even one that looked as much like a motel room single as this one.

– I know what you're thinking, she beat him to it, once the initial awkwardnesses were out of the way. She pushed some brie towards him with the back of her fork. – How can she afford this?

This wasn't the first thought in her father's troubled mind at all, but she hurried on, as if she wanted to put his mind at rest about the important things.

– Well I've made a friend. A mate. He's one of the wheels who's been putting this place straight. He got me in here at what you might say was the wholesale price.

She galloped on again, as Hector choked the cheese down, and tried to get an opening.

– Did you clock the nurses?

Hector had in fact been unable to take his eyes off the legs of the one showing him to the room. The girl should have been a model, the way she walked like a mucky thought. Angels of Mercy came pretty sexy in the private sector.

– Only they don't like you calling them nurses. Nurses might make you think of hospitals, and hopsitals might make you think of being ill. And thinking of being ill, might lead you to think of dying, and they don't exactly encourage mention of the Big Red D here. See the sign above the bed? Strictly No Croaking On The Premises. Well I mean—anyone in here, with maybe the exception of your loving daughter, is far too busy or important or well-insured to cop for the Big Red D.

– You look so well. He finally got it out and was about to ask the next question, the one he dreaded, when she beat him to it again.

– Ground rules. You never ask me why I'm here. I haven't come back for sympathy. I'm back, and I'm here, and that's all there is to it. Got it?

Couldn't he even ask about treatment? And, most important of all, from a father's point of view—pain? Was there danger? Was there pain?

Another no-no.

– If I say there isn't, you'll think I'm lying to you, being brave, and that'll worry you. And if I say there is, you'll think I'm looking for sympathy, putting the hooks in. So I'm saying don't ask. Don't ever ask. And don't ask me how long I've had whatever I've got, if anything, which I'm not admitting. Or how long I'm likely to be here. I'll just say—I never knew before what it was to watch the clock go round.

– Fancy a lift?

Dev fancied a lift. His car was a terminal case, and ever the sharp dresser, he didn't want to test the rain-proof qualities of his Italian boots down the wet back streets.

He slid into the Porsche beside Nesta.

– Where?

With nothing much else on that afternoon, Dev leant across and kissed her hard, while his hand moved under her seat belt.

He waited for the smack in the face, or the hand between his knees. You never knew. But finding out was one way to start an afternoon off.

The tray was finished in the clinic room, and so, it was plain to Hector, was any hospital bedside talk. Connie wanted to talk business. She'd looked round the factory when she went to see Bea, and hadn't been impressed.

Hector didn't want to talk business.

– Let's talk about you, then. Still got those ten thousand hot pants?

He especially didn't want to talk hot pants, either. Hot pants had been a sore point with him, ever since he'd got lumbered with ten thousand the weekend before the hot pant craze died as suddenly as it flared.

– Mark my words, the day of the satin hot pant will come again, and when it does, I'm poised to make a killing, was all he wanted to say on hot pants.

Connie was right when she thought she detected some disillusionment with the fashion business.

– I'm getting on, he sighed, oblivious of the comedy of his complaining at someone else's expensive hospital bedside. – You change. I'm getting too old to be in a business founded on lies.

Wasn't that a definition of any business, she asked?

– Maybe. But I'm sick and tired of manufacturing disguises, and selling them through fraud. We say to people—you—you're a fat smelly bird with a face like a rivet catcher's glove. But wear this, and you'll look like a dirty movie starlet. Or we take a fella who it's a toss-up with whether his skin condition is worse than his bad breath. We tell him all he has to do is get into these jeans and this jacket—and he'll be up to his neck in discarded knickers.

The problem for Hector feeling like this was, as Connie forcibly pointed out, what else could he do if he left the knitwear? And he knew, as well as she did, that he wouldn't get out of it even if he could, because the business was an addiction, as well as a job. So he was stuck with the House of Bea, just as she was stuck with whatever was the matter with her. If anything. Which, she reminded him, she wasn't saying.

And talking about the business in general, and the House of Bea in particular, brought her on to something she had to ask him.
Which he knew he wasn't going to like at all.

Dev had got the lift, rather than the smack in the face. Not to his place, but to Nesta's. On the way there, with Nesta driving even faster than usual, he'd thought of a way to turn this kiss-and-promise into something more than an afternoon romp through stranger sheets. He waited until the woman, slightly flushed and tight for breath, had shooed all business away for the afternoon. Until the door was shut on the two of them, and he followed her glance at the spiral staircase.

Time to cool things.

Time to make his offer. On demand.

– Give me a job. Take me on.

Nesta was wary.

– I was a designer. I was a bloody good designer.

– Was, she noted. – Where have you been for the past few years?

– I can come back. Designers do come back.

She shook her head, and wished it could have been just as she'd imagined it was going to be, as she drove him back. Straightforward sex, with no commitments. Of the pocket or the heart.

– Let me buy for you, then. Dev had taken himself by surprise as much as her. Now that he was in the ring, fighting for a proper job in the business, he knew how much he wanted it. – I've got the eye. You never lose that, not even if you've spent your time teaching theory.

Nesta looked towards the staircase again, down which the job prospect had left those days before. That had been one of those straightforward afternoons. An idea struck her.

– I do have a job open. But it mightn't be what a creative person like yourself is looking for. I'll tell you about it. Up there. And she jerked her head towards the staircase.

As he followed she explained what was required of her personal nark. Made no attempt to pretend it was anything but an administrative job, with no creative involvement. Or disguise that what she really wanted was that old rag trade queen with hands like white butterflies, who knew every dirty wrinkle in the game. But the job was there, if Dev wanted it. If he needed to scratch that itch of working full-time at the sharp end of the clothing business again.

And if he passed the job interview.

Which Nesta made very plain as she reached for his belt buckle, would take place horizontally, on the black silk sheets.

– Take you back in the business?

Hector choked on his Blue Mountain coffee, and dabbed a scorched lip.

– You're asking me to give you a slice of the House of Bea?

His daughter helped herself to more coffee. Very black. Very sharp.

– You owe me. You voted me out, which is why the bitch has got my shops. I want you to go back to Bea and tell her I'm willing to come and work for the House of Bea.

Hector protested that these days they could hardly pay the wage-bill for the crew, let alone afford to carry passengers.

– I'd graft. You know I'd graft. I'd graft like Bea's too old to, and you never knew how to.

The main objection to taking her on appeared to Hector. It was so obvious he could have kicked himself for missing it in the shock of her request. He didn't want to be indelicate, or lay too heavy a welly on her—but could he point out she was in a hospital bed?

– It comes and goes. She dismissed it. – One day up, one day down. I get paid by results, and I don't get paid for time I spend flat on my back under a saline drip.

He couldn't do it. Much as he would like to, because she was his own daughter, and because she was indeed a grafter, and that's what the firm most needed. There was no way, especially at this moment, that he could approach Bea with a request like that.

– I'm here for some time, dad. She told him not quite the truth, but certainly no lies. – And I don't intend to go round the bend with time on my hands. I need to work. It's self-respect, as well as that itch to be in the business again.

He suggested that she fly Georgiou over, to share things with, if time was going to lie on her hands, in hospital and outside. But she didn't rise to that. How could she lay that on Georgiou? The Greek had many qualities, but a bedside manner wasn't one of them. No. She was here to face this by herself, and she needed the job. Not, she'd have him understand, for financial reasons. But for inside ones. Reasons of the heart. A heart that was still firmly hooked on the daily ups and downs of being professionally involved in the making or selling of fashion.

But he wouldn't budge. The chin that was usually so weak firmed, and the lips closed tight. He wouldn't, and he couldn't. And that was final.

She leant back, in the bed, as if the effort of trying to persuade him was taking too much out of her. He didn't relax. He was flesh and blood after all. And rightly suspicious of any sudden retreat by his determined daughter. Who shared with him a family urge, on entering a room, to fight all the fellas and screw all their birds. Only the other way around with her, of course.

She was reflective. Musing on how good it was to see him for the first time in those eight absent years. Except that it wasn't exactly eight. For hadn't he come out to see her, the first year of her exile?

He remembered.

– Remember the late nights, watching the ferry boats pull out across the Aegean, with all their lights on, like castles on the water?

He remembered.

– Remember the noise and clatter of the taverna, and the drinks and the eating, and the dancing, and the breaking of plates?

He remembered.

– Remember the girl from Oslo you met there? The one you went off to do a month's island hopping with, when Bea was in the States looking at West Coast sportswear?

He remembered.

Looked like Hector would be taking her request to Bea after all.

Four

As Connie was talking her way into a job, Dev was turning one down. The same impulse that had led him to provoke the woman in the car led him to turn her down, once he was in her bedroom. Not just turn her down. Knock her flat. By refusing her as a woman, with the same breath he refused the job.

He waited until she had everything off, and had made that awkward sideways slide between the sheets, to hide the extra weight she was carrying despite all her exercise classes, and work-out tapes. Not that she was fat, or out of condition. But a life spent chasing deals in the cut-throat world of women's retail fashion meant a lot of snatched meals, junk food.

– I don't want your job.

He watched her, wondering how she would react as his shots went in. Would she crumple? Would there be tears?

– You're not worth it.

He let his gaze stay a moment on the white flesh showing under the rucked-up sheet. Defenceless and cold, against the grain of the black sheets.

– You'd be worth it maybe for the designing job. But not for anything else.

He didn't get tears. He saw the face freeze for a moment, and wondered, somewhere in the back of his mind, why he was being so cruel.

– So thanks for the offer, but no thanks.

And he checked the buckle on his belt, and went quietly down the stairs.

Nesta sat very still in the bed for a long time. She got colder, but didn't notice it. The phones rang downstairs, personal and business. But she didn't answer. When she finally got out, feeling foolish and fat, and all the things you feel when someone has taken you that far, only to walk out, hitching up their trousers, she was very calm. Not thinking all that logically, because that's hard to do at a time like that. Thinking logically, she couldn't have confused what Dev had done with the threat that Connie had to represent. But she knew that she had two problems on her plate now. Two people to be sorted out, in between attending to business.

Calm, and thinking straight if not completely logically, she first of all tried to phone the clinic to see if Connie had anything to do with her humiliation by Dev. Then, when told that all admission information was confidential, she phoned the School of Fashion.

Dev wasn't there, as she'd guessed. But she did get to leave a message with a very intrigued secretary in the Design department.

– Tell him he needs me, because Connie's back, and nothing's the same this week to what it was last week. Tell him he's on her shopping list, like I am. Tell him, Nesta says – See you, Dev. And I'll have him upstairs on those sheets he walked away from, or against the door of my office, or on my desk. I'll have him, and he'll say anything, Nesta, anything. Just so long as you help me pay her back. Tell him, Nesta says – See you, Dev. And that's more threat than promise.

Bea loved Hector.

He was an old villain, a moral hooligan, and she could see through him to the label on his underpants. But she'd found him late, and she was going to keep him. Because she loved him. He knew that, but it was risky to play on it in the matter he now had to fix. Getting his daughter a slice, without bringing Nesta down on his head, even if Bea approved.

His natural preference was for the crabwise approach, but he was an amateur in that when up against the women in his life and at the House of Bea. He decided to rely on Bea being as daft about him as any seventeen year-old for her spotty herbert. And an appeal to her motherly instinct. Though the black she favoured for wear at home and at work said Black Widow spider, rather than Cuddly She-Bear.

– My daughter is back. He hoped he hadn't pushed the preamble of how he had found her, and what she'd said, or failed to say about her illness, too far towards the sentimental. – My little girl is saying to me that she wants to be with me until whatever happens. What do I say to that? What would you have said to it, if it had been your blood daughter asking? Picture her—lying in that bed, looking up at me. Pleading for a chance to fill her time in by helping her old dad out, at a time in his business life, when God knows, he needs it most. Could I refuse? Could you?

So Bea had been right. The little madam had been casing the joint at her visit. Only from the highest motives of family feeling, it seemed, if Hector was to be believed. But casing it, nonetheless. She probably knew what the firm was doing to the nearest dozen.

Hector interpreted her grim smile of self-satisfaction as indication that she wasn't buying, and redoubled his efforts. With emotion in his voice he word-painted the hospital bed, the wan patient, her quiet plea to be allowed some months of usefulness. It would have been an affecting portrait, if Bea hadn't known him better. Hector could weep tears over spilled chips, she knew.

– Knock it off. She's got the job.

His eyes widened.

– She's got the job because God knows we need even the halt and the lame risen from their sickbeds to help out. New blood, however weak, might just be what we need to turn the corner.

And it was Bea's turn to paint a picture of the next few weeks. Connie would be the first in in the mornings, and the last out at nights, and if anyone had to pass up on their dinner hour, guess who it would be? She needn't think she was coming in to sit behind a big desk, polishing her nails. When she wasn't out on the floor she'd be expected to be on the phone, selling. Or knocking on wholesalers' doors, looking for orders.

And so on.

Hector listened, with less joy than could have been expected of a father who'd just swung a job for his only daughter. Blood daughter. Bea lighting up at the prospect of getting someone in to work all the hours God sent for next to nothing meant there was no risk of her getting to know about the girl from Oslo, and that wonderful month island-hopping. But it also meant another strong-willed woman at the factory, and in his life.

Weeks later, when Connie firmly had her feet under the desk, she asked Bea point blank why she'd given in and let her have the job. Despite the reservations and suspicions she must have had. Especially knowing how very much displeased Nesta was going to be.

– Greed, said Bea, knocking ash off the black of her dress. – Just that. I wanted to feel what it was like to sign blank paying-in slips again, instead of cheques. Just that. Just that best of all reasons. I knew whatever else you were, you were a grafter. And why ever you were back, you were here to work.

Connie didn't wait long, after Hector closed the door, having given her the good news. She wasn't the type to enjoy lying around in bed alone all day, even in these plush surroundings. Not even if she'd really been ill. She waited until his Rover had crunched out of the gravelled drive, dressed, and left. She signed the bill at reception on the Siggins Bowser and Comer account, and took a cab straight to the hotel.

Jamieson wasn't there, as she'd planned and hoped. Today he'd not been able to put off a trip to London, where he was expecting an uncomfortable hour or so, explaining what he'd been up to for the best part of the week. Or rather, not explaining, but selling them an acceptable pack of lies.

Connie had urged him to get in touch with his wife as well. She was the other woman in this brief affair, but she really did think he ought to do the decent thing by her, and set her mind at rest. Tell her he'd been held up for longer than he expected, but he'd be home sometime.

The man hadn't asked for her advice on the domestic side, but she hoped he'd take it. Some time, after all, he'd have to go back. And it would sound pretty thin to claim his plane had been fogbound at Zurich all this time.

With him away, Connie could take steps to make sure that he finally snapped out of it. Started attending to his wife and his career again. Picked up the broken threads from that day she'd pinched his car and driver at the airport. Knowing it was for the best, and that for once what was good for her coincided with the same for the man entangled with her; she took off the dress he'd paid for. The cotton print was the only thing her side of the wardrobe door, and she put it on even though she knew how cold she was going to be in it. Until she had time to put some things on her own back, with her own money.

She left the bathroom tidy. It would be cheap to leave him with the bathroom shelf cluttered. She drew the curtains across, and tuned the music station on the bed-head radio, under the dim glow of the bedside light. He was going to be hit hard, she knew, but the right ambience might make it seem not so bleak. When all was ready for her leaving she opened the bar-fridge and took out the half bottle of champagne. She drank a glass of it straight back, and then placed the other glass beside it. Propping a piece of paper against it, where he would see it straight away, and be under no illusions. Her farewell note.

She was out of practice writing Dear Johns, but she'd kept it simple.

With a last look round the hotel room, for old times' sake as well as to check if she'd left the stray pair of tights, she turned. Just as he came through the door.

What could she say?

– I was going to do a bunk.

She had her flight bag in her hand, and he his calf hide briefcase. He was slightly out of breath, as if some urgency had propelled his steps. As it had. From the clinic to the hotel room.

– And you hate big farewells?

She nodded. She hoped he was going to make it easy.

– I'm allergic to Hawaiian guitars and heavenly choirs.

He lifted his shoulders a fraction, accepting it, and stood aside, as if to let her leave.

Perhaps it was that which made her want to say something in defence of herself, and the cowardly way she was sneaking off.

– You'd have been clearing off yourself soon. Taking the back way out, underpants and shoes in your hand. Back to the little lady. Deny it.

He didn't bother to.

– And I will settle up. I'll pay for everything, even that dress, if the shop won't take it back.

– Does that include your bill at the clinic?

She knew now why he was out of breath. He'd had a phone call in London. Headed straight to the clinic by very expensive cab. Found her gone, and hared back to the hotel. Where he'd taken the steps four at a time.

– I needed that hospital bed for an afternoon. Private business. I take it I'm not disqualified for life from private medicine just because I once spent a few nights with you?

He moved his head once, sideways. No. But he'd have preferred her to check with him first. Especially since she'd used his name, and signed on the SBC account.

She looked concerned.

– You mean you could get into trouble? I never thought. I took you to be such a wheel at SBC.

It was no trouble he couldn't get out of. Even though he didn't wield such power in the firm as she appeared to think.

– Well that's that, then. She concluded. – No harm done. Except to my perfect exit.

– I saw my wife.

She stopped him. On her leaving line, she wanted no talk about his domestic complications.

– I saw my wife, and some other people. He pressed on. Somehow, in his business suit, with that briefcase in his hand, he could handle her better. Wasn't quite so reluctant to push against her shove. – I want you to look at something.

The briefcase was open, and Connie could never resist looking into other people's luggage. She watched him draw out a buff envelope, and spread its contents on the bedside table. As if annoyed by the music, he switched it off. So much for her trying to break it gently. She took the champagne and drank it as she looked at the brochure. It was estate agents' standard glossy, showing a small country cottage, in the expensive septic tank belt. Tucked into a lane, behind huge hedges.

– Like it? I love it. And so will your missis. She sipped the champagne, and wondered whether she could palm the farewell note, which he still didn't appear to have spotted. – But isn't it a little far from London?

– Yes, but it's not for her. It's for you and me.

He took the glass off her, glanced at the envelope containing the note, dismissed it, and sat her down on the end of the bed.

– You need me. He told her. Making sure of every word before he said it. – You need a place to stay, you need some mug to use as a punch-bag when things don't work out with your family. And I need you. For all the reasons I told you about that first night here. I can't afford to keep you in a hotel room against the days I can get to see you, not even at midland rates. And I have to start turning some hours over at the firm again, if I'm going to keep my job.

– So you take a country cottage on a six-month let, with me included?

He nodded. There was no way to fake it. That was what he was offering.

And the upcoming Number Two in the European Division was only going to give her fifteen minutes to make up her mind to say yes. Because in fifteen minutes a car was arriving to take him to the railway station, and out of her life for good.

Connie's turn to sit in a quiet room, weighing up the questions and the answers. Knowing a clock was ticking in the bar, which would alter things for good or bad. For a long time ahead. The last thing she'd wanted when she hit the airport was an immediate affair with a total stranger. Especially one who seemed determined to turn a casual afternoon's love-making into the love-job of his life. But there were practical considerations. Like she didn't have any place to stay once she left the hotel. Except with Hector. And that was going back to Dad, with all that implied in loss of freedom and self-respect. Like Jamieson might be acting like a mug, but he was a mug with prospects. If he was willing and eager to throw his money into a six-month let, who was she to adopt a superior moral position and turn him down?

And besides, the winner, the killer, the deciding factor—she sort of liked him, in an on-the-rebound sort of way. If only because he was so different from the unshaven love-machine she'd punched up in the taverna.

She made the bar as he tilted the gin and tonic glass for the last time.

– But understand, she made sure of every word before she said it, too. – Only because I want in the water with the other sharks. Only as a temporary let. I told you nothing in trousers or out of them is ever going to get in my way again.

She bit into the lemon wedge, as if to emphasise her point.

– Six months. Then it's over.

He nodded.

– If it lasts that long. And don't worry. I won't let you wreck my life.

– Reckon? she asked, turning the question round as if it didn't concern her personally.

– Reckon, he said, with finality.

Surprising Mr. Jamieson was finding his feet quicker than he expected in this love-job of his life.

Five

There are a lot of lonely women in the fashion business. It couldn't operate without them. With no man to go back to, or family to care for, they've no reason not to stay on at the office or the shop or factory until the late late hours. From one point of view that's taking advantage of them. From another it's a sort of social service for the widowed and divorced and single career girls who've turned, without even themselves noticing, into career women. For what else would these high-heeled women do in an evening after hours, but drink too much, or screw around too much, if there wasn't always more business needed doing than there were hours in the working day to cover. Or get paid for.

Maggie Greer was one of those high-heeled women who'd passed up, without really making the decision to, on home, husband and family. She was a survivor in the business, but when she stopped to think about it, a walking wounded so far as her personal life was concerned.

She'd started in the good old bad old days, when the Manageress could line her sales force up in the morning to be checked over, from finger-nails to stocking seams. In those days there were second, third and fourth assistants, a proper pecking order. Girls could be sent home for not making a sale, to encourage the others and themselves to higher effort. The customer had to be served, and advised, and wooed. Not just glared at, as so often in even the better boutiques, as an intrusion into the sales girls' coffee breaks, or boy-chats between themselves.

Now all an assistant was required to do was bag the goods, and punch the till. And they didn't even have to work out the change. The electronics did all that for them as well. Which was just as well, she often reflected, surveying her own staff—because all they seemed to have learned at the local comprehensives was gum-chewing and sex.

Even the position of Manageress wasn't what it used to be. She didn't even get to order her own stock, the computer in Nesta's office handled all that. All Maggie Greer did, as Nesta's manageress, was supervise the bagging of goods, the punching of tills, and break into muck sweat every time Nesta appeared to find fault with how the operation was run.

The flame thrower had always been Nesta's favourite management tool. And if anything, she applied it more freely to the extremities of her senior staff, than to their underlings. There were always more gum-chewing boy-chatting jobs for them. The Maggie Greers had put so many years into making their careers in retail fashion that they had nowhere to go once they were fired. Like her, most of them were well into their mortgage years, with hire purchase outstanding on the car.

There were, however, little tickles which the Maggie Greers could set up for themselves. Over and above the twenty pound or so private take from the till, and the Christmas bonus a manageress could always arrange by fiddling the stock books. It was risky, even though most owners turned a half-blind eye to the practice, so long as it remained in reasonable proportions. But the low basic pay in retail could only be got away with, so long as there was the escape valve of staff thieving, on top of staff discount.

Not that anyone saw it as thieving. It was something which had been accepted in the business, and it was in no one's interest to bring it to a stop. Except the customer's, because she picked up the bill in the finish.

Maggie Greer had made her own moral adjustments long way back, so when Nesta left an Italian piece of knitwear with her that looked as if it was worth pirating, she didn't hesitate. The grapevine had told her that Connie was back, and in manufacture, and she knew Connie of old. Had been the manageress of the very second shop she opened. Stayed for five years, during which they had their ups and downs, but never once had she been found with her hand in the till. Which had to be a record.

– Hand in the till? Up to your elbow in it, more like. Connie grinned, as they talked about old times, professional rivalry now a thing of the past. – But I never could catch you at it.

Not that she would have done anything about it, had she known, for sure. There are rules. And not rocking the boat for your senior staff, so long as they don't get too greedy, is one of them.

After old times they talked about Nesta, and the new times. Connie kept tight lips, not wanting to run down family in front of someone who at the end of the day was only a business acquaintance. And wondering what this invitation for coffee and cakes was leading up to.

– Like it?

She looked at the sweater casually handed her across the onyx coffee table. She liked it. This was the very best of Italian knitwear, which for design, and at the very top end of the scale, making up, is the best there is. This one sweater would retail at more than the average man's tailored suit, Connie knew just by the feel of it. It was a classic, and only a very few lucky women would ever know what it was like to wear it.

– Nesta picked it up at a trade show in Milan. She likes to put the occasional good piece in the window, with all the tats. She can kid herself she's up-market.

Connie knew the symptoms. She'd treated herself like that in the past.

– Now if I knew someone in manufacture, I could let them have a loan of that while she's away at another trade show in Frankfurt . . .

She let the dots run on.

Connie knew why she'd been asked. And it wasn't just to admire the coffee maker.

Hector had been showing Jamieson round the factory that Saturday morning. There was a shift of sorts working, to fill a discount warehouse order that Connie had fought for till her nails ran red. Jamieson had been expecting another quiet country morning, but found himself at the factory, instead. Kicking his heels, and waiting for her to get back from the sudden visit she had to make downtown.

Being shown the plant by Hector hardly seemed an adequate substitute for being in the sheets with the woman who was possessing his thoughts now as much as on those first few days he knew her.

– Any of it make sense to you? Hector demanded, having explained at more length than his visitor would have wished, the production process. He got a shake of the head in reply. – All you have to remember is it all hangs on the latch needle. Hector reached in a tin tray of broken ones. – The latch needle. A knitting needle with a short hook instead of a long spring beard point. The distance to the shaft bridged by a latch, enabling the yarn to be locked into the needle so the knocking over of the old loops can be done without a presser bar. Got it?

Jamieson, in line for the European Number Two spot though he was, shook his head.

And Hector would bet he didn't know what it meant when it was invented in Leicester a hundred and forty odd years back.

Jamieson admitted that, as well.

– It meant you could mechanise the old knitting frames, power them by steam, turn cottages into factories, turn farm labourers into mill hands. It meant the bringing about of mass production, flow lines, the track, the motor car, the modern world. And it started here, in the knitwear business. So don't look down on us. This is backbone.

Jamieson attempted to protest that he hadn't looked down on the business, or the people in it, despite the run-down premises. But Hector was intent on showing him more of the plant.

– Chemical wool. He indicated the stock room, piled almost to the ceiling. – Man-made fibre so near the real thing, if you listen hard you can hear it go baa. It comes in here dyed every colour of the rainbow, and a few that God never put there, through the frames and on to the –

– Overlockers.

– Interlockers, Hector corrected him, but pleased he'd picked something of the process up. – A very important part of the team are the girls over there. Without them your sleeves would fall off your pullover every time you put it on, leading to inconvenience and embarrassment.

He pointed out, as if it wasn't plain enough, that all the interlockers were female. An interesting statistic, which Jamieson and his pocket-calculator mind might like to know, was that throughout the garment trade there were three women to every man.

– So you take those three, and I'll take them, and we'll work in from the outside, meet in the middle and swap.

They walked on, and turned into the yard just as Connie hurried through the fire door, a parcel under her arm.

– Ahead of you, the dispatch shed, a listed building, would you believe, that we wouldn't be allowed to knock down even if we had the money to redevelop. It is in the dispatch shed that the final act of this great commercial drama takes place every day, when Leroy, our transport manager –

Leroy scowled from under his felt cap, and spat on his hands massively, about to lift the twelve-volt battery into the front of his van –

– Carefully clips the wrong delivery note to each order and hurries the longest way round to our eager waiting customers –

There was a moment's silence after what happened next, then both the watching men's faces made exactly the same universal expression of shared pain at another's suffering.

Leroy wouldn't be hurrying any way round to his waiting customers that afternoon. Leroy had just dropped the twelve-volt battery on his foot.

Bea was hesitant at first. What Connie was suggesting was theft, was piracy, was commercial malpractice. Was also, more important, likely to come to light.

Connie denied it. And even if it did, and whoever had the sweater ripped off traced the copy back to the House of Bea, there was no legal remedy. The legal position was that you couldn't watertight copyright shape, stitch or pattern. The thing could look as near the original as effectively made no difference, but if a button was different, or a small part of the repeat pattern varied, there was no case. She had reason to know, having been burnt once or twice herself. If you copied a Paris designer number down to the last stitch, but left one button off, and labelled it Fred Balenciaga, 2 Fish Dock Rd., Grimsby, the Home of High Fashion, you couldn't be touched.

Bea still was reluctant. It wasn't the sort of thing the House of Bea had done, even though half the factories in town spent most of their time pirating ideas. Connie pointed out that it was probably because of that, that there was a gaping hole in the machine-room floor, where the frame had been taken out.

– You guarantee there's no way whoever you ripped this off is going to find out?

Bea was weakening, thinking of those paying-in slips, if they could shift a couple of hundred dozen.

Connie, seeing that, didn't reply. And Bea didn't notice. The figures made too much sense, she saw that, even idly doodling them on the blotter. If they just ran five hundred dozen off, strictly as a one-off job, to get the frame back, they could start pulling down the bigger orders that Connie's aggressive new approach to sales was already starting to win.

And once they got the big orders coming in, they could plan, months or a year ahead, to open the shed Leroy lurked in at the moment. That was Bea's secret ambition, hidden even from Hector. She wanted to open it up, so that she could hand the House of Bea on, some day, as a going concern. To Nesta, of course. That was the piquancy of the situation. Which Bea's palate for the sharper tastes was fully enjoying. Here was Connie, Nesta's sworn enemy, working every hour God sent, to build the business up, which ultimately Nesta would inherit. Less Hector's third, of course.

Her jaws snapped on the deal.

– But keep me out of it. It's your baby. And you're in for ten per cent for bringing it up.

With the business out of the way, and a final warning that Connie would be thrown to the wolves if anything hit the fan on the crooked deal, Bea turned to personal matters. She got nowhere with her enquiries as to the current state of Connie's mystery illness, so turned to her relationship with Jamieson. Did that mean that Georgiou was out of it? Had Connie finally split with the slick spic with the suntanned whatsit?

Connie gave nothing away. Like Hector, Bea concluded with a sigh, she could be as tight as a shark's backside at fifty fathoms, when it suited her.

Hector had slid into the office almost unnoticed, as they fenced. When asked sharply what he was looking for he said the Accident Book.

– Some silly tart hasn't gone and put her foot through the floor again? Bea was not the most sympathetic of employers at news that one of her girls might have injured herself.

– Leroy's dropped a twelve-volt battery on his foot. Hector located the Accident Record down the back of a filing cabinet, and prised open two pages gummed together with something peculiar that smelt horrible.

Bea exploded a sigh. She was due for a round of golf that afternoon, and Hector had to be in Manchester checking a complaint on a batch of sweaters they'd dispatched earlier in the week. She'd particularly promised delivery in the next couple of hours. And now Leroy had demonstrated his total lack of gratitude for being taken out of the dole queue and kept in worthwhile employment by dropping a battery on his foot. Probably deliberately. Bea

c.—3

wouldn't put it past him. She wouldn't put any act of self-mutilation past any of her staff, just to upset her.

Hector whistled as she raged. When she finished he explained, trying to keep the smug note out of his voice, that all had been taken care of.

– Flexible management in action. Crisis control. Hector took all the glossy business weeklies and monthlies. He may once have been caught out in a bear market for hot pants, but he took his responsibilities as a management staffer seriously.

– He took on a casual? Bea slapped her forehead in an oddly Italian gesture. – We can't afford a Sunday joint, and he takes on a casual.

Hector hadn't. He'd sent Jamieson.

Connie now saw her weekend disappear. No consolation that Jamieson might make a good job of it, a better one than Leroy usually did, even though he was having to work from maps. Then she caught Bea's eye. She had agreed to put in seven days a week, if need be. No one had begged her to take the job on. There were still five months left of her deal with her fancy-man. Five months of Saturday afternoons, spare weekends, and every bank holiday away from his wife that he could fix.

She sighed, accepted it, and picked up the delivery documents by the Accident Book. She flicked through the copies, and stopped.

– Thanks, dad. Her jaw was the same grim line that featured in The Look. – He's got a load to drop off at Mansfield market. For Arnie. You've just sent my current round to see my ex.

And it was one of Connie's golden rules, born out of long experience, that current lovers and ex-lovers were best kept as far apart as geography would allow.

– Message.

It hadn't taken long for Arnie to work out who the replacement driver was. He'd been expecting him to call, if not in these circumstances. On Connie's arm, being flaunted. Or by himself, to size up the man who'd previously lived with her. Arnie knew the urge to check out the previous men who'd shared the body in question with you. Women had the same curiosity, which was why it had been a bonus for Connie to have seen Babs.

The girl, luckily, was on hand when Jamieson showed, looking out of place in yet another suit as he lugged the knitwear towards the stall. It was good that she should hear this.

– Message. He repeated, after signing for the documents, and checking Jamieson's signature. – I'm in trouble with the VATman, I'm down the tax office so often I get invited to the Christmas parties, people are chasing me with everything from sawn-off shotguns to crown court summonses. But I'm happy. With my bird. Make sure she gets that.

Jamieson asked what that had to do with him. That stopped Arnie, dead.

– You're her new fella, was all he managed.

Jamieson put him right on a few things. Not in a loud voice, not grabbing his lapels and bending him backwards, knee in the crutch, as he made his points. But making them effectively, all the same. The main one being that he wasn't signing up for a family war, just because he happened to be in bed on a regular basis with Connie.

– You mightn't want to be signed up, but you are. Arnie assured him. – You mightn't think she's taking you for a mug, but you're just one in a long line.

Jamieson put him right on that. He was doing the van round because it was a novelty. He'd no intention of spending every weekend as unpaid labour for the House of Bea. Likewise, he'd gone into his relationship with the woman with his eyes open, after the first heady night and day. He tried to correct an impression that seemed to be gaining on everyone who knew of his affair. Especially family. Or ex-family, as in Arnie's case. The impression being that Jamieson was a straw-sucking hay-seed who would be taken for a ride and stripped of everything but his underpants before being kicked out with not so much as a thank-you.

He hadn't spent eight years working on a failing market barrow, he pointed out, not wanting to wound, but having to risk the personal. He'd been consultant in business efficiency to international companies whose turnover in some cases equalled or exceeded that of the gross national product of several of the countries at the United Nations. He wasn't any number in a long line, but in a queue by himself. At the head of a queue of one. With all his wits about him, his feet on the ground, and eyes as sharp as lasers, for anything Connie might do across him.

He could take care of business, and take care of himself. With no advice needed, least of all from an ex. And an ex like Arnie, at that.

And as he said it, he almost believed it himself.

Arnie dusted himself down. He'd been surprised with the force with which the man in the boring suit had come back at him. So had Babs. But it had been good that she should hear her man put down the woman she thought could still represent a threat to what they had together. Babs had no wish one day to find Arnie gone, and have to make her way back to that south-bound lay-by where Arnie had found her.

– Wait until Connie starts in with Dev again, Arnie muttered, in Jamieson's departing direction – That'll fix you.

Because he knew, better than anyone, that Dev got Connie where it mattered. Eight years on, it might be, but if Dev ever swung his hip Connie's way, he would take money she'd fall.

Which was why it was good for Jamieson's peace of mind that he didn't see Connie pull up outside the Fashion School three days later.

Dev was on the roof, trying to persuade one of his design students not to throw herself off it.

Most of the time Dev got away with it. The pick-up, the betrayal. Sometimes there would be phone-calls in the night for weeks after, but on the whole he'd been lucky. There had been no operatic scenes, no wrist-slashings, nothing to draw the attention of the Head of School to the perks of female flesh which Dev had come to regard as his right. When anything like that threatened, he was good at talking his way out.

Dev wasn't above pointing out that, the way he saw it, being cheated on by their tutor was an essential part of a fashion person's education. Fashion was all about deception, he echoed Hector. About lies and deceit. Who better to learn it off than him, and what better time to learn about it, than before going out into the real world? The real world of buying and selling, in a business that was based on fantasy.

It took a little longer than usual to persuade the girl he'd had to chase up to the roof to see things that way. She'd had a rocky time of it altogether with Dev. Throwing herself off the roof in her lunch break seemed as fitting an end to the unsatisfactory affair as any. Instead of which she ended up pinned against the lift-housing by him, surrendering again. Dev did have a way with words, especially when his brain was working overtime to prevent one of his star students going jogging vertically on campus.

They made love against the lift-housing, among the city pigeons, above the bald heads below, and the girl promised never to do anything so stupid as to threaten to throw herself off the roof. Until the next time she caught him cheating with one of her best friends and class-mates, of course. Or she got the itch to do it sky-high, yet secret, above the campus paving again.

Connie knew none of this as she waited for him several floors below. Not that she would have been surprised, had she known. The campus roofscape was just his sort of speciality. He'd pressed her back against a few lift-housings in their time together. Just as she'd pressed his.

Never one to waste time, Connie looked through the work on display on the pin-boarding. She was impressed. The School had a reputation to maintain, and seemed to be more than capable of it. Even in Connie's day most of the designers were destined never to work in England, but were immediately on graduation whisked abroad. To France, or Germany, or Italy. And increasingly to the States.

Her visit was meant to be a chance to look over Dev, to see what the eight years had done to him. She knew there was a risk in that, because she'd never fooled herself that Dev had done her in once, and that his sexual athlete's body could do it again. She'd been putting it off, telling herself she was too busy at the factory, or on the road during the week. And at weekends, of course, when there wasn't a rush on at the House of Bea, she had her time with Jamieson.

Today she'd grasped the cattle-prod with both hands. Excused herself for the afternoon, the first one she'd taken off since she'd started work, and headed for the campus.

As she looked round the work on the walls, however, an idea got up on tiny legs and started to run around inside. And an idea was certainly welcome, at the moment. Bea was getting increasingly nervous about the extended production run of the sweater rip-off. They had several thousand dozens in circulation now and could off-load as many as came off the frames. Bea was concerned that their good fortune in not being nailed for pirating such a conspicuous and conspicuously good design might soon come to an end. With a bang. She knew all the legal side, of course, but knew it never made sense unnecessarily to annoy the big people, the white folk at the top of the business pole.

So Connie needed inspiration. The production run of the knocked-off sweater had shown her there was a steady, if limited, market for distinctive gear. That sort of gear sold at a higher mark-up, being a fashion line, than did the bread-and-butter numbers. Another couple like that would prove her indispensability to the firm. And indispensability was what she was after.

Connie didn't find it as piquant as did Bea that she was working her buns off only for Nesta to pick up the revitalised firm in five or ten years' time. She found it highly unpleasant as a thought. And unacceptable as a fact. And was working towards changing a few things in that area, provided she could dig her feet deep behind the office desk.

What she needed to come up with was a range of high fashion items designed by a young and lively mind. The firm wasn't big enough yet to carry its own designer, and wouldn't have given untested talent a chance, even if it had been. What was needed was a portfolio containing the best of what was displayed on the walls here. What was pinned up was of course last year's stuff. The latest would be kept under lock and key in the plan drawers and cupboards of the design department.

Like in the plan drawer she was standing next to at this very moment.

Dev checked how he looked in the window glass before pushing the door open. The message left in the staff room had been that Connie was waiting for him, and he wanted to look as if he'd been on the way up for the past eight years, and not headed down.

He must have kept her waiting too long, he decided, after looking everywhere from the Silk Screen Print room to the Footwear Design department, and its odd litter of wood and leather. Damn Annie. Dev was as eager to see whether he could still do the trick on Connie, as she'd been afraid to put it to the test.

Was so annoyed, in fact, that he failed to note the splintering of wood around the plan drawer by the window, and the bent metal around the cupboard lock where the girls' latest drawings and notes were kept for safety.

He had his meeting with Connie, though. Two days later, when he found her in the Design department room, when he turned up to collect some photostats. And the same day of the following week, when he again came on her unexpectedly. Nothing came of her showing up, so far as roofscapes and lift-housings went. But he knew that was only a matter of time. She was back, and she couldn't stay away from him, and sooner or later, whatever her half-hearted arrangement with the new stud in her life, he knew she'd fall.

He could afford to wait, because he was Dev. There was enough on his plate at the moment anyway, what with Annie and the continuing suicide threats. Plus the annoyances at the work place, which was being plagued by a seemingly random series of minor burglaries and small thefts . . .

Six

Ironically enough, it was Bea who pulled the roof in on their heads. The same Bea who had never rested easy every time she'd been persuaded by the latest figures to keep the pirated lines in production. It wasn't business morality, as she kept protesting to Hector, it was commonsense. But she did love filling in those credit slips, so went along with it. Knowing sooner or later she'd be knee-deep in rubble, the light-fittings round their ankles.

It happened the afternoon Nesta called round, for her every-so-often prowl round the property she confidently expected to inherit. Things were looking up, she was happy to admit. But not so happy to admit it was all down to Connie being lean and keen to do business.

– If this is what she can do with a mystery illness watch her smoke when she's fit and well. Nesta's expression, as she bit the meringue in two, indicated her scepticism about the convenient illness.

Bea couldn't add anything to what was already known about that. It came and went, was all she knew. For weeks now it had stayed went, but who knew how long Connie would be able to keep up the pace?

– Until she fancies being shafted by the wop again? Nesta suggested, as sweet as the filling between the meringue shells.

Bea had nothing to add on that, either. She wasn't altogether displeased by Nesta's sour reaction. It had long been apparent to her that there was an advantage in playing the two women off each other. It was noticeable that Connie grafted even harder every time Nesta was due to make a visit. As if to infuriate the step-sister with the latest success story marked on the sales and profits charts. Which she always succeeded in doing, even though those rising lines showed the financial outlook for Nesta was even rosier, week by week.

On the grapevine Nesta had heard the firm were trading up. She didn't like the sound of that. Experience taught that firms like the House of Bea started trading up as a last resort, a final throw of the dice. The bread and butter lines were the pink acrylics for the old boot trudging round the supermarket with a fag in her gob, and her stockings round her ankles, she reminded her mother. Using the unflattering, but very useful definition of their targeted customers which Hector had come up with. They were in the business of high volume and low mark-up. Sooner or later any firm desperately chasing the low volume, high mark-up trade came up against quality control problems, and bust.

– We're not losing sight of the bread and butter lines. Bea assured her. – But the occasional limited run of the other gear helps with cash flow.

And to keep the needle in there between the two, to demonstrate how invaluable Connie with her new ideas was proving to be, Bea pulled out a box of the sweaters.

When the dust had settled, and the shouting was over, when Connie had been called out by Nesta, and Nesta had been dragged around by the hair by Connie, Bea poured herself a large Tia Maria and sank back in her chair. She'd acted in good faith. That she knew. She could keep hold of that. Maybe it was a little unmotherly to want to wind one daughter up against the other, like that. But she wasn't just a mother, she was a mother in business.

Should Connie, then, have confided in her exactly who it was she'd ripped the sweater off from? It would have saved the knock-down and drag-out row they'd just had. But she couldn't honestly hold Connie to blame for not telling her. For one thing, she'd have turned the deal down flat. And the deal had already paid for the dunned knitting frame to be moved back into the hole in the concrete. All paid for, in hard cash.

This appeared to be one of those uncomfortable and unsatisfactory affairs, where no one could properly be saddled with blame.

It had been unfortunate that Connie had been on the premises just then. And that Hector's attempts at peace-making had only fanned the flames. But there you were. Family businesses meant that business rows could turn into personal squabbles. With mud being stirred up in both histories which you hoped had long since settled on the bones of long-dead quarrels.

Sucking the drink back, she knew that not only had Connie enjoyed the fact that it was Nesta who was being ripped off, but that she'd been looking forward to the day when Nesta found out. She had a strong suspicion that if she hadn't blundered—she admitted the word—into the exposure, and so scored an own-goal, Connie would not have rested content until Nesta found out. For the row, and for the look on Nesta's face when the cat was out of the bag. Or the Italian sweater, in this case.

They had slugged each other to a standstill. Connie demanding half of the firm she still said had been stolen off her when she wasn't emotionally capable of fighting back. Nesta telling her in no uncertain, and very shrill terms, that all she was going to get off her was a one-way ticket back to the Med and her greasy boyfriend. And that offer wasn't going to stay open for ever.

Hector, seeing a chance for some high-level shuttle diplomacy, had darted between them, suggesting a compromise. How would it be if Nesta gave up one or two shops? The ones that were proving to be duds, say? So that Connie could start over, at the same time as Nesta benefited by losing the weakest part of her empire?

That suggestion curled and crisped in front of his eyes, as the girls turned on him. He took a ringside seat, and sat on his hands until the wrangle ended, with Nesta storming off. So much for trying to act like a one-man peace-keeping force, when two women got at each other's throats.

Bea poured another shot of coffee liqueur. And eyed Connie broodingly as the flushed woman came into the office.

– Anything else I should know?

– The other designs. The ones we've been selling to the boutiques –

Bea lifted a limp hand. She didn't want to know.

But she did. And sooner than she or Connie expected. Because Dev was stood in the office door.

– I know why you've been at the Fashion School so much. He was tense, but controlled. He wasn't going to make a fool of himself. He just wanted to let Connie know that he knew.

It was an interesting question who had lost the most. Dev, because he was now suspended without pay, since the scandal of the stolen designs broke, incriminating him. Or Eva, the girl whose competition portfolio Connie had lifted down to the last drawing. Drawings which had now come to life as living, breathing knitwear, and were making a substantial contribution to this month's already in-the-black figures.

True, Eva had lost the chance to show the portfolio in competition. Which might mean losing out on a prize that would secure her a glamorous start to her design career on the Continent, or in the States. But she was young. And she'd learnt a useful lesson about the morals of the industry she wanted so badly to work in. Ideas were still bubbling up in her young and lively mind, the way they did in the first heady years of your career. She could work night and day to complete another portfolio, which, who knows, could well turn out better even than her first.

On balance, Eva might not have done so badly.

Dev, by any reckoning, was in a much worse case.

Now that the pirated designs had come to light, spotted by another tutor on a buying trip to the London boutiques where Connie had been careful to place them, the wheels of a major investigation were turning at the college. Already Dev was suspended, and it didn't look hopeful. Starting with Rooftop Annie, a succession of old dates and jilted conquests, students and staff as well, had been wheeled into the Head of School's office. And now the Principal was involved.

The thread by which Dev's career had hung was beginning to twang ominously.

– It's tough all over, was Connie's only consolation. – It was tough for me, when you dumped me eight years back. You get over these things. I know. I majored in getting over things. Especially losing you.

– I need those two half-days a week.

Connie nodded. Of course he did. With them he could still kid himself he was part of the fashion world. When he was bounced out on his ear he'd have nothing to hang on to. Like she had nothing to hang on to, when he'd walked out on her.

– You've been carved. She made no apology about it. – You thought you were going to get your leg over again. But like I keep telling somebody else—nothing in trousers or out of them is going to get in my way this time round.

There are a lot of lonely women in the fashion business. Well into the mortgage years, with hire purchase still outstanding on their little motors. Who'd do anything to hang on to their jobs, work any hours, take any amount of bad-mouthing by their bosses, the owners of the business.

Nesta knew that. Despite her annoyance at finding that she of all people had been ripped off over the trade-show designer sweater, she was canny enough to realise that gave her a hold over Maggie Greer. Good manageresses of the old school were few and far between these days, and in the older woman she had one of the best.

The scene between them left Maggie Greer's blood spattered on the walls and ceiling, but at the end of it she still had a job. And was under no illusions as to how hard she was going to have to work to keep it. Not that it had been an easy ride before. She smoothed her stylish but simple skirt back down, tucked her head between her shoulders, and buckled down.

She'd got her fingers burnt. Been found with her hand in the till up to her shoulders, and so had to pay the price.

And the last person she expected to find knocking on the delivery door of the shop at half nine at night was the person who'd helped push her hand in the fire.

– Tough, said Connie.

– Tough, agreed Maggie Greer. – But it happens.

Connie agreed that it happened.

– The way I heard it, I got caught up in somebody else's family row.

Connie lifted her shoulders.

– Sort of.

The neatly dressed woman opposite her didn't push it further. She'd taken her shot, lost out, and wasn't complaining. You didn't get involved with someone like Connie, if you were the complaining sort.

– She's keeping you on?

– I've five years left on the flat. It's hardly home. You need other people to make it that, but it's somewhere I can kick off my shoes, and unpeel the professional smile. You wouldn't know about that, not now you've got your fella.

Connie passed no comment. The other woman had no way of knowing that was far from the case at the moment. Jamieson hadn't shown for two weekends. There hadn't been a phone call or postcard. She was beginning to know just what sort of evening Maggie Greer had ahead of her. That night, and every night, when she switched the lights and the electric fire on herself.

– I'm surprised she kept you on.

– I went down on my knees and I begged her to keep me, Maggie Greer told her. – Which is why I'm in with the milk most mornings, and here at half nine tonight.

– Can I help? Connie offered. – If she's making it tough, maybe I can get you something with the House of Bea –

– Only to be kicked out when she inherits? She shook her head. – Thanks for the offer, but it's no offer.

– You ran the second shop I ever opened, she reminded the tired manageress of the miles they'd put on the clock together.

– I'm not taking the ride this time, ta.

She looked through the plate glass at the front of the shop. Was Connie's fella out there in the rain somewhere? Why didn't he come on in?

Again Connie passed up the chance to lean on a shoulder. Jamieson was in Zurich, or Berne, or most likely, back with his wife in their garden suburb. Probably this minute penning his farewell note. She wondered what would happen about the cottage, to which she was getting attached. Could she afford to extend the let? Or maybe even make an offer for it, if things kept going well at the factory?

But the rain on the glass somehow reminded her that there was nobody to go back to. Not tonight. Not for the past dozen and more nights. And likely not for the rest of the time she was due to spend there.

There are a lot of lonely women in the fashion business. And Connie had joined the sad ranks.

– Can I borrow your office ten minutes?

Maggie Greer froze. So this was why Connie was round, dripping sympathy. She was up to something.

– Finishing something off, said Connie. – A girl has to make a living. And could have added, under her breath, even when her fella's done the bunk she forecast he would. Which didn't help.

– I ought to throw you out. Even as she said it, Maggie Greer was grinning, despite herself. There was something engaging about downright cheek. Which was why Connie had got away with so much in her business life, as in her personal. There had never been any pretence with her that she was out for anyone save herself. And after the hypocrisy, evasions and self-deceptions of most people, that was refreshing. Even if it did mean danger for those around her.

The girl stood blinking rain out of her eyes. She'd been standing in the shopping precinct for a half-hour, deciding whether to keep the appointment or not. In the end, the rain down the back of her neck and the absence of buses headed her way home, made her cross the deserted flagstones and rap on the shopfront.

She stared at Connie a long time.

– What can I say, Eva, but sorry, kid. Connie offered no defence. – I ripped off your designs. It would be too much to expect you to be flattered right now. But maybe in a month or two –? And this cheque might help.

The girl looked at the cheque on the desk, but didn't touch it. It was for a lot of money. More money than she ever imagined she could make for doing exactly what she wanted to do, which was draw clothes.

The money wasn't important.

– I spent three terms working up that portfolio. It was my best work, my competition work. Now she was speaking, it was coming in a rush. – I could have gone anywhere, if I'd got a place. Now I can't even enter it, because they don't allow work that's been in the shops already. It's that I mind more than the money, or being cheated. I might never get the chance to work abroad, make my name where it matters. You stole my designs, and it was because of what Dev is that you were able to, and I'm not taking a word back of what I told the Head of School. Nor is anybody else.

Did Connie want her to withdraw what she'd said? Had she asked her to –?

But Dev had fixed this meeting, hadn't he, the girl asked, confused. With tears in his eyes he had told her Connie had agreed to see her and explain.

– Let me tell you something, Connie pushed the office door shut. Not to keep its proper occupant out of things, but to make the mood more intimate. More confiding. – Let me tell you why I'm as obsessed by fashion as you are, and why I think I could have an offer for you. Despite what I've done across you.

The girl choked at the thought of Connie, of all people, having the nerve to talk about offers, but Connie had her feet on the desk and was away.

– I always knew I was a looker. That was nothing I could take any credit for, that was just how it panned out. I pulled one of the lucky tickets.

Eva could see this was a statement of fact, not romance or wishful thinking.

– I wasn't complaining, don't get me wrong. Better by far to get into the sort of trouble lookers can get into, than not pull that lucky ticket at all. But my problem was that I just didn't seem to be landing on the sort of fella someone with my looks should have. I've had some low-life fellas, believe me. She shook her head, as if awestruck by some of the memories. – I've had a few shouldn't have been let out by their mums without a bin sack over their heads, and their arms tied to their sides.

Then she made the breakthrough. Or so she'd thought.

– A dentist, he was. Well, a trainee dentist. Or at the very least he said he was a trainee dentist. And he did have big hands. I've clicked, I thought. I always knew I wasn't the scrubber the low-lifes always ended an evening trying to treat me as. And then, after a nice night out, with none of the usual inexpert gum-sucking or amateur obstetrics, he went crazy.

She emphasised it, so there would be no mistake.

– I mean, this trainee dentist, this nice boy went mat-chewing mad when I pulled him off me, and said could he call me a cab. He didn't call me a cab. He called me lots of other things, like tart and whore and scrubber. But not cab. It was a night I could have done with the nine-inch hat-pin and cast-iron corset, I can tell you.

He'd told her she'd no right to play the virgin, the way she'd dressed for the date. All her traffic lights had been blinking amber and green, and what was a trainee dentist to do when he suddenly ran slap into a red?

When she got home that night, with a blackening eye and feeling as if she'd just fought off the Giant Squid from Sixty Thousand Fathoms, she looked at herself in the wardrobe mirror.

– The fella was right. There was a tart in there, looking back at me. And in that moment I said to myself, from now on how I dress is going to tell the world how I feel about me inside. I'm a class bird, not a scrubber, and from now on, nobody's going to make any mistakes about it.

She reached a scotch across, from the bottle Maggie Greer kept for those times when being Maggie Greer was too much for her.

– I drink to you, Eva, and all the others like you. All those who have the gift, the hand and the eye, that makes it possible for all the class birds in the world to show they're class. Who help the lookers get their due, and those who aren't lookers at least a crack at dressing as if they are. To fool the enemy. Which is all the fellas out there.

They touched glasses, and drank.

As the young girl swallowed, Connie knew she had her. She knew which was the right button to press, because she had been that young girl once.

Now for the offer.

Dev had been kicking his heels at the factory for two hours when Connie showed, as promised. His confidence that Connie could pull it off had wavered, then restored itself. What he never doubted was that he'd read her right. He still got her inside, he knew. Dev was never wrong about those things. She'd do the favour, despite those hard words. Just like she'd turn the trick when he got round to getting interested in having her do it for him again.

Maybe tonight? Maybe he should show his gratitude for her getting Eva to withdraw her complaint by taking her when she showed? On the roof, perhaps? In the rain, on the factory roof. That would be symbolic of something. Exactly what, he didn't know. But of something.

When she turned into the narrow Victorian lane, down which generations of tired feet had gone before her, she seemed low. As if all the history of the place had seeped into her walk and her mood. This was two hundred yards from the main road, but there was no one around, and no sound of anything except her tip-tapping towards him. He waited, confident. She stopped yards from him. Maybe, he told himself, because she wants to risk coming nearer, and yet doesn't. That sixth sense that develops between hunter and prey was stopping her right there.

Without a word she opened the yard gate and walked through. He followed. They could be on for the roof, then. Or what about nice and dry in the office? Or against one of the machines? Or in the soft piles of fabric waiting to be overlocked?

They were in the oldest part of the factory, the decaying listed building which had seen the Victorian street-plan lap up against it, blossom with new business, and then slowly start to have the corners fall off it. There were four new knitting frames, still under tarpaulins, waiting for installation in the next working week.

– I got these back here. Me. Nobody but me. There was no triumph in her voice. What should have been a significant moment in her fight to wrestle at least part of the firm out of Nesta's hands had gone flat. Sometimes she wanted to walk away. Sometimes she felt she could pick up the entire factory, and all the people in it, who'd carry on with their busy pointless little lives and never realise. She'd hold it there, and then take one step back and let it smash.

She felt that especially these days, when there was no one to go back to, after a day of carrying on with her own busy pointless little life and career.

But she knew she'd never do it. Because she was one of the grafters. She had Hector's flash, and Bea's lust for work. The House of Bea had her hooked, well and truly. Fashion had her hooked and gaffed.

– You saw her? Dev felt he had to kick the business of the evening into touch, before getting down to the personal, the intimate side. On the roof. Or maybe smack centre of the factory floor. That could be a turn-on.

She had.

– And let me tell you something, Dev. That kid's a natural. She's got perfect pitch for clothes. Unlike you. Let me tell you something else, just before I bounce you out of my life for good –

He froze in the act of sliding his hand across to her. Having decided to take her suddenly, once she reported what he wanted to know. Leave her no option, but to give in dead in the smack centre of the concrete floor.

– You were never up to much as a designer. I used to fake your sales figures. You didn't know that, did you? You were rubbish. I mean a bad joke. I mean not very good.

The girl, on the other hand, was born to the business. And to sweeten her introduction to it, which so far had been more than usually bruising, Connie had offered her her own label, on the House of Bea frames. Any time she wanted to run something off, experimental, or main-stream High St. fashion line, to see how it looked, she'd be welcome. All Connie asked in return was first refusal in anything she thought sellable.

It was an offer no high-flyer could afford to turn down. How many got the chance to break into the real world of buying and selling, while still learning their skills in the protected world of college? It was a relationship that would benefit everybody. The girl got used to the everyday rough and tumble, where the bottom line wasn't the thought behind the design but how well it sold; and the firm got an input that would keep them in touch with what was going to be selling tomorrow, and the day after.

Eva's label was never going to be the main selling line, because the bread-and-butter was still the pink acrylic for the old bat trudging round Tesco's—but Connie one day intended the business to move a little up-market from that. You had to keep dodging and twisting to stay alive these days, with a fashion market that changed three times every season.

– And what about me? Dev had listened impatiently, as Connie, without a trace of gloating, outlined how she'd done the snow-job on the model pupil. Who in a world where there was any justice, should next be seeing Connie in court, suing her, rather than meeting her in a solicitor's office, to sign a contract.

– You? Connie looked as if the suggestion that he should have figured in any conversation between her and his star pupil came from left of left field. – We never mentioned you, Dev.

– I fixed the meeting. You said, you promised you would see her for me.

– I said I'd see her, if you could fix it. She reminded him. – I don't think I said or promised anything else.

There are a lot of lonely women in the fashion business. Who end up a hard day's grafting, and buying and selling, and twisting and turning, and winning and losing, sitting by themselves, in empty offices, with the shades down. Trying to summon up the effort to go home to that empty flat or cottage, knowing that there is another day of hard grafting, and buying and selling and all the rest of it starting first thing tomorrow. And another lonely night at the end of that.

What was winning out over Dev, and snowing Eva, and proving yet again to Bea that there was no hole she could dig herself into that she couldn't also dig her way out of—if dinner was for one, and there was only the hot-water bottle to tuck up with, at home?

She slammed the desk drawer shut on the bottle she'd decided not to drink from, in case she got maudlin, and started on the long slope that got steeper with every bottle a lonely woman could put away. Turned, and there was Jamieson.

– Look at you. She recovered fast. Not giving anything away. And not knowing but that he wasn't back to take aim, and fire that bullet. Confirm it was going to be dinner for one, from now on – You stay away for a few days, and you're back looking the picture of sartorial incompetence again. No one under eighty or outside a pine box should be seen dead in a vee-neck pullover under a suit jacket.

– I've been to see Sonia.

The name took a moment to register. Sonia, his wife. The other woman. Or was she the other woman? Properly, she supposed she filled that least flattering of all job descriptions. She could take it. If he was back to fire the bullet, Connie wasn't the sort to ask for a blindfold.

– Don't tell me. I'm there already. You fell on the mat, explained all, begged forgiveness, and made love in an ecstasy of reconciliation until your eyes boiled.

So was he back to do the decent thing, the Cashmere Kid thing, and tell her it was over to her face? Or did he want to rearrange their relationship? Make Connie even more of an occasional thing? Keep her on at the cottage until the let was up, but only see her when he fancied a quick poke, a sudden bash?

He was talking about a file. A file his wife and he had kept, from the first months of their outwardly perfect marriage. A company marriage. Reflecting his dedication to his career, of which a wife was such an important part, if it was always to be onwards and upwards through the executive ranks of Siggins, Bower and Comer.

– We entertain a lot. Business friends, bosses, overseas visitors. We keep a file on everybody. Their favourite food and drinks and special interests. What they like to talk about, what they don't like to talk about. Cross-referenced against details of who's sleeping with who, in the firm, or who would like to be sleeping with who.

This was all very interesting, Connie intimated. But what did it have to do with her? Surely he hadn't opened a filing card for her. Not that it wouldn't have been eye-popping to have come across it.

– That file is everything I've come to hate about the way I lived before. Neatly, tidily. Hanging up my trousers in the same way every night, after taking all the change out. I want to live untidily. I want to live in the same sprawling way you do. Weekends and stray days with you just aren't enough any more. It's got to be full-time. I've left her. For good.

Seven

Those first couple of months Connie was back nothing could go wrong for her. She had only to pick up a phone, and someone would give her an order for a thousand dozens. If she called in person to see someone who'd been getting touchy about outstanding bills, they called off the dogs, and offered a further credit line. The same golden touch was working in her private life. Whatever the ongoing state of affairs with her Greek boyfriend, she now had Jamieson poodling after her. Still keeping down his job with the firm, but commuting from the cottage. And not above turning a few hours in for the House of Bea at weekends, and days off.

Hector was pleased. Not only because she was his daughter. But because the rising sales and profit figures meant that Bea was less inclined to take out her financial frustrations on him. The firm was some way from being an obvious take-over candidate for one of the giants, but the dark days were lightening by the week. Business was good, Bea was relaxed. And Hector was left free to pursue his out-of-hours amours. Connie hadn't even had to get involved with a messy matrimonial break-up involving Jamieson's wife.

The businesslike exec had approached things coolly, sorting out the property and financial things at the same time as the inside things. In previous similar circumstances Hector had always left messily, and had female furies pursue him for months, or weeks after. Secretly, he rather thought that was the only honourable way for these things to end, and that there was something chilling in Jamieson's level-headed, wall-plan-charted approach. But it did keep things neat and tidy. With no danger of sudden outbreaks of recrimination or even violence weeks, or months, down the line.

Connie was back, and things were going sweet as sugar-lolly for her, and that was spreading a warm glow all around. For everybody, he supposed, but Dev and Nesta. But was that a bad thing? Those two well deserved some grit deposited between the cogs of their usually super-smooth maraudings.

Life, and women had taught the dapper lady-killer that the

engine is at its sweetest, and the propellers churning most faultlessly through the blue and undisturbed water, as the ship is on its way to meet the iceberg. But try as he might, he couldn't see anything to cause pain, anxiety and grief in his business or personal affairs, in the foreseeable future.

So Hector turned away from his overview of what Connie's still unexplained return had meant, and decided to enjoy. Even if he had been more narrow-eyed as to the prospects ahead, he would not have guessed that the storm would come from Arnie's direction, of all people. And would figure another Greek. Not Connie's Greek, but one far more dangerous than that slick spic with the suntanned whatsit.

The morning Arnie was beaten up he'd been knocking his brains out trying to drum the rudiments of working and selling on the barrows into something with pimples. It had taken the Job Centre three weeks to come up with a suggestion, and his heart sank at the prospect when it showed. Ever game, and knowing that the gift of the patter descends on the oddest people, he decided to give it a try. Babs was stalwart on the standing around and looking good side of things—but she just didn't have the killer instinct you need to be a successful closer of a sale.

And every so often, the little mystery he'd picked up on that lay-by headed for it again. Part of the deal they had was that he wouldn't ask where she was headed, and who she had to keep in touch with. It was killing him that he didn't know, and every time she left he pickled himself in the hard stuff, trying not to think what he'd do if she didn't come back. But that was the deal, and he was sticking to it. He'd had one with Connie before, that he hadn't stuck to. Which was what he was doing with a caved-in face, boozer's eyes, on a market stall.

The Job Centre's star didn't instantly inspire confidence, gazing about him, as Arnie thought, with all the inner sparkle of a lobotomised camel. But he gave him the benefit of the speil anyway.

– Lesson one is wrap up warm.

Odd how many people never clocked that one. That was an essential. It just wasn't possible to sell a pair of strides if you were freezing in your own. Arnie strongly advised the lad to invest in a pair of long johns from the Army Surplus stall, or, if he was that way inclined, to borrow a pair of his girlfriend's old tights.

He then moved to the general principles of choosing a market pitch, unaware that even as he spoke a mud-spattered Rolls Royce was bringing down on his head someone who would shortly make the choosing of one an academic matter.

– You can have the best pitch on the site, which is usually the line from the car-park to the bogs or hot-dog stand, but you've still got to get noticed. That's why Babs is handy—He brought the dreary youth's suddenly vitalised attention to Babs, who was bent over stacking jeans some feet away. – No one's going to miss that backside in stretch denims, are they?

Arnie strongly believed in getting noticed, as the one necessary preface to making a sales pitch. After Connie had gone to Greece, and he'd blown his share of the settlement, and he'd dried out half-way, and decided he needed something to give him the motivation to keep going to the end of the treatment, he'd bought a box of seconds for a fiver. It was February. He'd stood in Loughborough market, in a drizzle, and started a strip. Jacket, shirt, shoes, socks. When he was down to his underpants he'd started selling the crowd who were standing around watching, and he'd never since moved knitwear so fast.

He told the kid with the gaping mouth and the face that looked like it had come off the top of a pizza about women. The stall dealt in men's clothes as well, but so much shopping was done by women for and with their men, that knowing how to sell women was all important.

– You sell the woman who knows how to wear clothes easier than the woman who looks like a dog. And the difference between them is in the walk. If a woman can walk, she can get away with a torn sheet round her hips, and a dishrag on her head. If she can't, then a Paris original is going to look like your grandad's old mac on her. And she's hard to sell because she doesn't look good in anything, and she'll take that out on the salesman.

The most important thing to know about women was that whenever two of them met, without exception, not even two nuns, he'd swear, there was a battle going on. They summed each other up in ten seconds dead, always starting at the face. Unlike with men, who they started off judging by the shoes. There was always the one result—one came off the winner, and the other the loser. And they both knew which.

– So you're helping out whoever you're selling in that life-long punch-up the girls are having around us fellas, every hour of the day, without us ever noticing. You're in the ring holding a towel for them, and you've got to care for them. Care? You've got to be obsessed by them. They're your bread and butter, and the magic mysterious tree of the ultimate secret of life. Got it?

The youth didn't reply. He was quite content to stay on the dole, doing his little bit to bring down the government by adding to the unemployment statistics, and standing round in the rain six days a week didn't appeal to him at all. Helping birds into and out of their gear behind a make-shift screen was something he wouldn't say no to, but he could always work on that in his own time.

He tried to figure out a way of phrasing his refusal of the job offer that wouldn't bring his benefit to a sudden stop, but needn't have bothered. Because Arnie's attention was suddenly taken up by something else. The arrival of a Roller containing a middle-aged Greek and what looked like a wholesale buy of mean-looking cousins.

Kyprianou had got tired of taking dud cheques and fast-talking promises off Arnie.

He'd come to collect.

From the staff, and out of Arnie's suddenly very-white chin.

Someone else collecting that morning was Nesta.

She'd told Dev he'd be back one day, and he was. She'd said – See you, Dev, as he'd made off down the spiral staircase, and so she was seeing him again. In the office. And he was asking for help in getting even with Connie. Like she'd said.

It wasn't essential that Dev give her all the details of why he wanted to get his own back, but she insisted. And could only admire, in a twisted sort of, Nesta sort of way, her step-sister's adroitness in taking advantage.

What was Dev offering, apart from resentment? What that was useful to her?

He lifted his shoulders. And let his eyes flicker a moment towards the corner of the room, and that staircase.

He couldn't think that was enough, Nesta asked him? He surely didn't think she was going to go out of her way to screw Connie, because he would screw with her? Even if it was to be on a regular basis, a boy and girl basis, a steady, dating old-fashioned basis, and not just a casual affair? Having established the price he might have to pay, she sat back and watched him try to come to terms with it.

Okay.

That hadn't been the sort of deal he was after, but if she insisted. If Nesta wanted someone to be on her arm, and in her bed on a regular basis, he'd hack it. He had to. He was about to be thrown out of his flat, and couldn't see that he had any choice. Not if she was offering.

She turned the knife a little more.

– You think I need a fella so bad I'd take him on and feed him? You haven't got a job. Not even the pretend one at the college.

That was true. He wasn't denying it. But he was looking for something. There were offers. He couldn't say what, she'd understand that. But any day now he expected to hear good news.

– Or any week? Or any year? Or any lifetime?

She was offering him the job he'd turned down. The travelling nark's job. The job of the fella who tuned the staff up with a blow-torch, preparatory to Nesta going in with the flame-thrower, and burning bits off. To encourage the others.

– This is a suit job. She warned him, turning the knife again, watching his eyes. – You get that? It's an admin job, not a designing job. I can't offer you a designing job, because you're no good. You never were any good. You're a wash-up in that line. Did Connie make that clear enough to you?

Connie had. Which was one of the most livid scars he still carried from his run-in with her.

– I want the job. I want you to pay her back.

That was his bottom line. She knew she had him, by the way he said it. With a venom that came near to her own, whenever she spoke of Connie these days.

– Let's go for it. She nodded, accepting his offer and his surrender.

But first there was a formality. He'd not completed the job interview the last time. It was Nesta's practice never to take on staff, however much she fancied them, unless they passed the practical. The last time he'd been to see her, if she remembered right, he'd chickened out. This time, he'd better show a little more determination. A lot more determination.

In fact, there was still a chance, if he didn't pull all the stops out on those black silk sheets and leave her wide-eyed and legless, that he'd still be leaving here without a job, woman, or roof over his head.

He passed.

It left him limping for three days, but she gave him an A-plus.

Dev was in business again. Working full-time in fashion, even though not on the creative side. It looked like Arnie was out of business. For good.

They hadn't worked him over badly. You could almost have said he got that fist in the mouth by accident. As he tried to stop one of the cousins from grabbing the money bag around Bab's neck, to go with the contents of the stall. He'd been able to accept everything else but that. Babs had been about to give the cousin two fingers straight in the eyes, maybe revealing what a hard school she'd been brought up in, before hitting the road which led to that lay-by.

Ever the knight, Arnie had got in the way. And been bounced a little for his trouble.

By the time Babs had pinched off the bleeding from his nose and decided that the teeth put through his lip wasn't worth going to casualty for stitching, the Roller, everything on the stall, and Kyprianou were long since gone.

He'd got away lightly, if you believed all the stories you got told about the Greek.

Hector always regretted the accident that Connie was in the factory when Arnie came around begging seconds to open up the stall with again. If she hadn't ear-holed that, all the following unpleasantness would not have occurred. True, it turned out well in the finish, but he could have done without the moments that turned the juice in his stomach sour.

She always made a bee-line for what would give her most trouble, like he had done all his life. The difference now was that he was looking forward to a cushioned retirement in five or six years' time. Sooner, if Connie kept cracking the whip. He could do without the excitement of getting involved with Kyprianou. He'd heard the stories, too.

Connie hadn't, of course, because she'd been away eight years. She'd missed the splintering of the business, as different ethnic groups moved into it, and fought for sales, outlets, and suppliers. The clothing business, like catering attracted immigrants, the new starters in a strange land. The rule that said by working twenty-four hours a day over one knitting frame, you could in five or ten years' time look forward to owning a factory of them, applied to people straight off the boat.

Kyprianou wasn't exactly that. His family had business connections in the country going way back. Kyprianou was the first, however, to put a toe into the garment game. A toe in a steel-tipped boot.

The stories said he was a thug, and a shotgun merchant. That people who crossed him got hurt much worse than Arnie had been hurt. That fire-bombs came through his rivals' windows in the middle of the night far too often for it to be coincidence. That he wasn't above putting the torch to his own premises for insurance.

– It always happens to friends of friends? You never meet somebody it personally happened to? Connie was sceptical, even after Bea and Hector's lurid painting of the background of the man Arnie had come off second-best to.

Bea admitted Kyprianou attracted rumours. But even if you discounted the wilder of the stories, you were still left with the fact that he'd locked up what knitwear business the Asians hadn't, supplied all the party plans in the North-West, and ran a dozen wholesale discount stores that were priced keenly enough to hurt. There was also the undeniable fact that he was usually seen in a swarm of mean, keen, nasty and lean cousins, who watched every move he made in his second-hand Roller and out of it.

– A man like that should be avoided like head-lice, was Bea's firm conclusion to the discussion, as she ushered Arnie downstairs to take his pick at the seconds, for old times' sake. Hector concurred, more than whole-heartedly. He got a shiver all the way up and down the yellow streak along his spine, just hearing the man's name.

But Connie left that night, thinking that a fella like that was just the person the House of Bea needed to get into bed with.

Jamieson had a couple of days' leave owing. If Connie could get away from the factory they were going to tool round the Lake District, or to the West Country, well away from streets of shops selling knitwear and factories making it. He was developing an interest in the piratical nature of the business, but you could have too much. Connie had to live, eat, drink and breathe it six and sometimes seven days a week. He wanted her to share his days off, doing something well away from it.

Connie had other plans.

She was going to be working that week anyway, she told him, in between forkfuls over another rushed dinner. He was just back from Berne, she'd sprinted to Newcastle and back in a day. But she wasn't prepared to have him lounge around the cottage. Who knows, but he might get to thinking what a crazy thing he'd done in throwing his past life over, to risk all with her. What he needed was to be kept busy.

Did she have anything busy in mind?

He needn't have asked.

Of course she did.

– There's this guy called Kyprianou. Not my Greek. Another. I've been hearing a lot about him. One or two good things, like he smacked my ex around the other day, and that might knock some sense into him. But mainly bad.

She ran through the list of bad.

– Where do I come in? Jamieson was puzzled, and rightly so.

– I want him zapped. Once, for what he did to Arnie. Who may be a shit, but who's still family. And in this business you can't afford to let it be seen your family doesn't protect its own. Twice, because somebody like that shouldn't be allowed to get away with it. If he does, then the honest businessman doesn't have a chance. The Beas and Hectors go to the wall.

A bemused Jamieson pointed out that Connie's shop-gossip was all about the latest stunts, tricks and cheats that she, Hector and Bea had put across the opposition. Hadn't there been a small matter of pirating designs, not too long back?

Connie impatiently tried to describe why that was different. That was sharp business practice, staying well the right side of the line. What Kyprianou was alleged to get up to was something very different. That was shotgun merchant stuff. And if, as she hoped and expected, Jamieson came back with a nil report on that aspect of his trading methods, he should still be hammered for getting an unfair advantage by encouraging those sort of stories.

She sketched in Jamieson's credentials for the job of sleuthing the Greek. He was used to big business, accounts, handling people and figures, working out where the money was going. Admittedly, up to now it had been very gloves-on, with respected national and international names. But surely that meant taking on a tin-plate gun-man like the Greek would be easy? How could there be any contest? He'd chase him for a week, bring back a report, and that would be that.

– What would be what?

– I'd walk in on him, confront him with it all, and see him off.

– Just like that?

Connie nodded. Jaw set. Eyes sparkling. Just like that.

How could he refuse? Hadn't his entire business career, from business school onwards, been training him up for this one assignment? This little assignment. This assignment that meant he'd be in hardly any danger at all. Because she didn't believe for one moment he really was a shotgun merchant. No matter what the rest of the world did.

All this was very interesting, and indeed flattering. But it didn't add up to half a reason why Jamieson should give up the cottage and its comforts for an hour, let alone a holiday week, and race round the country, hot on the heels of somebody who may, or may not, have had a lifetime love-affair with shortened shotguns.

Connie used the clincher.

Once the six months were up she had a decision to make. He'd burnt his bridges, but that didn't mean she had to follow suit. And she couldn't guarantee to stay on indefinitely with him, if he didn't get more acceptance from the family. To be sure, he got by on rubbing-along terms with Bea and Hector. But someone who believed so strongly in the family virtues as her, needed to feel that her fella was one of them.

Ignoring what she knew for a fact, that Hector would explode at the first mention of what she was up to, she spooned the cassata ice-cream down, and waited for his answer. It seemed to her, she sweetly prompted, that someone in his position, who'd taken so much time and trouble to rearrange his property and financial affairs, would feel very foolish having to unscramble them. If, as could be unless he said yes, she walked out on him once those six months were up.

Hector went through the roof, which wasn't in too good a state of repair anyway, when Connie broke the news at Jamieson's insistence. She was all for him leaving quietly, then bringing his report back as a triumphant surprise. But canny Jamieson said if he was doing this for the House of Bea, he'd like board approval.

Bea had her doubts, but choked them back. It wasn't that she was taken in by Connie's claim that she was doing this to preserve the good name of the knitwear business, and the ground rules the small and decent people in it had a vested interest in keeping. She'd seen the sense of making a deal with someone like the Greek, to take the extra volume the new frames in the listed building section of the factory were capable of turning out.

The Board went along with deputing Jamieson to go after Kyprianou, so long as he did it quietly, and kept at a safe distance. This Jamieson was only too keen to promise. He had a list of the names who figured in the more enduring of the shotgun and petrol-bomb stories, and they were to be his first points of contact. Thereafter, it was up to him.

– Madness, was Hector's verdict on the whole thing. – Suicide. You know what the insurance is on this fire-trap already? If a bomb through the back window didn't wipe us out, the increased premiums would.

But the Board, in the person of the majority partner swung, if a little stiffly, and feeling that it had been faced with a fait accompli, towards Connie.

She could set her dogs on to the Greek. But if he turned round, shotgun at the ready, she'd be on her own. Her and her boyfriend both.

It was what Bea had to say, or rather, didn't have to say about this latest extravagance of Connie's, that caused Nesta to set Dev on Jamieson. She was just too damn mysterious, and pleased about something that was going forward at the firm for someone of Nesta's sharpness not to have picked it up. After they'd played their eighteen rounds, and a reluctant Nesta had picked up a tenner for every hole she'd won out over, she headed back to the shop and office very thoughtfully.

She knew that Bea enjoyed playing daughter off against step-daughter. Every time she dropped by at the office, or they played their weekly round of golf, Bea had some further titbit for her. How Connie had pulled off an impossible sale. How she'd found a way to fiddle the interlockers' piece-work rate in the management's favour. Always some more needle for Nesta. Knowing that would make Nesta work harder in her own line of business, and that would be a spur to Connie, to rival, equal and exceed.

Today, however, as Bea swatted and hacked her way around the fairway and greens, determined to get her money's worth out of the year's subscription, even though she hated the dour game, there was another flavour to the needle. Bea was keeping something under her hat, and it had to do with Connie. Whenever Nesta tried to swing the conversation around, Bea parried her. Asking how she was getting on with the latest, if darkish flame in her life. Or questioning her closely on the mark-up in retail of the sports and leisurewear line that Nesta was now moving into.

Whatever Connie was up to now was a little more dangerous than usual, it seemed. And Bea was turned on by that danger, even though she was apprehensive.

Phone Hector? Pay him a surprise visit, to see if he was sharing the same feelings? Even if she found him alone, he'd be hardly likely to come clean. There was the tie of blood between him and Connie, however long they'd been apart. The same tie that was between her and Bea.

Try Jamieson? The new man in her step-sister's life seemed keen to keep her at arm's length. Not particularly because he was apprehensive of her, she rightly judged. But because that offered scope for complications, and he was in no hurry to get involved in a family war. If she was, however, to approach him in the right way, suggest she wanted to find a way to repair her bridges to her sister? Might he not want to help with that?

She still hadn't decided whether to approach him or not, when she got back to the shop. Dev was in the back, trying to look as if he hadn't been chatting up the blonde assistant with the brace on her teeth. She vaguely wondered if it meant you were getting old when the sales assistants started looking younger and younger.

This was a changed Dev. He was wearing a suit, and a collar and a tie. It made him look very different. Pulled him upright, made him seem stiff and uncertain of himself. He still looked as sexy as he ever did to her, but it was a different sort of appeal. The wolf had been crammed into sheep's bank-clerk clothing, and she sort of liked it. Because she knew the wolf belonged to her. She'd put him in that business suit, and she only had to snap her fingers to have him step out of it. Upstairs. On top of that well-trod staircase.

She tugged his tie straight. He could be excused for the untidy way he'd made the knot. It had to be years since Dev had to wear one.

He watched her, his face sour. It required a great act of will not to take it off, and throttle her with it, there, her back arched across the antique leather of her desk top.

Nesta knew what he was thinking, and that was a turn-on too. What was the use of a pet on a chain, if it didn't have claws? Dodging those claws, and sometimes allowing the animal to use them on you?

Afterwards, as she wiggled her toe into the suit-jacket and lifted it in the air, to check how well it was made, she made her decision. Dev wasn't going to get to go to Milan with her. She knew she'd promised him, and he'd been looking foward to it as a little holiday before he buckled down to getting out on the road six days a week for her. But something else had come up.

Dev was going to get stuck into Jamieson for her. Before she approached him, she wanted some spade-work done. Dev would find out what made Connie's fella tick. His turn-ons, and his no-nos. She wanted a map of the area, before she blundered into it.

– But that means I don't get to Milan. Dev caught up.

– Milan isn't going to go away, she promised him. – Stick with me and you'll be as sick of Milan and Rome and Paris and Frankfurt as I am.

But only if he showed he could do this job for her.

Which was why when Dev turned up at the factory, having driven Nesta to the airport, and saw Jamieson load two suitcases into his car, he wasn't sure what to do. Should he report to Nesta that he'd just missed him, and make the blonde assistant with the brace on her teeth? Or should he pile into his own car, and give chase?

Dev knew a meal-ticket when one was pressed into his hand. Sooner or later he'd not be able to take much more of being kicked around by Nesta, but just now he was enjoying three square meals a day, use of flat, motor, and her more than willing body. Which wasn't the greatest he'd ever been in bed with, but which was at least there. And willing. And grateful. After the years doing the job on the run, as it were, with a string of wide-eyed students, he was enjoying the luxury of making love with an experienced woman, with time to spare.

He also had hopes that one day, whatever she said now, she'd let him show her some designs. And come the day when she took over the House of Bea, if he was still in play, or had left her gracefully, who knew but that he wouldn't get his own label again? The easy way. Designers did come back, Dev passionately believed it. In his own case, as an exception to the general rule, yes, but he believed.

He was as drunk on the business of fashion as anyone else.

He reversed down the street and waited, feeling ridiculous at the private-eye feel of what he was doing. And made the left Jamieson made, and the same turn at the roundabout, and on to the motorway headed to the North-West six bumpers behind him.

Eight

Kyprianou was a great believer in the family. Witness the cousins. And the bedrock of family life was religious observance. Not the core of the religious experience. But exactly the observance. He hadn't been a whole-hearted believer back home, but like many exiles, once he was abroad, the tug of the familiar was too strong for him. Which was why Kyprianou the keen garment-trade man, and Kyprianou the keen family man, was also Kyprianou the keen supporter of his local Greek Orthodox church. Had, in fact, put a lot of his money into the fitting of it into the shell of a run-down Anglican parish church, which no longer had the waters of faith lapping against it.

That was as private a place as any to see the woman who'd been making persistent phone calls to his home as well as his business premises. She wouldn't say what she was after, and he'd run a blank on the check-list that came to mind. None of his cousins, or nephews or nieces could help out either. The woman was a mystery to them. It could be that one of the male side of the family had been playing around outside the tightly-knit Greek and Greek Cypriot community. But he would have expected, as godfather of the clan, to have been quietly approached on that.

After the fifth annoying, but polite call had insisted that it really would be in his interest to arrange a meeting, he decided he had no option. But the meeting would take place on the turf he chose, and at a time of his dictation. His persistent caller thanked him as politely as she had made her request over the past three days, and hung up.

A little worry grumbled away at him, on his way to the leafier part of town where the church was situated, blazing inside with un-English gilt and icons. He'd run down a dozen times the list of things he might have to worry about, over a meeting like this. But came up with no sensible answers. There could be danger, but he could hardly think it was physical danger. Not if the outfit he was dealing with allowed a woman to front them. If there was an outfit.

But the very fact they had fronted with a woman might mean they were more dangerous than he'd given them credit for. Perhaps he was intended to wander in with his face shiny and his willy hanging out? Thinking he was dealing with a single woman, or an outfit so wimpish they allowed a woman to do the talking for them?

No chances.

No shotguns. He didn't own one, and nor did any of the cousins. He'd seen too much of firearms back home, where the embers of family feuds and civil wars still burst into flames from time to time. But with a car-load of cousins behind his Rolls, and another in front. And a tight packing of two others either side of him in the back seat, behind the darkened windows, with the little affectation of a sun-blind pulled down as well.

He even made the drivers throw a dog-leg into the route from his out-of-town house to the church. Feeling, as he gave the order, much the same as Dev had done. That he was acting a part he wasn't very good at, in a movie that he wouldn't have bothered to see anyway.

What Dev most of all wanted was a shower, and clean sheets. After two thousand motorway miles, trying to keep in touch with Jamieson's back number-plate, and four nights in cheap hotels, his mouth felt like the floor of a budgie's cage, and his eyes were revolving in opposite directions. It wouldn't have been so bad if he had any idea what Jamieson's trip north-west, south, north-east and back to the Midlands was supposed to add up to. But he'd stuck to him, even at the price of only having been able to grab junk food on the run.

His head hadn't been back on the pillow in Nesta's flat ten minutes when the phone went. Nesta wanted him to pick her up at the airport. Now. And if he couldn't make it straight away, could it perhaps be because he was in bed with the assistant who was advertising her dentist's hardware?

He dragged himself down the spiral staircase and flopped into the car seat again. He fancied even the engine note said Oh Christ when he turned the key. The only consolation in having to break his beauty sleep was knowing that he'd performed beyond the call of duty for Nesta. Showed initiative, skill and dash. Surely even Nesta couldn't fail to be impressed with that?

Connie was impressed by what Jamieson had come up with. She scanned the file he'd put together. Her man had checked every lead, which had taken him to what seemed like every fire-trap, sweat-shop, dodgy wholesale warehouse, or union office in the country. The Greek was paying under the legal rate; employing minors and illegal aliens; ignoring every health and safety regulation, and chased the unions off his premises with curses, threats and big black dogs. It was all much as everyone had suspected for years, but no one before had put it on paper. All that was missing was confirmation of the shotguns.

– Nothing, Jamieson knuckled his eyes, looking forward to a shower and clean sheets as much as Dev had been. – But that doesn't prove there isn't anything to be found.

Connie agreed.

Which was why she had a dry prickle in her throat ever since Kyprianou had agreed to meet her, and had dictated the location. It would almost have been better to have known for sure. That way she could have taken precautions. Like keeping the hell away from him. But Jamieson had worked so hard on the report that she had to make use of it. Plus the other one he'd come back with. The dossier raised by a union official who had been trying to nail the Greek for years.

– Don't let it out of your sight, he made her promise. – Kyprianou would give a lot for that.

She promised, and kissed him on the tip of his nose. She was going to see the Greek alone, while Jamieson rested up. She'd started this, and she was going to finish it.

Even though she could be about to walk into Shotgun Alley.

Nesta wasn't impressed with what Dev had to report. Not entirely. She agreed with him that he'd put a lot of leg-work in. But leg-work wasn't enough. A monkey with a driving licence could have done what Dev had.

– I haven't had a proper meal or a decent bed for four days and nights. The injustice of it all choked him. – Have you ever tried to get a decent meal in Gateshead at ten at night? A room with a shower in Warrington any time?

But what was the point, if all he'd come back with was a random list of addresses? She could tell this hadn't been a straightforward buying or selling trip. Even if the House of Bea would have sent an outsider like Jamieson on such an errand. It wasn't that she was as far as ever from getting a handle on what Connie was up to. She was even further away and that was all down to Dev's being content to tag on behind, and not make the running.

How the hell could Dev make any running, he wanted to know, genuinely upset. What sort of running could he make? Hadn't it been enough that he'd come back with a faithful list of where Jamieson had been? And wasn't it up to superwoman herself to make sense of it?

There was justice in what he said, Nesta conceded. But only to herself. It wouldn't do for him to spot any chinks in her armour, so soon in their relationship. There was something she was missing. The list of factories, retail outlets and, most puzzling of all, the union organisers added up to something. But she couldn't see it.

– Now can I go back to bed? Dev pleaded. And could have added that he wanted bed, for once, as a place to sleep. Any more elaborate welcome home she wanted would have to keep.

He could go back to bed, she agreed. After he'd driven her to the factory, to tackle Bea head on. She had an interest in the business, didn't she? Or would have, when Bea and Hector decided they'd had their run for their money in manufacture. She had rights. Getting to the bottom of mysterious trips by the least likely candidate was one of those rights.

They got to the factory yard just as Bea and Hector were driving off. Jamieson sat in the passenger seat. Connie had sent him off home via Arnie, whom she wanted to have on hand outside the church. Because Arnie would want to be in there at the kill. When she took the Greek. Message delivered, Jamieson would have liked to do nothing better than head towards the country. Had in fact driven well out of town before he sighed, reversed in a farm track, and headed to the factory. He was disobeying Connie's strict instructions, but he felt that she shouldn't be allowed to keep the meeting to herself. He knew, of course he knew, that she could dig herself out of every hole she'd dug herself into. And he was very, very tired, and out of his depth when it came to handling people like the Greek. But all the same, if Kyprianou was turning up for the meeting with a team, the House of Bea should be going in mob-handed as well.

But what a mob. His physical tiredness, and the mental

imbalance that went with it, made the prospects for the three who comprised it, seem even more odd. Apart from himself, who was new to this world, there was the Hot Pant King and the Queen Bea. Both of whom were too old to get involved with racketeers. Even if the racketeers weren't in the event mobsters, and the only violence Kyprianou and his cousins wielded was that of the tongue.

This could be a massacre, he sighed, shrinking even further inside his creased suit.

Dev and Nesta stuck several car lengths behind. Dev was getting expert at threading through traffic after somebody else's exhaust pipe. He'd that much to thank Nesta for. It was a new skill to add to his c.v. If an even more useless one than designing clothes, in a business where everybody just knew, for certain and for final, that designers never came back.

Connie was passing up an opportunity that might never occur again, she knew. How often do you get a chance to walk in off a Midlands street, and find yourself by the Med? Outside were those English brick colours, and the air that felt like Sunday gravy with the lumps in. Inside was incense, and golds and blues and reds and royal purples that never did have any place in English worship. And somebody in a back room or crypt, it was hard to tell from the echoing fabric, was practising fiddly bits of a hymn. Or psalm. Or maybe just practising reading out the notices for the upcoming service. The Greek Orthodox did tend to lay it on with a trowel, when it came to the showy bits.

It was all very different from the pious gloom which had held sway in the mid-Victorian building before the Greeks had moved in. She warmed to it. It brought back memories of the Greece she knew, the chapel where she'd been once or twice with Georgiou, whitewashed, burning with colour inside, set high on the cliff over the impossibly blue sweep of the bay.

Georgiou.

She put all thoughts of him aside, as she looked round for the man she'd come to see. As she put aside any sociological reflections on the contrasting styles of church decoration, and all that said about the different images of the same god. She'd kicked her way into the room where the big game in town was being played. Now she had to show she was up to taking on the hard-faced men with the big cigars.

– Why are you doing this to me?

Kyprianou had good English, she knew that. But he made a point of having everything he said translated out of the demotic by a cousin in spectacles. Two others hovered by each exit. The gimmick was intended, she supposed, to add to the drama of the moment, and the sinister reputation of the man. It didn't work on her. It annoyed her, in fact, because it gave a slow-motion quality to the dialogue between them. Connie was a fast talker, and she firmly believed that the faster you talked, the faster you thought. Waiting for the rigmarole between Kyprianou and his totally superfluous interpreter could slow her brain down to a walking pace. And she needed to be speeding on a high at this moment, more than any other in her career since she'd come back.

– Mr. Kyprianou says why are you doing this to him? Why have you come into his life? Mr. Kyprianou says isn't business hard enough these days, without people in the business making things more difficult for other people in the business?

She ignored the cousin in glasses completely. Slapped the two files on the pew in the gap between herself and the man she'd come to see. Talk to the vent, and not the dummy, that was her approach.

– One of these files is a trade union round-up of all the pay and health and safety fiddles you get up to. With names, and dates, and phone numbers of people who'll be willing to stand up against you, when the file's thick enough.

Kyprianou flicked his eyes at the interpreter, but said nothing. You had to admire his self control, admitted Connie.

– The other is the nearest anyone has ever got to drawing a complete picture of the companies you own, and how the money circulates between them. I had it specially done by someone who's used to financial wheeler-dealing. How would you like the Inland Revenue and the Value Added Tax people to get a look at it?

Again he bit on the bullet, waiting for the interpreter. Connie realised that the ploy also gave him time to collect his thoughts, take aim for a reply that would be all the deadlier for the fact he had extra breathing space to shape it in. She couldn't allow that.

– And as an appendix, there's three pages on your frauds against the development agencies. You know those mugs who hand out taxpayers' money when someone like you promises to open a factory in a run-down area? And you open up shop, cash the cheques, then strip the place of its stock and machinery while the staff are at their lunch break?

A movement. A definite twitch to the left eye, a tremor of the lip. She was getting through.

– You've been able to get away with it because, let's face it, you've only been up against civil servants. So long as they're able to show some dent in the unemployment figures, however fake, they're happy. But now that I've had the details put together, I should say there's every chance a charge of conspiring to defraud could be stuck on you.

Maybe he didn't agree? Maybe he didn't think there was anything to worry him in the two documents she'd brought along? Of which there were plenty of photostat copies back at her place, be sure of that. If that was his reaction, okay, she'd pick her files up, and apologise for taking his time. As well as for the five phone calls over the past three days. And she'd see if anyone else was more interested. Like the above-mentioned taxmen, and the local police.

But if he did want to talk further, if there was something in the files which made him go ouch, first of all he'd have to bounce the interpreter. It wasn't only that his presence was a complete waste of time, with Kyprianou speaking English as well as she did. It could be embarrassing for him, as a good Greek, having to be seen and heard negotiating with a mere female.

The mob waited outside, while Connie waited inside, for his answer. You didn't go walking into somebody else's place of worship, just like that. You had respect. Especially if you didn't know the forms and observances. When to nod, or bow, or what parts of the interior to avoid. Double especially if the front door was firmly barred, and you had to excuse yourself past the two hard-faced cousins on the side door. Who looked as if they would need some persuading to let unbelievers through.

– Sure she's in there? Hector was all for switching the engine off and reversing in neutral back down the slope and away. He had respect for other people's forms of worship. Especially when the wiriness of the sidesmen perfectly complimented their tough features. They might be small, but so were the Japanese army, and the Argyll and Sutherland Highlanders. And everybody knew not to knock their beer over. Especially not in their own bars.

She was in there. And Jamieson was all for going in after her, once he'd had Arnie confirm that was Kyprianou's Roller, parked round the corner.

– He keeps it covered in mud to fool the tax people, Arnie gagged. He wasn't sure what he was doing here, but he'd go along for the ride. That was Arnie, all over.

On his way back to the van, where Babs sat waiting, as she so often sat in the van waiting for him, Arnie saw Dev and Nesta pull up. This was a combination new to him. Perhaps she knew what was going on? Or Dev?

Whatever it was, Nesta could assure him, he wouldn't have been told to be sure to be there, unless there was a slap in the trap coming up for him.

Just as Dev had got his.

Kyprianou had to understand why she was doing it to him. The grumble of worry had gone, to be replaced by intrigue. It was plain that he was up against somebody who wanted a business favour done, and not somebody determined to close him down. The fact that it was a woman was inconvenient, from the point of view of loss of face, if he had to deal. But he would have to ride that. He'd ridden worse losses of face in his time. Still remembered the shit he'd had to eat on his way up. Dishing it out now wasn't as big a kick as he'd thought it was going to be. Being boss had other, more subtle satisfactions. Particularly those of being able to find out exactly what made other people work. In this case, so taken was he with the aggression of the woman beside him, that he was willing to include women in the word people.

– Tell me why. And don't tell me because you want the business cleaned up, for the sake of all the decent little people. She was here to deal. He knew that. He could smell the offer of a deal, even with the air thick with incense.

– Because you slapped my ex-husband around?

She tried that on him, and it took him three goes before he even remembered the incident, let alone the names and faces attached to it.

– We never touched him. He pulled a face, and rephrased it. – We never touched him much. There was a girl, and one of my relations got a little too keen to show me he was doing a good job. And your husband –

– Ex, she very definitely corrected.

– Your ex-husband walked into a fist or an elbow. That was all. I wanted my money, that was all. I was happy just to pick up what he had on his stall.

– Leaving him with just the poles and canvas?

Even so, Kyprianou insisted he'd still come off worse. Arnie had such a poor eye for gear that the Greek still reckoned, despite stripping the stall, Arnie owed another couple of hundred.

– How ex is your ex? He wanted to know.

– Very ex.

She thought of sketching in her eight years with her own Greek, but that would be getting off the subject. They weren't here to talk about old times, or swap taverna recommendations. There was a deal to be made.

– So it's not really because of your ex?

He was pushing her back towards telling him why she was really doing this. It wasn't necessary for him to know, for the purposes of his business with her. But what was the point of being godfather, if you didn't indulge in a few luxuries. Like can-opening the tops of people's heads, and peering inside.

Connie told him. As much as she knew herself. Why she'd pricked up those ears at the mention of what he'd done to Arnie. Why she'd wriggled and fought to get sat here beside him. Not dictating terms to him, but insisting he talk business.

– My dad once told me he could never go into a room without wanting to fight all the fellas and screw all the birds. The same with me. Only the other way around. As soon as I heard you were a big cheese, I headed straight for a collision with you. Couldn't help myself. No more than Hector can. I heard you were numero uno, and those are the ones who've always attracted me. When I hear there's a number one around, I want to bed him. Or bash him.

He nodded.

– In my case –?

She grinned. Didn't he make a big thing about being a family man?

– You were going to get bashed.

– And you think you've bashed me, with those files?

She considered it. There was no way of telling whether she had or not, she admitted. But surprisingly, it didn't matter. He could have his heavies work her over for her cheek in breading him, but even if she spent the next year on a walking frame, she still would consider it had been worth it. Because no one else had had the balls to get that

C.—5

close to him.

– The deal?

– Straightforward. You collect these two files, plus the appendix. The House of Bea gets to fill its order books through your discount operation, at preferential terms. A business deal. No strings. We're not a shotgun outfit.

He let that ride. By rights he should have put her on that walking frame for the next twelve months. Or at the very least put the word around that the House of Bea, who she was fronting, was dead. But he liked what she'd said. She hadn't wriggled or twisted, or pretended altruism. She was scratching an itch she couldn't get rid of. And his human responses twitched favourably at that. She'd pitched it dead right. Those eight years with her boyfriend, his fellow countryman, paid off.

Kyprianou knew he should settle this in line with his family responsibilities. Take the files, run with them. Spread so much fear around that the photocopies would stay under lock and key, or be put through the shredder. That was clear. He owed it to the heavies on the side door, and to the cousins waiting out of sight by his Roller. Not to mention their wives and families, and the cousins of the cousins, who depended on him.

He hadn't known he had so many cousins, and dependents, until he'd started to make his way. He'd been doing all right, on his market stalls one day, and the next the place was wall to wall with relatives. Who needed jobs fixing and favours doing. No sooner had he fixed them up, than the taxman had hit him. He worked a straight year of seven-day weeks to clear the tax bill, only to have to do the same again on his VAT account.

Before he realised what was happening to the well-planned business mixed in with a little leisure he'd been looking ahead to, he was fighting for his life, just trying to keep in the black. All because of family. Putting in twenty hours a day, every day of every week including Christmas, the Greek Easter, and the English Easter. It was proving as hard to keep the money he was making out of his family's hands as it was to keep it away from the government. And the future seemed to offer nothing but more of the same. The treadmill getting stiffer to turn, the harder he tried to turn it.

Screw the family. Just this once, for the first and last time in his life, screw them. Forget them. This woman had opened herself up to him, in a very unEnglish way, and he appreciated. He knew his destiny was to graft until his balls broke for his family. But he was surely entitled to one little rebellion before he buckled down to family serfdom for the rest of his working life?

Connie got her deal.

It had been close. Nobody knew that better than Connie. But as even the shaken Hector had to admit, when the details of the scam were out, it seemed she could do no wrong. There had to be an angel or an imp taking care of her.

Arnie had his smack in the face with the same wet kipper as Dev. For the only thing worse than needing a favour done, is having it done, and being in debt for it. And there was the added complication that Babs had witnessed Connie sorting his affairs out for him. Bad enough that it had taken another woman to step in, and put things right. How much worse it being Connie. Who Babs still narrowed her eyes at, at the mention of the name.

Dev should have come out of the matter much better than he did. Would have done, if he'd been working for anyone less fire-resistant than Nesta. As soon as she'd recognised Kyprianou, as he and Connie came out of the church together, she realised what she'd been missing. The Greek connection. Although she was up-market of his side of things, she still knew how important he was on his own side of the tracks. And instinctively guessed that Connie had snatched a deal right out of his sharp teeth.

Hector and Bea were clear winners, of course. Bea had never made public her reservations about Connie jumping in the water, with a harpoon aimed for that particular shark. So she even kept her moral superiority. Hector tried to make light of his, but she knew all about the yellow road markings that ran from the nape of his neck to his underpants elastic. And it didn't faze her in the least, because she was in love with the guy.

Jamieson came out of it better than anyone. He'd even had the foresight to snowpake the names, addresses and phone numbers of the informants in the union file. Connie hadn't noticed that, in her haste to get the file on the table between herself and the Greek. For Jamieson hadn't believed for one minute her story that she was tackling the big bad Kyprianou, for the sake of all the woodland folk. He'd stopped believing in the tooth-fairy, and all those sort of tales, long before he'd met Connie.

There was a bad moment when Kyprianou found that out, but Connie was able to talk her way out of it. Claiming that she'd only been able to get hold of a censored copy. She didn't say who'd censored it, and the Greek accepted it. There was enough circumstantial information in the file to tell him who'd been talking. And was their fate anything to do with Connie? Didn't they have to take their chances, just like she did? And in her case, she didn't even have a union to back her up when things got rocky.

Jamieson scored brownie points all down the line. It was such a pity, then, to find the envelope with the Siggins, Bowser and Comer logo on the hallway floor at the cottage, when he finally made it back.

He stumbled into the bath, needing fifteen minutes up to his neck in boiling water, before he could even think about boring things, like the correspondence that had been mounting up since he'd been away. Playing cowboys and Indians, or cops and robbers, or spacemen and aliens, for Connie.

There was bad news in that brisk-looking envelope.

He took it right between the eyes, when he opened it next morning, when his brain was unscrambled, and his body pleasantly tired, rather than crazily so.

SBC had taken advantage of his leave to rationalise their management structure.

He was fired.

Nine

Bea had a gambling problem once. In between husbands. Pre-Hector. She'd grab a handful of cash every night on her way out, and throw it away. Long since under control. Since she'd found her fella. The only reminder of the urge which had nearly lost her everything was her insistence that she play for a tenner a hole with Nesta on their golf mornings. And she justified that by claiming it wasn't really gambling. How could it be, she was only learning the game? She believed in market forces, and didn't see how you could learn anything unless the learning cost you money.

Once in a while the niggle came back, and she took a sackful of coins and fed them one after the other into the one-arm bandits lining the walls of the country club foyer. But she always stopped when her sack was emptied. Never begged more off Hector, or raided the cash-box at the factory.

She applied the same approach to business, when Connie came back after a few days off, helping Jamieson get over the hand-off in the face from SBC. Taking the man on, as admin wasn't a gamble. She fell in with that suggestion of Connie's straight away. Sure, he was from outside the business, and she knew that you had to have fashion in your bones and blood. But as he'd be in charge of the figures and not the fabric, she didn't see what harm he could do. Saw instantly that he could be a bonus, and one that would come cheap. Didn't he need a job? Any job?

He did. And more than she could know, because his wife was now deciding to challenge the arrangements he thought they had agreed on. A little grit had worked its way between the cogs of his smooth running down of his marriage.

What Bea didn't fall in with with such appetite was the idea that they take advantage of the Kyprianou connection, and open up the listed building on both floors. Let alone that they look for a way to get round the planning limitations on it, and knock it flat.

Did Connie have no respect for all that was historic about this grimy corner of town?

She didn't.

What she had respect for was the fact that the deal struck with the Greek meant that for the first time they could rely on a high-volume base on which to expand. He'd promised to take all they could turn out, and Connie knew now she had a personal as well as business relationship with the man. He'd stick to that deal. To maximise the leverage it gave them, however, they had to get ambitious. And that meant building.

Bea pointed out that building cost money. Connie had done well since she'd been back, but there still wasn't enough money in the firm to rebuild with. Even if the planning consents could be wrangled.

– Go to the bank. It was simple. You didn't need to be a financial whizz like their new office manager, moving a desk into the upstairs office. Banks make money by giving it away, she pointed out. That was one of the happy paradoxes which underpinned capitalism. If they didn't spread the stuff around the likes of the House of Bea, they didn't get a return on it. Did Bea want to shake people's confidence in the banking system? Did she want to be responsible for a run on the West's financial institutions? On the desk, in front of the woman dressed in black, was a quarter's figures which would have any bank manager worth his briefcase break his leg to lend on.

– We are not going to the banks.

That was final. All her business life Bea had been up to one of her chins with banks. The banks had driven one of her husbands to the bottle, and another completely round the bend without the help of the bottle. For the first time in her business life, she was free of them. She was accepting no responsibility for the break-up of civilisation as they knew it by refusing to let the banks get their hooks into her again.

– It's thanks to me you're free of them.

Bea accepted that. She was properly grateful. What was on her face was a thankful smile. Not, as might at first have appeared, moonlight playing on the brass handles of a coffin. She was so full of gratitude she was upping Connie's bonus, and, if requested, would have Leroy paint the fact of her gratitude in three-foot-high red letters along the yard wall. What she wouldn't do was go to the banks or anyone else, for a loan. Even if there was any possibility of being able to demolish the crumbling relic of the past in the car-park yard.

And by that she wasn't referring to her beloved, but to that eyesore of an architectural gem.

Connie came back strongly. She wasn't talking about a hundred and twenty thousand square feet on a green-field site. She just wanted more floor space, and a chance to rationalise the work flow. Jamieson was already sketching out a plan to reorganise the production process, but there was a limit to what even he could achieve without more physical space and plant.

– There's no long-term future, Con. Bea tried to get her to see that. – People are always going to need knitwear, yes, but there's a lot of people out there making it. Brown and yellow and black and coffee-coloured people in Taiwan and the Philippines and Korea and God knows where else. They can ship it here cheaper than we can truck it, because they can pay their girls a handful of rice. Because their girls are hungry in a way our girls and us could never imagine you could be allowed to get so hungry.

– But we can turn the stuff over faster than them. That's our edge. We can spot something new on the street one Saturday lunchtime, and be piling it into Leroy's van the next.

– And that means graft. Hard, blinding graft. And why should I want it at my age?

– Because you're a grafter. You were bred to graft. Cut you and you bleed machine oil. Drop you on a desert island and inside a week you'd be undercutting the locals in grass skirts. You're Midlands, heartland, where the money's always come from, and where it's got to keep coming from. Or there's no future for any of the others, anywhere.

Great speech. Bea conceded that. A knicker-wringer. And Connie had said it like she meant every word. But the answer was still no. But Connie wasn't going to get to know the biggest reason for that no. The fact that Bea had spotted Hector getting restless again. And at the best of times, a woman needed all her energies and attentions devoted to him. If he wasn't going to throw himself, head first, off the straight and narrow yet again.

Bea was right. Hector was getting that itchy, squirmy feeling. He loved Bea, there was no question of that. She was the best thing that could have happened to him. His love life had been as disastrous as hers, a story taking him from nags to bitches and back again. And again. Bea had been the saving of him, and he was more than grateful. Was, in fact, as much in love with her as she was with him. But from time to time that itchy, squirmy feeling came over him, and his eyeballs and his hands took on a life of their own. As if they were dragging his reluctant body after them, determined to get him into trouble.

Trouble duly arrived in the shape of Lisa, a new interlocker. He didn't think Lisa was going to be anything other than one of the usual, casual, half-hearted affairs, the small change of life and love, when he came across her putting up her hair. In the toilet that had been used by the male and the female staff for the past two years, while the gents was awaiting repair.

Hector had put a spell in advertising, and had discovered a facility for jingle-writing. The long lunch-hours had put paid to any serious attempt to make his way in that business, but his head was still crammed with odd snatches of poetry and doggerel, which he'd had to read to get the juices flowing, when faced with a new piece of copy.

He had just the thing for this moment.

– Amarantha sweet and fair
Ah brade no more that shining hair –
As my curious hand or eye
Hovering round thee let it flye –

His foot back-heeled the door shut. This wasn't the most romantic of spots for an assignation, but Hector was a great one for sexual improvisation.

– Let it flye as unconfined
As its calme ravisher the winde
Who hath left his darling th'east
To wanton o'er that spicie nest-

To be on the safe side, he jammed a broom-handle under the door-knob, winking at the girl's reflection in the cracked mirror, with the cheap plastic frame. At least she wasn't screaming rape.

– Every tresse must be confest
But neatly angled at the best
Like a clue of golden thread
Most excellently ravelled.

The girl's hair wasn't exactly golden, but in this light what did it matter? Wasn't he entitled to a little poetical licence? Moving closer, and trying not to wrinkle up his nose at the sight of the disgusting state of the roller towel, he got ready for the vinegar stroke. The movement that might have her shouting rape, good though she'd been to now.

– Do not then winde up that light
In ribands, and o'er-cloud in Night
Like the sun in's early ray
But shake your head and scatter day –

And he let her hair down, and she made her mouth a little O, but apart from that, nothing.

– See this broke! – Within this grove
The bower and the walkes of love
Weary lie we downe and rest
And fan each other's panting breast –

There wasn't anywhere to lie down, but she allowed herself to be turned by him, her back against the crumbled plaster of the cubicle. He moved her slightly, so that the small of her back wasn't pressing into the cracked wash-basin, and let his hand unravel the last knot of hair. Hector had a horror of dirty hair, but this was hair which could have had that poem written for it.

– Here we'll strippe and coole our fire
In something something something higher –

He skipped over the bit that memory had blotted out. This wasn't a schoolroom examination, after all.

–And when all wells are drawne dry
I'll drink a tear out of thine eye
That sorrows thus we can deceive
Or our something something weepe
That joys so ripe –

And he moved his hand to the left-most ripe joy –

– So little keepe.

But it was going to have to keep a little longer. Leroy was kicking on the door with his steel-capped work-boots. The roller towel was due for changing.

Not surprising that Hector found it hard to keep his mind on business the rest of the day. Expecting the summons from Bea, who might have found some way of discovering what he'd been up to with the new girl. The way women did, which defied all the Newtonian, and post-Newtonian laws of physics. Or the girl giving some hint that she hadn't just been pleasing an old man's fancies. The open mouth she'd turned to him, as his hand moved to her, meant a very definite, very breathy yes.

Not surprising, when nothing happened, that he tried to take the tension out on Leroy. Leroy, the owner of the boot which had interrupted the nice little thing that might just have been about to happen between his boss and one of the girls.

The point at issue was whether or not Leroy's job description as van driver, covered shifting rubbish in the yard. It was stacked several feet high in a litter of old boxes, samples and discarded fabric against the venerable eye-sore, and Hector hardly thought it contributed to the firm's image. He'd also just had his backside kicked by Bea. And whose backside better to pass that kick on to than the lowest link in the chain?

The wrangle had fizzled on between them for an hour when Hector decided enough was enough. You can only sit around the table so long, arguing the toss. At some point an ultimatum has to be issued, backside kicked.

He was giving Leroy a direct order. Shift that rubbish. Whatever he was on the books as, he was temporarily transferred to garbage duty.

– Mr. Hector, Leroy looked thoughtful. He'd no wish to spend tomorrow at the Job Centre, holding the dole queue enthralled with stories of what it had been like to have a job in the England of the Eighties. But he did resent being called out like this. – Mr. Hector, if I called you a pillock, you could fire me, right?

Hector agreed that was right. And that he was itching for Leroy to do it.

– But you couldn't fire me if I only thought it, could you?

That was true. Obvious. You couldn't fire anyone for thinking.

– Mr. Hector, Leroy took his time delivering his line. – I think you're a pillock.

He'd battled to a draw with Leroy, but it looked like a win with Lisa. Lisa who was stood behind him, as he loaded samples into the hatch-back. The executive hatch-back, as he insisted it was known. Never an estate. Company reps had estates. Hired hands drove estates. Part-owners drove executive hatchbacks.

– Ancient person, for whom I
All the flattering youths defy
Lond be it ere thou grow old
Aguing, shaking, crazy cold,
But still continue as thou are
Ancient person of my heart.

She had picked up one of the books littering the shelves of the office, among the paperback Westerns and thrillers. Clever of her to have come up with this verse, of them all. Startling, if she understood what the words said, and meant them.

– On thy withered lips and dry
Which like barren furrows lie
Brooding kisses I will pore
Shall thy youthful heat restore.

She certainly seemed as if she understood what the poet was saying. Or poetess. He tried to remember the names of any female writers of the metaphysical school, but in the puzzle of the moment, his brain blanked.

– Such kind showers in Autumn fall
And a second spring recall
Not from thee will ever part
Ancient person of my heart.

This was all right. This was the sort of reaction he'd been looking for. And the passage that followed made him forget the danger of getting involved with someone who so quickly grabbed the main chance when it showed.

– Thy nobler parts, which but to name
In our sex would be counted shame
By ages frozen grasp possest
From their ice shall be released
And smoothed by my reviving hand
In former warmth and vigour stand.

Well, what could you say? That that school of poets had always struck Hector as the jack-the-lads of English poesy? That he was grateful to her for coming across a verse he'd somehow skipped, and that he'd certainly look out for more by the same?

All that. Plus the fact that he was headed off to Manchester for the afternoon. And if she wanted to plead a headache or sick budgie, why didn't she take the afternoon off. So they could talk literature and life on the way north?

Mug, he muttered to himself, as he waited round the corner for her, eyes peeled for Bea. Mug and fool, and dimwit. And all those other names he reserved for fellas of his age, who pulled girls this young. Especially girls who dropped everything and ran when the boss winked. He rattled through his ground rules, as he waited. The ones that had always made sure in the past that his depredations didn't get in the way of what he and Bea had between them.

No slagging off Bea. No imagining, even for a moment, that this could be anything other than just another casual affair, based on sex on his part, and cupidity on the girl's. No risk-taking. No promising to set her up in a flat, or fiddle the books to get her a little motor. No neglecting of Bea for her, for human reasons as well as tactical ones. No week in which he saw the girl more than two nights, at most. No screwing on the premises, even if Bea was abroad.

Even when she was in the car, at his request repeating those intriguing lines about reviving hands, he felt sure he could stick to those rules. He'd made them. He was sticking to them. No matter how much joy she gave him, just by sitting there in the car alongside him.

Hector being headed up North with his fellow lover of literature meant that he missed Connie's storming-out of the meeting with Bea. They'd had a ring-a-ding such as the firm hadn't had since the early days of him and Bea. Before he'd snapped into line, realising that much as Bea loved him, business was business.

She'd brooked no dictation from him as to where the firm should be piloted, and she was taking none from his daughter.

So Connie walked.

Bea wasn't too worried. Seeing it as a tactical withdrawal. Hard to take it seriously, when Jamieson was still left, at his desk, with his thumb stuck up his bum. But then, why should he have been expected to have walked out on a job he'd just walked into? It made his position uncomfortable, but did he have any choice?

He offered the sacrifice to Connie. Despite the fact that he needed the money Bea was paying him, and he could hack the tension caused by his woman's walk-out—he was prepared to throw it over, and side with her.

She turned him down. She needed someone wired in to the House of Bea, who could keep her up to date with developments. So that she could time her counter-strike.

– You do want back, then?

She most certainly wanted back. Really, at times, she despaired of him. And when she went back, it would be on her terms.

Ten

Nesta liked to keep a close and beady eye on what was happening at the factory. She still had every expectation of picking it up, lock stock and barrel one day. Save for the little bit that Hector had nibbled off for himself. But recently she'd been too taken up with her own business to poke her nose as often as she liked into the House of Bea's.

She'd have been able to pay more attention to this latest surprise development of Connie walking out on everything she'd helped rebuild, had it not been for Dev, who was turning out something of a disaster, even though he did look so nice in his business suit, with the tie he'd now re-learnt to knot.

Normally, someone with his track record would have been chopped at the second mistake. But the complication with Dev was that he'd managed to carve himself a little place in her emotional life. Had in fact opened that emotional life up again, after it had been firmly shut for years. It would be too much to say that she'd been sent spinning by her new rep, but something made her stay her hand, every time news of another cock-up or near miss came her way.

It wasn't that Dev wasn't trying. He seemed to be doing his best, out on the road during the week. As he'd do his best for her between the sheets come the weekend. But there was something wrong with his aim. Time after time he'd miss something in the accounts, or misread a staffing problem. When he should have come down with the heavy welly, he turned diplomat. And when he should have finely tuned his response to something amiss in the shops, he stamped down with size fifteens.

She'd known for some time that he wasn't a natural retail person. That couldn't be held against him. What had to count against her continued employment of him was that he didn't seem to be somebody you could teach to be a retail person, either. So much depended on feel, and the appreciation of the intangibles which gave a shop its distinctive ambience. However much a whizz he might once have been as a designer, he didn't impress at the sharp end. The buying and selling end. She could put it down to the fact that somewhere inside he was still rebelling at being on the shopfloor, instead of at the creative side. But what use was that to her?

And still she didn't fire him. He might have been on for the gold clock and engraved tankard in too many years to think about, had it not been for her hand being jogged. Despite herself. Over that business at Bournemouth.

– You checked the Bournemouth store last week, Dev?

He flipped through his diary, legs nonchalantly crossed in his weekend white slacks. The alarm bells hadn't rung. He took this as Nesta keeping him on his Italian-shod toes. Reminding him that even at weekends she had the right to crack the whip.

– Bournemouth . . . . Bournemouth. He found the page. – Clean and tidy, girls nicely turned out, rails neat, price tags all marked clearly, manageress helpful in the extreme. Bournemouth gets straight A's. Something he found the part-time teaching years still flavouring his reports.

– Everything hunky dory and A-okay?

That's what he was reporting.

– Then how come first thing this morning she cleared the shop out and took the first plane to Marbella?

Car keys.

Cheque book.

Plastic cards.

Dev placed his badges of executive rank on the desk, and Nesta scooped them into her drawer. Dev might do a sensational horizontal samba, but that wasn't enough. Not even in this business. It was as much her fault as his that it hadn't worked out. She'd known she really needed a rag-trade queen with hands like those white butterflies. But her belly had done the choosing of Dev, the rank opposite. She had the word out in the trade for the queen, and this time she'd choose with her head.

Now that circumstances, and that sudden flight to the sun, had forced her hand, she could concentrate on other things than making excuses for Dev. She'd keep him on, in the personal capacity he filled so well. Her appetite for him had grown in the time they'd had together. Sooner or later he would try to shake her off. But for now there was an extra something in their relationship.

For the first time there was no pretence about it. Dev was going to be her kept man. Other execs kept mistresses, on the firm's time and money, didn't they? Wasn't it the sign of a successful businessman that he took up with a mistress to go with his golf? She was serious with her career, she was serious with her golf. She could get serious about running a little piece on the side. And to prove it was her little piece on the side, she told him to get his ear pierced.

– Why?

– Because I want to give you a diamond stud.

And she did. Because diamonds said lots of things. And one of them was I own you.

Just as Nesta was managing to turn from personal worries back to business ones, Hector was performing the same evolution. Things were going very well with Lisa. There were one or two ground rules he was still keeping, but for the most part they'd all long since been smashed. The ones he was keeping referred to no running-down of Bea, with whom he was still very much in love. With another part of himself, that conveniently moved out of the way when Lisa showed. And he'd been canny not to promise the girl an apartment. That was something he was far too clever an old fist-fighter to get suckered into.

The business problems had started the week after Connie marched out.

As Hector and Bea saw it, being born and dyed small business people, the whole world was against them. In particular the official world. Out there, beyond the factory gates, was a vast army of people whose business it was to stop you doing business. Army? It was more like a secret police force, with orders to sniff out anyone making their own way in the world, without hand-outs or state safety-nets, and stop them. Knock on the door at four in the morning. Truncheon the entrepreneurial class to the deck, and stamp on its balls and boobies.

With all the political hot-air being talked, you'd have thought the pendulum had swung away from state control. That the little man or woman was to be allowed to bring home the bacon, and keep the biggest rashers for himself. Just so long as he didn't make his little fiddles, his necessary little fiddles too obvious. To the waged class. Or the professional welfare artists.

If you tried to trim your labour costs a smidgeon, for the greater good of the firm as a whole, the unions or wages inspectorate hit you. If you really couldn't stretch this year's hard-pressed budget to what were really cosmetic inessentials like guards on every dangerous machine, the Health and Safety people bashed you up. Bea and Hector weren't in favour of bringing back the eighteen hour day, and sending the kiddies down the mines again. They weren't saying that. They were just asking for a little bit of pressure to be taken off. Didn't Hector's glossy business weeklies and monthlies refer to their sort of people as the wealth-creators?

The trouble was that wealth-creating caused jealousies and resentments. People seemed incapable of watching somebody else rise from push-bike to Roller, via Rover, Jag, and all the stages in between, without feeling they'd been in some way done down personally.

That had to be the explanation of the anonymous letters. What else could it be? Here was the House of Bea, picking itself up from a very dusty floor, and trying to make a go of things. And out there was some sick and twisted little mind, with a hand and pen, writing venomous letters to the appropriate, or any, authority.

The first one had brought a letter from the Revenue, asking for another view of the accounts, going back to the beginning of the previous tax year. After Jamieson had broken the firm's traditions by replying promptly, another buff envelope had arrived, demanding an immediate interview and the production of the records going back three previous years. Jamieson had started the negotiations on that, only to be hit by the other glove, when the VAT demanded access for one of their inspectors.

Up to then, it could have been coincidence. The bureaucratic machinery had hiccuped twice, and thrown their names up for a routine check. Which quickly became anything but routine, once the bowl of spaghetti which were the accounts had been forked over. What couldn't be coincidence was the arrival of the Health and Safety Executive staff, followed by the Planning Department man, and somebody from the Fire Brigade to check on illegal fire door access. And all the other gobbledy-gook these people babbled, intent only on stopping the business class getting on with making money. On which they paid taxes. Or didn't, as seemed to be one of the points at issue. Out of which taxes, hurrying on, their wages were paid. The wages of all the busybody council and government apparchicks, who didn't realise that time was money in business. Whatever it might be in the dreaming towers of local government or civil service.

On top of that, the on-going row with Leroy as to the exact definition of his duties, and where he stood vis-a-vis the now monumental pile of rubbish in the yard, seemed unimportant.

He didn't get much sympathy at the clinic when he called on Connie.

There had been a brief flurry of alarm at the news that Connie had retired to the clinic again, when the news was first broken by Jamieson. He stressed that it was nothing for anyone to worry about. They offered extra bed capacity for non-chronic cases. For people who wanted to use their five-star facilities as they would a health farm. Connie had been working as hard as a drayman's horse since getting off the plane. There had been emotional adjustments to make, as well as business ones. She needed time to relax, unwind, and work out where her future lay, if the House of Bea had no further use for her.

You could pay your money and take your choice over that. Decide that she was being brave, and that the mystery illness which she'd brought back from the Med, had laid her low again. Or that she really was just resting up, after that bruising run-in with the big boss in black. But wasn't above floating a little suggestion that she might be, just could be, very possibly was in the clinic, because of that self-same as-yet undiagnosed but convenient illness.

Viewed from the end of the bed, in her splendid room, with its view of the gardens and lily pond at the back, Hector agreed she looked as fit as a drayman's horse, as she had worked like one for himself and Bea. But she spoke quietly, and had him tug the shades across before he sat down on the leather bedside chair. Removing, as he did so, the dinner tray whose size suggested her appetite had not been impaired by her stay in this abode of pain.

– Pain? She winced. – I told you never to mention that here. The rule still goes.

She asked how things were at the old firm.

– Old firm? It's not been a fortnight since you walked out.

– Was fired, she rephrased it, making him bite back impatiently.

– You weren't fired, Con. No way you can say you were fired. I've had this out with Bea. You had a falling out and you walked.

– Can you blame me? I offer you a cast iron way to put the firm so squarely back on its feet, not even Nesta could rock it, when she collects. And I'm fired.

– Not fired. He wished to establish this point. – Walked out.

Well whatever way it had been, it had only been two weeks since she'd been gainfully employed there. He knew she'd understand if he was a trifle impatient at being asked to sit beside her bedside, with her glowing red with health, expected to swallow a dying swan routine.

She looked at him over the designer bed covers. Really, her reproving eyes said. If she hadn't been so low, she might have had some bones to pick with him about that. But she merely sighed a long-suffering sigh, and asked again how business was.

It hadn't improved since the previous time he'd dropped in on her. Jamieson, as she should very well know, was putting in twenty-hour days getting the back accounts in order. While he and Bea were locked in with the solicitors as many hours, working out how best to defend themselves if the Health and Safety, Planning and Fire Regulations infringements came to court.

– Maybe they'll settle behind doors. She sounded the hopeful note, but in a voice that suggested the opposite would most likely happen.

He doubted it. And even if they did, what consolation was in that? The very next post would bring the fruits of another denunciation down on them. He was hard put to think who, but no doubt the government employed people to step in, when they'd run out of people to legitimately harrass small businessmen. And women. Not forgetting Bea, because all this had come as a blow to her. The more so because things had been going so well before.

– Before I left? Connie accepted it, with no false modesty.

Before she'd left.

And wasn't that an interesting thought, he suggested, watching for reaction. That things had been sugar-lolly while she was there, but had started to go spectacularly sour after the bust-up. Thanks to the anonymous scribbler who seemed to know as much as anyone did, about the inside workings of the House of Bea. Whoever he was. Or she.

– Poison has always been a woman's weapon. Nesta flicked her eyes in Jamieson's direction, making sure he heard her and read the implication. – I'd say it was some sick female. Some bitch with time to spare, and nothing to do but complicate other people's lives.

She wondered aloud, still zeroed in on Jamieson at his desk, who that description fitted. The office manager and general dogsbody didn't wait for any more. There was another pile of shoeboxed accounts to be looked over. And the suggestion that Connie had sent the letters cut too close to the bone.

Not that she would have sought to get her own back that way. He reassured himself with that, as he thumbed his way through receipts and invoices that looked as if they were stray fragments of the Dead Sea Scrolls. He knew her too well, for that. But did he? When it came down to it, their affair was only months old. How much do you learn about anyone in that time? Especially someone like Connie?

After all, he'd thought he'd known Sonia enough to be confident that the marriage termination would be smooth and as painless as possible. But every personal mail brought in a further complication. Just as every business mail brought a steaming little droplet of dung to the in-tray.

In the office Nesta picked over the thickening file of official post which the letter writer had been responsible for. There had been nothing for a couple of days. But by this time Hector and Bea dreaded the quiet days more than the ones on which they got another buff envelope.

Bea wasn't prepared to believe Connie was responsible. She wasn't ruling it out as a possibility, but she would need considerable persuading. Like a confession signed in blood. Nesta offered to go and obtain it from the clinic. But her mother was in no mood to get involved in another round of the Connie versus Nesta row. Her energy and patience were being sapped by this barrage from the world of official busybodydom.

For preference, she wanted Nesta to go and make her peace with Connie. She was serious. She blamed a lot of the worry of the past few months on Nesta's insistence on keeping up the feud with her step-sister.

– Worry? What worry? I thought she was the best thing since wholemeal bread.

So she had been. What Bea meant was that Connie had her attention continually on what Nesta was up to. However good the results she'd been pulling in, they could have been better. This ignored the fact that Bea had been only too eager to keep that rivalry alive. But she was working up to laying some bad news on Nesta, and felt guilty about it. Needed to be in a lather, no matter how trumped-up the charges she was making.

– I went down on my knees and begged you to make peace with her, Bea insisted, – I wept a mother's tears – and a step-mother's tears. She didn't try to explain the difference between the two. – Have you no idea how a mother feels?

Nesta hadn't. How could she? And she had no intention of ever being in a position where she could risk finding out. Her shops were her kids, just as the factory would be, bar Hector's insignificant slice, one day.

Which was exactly what Bea had to pick her up on.

Wiggle every way she could, she had to meet Connie's major stipulation for hauling herself out of that hospital bed, and making it down the narrow lane that led to the factory again. Connie was on for a share too.

Hector was glad he missed the scene that followed between mother and daughter. His luck seemed to be holding, in the matter of rows and dramatic upsets. He even managed to get out of the job of taking the news to Connie. There was an order in East Anglia he was committed to chasing up. So Bea had to swallow her pride and do the detailed negotiation herself.

Not that Connie made it difficult. She'd got what she wanted. Which wasn't unconditional surrender by Bea. Just a recognition that she had made out an unstoppable case. If they didn't rebuild now, they would have to do so in five or ten years time because the place would fall down round their ears.

And if she was going to put her muck sweat into securing the future that far ahead she had to be on the ship as something more than a deck hand. She was in for a share of the booty this pirate craft was now dedicated to making. The potential in the Kyprianou deal had concentrated all their minds wonderfully. There could be no going back to the lazy old days, when it was sufficient just to jog along, trying to keep one step ahead of the creditors. And often failing. There was a certain enjoyment in that approach to business, because it offered the time as well as the excuse, for whole days on the golf course, or trips abroad that turned into rubber-necking instead of sales.

When Bea left the clinic, she knew that those days were now

behind the firm. Connie was keeping her, despite her objections, to her vision of one day opening up the factory to its full revs per working hour. Now she was committed to that, it was a small price that she should have to take the knife to the cake and trim Nesta's take.

But a mother could justify that, and without trying too hard. Because couldn't she be allowed the fond hope that if the two girls—women, she corrected—were forced to work together, they might come in time to get on together as people? They'd done so once, before the demons of greed and ambition had been set loose.

That still left the problem of finangling a way around the planning limitations on the listed building, which remained as solidly and, to their jaundiced eyes, as ugly an obstacle as ever.

The gods, imps or angels had swung round behind Connie again, however.

The morning after Bea had struck the deal it was a sodden heap of timbers and sodden plaster, trampled flat by firemen's yellow boots.

Eleven

The blaze which so conveniently left a big hole in the factory yard, just ripe for building on, had also come close to terminating Hector's association with the firm. And with breathing. For some months he woke with the shudders at what a close thing it had been. And at the thought that next morning there wouldn't have been just one charred body in the damp embers. Two. His and Lisa's. And it would have been interesting to speculate exactly what position they would have been found in, and what people would have made of it. Especially Bea.

Hector had broken all records to his East Anglian destination, done his business on the run, and then headed the executive hatchback straight back to the Midlands. He was tempted to stop on the motorway and tell Bea the car had broken down, but his ears still ached from the verbal violence she'd dished out over the Paris affair. And what was the point of fixing up a full night with Lisa, when there was nowhere to spend it?

The girl still lived with her parents in some dismal council flat he had no intention of going within a hundred miles of. For conversational, let alone more intimate purposes. And there was no chance of sneaking her to The Grange when Bea was out of the way at, say, a bridge club do. The initial thrill of al fresco lovemaking, even with someone as enthusiastic as his Amarantha-Lisa, was beginning to wear off. The nights were drawing in, and a sharpish draught up your shirt could severely restrict mobility and entertainment for weeks.

So Hector broke another of the ground rules, and offered the girl a place of her own.

– Not straight away. We've a few big orders in the pipeline, and I've every confidence. But once we get set fair—you're on for a place of your own. It won't be a palace, he cautioned her, seeing her eyes light up. Probably he'd only be able to run at first to a little flat, out on a handy bus route. He had estate agent friends at the country club, who could see him right on that. Perhaps later on, when business really picked up, he'd be able to fix her up with something really nice. Even consider buying a place. In her name, of course. But for now, for starters, she'd have to be content with whatever he could find.

It would be clean and dry, of course. He wasn't going to set her up in something he wouldn't be prepared to spend a lot of nights at himself.

– And maybe a little runabout. A little motor for yourself. That would make a lot of sense.

As indeed it would. Anything that simplified their meetings and lessened the risk of detection made sense.

– Just a little car, he had to stress. – Not a sports model. Not a Jag. Maybe with a sun-roof. I think I might be able to stretch to a sun-roof.

He waited anxiously for her reaction. Couldn't tell it from her face, because he didn't want to risk a light at this time of night in the deserted factory. Never knew what interfering do-gooder might not be down the back streets, even at this late hour.

Did she approve? She mightily approved. Things were happening faster than she'd imagined, from the moment she'd coolly made the deliberate decision to play the boss along. He'd already spent more money on entertaining her than her father pulled down in his wage packet every week. And she did sort of like him. That was important for her to keep hold of. Found him funny, and quick-witted. A change from the grabbing gormless boys she'd previously been out with. No-hopers, every one.

Lisa never thought it could happen to her, and happen so easily. It was the sort of story her mother read in paperback, with a fag in the corner of her mouth, and a small bottle of stout to her hand.

It couldn't last. Of course it couldn't last. People from council estates stayed on council estates. Once in a while you might get lucky, and get a sudden glimpse of the world outside. A world where people made things happen for themselves, rather than had to wait for things to happen to them. The door would slam shut on her, once the boss got tired, but for now, she'd go along for the ride. Not grasping, but very definitely taking.

So Amarantha-Lisa had no reservations in saying yes to the flat, and yes to the little runabout, sun-roof or not. And yes to letting him pour two glasses of Tia Maria from Bea's drawer, as a toast and pledge to their future together, and yes to him clearing the desk,

Jamieson's desk, of its clutter of shoeboxes and files. And yes to everything else that her decision to string the boss along was going to mean.

And it nearly meant frying in that office.

– Moonlight. Hector was stood on one leg, shaking his loafer off. – It's sort of – isn't it?

She knew what he meant, even though it was hardly the most pellucid line. Moonlight was still and blue and cold, and there was something about it. You had to admit that. Even half-naked on an office desk. Watching the moon through the skylight. And the dull red glow through the frosted glass pane in the office door.

There was no question but that Connie had torched it herself. No jury would have acquitted. Even her defence counsel would have been unable to deliver his summing up in her favour and keep a straight face. The listed building had stood in her way, so she had reached for the petrol can. She could be forgiven for not knowing that her father was inside at the time, working late on the accounts. But that was all you could say in her favour. She could just about manage to squeak out of the attempted parricide charge, but never the arson.

And her denials were just so much a matter of form.

Arnie knew she'd done it. Admitted surprise that she'd finally put her toe over the invisible line. But then, hadn't she been keeping close company with Kyprianou? Her life to date, and the episodes in it that involved him, had been leading up to this moment. He knew how close she'd sailed to the wind with her shops; it was inevitable that she'd end up doing the plainly criminal, and not just the commercially questionable.

Nesta knew she'd done it. In some ways fire was as much a woman's weapon as was poison. There was a part of her which had a sneaking admiration for the bold approach Connie had so plainly decided on to this particular problem. But on the whole she thought she disapproved. The trouble with that sort of thing was, it was catching. Witness the stories about the Greek she'd become pally with. You get away with one torch job, the next time you had a business problem, instead of thinking it through, you paid a visit to a garage where your face wasn't known. Result? You stayed in the black for longer than you otherwise would, but sure as hard-boiled eggs, you one day ended up gripping the bar of the dock.

Hector had to disapprove. Not only because he'd so nearly been caught in the pyre, but because a fire in circumstances like this only brought more officialdom on your head. Insurance assessors. More Planning Department sneaks. Another regret he had about that night was the fact that once again he had been shown not to keep his wits about him in a crisis. He'd been presented with a golden opportunity to consign all the extant VAT and tax records to the flames. Instead of which, as Bea pointed out, true to form, he'd only thought about himself.

Bea wasn't surprised that Connie had crossed the line. She was upset and angry that she should have been so careless as not to have checked the place was empty before striking the match. Very unbusinesslike. She was also niggled at her inability to break Hector's story about what he was doing back at the factory at that time of night. On the whole Bea thought the fire a mixed blessing. The site was now clear, and they could proceed with the rebuilding, even if Connie had been careless, and got put away. But if she did get put away, who would they get with the drive and energy to carry the rebuilding through?

Jamieson didn't know what to believe. But the very fact that he could entertain the thought that she might have done it worried him. What worried him most was that he couldn't honestly say that deep inside, he confidently rebutted the charges against her.

– I didn't do it. She insisted, packing her case, ready to leave the clinic refreshed and fit. As much as the number one suspect in an arson case can be.

– The fire brigade haven't asked me any awkward questions—the police haven't been round. They don't suspect me. Why should family?

The answer was that the family knew her. She had a record long as her arm with them, no matter that she was clean as a whistle to the police.

Risking having her blow up in his face, Jamieson took her through the evidence that had made the family suspicious.

– Bea fired you, and you came straight here.

– She didn't fire me, Connie snapped, over her shoulder. – I walked out. We had a professional disagreement and I temporarily resigned.

– And then the mysterious letter-writer starts throwing the shit at the fan for Hector and Bea.

Did he want to search her room? Look for the typewriter or pen those anonymous letters had been written on?

– That drove Bea to asking you back, on your terms—

– Which were only fair, seeing the work I've put into the firm, and the amount I've got to do now.

He sighed and nodded agreement.

– And all that stands in the way of you starting that work is one eighteenth century eyesore. Which is now a smouldering heap of ruins.

– Coincidence? She suggested, smiling brightly.

More like direct intervention by the Gods, he allowed a sour note into his voice. – Greek gods?

– Connie, I know you didn't do it. He held her arm back, just as she was about to land the blow. – You didn't write the letters, and you didn't fire the building. For a start you were here in the clinic that night.

– Checked?

He admitted it. He had checked at reception. It didn't mean that she couldn't have got Kyprianou or one of his cousins to do the job. But he wasn't prepared to consider that possibility. Nor that it hadn't been her idea in the first place. That, say, one of the cousins had approached her with the idea. Maybe putting the thought into play, but leaving it unresolved. So that she'd been as shocked as the rest of them when it happened.

– Wait a minute. You're saying this is what you don't believe? She'd got a little confused, so carefully was he picking his way through the minefield.

That was what he was saying he didn't believe, yes.

– But what do you believe? Can you put your hand on your heart and say you believe I didn't do it?

He was spared answering and feeling the ground rise green and orange under his feet by the nurse–receptionist arriving with the bill.

– Tell me, Connie flashed her most winning smile at the girl. – Do I look like an arsonist? My boyfriend thinks I'm an arsonist.

She was looking forward to getting back to the cottage, even though she'd been branded a poison-pen writer and an arsonist. Despite the food and comforts at the clinic, she was rested up and raring to go.

In bed with him, as much as at the firm. Where she was also known as a poison-pen writer and an arsonist. It was a distinction of sorts, she supposed, as she waited for her credit card to be returned. Not many people would have had the character to support two vices like that. Flattering, in a way, that she was considered so dangerous that she'd automatically be accepted as a suspect. Or was it? Poison and fire were cowards' weapons, more than they were women's weapons. Maybe she should be even angrier than she was.

But, walking towards the exit with Jamieson a sneaking sense of fairness held her back. Hadn't she told him she was an all-the-way person, and if he was coming along for the ride, he'd best hold on to his toupee, because it was going to be a fast and bumpy one?

Maybe she did deserve the suspicions.

But what did she care, so long as that site was wall to wall carbon, and she could press ahead with getting some drawings out of its replacement?

– Very stylish. She stood a couple of yards from the van, not impressed. You spend two weeks away from your fella, admittedly voluntarily, but two weeks' absence was two weeks. When you sign yourself out, you expect to be collected by him in something ritzier than the firm's delivery van.

Jamieson was unapologetic as he swung the rusted doors open. – I've got a run to Kent tomorrow. I'm delivery boy now, as well as everything else.

Where was Leroy?

Who knew?

Leroy hadn't been seen since the day after the fire.

They all kicked themselves for having mised it, once Leroy had been conned back to the office and confessed. Hector had been chewing Leroy up about the rubbish piled in the yard. Someone had put a match to that rubbish. The blaze had got out of control. Leroy hadn't showed the very next day. Nor the ones after that.

His attendance record had been so checkered that no one had put those two facts together in the confusion of the mopping up and reorganising the undamaged part of the factory for a limited and limping production run. Not until Connie spotted it, refreshed after her lay-off.

He was conned back to the office by Jamieson, who said there would be a couple of weeks in hand, and perhaps some holiday money due to him. Not a word about the fire. That bullet was saved for Connie to discharge, when he walked through the office door to find them all sat round waiting for him. Hector, Bea, Arnie, Nesta and even Dev. Connie wanted them all squished into the office to hear this.

He coughed, seeing there was no option. But not before a baleful glare at Jamieson, who'd suckered him along. He made a mental note never to trust the dogsbodies.

– I like a few beers. I mean, who doesn't like a few beers?

That one particular night they were interested in he'd been taken short because of his few beers, on his way home in a friend's car. What should he realise when he was stood against a wall, straining the sweet potatoes, but that the wall belonged to the House of Bea? In the dark he'd managed to arrive at where he worked during the day. Where his life was currently being made a misery by Hector.

– He was laying welly on me. Threatening to fire me if I didn't clear the garbage as well as drive the van. So I thought sod it. And I dropped a match on it.

No one had wider eyes that night in all of the Midlands, than Leroy, when the entire pile went up in a sheet of flame and a very loud whoosh. The Great Fire of London wasn't in it. Exploding supertankers came nowhere near. He'd fallen back, aghast at his own handiwork. Then his sense of self-preservation had overtaken his feelings of civic responsibilities. He'd legged it to his mate's car.

How could he have known there was somebody in the office at that time of night? The lights were off. He'd seen no lights. This raised the interesting question as to how Hector was attending to accounts in complete darkness, but he got away with it. Indignation at Leroy's conduct swallowed up the fact.

– You legged it? Letting it burn down?

How could Leroy have known it was going to burn down? He'd thought, once he was safe in the car, that it would burn itself out.

– A ten-foot wall of flame? An exploding supertanker?

Maybe he'd exaggerated how fast and how violently the first pieces of scrap had ignited. But now that the facts were out, what were they going to do about it? Call the police? Sack him?

The latter, very definitely. There was no way they could take him back, when every time someone lit a fag up in the yard they'd freeze with shock. And would he really want to work in an atmosphere where he was regarded as a potential assassin?

Not that he was going to fight it. He'd been badly shaken by the fire and even more by the realisation of what a deathtrap the House of Bea could be.

– You could get killed working here, he said, with just sufficient indignation in his voice to exasperate.

The police were a different matter. It didn't seem worth all that trouble to involve them when there wasn't any offence he'd committed. Save that of being a pillock. He was old enough to be allowed to play with matches, even if he should never have been let near a box. Was there any point in hauling the boys in blue down, and taking statements, and stirring up the Insurance company and their assessors again—? Wasn't it better to let sleeping dogs lie, and keep yards away from their dozing tails?

Hector thought so.

Arnie thought so.

Nesta and Jamieson thought so.

And so did Bea, which clinched the matter, after Connie gave her nod as well. Leroy was dismissed with a month's hush-money, without a stain on his underpants. But Connie assured him, as she held the door open to see him safely out, that she'd stay away from any bonfire night party he'd ever throw.

– So virtue triumphs again? Nesta said it just loudly enough for Jamieson to hear, as Dev held the car door wide for her.

– Looks like it, he smiled back.

– Or quick thinking? And making bloody certain Leroy knew his lines backwards?

And as Jamieson watched the car leave the yard, he knew he'd never really one hundred percent be certain what he believed. She was an all-the-way person, and he'd signed up to go all the way along with her.

– What it doesn't clear up is the poison letters, Hector paused, about to throw the main switch, the revelations of the day over. These days, he was scrupulously careful about things like that, which before had seemed eminently missable routine.

Bea concurred. But she had a feeling they'd be hearing no more of the anonymous scribbler.

– You don't think—

He started again.

– You never thought—

And again.

– Do you think—?

She completed the thought chain for him.

– Connie? I've no idea. And like you, I'm scared to ask.

Lisa supplied the answer. A week later, which was the very next time Hector could get away. He was showing the girl around the flat he'd already signed for. One-bedroomed, above a launderette, a couple of miles out of the city centre. But dry and clean. And discreet. In the kitchen something shadowed her face.

– Is this the place you had for Maureen?

Maureen? Maureen? He was genuinely perplexed. Did he look the sort of fella who would know any birds called Maureen? Let alone rent places like this for them?

She pressed the point, and he did recollect a Maureen. Maureen the interlocker. Maureen the balloon smuggler. Lisa had nothing to worry about there. That had been just the usual harmless slap and tickle among the knitting frames. It might have been that the girl had taken it more seriously than he'd intended, but it had never been meant to come to anything.

– She was expecting it to.

Hector dared say she might have done. But he couldn't be held responsible for the erotic fantasies of his staff, could he?

– The girls get crushes. They get odd thoughts. Especially about the boss.

– It was her wrote those letters.

Hector nearly pulled the handle off the door he was opening. What letters? And what did she know about them? If there were any letters? Which he wasn't admitting to, one way or the other.

– Those anonymous letters. She thought you'd been making a fool of her.

The word Maureen wanted passed on was that it was over now. She had suddenly realised there was no point mooning over what might have been, when Lisa was so plainly the favourite at Hector's little court. Besides, she'd found herself a fella. A cable-layer. It was true love, for Maureen.

– Did she cause you any bother?

Hector considered his reply, and shook his head.

– Not so you'd notice.

But he asked Lisa to remind him to buy Maureen a Bloody Mary, and her cable-layer a pint of whatever cable-layers drink, if they turned up in the factory pub one lunchtime.

For now, they had domestic things to attend to.

Like celebrate her acceptance of the new flat in the most appropriate way.

Twelve

Babs swung a mean body into and out of lorry cabs. She never had any trouble picking up South-bound trips for free, when she reached for her case, and went. Nor returning North-bound heavy haulers and artics, when it was time for her to head back. Once in a while she was bothered by a groping hairy hand, but she kept her nails long and never got into anything she couldn't scratch her way out of.

She didn't have to hitch lifts. Arnie was still waiting for the one big deal which would lift him out of the market rat-race for good. But there was enough coinage jingling in the bag at the end of every week to have paid for a train or bus ticket for her. Except she liked thumbing her way off lay-bys. There was a lot she'd given up for Arnie that he didn't know about. She'd signed a lot of freedoms away when she signed up with him. The lottery of making your way on your thumb was one she still got a kick out of.

In exchange for allowing her that freedom, and no questions asked, Arnie demanded one for himself. The freedom to get legless every time she went South. She was entitled to preserve a little mystery, so he was entitled to do the one thing he liked best. Hitting himself time after time on the head with a bottle, for as many days and nights as she was away.

Arnie was a great believer in the bender. People, for Arnie, divided themselves into those who needed benders every so often, and those full citizens who managed to get by without. Now and again you needed to lose the use of your limbs and frontal brain. Just as you needed to rest up the motor every so often. And if part of having a bender was getting your face poked after a pointless row in your local, he accepted that too. It wouldn't do for the straight citizens who didn't understand the bender. But it was almost a necessary part of Arnie's routine for getting through the irregular absences of the young girl he was crazy about.

Which was why Babs always headed straight to the market bar when she swung down from the returning cab. This time he wasn't slumped in the corner, his head resting on the juke-box's throbbing side. The barman nodded, and she went through to the passage. Arnie was sitting there, sideways on a barstool, dabbing blood from his lip.

He waved a vague hand and turned his attention to another trickle of blood coming suddenly from his nose. Time for more elaborate welcomes-back when he was patched up.

She did the patching, in the van. Uncomplaining, because she loved the guy. He was a mess and a boozer. But she had come back this time. Like she would keep coming back. Because he was the best thing could have happened to her. Just like Bea had been to Hector. And when you're stuck with that, the little things like patching up your fella don't bother you.

Unless in the back of your mind you're thinking your fella has someone else on his mind. That he's not been drinking just because he's trying to keep you in mind. Because he doesn't want to think of someone else. Who didn't swing perhaps, such a youthful body around anymore. But who had experience on her side. And who had, after all, gone a few rounds with the fella before.

The last person Nesta expected to see in her office was Babs. Her first reaction was that she had come to ask a favour for Arnie. A favour which wouldn't be allowed. Arnie had nothing to offer in exchange. And now that he wasn't kosher family any more, she only handled Arnie on a business footing.

Babs hadn't called round to ask help in baling Arnie out of trouble. She took her time saying why she was calling. Getting the feel of the office, nerving herself to make the offer to Nesta. That big bad bitch, who featured so prominently in all Arnie's horror stories of the complications of family life. She knew, for example, that this had been Connie's own office. And that when Nesta was Connie's number two, she'd seen to it that Arnie was never lacking for female company if the action was slow.

Nesta was thinking at the same time that the girl opposite, who looked like she got her clothes out of an aerosol can, had seen a bit of action at some time herself. For someone so young, she had put some time in. Nesta could read these things. There was something around the eyes. Bruising that only another woman could see. And only a woman whose job it was to know about women. For you have to know about them, to sell them.

There wasn't a word for what the two of them were to each other, was there? Nesta kick-started the conversation. Not one portmanteau word that covered the relationship of step-sister's ex-husband's bird. Did Babs know that African tribes had names for that sort of relationship?

There was a word. Babs insisted there was a word.

– Allies. Against her.

And Nesta knew at once what 'her' they were going to talk about.

Nesta put her straight on one thing. Maybe the most important thing.

– I don't think he'd go back to her. I don't think that's what he wants.

There was no way to be sure, of course. After all, he was only a man, a moral hooligan, an unguided emotional missile. But from what Nesta knew, all was over between them.

– But while she's here, Babs faced her out—there's the danger. And he's a different fella now she's back. It's like he was doing that Jack the Lad routine at the bar—

Nesta knew it. The one where Arnie, glass in hand told everyone who'd listen that he didn't give a monkeys, even though he was in trouble with the VAT and the Income Tax, he was down there so often he got asked to the Christmas party, the last time he'd paid the HP on the van was in LSD. Yes. She knew that routine.

– And then Connie walked through the door, and he stopped dead. Saw himself for what he is. What's happened in the time she's been away. That he's just another bigmouth on the barrows, and he can't take it any more.

Arnie was a loser. She knew that, and it didn't matter. She'd known winners in her time, and give her the losers any day. But how did you get a loser to believe that?

The problem was that no one knew even now just what Connie was up to. Was she back for good? What about that mystery illness, which had presumably struck and put her in the clinic prior to the fire? Where did Jamieson stand? Was that permanent? It looked permanent, he certainly acted like he believed it was. But where did Connie stand on that?

It was a surprise, and a shock, to realise that they were no further forward regarding Connie's long-term intentions and motivations than they'd been the day she flew back.

Leaving her Greek boyfriend in charge of the taverna, yes, but what else? Her heart? The part of it she hadn't given to Jamieson?

What they needed was to get someone out to the Med, and find out first hand. Maybe Nesta could manage a week in a couple of months. That wasn't very satisfactory, but it would have to do for now. There was no way Babs could turn round to Arnie and tell him she was flying out, was there?

– Months?

– Months. Nesta spread her engagement book for the girl. That rag-trade queen with hands like white butterflies was proving difficult to get hold of, so she was even more of a one-woman band than usual.

Dev? Babs had heard the word on Nesta's relationship with the ex-designer. Nesta merely pulled a face. This was no place to go into the details of her increasingly stormy relationship with Dev.

Failing anything coming up in the meantime to short-circuit the need for Nesta to head for the sun with pocket tape recorder and notebook, they agreed to meet every week. Take a sauna together. That would help keep their very private alliance that much more private. Besides, Nesta wanted to see if Babs' amazing skin went all over.

– We take our weekly sauna, and wait for something other than perspiration to drop into our laps.

There was another word, apart from allies, that from now on said what they were to each other. Blood sisters. Each with an oath sworn against Connie.

That something dropped into Nesta's lap a lot sooner than she expected. Half an hour later, precisely, when Dev turned up.

Nesta had been getting serious about doing something about the threat Connie represented, even before Babs had showed. She had a slice of the business. How long before she conned or bludgeoned Bea into giving her another? And one after that? So that in the end it would be Nesta who picked up a nominal share of the business when the Founder and her kept man decided to call it a day.

She had got something and nothing out of sending Dev out with orders to stick to Jamieson. His head was so far stuck into the accounting and office procedures reorganisation at the fire-damaged plant that she had written Connie's fella off. No approach to him, for the time being.

But Dev had showed himself a faithful poodle on that assignment. And it had been her fault more than his that she nearly missed the significance of what he'd seen, those days he'd followed Jamieson. All right, admit it—she had missed the significance, until the very moment when Kyprianou had walked out of the church on Connie's arm. She gave him another assignment. This time she didn't intend to be caught napping when Connie made a move. Dev was to wriggle his way up close to her again, whatever the cost to his self-respect. And if he couldn't do that, Nesta gave him carte blanche to get access to the factory low-down from any source he could.

– Pillow talk?

That sort of thing, she agreed. But without ever having to put his head on a pillow. He could chat up as many of the silly young tarts at the factory gates as he could. Buy them as many snowballs and harvey wallbangers as they could drink and still stand up at the lunchtime pub. But he was on no account to lay them. Not even in the course of duty.

That was the sort of job brief that Dev hankered after. But the whole thing had soon turned sour. Connie just wasn't around.

– She has to be. They're turning out knitwear, aren't they?

That was true, he'd told his boss and keeper. But on such a fire-reduced scale that Connie wasn't needed. She'd asked for a couple of weeks off to concentrate on the planning aspect of the thing, and hadn't been near the factory since. Nesta knew there was no point trying to sucker the information out of Bea during their weekly golf massacre.

Since the fire an even greater wariness had come to hood Bea's eye.

If Connie had gone underground, Dev had to go there after her. So on the morning of Babs' visit he'd aimlessly driven round every place where he thought she might be. Markets, shopping streets and precincts, up and down the endless red-brick terraces where knit-wear was made. And drawn a blank.

– So far as Connie goes. He floated the line just in time to stay Nesta'a verbal assault on him. And took his time delivering the goods.

– What would Hector be doing carrying furniture into a flat above a launderette, a couple of miles out of the city centre? And a dozen red roses, on top of them?

His step-daughter didn't know. But she was damn sure going to find out, as soon as her flame-red sports car could get her there.

The stereo was a cheap one, probably knocked-off, that Hector had picked up in a second-hand shop, down the road. But it worked, and it was a stereo. He'd smuggled a handful of his favourite LPs out of The Grange, and one of them was playing softly as he waited for Lisa. The table set, the lights low. Ella Fitzgerald caressing the words and music of 'Someone To Watch Over Me', and hardly a crackle or a hiss.

Hector moved to the door with a brimming kir when the bell rang. He spilt a lot of it over the lip of the wine glass when he saw Nesta stood there.

She walked in and waited until the record ended.

– Who looks after the one who looks after you, dad? She put all the sting in the last word. And as he fought for breath and explanation, she high-heeled the door closed behind her.

Was he going to tell her this wasn't what she thought?

– It's not what you think.

– Tell me you love her. Go on. Tell me the old old story . . . You love her, and this time, with this one, it's different.

It was.

– It started off as just another bit of leg-over. Then you woke up one bright morning and realised love had poked you in the eye. The roses never smelt so sweet, and the birds were singing fit to throw up.

It wasn't what she was thinking, but he didn't have to explain. and would she now please leave? To be fair, he didn't put much conviction into it himself, so you could hardly blame her for just curling the lip at him.

– Bit quick off the mark, aren't you, dad? She underlined the relationship again. – I shouldn't have thought there'd be the readies for this sort of thing until after Connie swings the rebuilding.

Maybe, she hazarded, he was putting a bit aside, the crafty old ram. Cutting down on the drinks bill, or skipping a service or two on the executive hatchback? Or maybe just straight thieving from the firm. Which was in fact what he was doing, and why he was not keen that Jamieson should be able to fully rationalise the accounts. Messy accounts meant you could slip things through. Like the flat, and the little run-about with the leaky sun-roof.

Nesta had the initiative and wasn't easily going to let it go.

– Is she preggers? Or pretending to be? Has she tried to sucker you with that one? I bet she's got her hooks into you for the car though, hasn't she? And the allowance to keep it on the road?

She was dead wrong, he rallied faintly, the kir still wobbling in the glass in his hand. He knew it looked bad, but there was a simple explanation.

She pressed on. Where did he meet this one? Hotel bar? Bank steps? Or was she another in the long line of House of Bea interlocker starlets he'd taken in hand? A fatherly interest continued after hours.

– I want to know where you met her, dad. And again the stab of that final word. – Where was she sat, showing everything, her hem up to her thighs, when you walked into her gun sights, you silly old sod?

Just where had this particular scrubber crawled out from?

Hector got some space. It was time to establish the ground rules.

– I love your mother. I care for her. We're the best thing that could have happened to each other. Whatever this is, and I'm admitting nothing—it's nothing to do with me and Bea.

Nesta begged leave to query that. The matching mugs for late night drinkies queried it. The sporting print table mats queried it. As did the raffia drink coasters, and, she did believe, napkin rings. It was all very cosy. He'd brought this one more than he'd brought her mother. Hadn't his cupboard been pretty bare when he conned Bea into saying Yes?

– In your mother I have the love of my life, and something I didn't expect or deserve. But that's not enough. The love of your life is not enough to take all the love that's in you. Not if you're made like me.

She was still checking the contents list. The comfy chintz cushions on the sofa for those late night chats. Everything for two in the kitchen. It had the look of a commitment. So did the bedroom, with the king-size duvet, and above the bed, a mucky picture of a swan and a bird with no clothes on. What next? 'His and Her' shower caps and soap-on-a-rope? Door chimes that played the melody line of Play Misty For Me?

– I've always played fair with your mother. I'm playing fair now. I can love the both of them, at the same time. With exactly the same bits of me, without cheating on either.

And he meant it. He did feel that. It wasn't a line he was shooting.

Nesta wondered if he could be using the word cheat in the same sense as she understood it? If he was describing some sort of complication of love, he was wasting his breath. Nesta didn't talk that language. She'd missed out on that, somewhere along the line. Even this thing with Dev that had started to possess her was at bedrock an infatuation, she was clear-eyed enough to know.

The little speech that Nesta allowed herself on that, enjoying the luxury of personal bitterness at the same time as paint-stripping the man in the bedroom with her, allowed Hector to get his mental breath back. Say what you liked about him, he recovered fast. Life had so often pushed him on to the back foot that he delivered his best shots from there. A counter-puncher was Hector. Just as Nesta was a server with a smash that could burn holes in the opponent's racket.

What did Nesta have on him, anyway? There had been half an admission that he'd lost his head over a girl, but where was the evidence to take to Bea? And he imagined that was what Nesta was here for. She couldn't damage Connie directly, so she had to be trying to nail her through her dad.

A lifetime of thinking on his feet without babbling incoherence came to Hector's aid. He even impressed himself with how he managed to stitch the story together, on his toes.

– What you've overlooked is that once we rebuilt we'll be going up market, after the multiples, the High St. chains. You know what a row some of them make if their suppliers get caught out running sweat-shops. Not that anyone gives a monkey's about them as is being sweated, but it's bad for the corporate image.

As Board member with responsibility for staff welfare, Hector was instituting an innovative and enlightened approach to personnel management and good staff relations. The House of Bea was now going to subsidise digs for staff. Did Nesta know how hard it was for young people to find accommodation these days?

– So it is a bird from the shop floor? Nesta was in quickly, but couldn't face him.

– I have no doubt this apartment will first be let to some deserving case, probably female. Which is the sex of the bulk of our staff, as you well know. Someone who's had a row with her parents, or is nobly trying to get by on her own.

This was only self-interest on the management's part, he hastened to say. How could staff give of their best at their machines, if they had personal accommodation problems hanging over their heads?

– You haven't mentioned this sudden out-of-character burst of philanthropy to Bea yet? Nesta didn't try to keep the cynical note out of her voice. She remembered the unisex toilet facility that Hector had not put off remedying for over two years now.

– Much better to present her with a fait accompli. Your mother has many excellent qualities, but she's one of the old school. I take all the glossy business weeklies, you know. And the monthlies. I'm more up to date in my attitudes to dynamic man management.

Hector could see he wasn't impressing his step-daughter, but her lack of a robust come-back suggested that he had baffled brains with bullshit, not for the first time in his personal and business life. He decided to apply the screws. Nesta was still free to go and retail her suspicions of the apartment to Bea. But would Bea thank her? Do you thank the person who puts the worm of distrust into a relationship? Even if that distrust turns out later to be justified.

– If she has to face the fact I've been fooling her—and he was admitting nothing—she has to face the fact her fifth marriage has been as big a disaster as the other four. And what does she have ahead of her? Listening to her own footsteps in that big house? Having only the hot-water bottle in bed with her?

Given a choice, he'd bet that Bea would plump to believe him, unless the evidence was overwhelming. Whatever way it fell out, Nesta wouldn't be doing herself any favours with her mother, by bringing her suspicions to her attention.

Game set and match to Hector. After initially being knocked all over the court, he'd taken advantage of not being able to get a word in edgeways, and came back strong. It wasn't often that someone came from behind to win out over his step-daughter. But he'd done it.

And would have got away with it, but for the fact that Lisa chose the moment he was holding the door open for Nesta, to arrive.

– I've got some drink coasters to go with the table settings, and a lovely lamp. She burst through, too excited to notice the expression on his face as she dropped her bundle of parcels on the armchair. – I spent far too much on the bits and bobs for the bathroom, but you're not angry, are you Hecky? You know I'll make every penny of it up to you through here.

Through there being the bedroom, and only then the girl realising there was someone else in the flat.

– Close the door, there's a pet. Nesta gave one of her nicest shop-smiles. She made herself comfortable on the sofa, and suggested they all have coffee. Lisa could make it. Lisa of the long legs, and armful of goodies, who was going to make up every penny under and on top of the king-size duvet. She and her step-dad had things to talk about.

And Connie's movements while Dev had been supposed to stalk her? Where had she disappeared to, briefed to find a way around the planning block on the redevelopment? Not even Bea knew that. Bea was keeping at arm's length, since it was clear Connie had a plan worked out, following the refusal of their outline plans. The objections were technical, but damning. On access and lorry-parking grounds. On the residential zoning of the area. But every problem turns out to be technical in the end, as the man said.

Connie had something in mind, and Bea let it go at that. Clapped her hands over her ears and insisted she not be told of a single move Connie was making. Come the day when she could present the House of Bea with the planning go-ahead, Bea would clasp her to her bosom and press rare wines on her. But just for the moment, in case anything went wrong, she didn't want to be involved.

Fair enough. Connie accepted it. As some people were born knowing design, or selling, so others have a gift for wrangling about property. Connie had cut her teeth on property when she was developing her shops. That had been in the looser and easier days of the sixties and seventies. Before a lot of fingers had been burnt in local government and commerce, and a lot of porridge flowed under a lot of previously well-respected citizen's bridges.

She accepted that, but still felt that given a fair wind, she could get her old touch back. But first of all she had to catch up on what had been happening in the town in the past eight years.

She explained it to Jamieson. Not that he took much of it in, because he was putting in twelve-plus hours a day. The filing and accounts system was proving a tough one to crack, even for a previous forty-thousand a year man. The principles of double-entry bookkeeping had been invented in Genoa in the fifteenth century. But so far anything but the rumour of it hadn't seemed to reach the Midlands. Not Hector and Bea's Midlands anyway. Getting things straight was now a physical as well as intellectual demand on him, but he was sure he could hack it.

Connie ignored the fact that he was about to fall asleep, and carried on. She needed to hear it herself, to make sure she was on the right track, before she launched herself off.

– It took me just a month to find my way round that village in Greece. You soon got to know who counted. Who was the biggest landowner, who had the local fuzz in his pocket, who were the families who mattered, and who were even more dangerous because they were trying to be the families who mattered. It was all there in front of you if you had the wit to see it. You could work out the pecking order just watching the big parade, the volta down the main street every evening.

It wasn't so easy here. Here people lived closed-up lives. They were hard to prise open. The deals were that much more secret, because the personalities that lay behind them were that much more invisible.

So she was going to draw for herself a wiring diagram, a street plan, a map of the sewers. Whatever you wanted to call it. She was going to read her way steadily through eight years' back issues of the local paper, and eight years' worth of council minutes. Her backside was going to hurt, and her eyeballs feel like they'd been rubbed raw on yellowed newsprint. But it was the only way to set about familiarising herself with who was who, and what they did to and with each other.

It wasn't something she was looking forward to, she assured him. Who would? And she was the active type, the doing type. She might burn her eyes out and need to wear pebble-thick glasses at the end of however long it was going to take her. Would she still be loved, in pebble-thick glasses? She nudged against him, flicking the TV on to the late show. Would she have to take them off before they made love? Or would he get a kick, to start with anyway, taking advantage of a woman who couldn't expect to have passes made at her, because of her glasses?

He didn't reply. Fast asleep. Dreaming, no doubt, of dancing figures, and the computerised system he was determined to install to get rid of the shoebox method of keeping accounts for ever.

Sitting on those hard chairs was the toughest thing she'd had to put herself through since she came back. Yet again the difference between hard work and working hard was borne in on her. She worked hard at the factory, on the road when she went out selling, and at her deepening relationship with her man. But it wasn't hard work, which had to be something you'd rather not be doing. However much effort you'd be putting into whatever you'd be doing instead.

By the time she'd finished, she thought she could draw from memory every pimple on the face of the girl who handed her the papers file every day. And the hundred and fifty varieties of wheezes and farts given off by her fellow ploughers through the council records.

If it didn't pay off, she was going to be one very pissed-off paper spider, indeed.

With Connie busy coming on like an investigative journalist following up a story she wasn't even sure existed, and Jamieson having more downs than ups on the office side, it wasn't surprising that they missed Hector's sudden absence. Later, after the reasons for that absence became so painfully clear, Jamieson did recollect Bea mentioning something. To the effect that Hector had been looking a little peaky over the last few weeks, and that a rest would do him good.

If he thought anything at the time, it would have been that Hector was going to get sent out on a sales trip, because that was what Bea usually meant by a rest. But he'd let the remark go by, and Bea hadn't lingered on the point. For she had her reasons for going along with his suggestion that he take himself off to Greece, now there was a slack period at the firm, and find out exactly what had happened between Connie and Georgiou those months before.

Bea was impressed that Hector had thought of this himself. It showed how he could be underestimated. She also realised with a jolt that the question of why Connie was back had never been cleared up. If you discounted the story of the mystery illness, which had now been finished with. Its disappearance had been one of the conditions she had set, before Connie was allowed a share of the business.

She was suspicious, on reflection, that perhaps Nesta might have had something to do with it. But she was unaware of any basis for a Nesta–Hector axis. Connie's return had put a strain on a relationship that had never at the best of times been one of fulsome mutual admiration. She could see no reason why Hector, of all people, should have taken up with a plan of Nesta's.

So Bea agreed with him that he could do with a couple of days in the sun, and personally drove him to the airport. He'd half-heartedly suggested that she come with him, but someone had to mind the store. Besides, Hector had been over to see Georgiou once before, eight years back. He could build on that meeting, get the taverna owner's confidence and the dirt on Connie's now extended homecoming.

Bea wasn't a mug. She'd long since known that Connie was estranged from the man and had probably lost all her money to him. But was the Greek angle still closed for the new partner in the firm? She had to be sure, against the day when Connie came up with the goods on the planning side. No point getting into a possibly bent commitment to go ahead with the rebuilding, with all the heartache and graft that would entail, if at any minute Connie might take off. Head back to the Med, to patch things up with her greaser.

– And keep clear of the topless beaches, was Bea's last command to Hector, as he tried not to look as elated as he felt at the prospect ahead of him.

He didn't get to any topless beaches. There was no time in his crowded itinerary for that. He had four days in Greece, one of which was taken up by travelling—by plane, ferry hydrofoil, and local rattle-trap bus to the beach on which the village sat. The rest was lost in a multi-flavoured mist of booze, drink, dance, song and laughter. When he went out, there was no thought in his mind of doing anything across his daughter. Bringing Georgiou back to England with him was the last thing he intended.

Nesta wanted the low-down on the bust-up, if it had been a bust-up. Bea jumped at the chance of getting the same. Very well. He'd take advantage of their voracious female curiosity, and come up with the facts. But nothing more. If they hurt Connie, that was too bad. He couldn't see that they could hurt her, but he had to take that risk. Because otherwise Nesta was perfectly capable of blowing him sky high for his love-nesting with the girl.

But he did bring Georgiou back with him. And knocked Connie flying. Not to mention Jamieson, who had to pull his head smartly out of those shoeboxes and start fighting dirty.

Thirteen

Feeling as if someone was playing a blow-torch down his throat, and wishing that he'd risked something lighter than a Donegal tweed suit, even this late in the year, Hector surveyed the taverna. The shutter hanging by one hinge said it all. And for confirmation was the lizard basking in the autumn light on the upturned umbrella table on the fly-blown patio at the side.

The shutters had finally slammed shut on the taverna, and when he found Georgiou asleep in a caique prow, he knew the shutters had closed on him as well. It took the Greek half an hour to come round from sleeping off the morning ouzo, and as long again to recognise Hector.

It was of course necessary to greet the unexpected visitor at the one taverna which stayed open all the year, tucked down a back-street, well off the tourist drag. The last thing Hector clearly remembered between going into the low door of the local bar, and walking groggily down the plane steps with Georgiou behind him, was how many brothers Georgiou seemed to have. And how hefty looking a bunch they were.

Hector had met quite a few brothers that afternoon. And evening. And cousins and aunts and nephews and nieces that night, when he was taken to some sort of celebration in the mountains behind the village. The three-hour ride in the back of a Japanese four wheel drive jeep would have splintered his spine, had it not been for the fact that he was continually pressed with variations on the local fire water. Including a raki especially brought over from Crete for the occasion. Afterwards he was never sure whether it had been a wedding or a christening, or even a funeral. All he knew was that he had had a lot of wine to drink. A lot of toasts to respond to, and a lot of dance steps to master. And that the booze thankfully blotted out the return journey by the same jeep. And when that was driven into a ditch, on the back of a borrowed mule.

There was a definite feeling in the village that Hector's arrival was the biggest thing that was going to happen between now and the

returning tourist buses in the summer. And man, woman, child and the village dogs were prepared to squeeze themselves into the taverna and make the most of it. There may have been a hard wet Greek winter ahead, but there were going to be some Hector-carnival memories to look back on.

It was impossible to say exactly when the idea that Georgiou should come back to England with Hector was first put about. Or by whom. Hector would swear until he was blue in the face that it hadn't been his idea. But he had to admit that it must have been what he'd said that started the idea running.

They were such an expansive people, that was the trouble. They lived loudly. You responded to their peasant heartiness. And part of that response was to exaggerate how well Connie was now doing. That was a back-handed sort of tribute to Georgiou, wasn't it? It helped him keep face, because he got all the kudos for keeping such a high-powered businesswoman in the taverna for eight years.

Hector leant back in the hand-carved chair, and built up such a glowing picture of how well Georgiou's ex was doing that he almost believed it himself.

But how was she inside? Was her success helping her get over the row she'd had with the Greek? The details of that row were never quite made plain to her father, but he guessed the facts weren't flattering to Georgiou.

What could Hector do? Tell the man to his face, in front of his brothers, his very stocky brothers, with the wire-wool hair on their stubby forearms, that she was now shacked up with somebody else? That wouldn't go down well. It would lose face for Georgiou, and who was Hector to introduce a sour note when they were all getting on famously?

So he avoided mention of Jamieson, and dressed the facts up a little. Hinted that Connie hadn't quite got over the separation. That there was every possibility that deep in her heart (who knew with women?) that she regretted him. That one day, having made her pile, she may intend to throw it all up and come back for him.

It wasn't that Hector believed all that crap. Nor that he told it as a pack of bare-faced lies. He blushed even as he retailed them. But this was the land of Homer, after all. These people lived and breathed legend, and never mind that a story was larger than life, so long as it was well-told. And Hector, in between the boozing, the

eating, the dancing and the winking at the pretty giggling girls, told his tale so well that Georgiou followed him on to that plane, and down the steps four days after.

And what could Hector do? Force him back on the returning flight? Mightn't he be doing Connie a favour, after all? Perhaps his paternal instincts were right—the woman was waiting for something like this to happen? Perhaps she did go to sleep in Jamieson's arms every night dreaming that they were the Greek's?

He didn't believe it. Couldn't make himself come near to believing it. But it was some sort of comfort as he sat in the taxi with the man on the way to the House of Bea. This was some swarthy bunny, with impossibly white and regular teeth, that he was pulling out of the hat.

It had been a good morning for Jamieson and Connie up until then. It was her first day back, and she felt she was on to something. Something had turned up in the files and council minutes that was well worth looking into. Being away eight years had turned out to be a distinct advantage. Just as the street-names and high prices were new to her, so the town had been. So she saw things much more clearly. Had picked up the sniff of scandal in the files, and in the newsprint. Which could short circuit their planning rejection appeal.

Bea stayed tight-lipped. She hadn't heard. Didn't want to hear, not until the consents were through and the first paddies arrived to dig out the footings.

And Jamieson had reason to smile as well, because Bea had agreed to the computerisation in the teeth of Hector's strong reservations. The new office manager knew by now that Hector had been up to no good in the accounts and wanted them kept in a mess for strictly practical reasons. He kept quiet about it. That knowledge might come in useful further down the line. Jamieson was learning how the game was played at this level. Didn't footballers agree it was tougher in the fourth division than the first? The tackles were that much more desperate, the elbows in the face that much sharper?

Bea decided in his favour, and he reserved one crunching tackle and one teeth-spitting elbow for Hector, should he need it later.

And then Hector walked in with the Greek behind him.

And all he said, as he stood in the doorway, leaning slightly against it, with his stubble of beard making him look even more the

villain, was—Hello Connie. I have come to take you back.

And all she said, his all-the-way person, who lived life at the gallop, and had promised him nothing but trouble, after that first heart-stopping moment was—Sorry. And—See you, pal, as she walked past Jamieson, and down the steps with Georgiou.

Sorry and See you, pal were hardly the all-time great lines on which to end a relationship, but it looked as if they were all Jamieson would be getting. Very Connie to snap a decision like that. Very Connie to give in to that urge to do the dramatic thing rather than the sensible. She was out and away before Jamieson had properly taken in who the dark stranger had been. Contrary to what he might have expected, there had been no flash of telepathy to tell him this was a rival, this was danger. He'd stood with his thumb up his bum while Connie had reacted, and got to the door second to Bea, when he recovered.

– Sorry, pal. I got there first. And Bea slammed the office door shut and was off after the lovebirds. Which was very Bea, in addition.

By the time Jamieson had unscrambled things, both cars were off the grid and he was left with his thumb still in that uncomfortable position. With Connie gone, her words sinking in, he was beginning fully to realise their implications. He turned back to Hector. Hector, who had so obviously been the root of all.

The old fox was trying to sneak out the back way when Jamieson caught up with him. Needing a shower and a shave and some wholesome, dull English food. Needing most of all not to be around now that Jamieson had caught the bullet between his teeth.

– Why?

Hector could only roll his shoulders. Even that somehow seemed to damage his head. He could see why the making of raki was outlawed in mainland Greece. Tiredly, he explained about the shuttered taverna and the dozing Georgiou. And then how things had got livelier, and he'd met more and more relatives, each of them anxious that he honour them by sampling the family moonshine. And how he'd grown expansive in his cups. And how it didn't seem very polite, or safe, to turn down the suggestion that Georgiou accompany him back.

His half-hearted suggestion that Jamieson try to shrug it off and wait for Connie to come back didn't go down well. Not that he'd thought it was going to.

– You didn't come up with this yourself, Jamieson was certain of that. – Was it Nesta? And if it was Nesta, what did she have on him? He guessed at a bird, and took another guess that the secret of her identity, and what Hector was up to with her was hidden in the shoeboxes. That was shortly going to change, though. He was on the track of various sundries that Hector had been making a practice of slipping into the business accounts.

So buoyed-up by the sense of his own grievance was Jamieson, that he was taken by surprise when Hector came back at him. Hector took himself by surprise as well. He would have thought he was far too tired to get involved in a slanging match. Especially with someone who, at the end of the day, was a mere hired hand, who he could fire at will. If he got Bea's say-so.

Jamieson had best accept what had so joltingly happened to him as yet another indication that he didn't fit in their world, and never would.

– You're not made of the small business staff. You may have been a forty-thousand a year man, and a right hard-arse for your boss, but you had a boss. You're the sort who needs a boss. You can't think for yourself, and you shouldn't try to mix it with us. With me. Because I'm an entrepreneur, someone who has always lived by his wits. Who's had to grab what's going in his personal life as well as in business.

The fact that he may have often been a spectacularly unsuccessful entrepreneur was neither here nor there. It was the acceptance of those qualities that counted.

– Unlike you, I've never been in business with a safety net. Never used one in my private affairs, neither. I said to life at an early age that I would not pilot a small car carefully down the slow lane, observing all the requirements of the road traffic acts, safely belted up. Nor will I ever. I will do a ton-ten in the fast lane, with six double scotches inside me, and damn your safety precautions.

He needed to live on the edge. Like Bea. Like Connie. Who he had just seen turn on her heel and walk out on him. With hardly a word.

– Me and my girl live headlong, and if you try to mix it with either of us, you'll get roughed-up. Got it? Keep your pointy nose out of my accounts, and forget doing anything to screw up her and the Greek. Chuck the job, go back to your missus, and see if they'll take you back where you were before. Even as a teaboy. There's more future for you in that than there's ever going to be here.

Because here was the real world, where you played tag with hatchets. Or didn't turn out in the playground at all.

Connie certainly felt that she was doing ton-ten in the fast lane, and with more than a couple of scotches inside her. Wasn't too sure why she was doing this. Didn't know how it would turn out. Was sure it was the most irresponsible of all the options to take when the Greek showed up again. But was enjoying the sensation of lifting her hands clear off the steering wheel as the car hurtled along, and seeing where it took her.

She used to do that in real life. When Arnie was being more of a fucked-up pig than usual. She'd take one of the boy racer motors out of the four-car garage, and rev it up and down the country lanes around their ranch-style eyesore of a house. And turning into the darkest lane, switch all the lights of the car off, and take her hands away from the wheel. It was terrifying, it was insane, but it was exhilarating. She couldn't say she felt better for it, just as she couldn't truthfully say she felt better for grabbing the Greek and running. But at the least it was feeling rotten in a different way.

And hadn't things been getting samey? And didn't she miss the easy sprawling days with the Greek, just a little bit? Very soon she would have to start chasing up the scandal she claimed she'd found lurking in the council minutes, and the local rag's columns. Once she did that she was committed to seeing the rebuilding through. And that meant she could sit down now and write up a five-year diary in advance. Because it would take her that long to get things buzzing how she wanted. And every day would be like the day before it.

There was another reason why she'd lit out on the spur of that sudden moment. No Englishman could wear white linen slacks. And Georgiou's pair, though creased by the flight and ride from the airport, brought back memories of happy days. And particularly nights. And more especially mornings. And long, slow happy afternoons, making love and being made love to like she never had since her time with Dev.

Which was why she wasn't too pleased to be called urgently to the hotel reception, just as she was about to slide into the bath on top of Georgiou. And even less pleased to find Bea there.

– You've walked out for good? On your fella and the House of Bea? She came straight to the point.

It was possible that the next morning Connie would have given a different answer to the one she did. That one night of lovemaking would have scratched that itch. But defiance, and a feeling that she'd look foolish undercutting her knockout exit, made her tilt that Connie chin. It was That Look again.

– For good. I can fill you in on what I found in the files. But you'll have to handle it yourself.

Bea brushed that aside. What she had to know was that Connie was finished with Jamieson. If Connie could tell him properly to his face it was over, she'd believe it. For Bea knew the heady attractions of the big bold gesture. And the remorse that often followed giving in to the glory of it.

Bea insisted, and Connie gave in. She knew the older woman was perfectly capable of making a scene in the hotel foyer if she didn't get her own way. She sent word up to Georgiou that he should bath and rest, and order up some food. Room service, of course. He was to have whatever he wanted, on the bill. Even take a stroll in the shopping galeria, if need be, to get himself a shirt of two. The next couple of days she'd see him all right for a new suit, more fitted to the English climate. And shoes. And underwear. Go shopping with him for all those private things he needed.

She left with Bea to face Jamieson. With That Look bolted on.

– Can you see me going back to Sonia? He asked it as if it was a matter of no particular moment. Overplaying the Mr. Cool as he faced her in the office. With Bea looking on. He'd objected to her being there, but Bea had after all fetched his woman back for him, hadn't she? That gave her some rights. – Can you see me, after living with you, going back to the storm porch, and the file? The file we kept on everybody I ever had to entertain for business? – Don't whinge, Connie told him. And that stung because he'd thought that was the last thing he was doing. He was just calmly setting out the facts of his position.

– Can you see me saying hello, Guess Who?—I'm back, and lets talk storm porches and kitchen units and built-in cupboards again?

What he saw himself doing was fighting for her.

– I told you the day I hijacked your car and driver I would be bad news for you. I live an untidy life, and you've just got caught up in that untidiness, even though you were warned.

Was it because he was too cosy and comfy? Too slippers by the fire, and cocoa for two? He had to know.

It was that, but it was more than that.

– He's only here because he thinks you're loaded. Connie took that on the chin. Was this meant to be news? Didn't he think she could work that one out for herself? Too right she never had so much as a postcard from the Greek from the day she'd left him. Too right he must have sat in the car rehearsing the plaintive look, and the way he'd slouch in the doorway as he delivered his—I have come to take you back gag. But it didn't make any difference. She felt her knees buckle when he walked back into her life. And she was keeping hold of him. However much it meant throwing over. That's how she'd always promised herself to live.

Bea chimed in. Now she was faced with it, she didn't want Connie to leave the firm, however much that would smooth things over between her and Nesta.

– You're not just taking him on, she pointed out. – You know the Kyprianou syndrome. You're taking on his brothers and his cousins, and the family friends. There won't be a cardboard suitcase left in Athens. They'll all be headed here. He's no intention of letting you take him back to Greece.

– But we're going back. I'm going to book two tickets first thing tomorrow.

And if as soon as they got back, Georgiou was all for getting on the plane again, that was all right by her. This was surrender on her part, didn't they realise? It wasn't making a cool and calculated decision on the odds. It was sheer lunacy. Lifting your hands off the wheel just when things were going well. Because she loved the guy.

Jamieson didn't threaten. The time for that was past. His shoulders slumped, and he let her go. Thanked Bea for going to the trouble of fetching her. And asked if he could take her back to the hotel.

That wouldn't be such a good idea, Connie parried. It would mean he knew where she and the Greek were holed up. And she didn't put it past him to nobble the fella.

He didn't threaten, and Connie didn't say goodbye. She left without a backward glance, but inside she was asking herself why the hell she was doing it. And then she remembered those white slacks, and that long lean sun-baked body waiting for her in the hotel. And she knew.

Except it was Nesta's body waiting for her in the foyer. There seemed to be a regular traffic jam of people queuing up here to talk to her. Threaten her. Cajole her. Or congratulate her.

– Congratulations, Nesta pecked her on the cheek. How nice to know that love stories sometimes had second instalments. That the lovebirds got reunited in the very last reel. Nesta had bumped into Hector, and Hector had told all. So Nesta had quickly checked the only worthwhile hotels in town, and come up with Connie's reservation.

– And now I'm going to my room, Connie grimly told her, moving to the lifts. – And when my fella gives me time to breathe, I'm going to ask myself questions about you and my dad.

Nesta said they had nothing to hide. What could she possibly be suspicious of? She didn't think that Hector had been sent a thousand miles at the snap of her fingers? Connie didn't know what to think now, and had other things on her plate. And in her bed. But Nesta kept her finger on the button, as Connie stood in the lift.

– He's not there. I've hijacked him.

Connie came out of the lift even faster than she'd gone into it.

– I'm thinking like a sister, Con. Nesta assured her. – As soon as Hector told me you'd put him in here, I wanted to take a look at him. But when I found Bea had whisked you away to the office, I didn't think it was wise to leave him here. You never know what sort of bother fellas can get themselves into in hotels.

– Where is he? Connie was prepared to smack her around to get the answer. This far was far enough. If it had finally come to them rolling on the fake marble floor and hitting each other with the foyer pot-plants, so be it.

Nesta had made sure he was safe. Away from temptations, like early-morning chambermaids, or linen girls. Georgiou with the white slacks and teeth to match, was well and truly boxed off, away from prying eyes. Like Jamieson's. But did he have to be locked away from Connie's hands as well?

– You know what you're like, Con. You've no sooner made your mind up one way, than something makes you charge off in the opposite direction. What you need is a night without either of them, so you can be sure in your own mind you're doing the right thing.

Wasn't that so sweet of Nesta that it made your teeth fillings shriek? She ought to have a saints' day named after her. Or a disease.

Nesta looked disappointed. This really was not the attitude she'd expected. Not after she'd taken so much trouble to protect Connie's interests.

And where was the Greek? Another hotel? Some crummy boarding house? Surely not locked up in Nesta's own flat with a gag in his mouth and his hands tied to his ankles with a pair of her tights?

Somewhere safe, was all Nesta would say, with that same maddening smile that was saying I'm meant to reassure, but I also know I'm driving you crazy as hell, sister. Nesta had him under lock and key, where neither accident nor design could locate him. And there the fella was staying until Nesta drove Connie round to collect him the next morning.

– I haven't even booked the flight, Connie protested.

But Nesta had.

Two first class seats, with her compliments. It would all be fiddled through the books of her shops, of course, but she was only too pleased to be able to speed things up for the lovebirds.

Wasn't that sisterly of her?

Hector had been looking forward all day to dropping by on Lisa. Just that, if it had to be just that. Time for a peck on the cheek, and a coffee. Before going to report to Bea. If there was any chance of anything else, he'd take it. But he would settle for the domestic comforts. It was that sort of relationship. The odd mix of characters, the old fox and the inexperienced girl was working out.

She brought him joy, and he was bringing her something over and above the little gifts. He knew that. Was sure he wasn't fooling himself. It had started out as a casual affair, but he'd been tripped up. This looked as if it could turn into the love job of his life. And though the prospect terrified him, it also brought him new life and vigour.

So it was all the ruder a shock when he opened the door, intending to surprise her, and found Georgiou sat in his vest, watching her, as she made coffee. For two. The other cup very definitely not for the guy who paid the rent.

Fourteen

Arnie was no master of timing. That was one of his charms. But even those who didn't particularly care for him would have winced as he confidently trotted up the wooden stairs to the office. Out of which Bea had just followed Connie for the second time. In which Jamieson was contemplating the ruin of his personal life and career.

Geometrics were going to be a big line. Arnie had had that feeling. The one that gripped him every so often. That said this was going to be it. He'd finally sniffed which way the market was headed. If you didn't get heavily into geometrics, you'd be left standing with a pile of stock as big as your overdraft.

Babs had tried to talk him out of it. She knew only too well the results of his previous hunches. Still remembered the canvas loons and the anoraks with the fun-fur collars that they'd only shifted when Kyprianou had forcibly stripped the stall. But the rule of the game is that the man who has his name above the stall calls the buying shots. Arnie had punted heavily on geometrics, and when they hadn't happened at least had the sense to clear the stall of them at give-away prices. Dish-rag prices. Even then he'd had to let some go for tats, to the rag-pickers.

It was the old routine—there was no point being able to shift stuff off the front of the barrow if you weren't also capable of buying it in at the right price, and in the right range, at the back. Hector's hot-pants plunge should have been a deadly warning, but Arnie just wouldn't learn. Couldn't learn, Babs sometimes thought. He'd go on plunging in on his hunches until he lost the lot.

Except her. She'd be with him, right the way through. And now that it looked as if Connie was on her way back to Greece, she was feeling better than she had done, since the black day of the ex's return. In her jubilant phone call breaking the news, Nesta had insisted they make the weekly saunas anyway. They were blood sisters now, after all.

Situation desperate, but not critical, was how Arnie read the trading position. Not yet aware that the floor had opened up at

Jamieson's feet. At the end of the day, when all else failed, he could wangle stuff out of the House of Bea at better-than-discount rates. That was one of the few advantages of his ever having been family. Hector had said any time, Arnie old son, any time.

– But I don't have a note here that says so, Jamieson picked through the orders and memo pads.

– Verbal agreement.

– I've instituted a new policy here with regard to paperwork, the less than welcoming Jamieson snapped. – We now keep some.

Something had gone wrong with the idea of the extended family in the West, Arnie lamented.

So somebody had been saying in the market traders' bar the other night. He'd got it from the telly. Something to do with the Industrial Revolution. The unit breaking up. The change from an agricultural life style, where every generation had its place in the scheme of things.

Arnie didn't follow it himself. But he got the general outlines. You take Kyprianou, and all his cousins. Typical peasant, despite the Roller. There was a network of obligations he could fall back on, just as he had a range of understood duties to perform. Back scratching. Barter. You wanted a new roof on the house, so your second cousin third removed did it in exchange for you shoe-ing his half-sister's uncle's mule. For which he was entitled to a free brain operation next time he was in Athens, off his niece's brother-in-law the brain surgeon.

And in the West? In the Midlands? He wanted a five minute rummage through the seconds box, and Jamieson was empowered to say no. Typical, just bloody typical.

– No wonder we're getting squeezed out of the business. He didn't want to sound a note of racial prejudice, just state the facts. The indigenous grafter didn't stand a chance, in the face of the extended family system the immigrants, of whatever shade, could call on.

– Take Kyprianou. You know him better than anyone. Importing cousins wholesale, by the container-load, employing them illegally, working them every hour God sends, and any bother out of them, it's a quick word with the immigration people and they're back on the silver bird.

Yes, Jamieson did know the Greek better than anyone, and that was a fair summary of his business methods. It was unfair that he should have such an advantage over the true blue grafters like Arnie but there it was. Now would Arnie clear off, and leave him alone? He didn't want to go into details now, but it had been one of those days.

– Funny, isn't it? Arnie, having lost out on the business deal, was prepared to wax philosophical. – We're still the Promised Land to those yellow and black and polka-dotted tribes, aren't we? No matter how rough it gets here, it's never going to be as rough as if they'd stayed at home. Makes you think. They'd fall over themselves to get a crack at even working for a shotgun merchant like Kyprianou. It does make you think.

Jamieson was sure it made you think. But he didn't want to think about it just now. He saw Arnie off the premises, and was shrugging his top coat on, when one of the girls showed a caller into the office. A black face, above a muscular body. For a moment he thought this was someone from the Job Centre, come to replace Leroy. Then he realised his visitor had to be pushing his early forties, and looked too sleek and well-dressed to be chasing a van driver's job. The guy had to be a sales rep. He'd not seen a black one before, but there was always a first time. It stood to reason, and was long overdue, he supposed. There were so many minority groups cutting themselves slices of the fashion cake, sometimes you felt out of place being white.

– We only see reps by appointment. Sorry. Leave your card.

The visitor ignored it.

– Looking for a Connie. Of Hector Bea and Madam Bea. Fashion Knitwear. Baby Bea, Infants and Childrens Wear. Busy Bea, Sports and Leisurewear.

This last was a new line that Bea was pushing, having been convinced by Nesta that the market sector was growing. She'd had copied most of her daughter's best selling lines, with a few changes in pattern and colourway here and there. The line wasn't breaking any sales records yet, but it was building.

– Just missed her. Jamieson pointedly indicated the door.

– And I'm headed home.

The caller wasn't to be got rid of so easily. Could Jamieson help? And did he mind saying exactly who he was, and what was his position in the firm?

Jamieson was too tired to throw him out, and answered the

question as he sorted papers into his briefcase. It was going to be a long and lonely night. He'd take work home with him to share the empty hours, and the bottle of malt.

– Office manager, accounts, general dogsbody. At the moment, who knows what tomorrow brings?

Just the man the caller needed to see, if Connie wasn't going ahead with the business. They could settle the account on the spot.

– You said you weren't a rep.

– I'm not. But I still get a half day's expenses, plus mileage for showing up. I'm not taking a financial penalty because this woman can't be bothered to hang around for me.

– Expenses for what?

The caller weighed up the accounts man. Although he was here in strict confidence, he could see he wasn't going to get his money unless he gave a little more.

– She wanted a planning committee matter looked into. Inquiries of a confidential nature. Indications to be followed up that something is wrong in the planning sub-committee.

He didn't say that he'd jumped at the chance to handle what looked like real police detective work, instead of just chasing bad debts, or process serving. Looked like it wasn't going to happen. Had been too good to be true, from the top.

Jamieson clicked. So that was how Connie intended to swing the planning consents. Step back and set a bloodhound on the trail of whatever she thought she'd found in the council minutes, or newspaper columns. He apologised, as he reached for the cash box. It was a shame that Mr. Jardner of Jardner Security and Investigations International had had a wasted trip across town.

International? He queried that, just out of interest.

– I did a case in Wales once, Jardner grinned, writing his itemised bill. Was there nothing he could help out with, now he was here? It was a forlorn hope, he knew, but you had to keep asking. Or was there a chance Connie would want to pursue the matter when she was back in circulation?

Not a chance, Jamieson told him. But if he wanted to be one hundred per cent sure, he'd have to find her and ask her.

– No problem. Finding people is my speciality.

Jamieson snapped the cash box shut. That was true. Private detectives were in the business of tracing people who didn't want to be located. Maybe, if the big man opposite had nothing in his private eye's diary for that afternoon, he could help him out with something? For the usual expenses, and the mileage.

The private eye had nothing in the book but ruled lines with not a thing on them.

What was the job?

Jamieson got back to the cottage late that night. But there was no 'welcome home' light in the hall, and no one to share supper and the bottle of scotch with. He lifted a glass to Connie, wherever she was that night, trying hard not to think what she was probably doing at that minute. He was more hopeful now than he had been since the door opened and Georgiou sashayed back into Connie's life. And his. Because the two ran braided together now. And he'd fight as dirty as he had to to get her back.

Connie nearly picked up the phone half a dozen times that night, in her solitary hotel room, to ask him to come and fetch her. And no sooner did she start reaching than a wave of longing for Georgiou came over her, and her hand was stayed. The hotel bed felt very big, and she rattled around in it like a pea in a pod. Such a waste.

Hector had just as bad a night. Even though Nesta had explained what Georgiou was doing holed up in Lisa's flat, he couldn't get the picture out of his mind. The Greek with his strong brown body, watching Lisa's backside, as she moved around the kitchen. Getting his range. Working out his best angle of approach. Of course the Greek would spend the night on the sofa, and Lisa would keep a chair against the bedroom door. But all the same. Disturbing. He was so brown and his teeth so white. And you never knew with women, did you? Of course the girl knew what side her bread was buttered on, and she had far too much respect for her protector to fool with a ship in the night. And yet. And yet.

Nesta, it went without saying, slept the sleep of the just. Woke refreshed, hummed all the way through her shower, after taking the still sleepy Dev twice, and even brought him breakfast in bed. As she buttered his cinammon toast she told him a story. He struggled through the blear to understand the point of it.

– Pat gets a weekly letter from his mother. At the end there's a PS. 'Dear son, the goat fell down the well, and had to be destroyed'. Now this had been Pat's favourite goat, and he was very upset. So he writes back and tells her that's no way to break bad news. She should have written first and said they hadn't seen the goat for a couple of days. In the next letter reminded him of the old well in the back yard. Then that his dad had a mind to look down that old well she'd mentioned in her last letter sometime. And finally, the letter would come saying the goat was down the well. That way it wouldn't have come as such a shock.

Dev started panicking. Had something happened to his brain in the night? Or had what Nesta had just done with him, as he lay half asleep, affected his nervous system.

– Pat gets a letter by the next post. There's a PS. 'Dear son, your granny went up on the roof this morning.'

Nesta got to the point. She was going to be out of the office all day, fixing and finalising a very tricky matter, which involved the family. She hoped she'd closed down all the angles, but you never knew. Dev was to keep his eyes and ears open, and be alert for any sign that granny was on the roof. Especially where Jamieson was concerned.

Dev was a trifle rebellious that morning. Itching for a row. He'd something planned for himself that day. Nothing important, just a couple of games of squash and a work out in the private gym she'd taken out membership in for him. He was getting a little lazy, with this pampered life.

– You're pretty damn sure I'm going to keep taking being treated like this, aren't you? He moved her hand away from where it had fallen. – You think the stud in my ear says you own me?

Her face hardened. Just like the little trollop to make a fuss and spoil the start of the day she'd been looking forward to for months. The day she was finally going to see the back of her step-sister. She knew he'd take it, and worse. He'd take anything and everything she chose to dish out to him. He might not have much of a deal going with her, but it was a better one than he deserved. And a better one than anyone else would hand to him.

– I could walk out. I could walk out on you like Connie's done on her bloke.

– Your walking-out days are over, Dev. In the game you're a clapped-out designer who'll never work again. On the game, there's only so much time your very specialised and uncommon talents can buy you.

He'd take it, until she was through with him. Then she'd have him through the flat and shop door so fast he might leave his ears behind. She was going out. He'd cancel all appointments, and look after business in her absence. And most of all, he'd wait and watch

c.—8

for any sign that granny was shinning up the drainpipe.

Jardner had no trouble finding the hotel where Jamieson was waiting in the coffee shop. He'd done five years in the CID, before the itch to work for himself had got too strong. There was also the fact that he was pending disciplinary charges, after a squeaky-close acquittal in a drugs trial. A little matter of some smokes disappearing between the bust and the forensic lab.

It wasn't so much that he'd developed an allergy to blue serge, or that the force had developed one to him. There were advantages to both sides in him being the colour he was. But he'd done his bit. Clocked up a reasonable pension, and decided to give private enterprise a try. Which he'd dabbled in, with the drugs business, but for some reason the force frowned unfashionably on the profit motive. So far as serving officers were concerned.

And there had to be scope outside. There were now ethnic banks and travel agents. Why not an ethnic private investigation service? God knew that coloured people got into matrimonial and business tangles as well as run-ins with the law. They needed summonses served, or got out from under. There was immigration work. And now and again, as he'd kept up his contacts with his old pals in the force, there were earners from that direction. His face could fit where theirs couldn't. In exchange he got the occasional drop, but mainly was able to pull criminal record and other confidential files, which gave him a lever over his rivals.

Despite that, business wasn't great. Was dismal, in fact. White clients baulked at the idea of putting their business into the hands of someone so conspicuous. And the blacks didn't seem to have the money to hire him in anything like the numbers needed to keep the rent paid regularly. Even in his poky office, above the Chinese restaurant in the city centre.

It was mainly matrimonial, and he often had to threaten to break legs to get paid, even when he came up with the goods. The prospect of getting his teeth into a severe case of council corruption was bracing. But that had fallen through, and though tracing the woman to the hotel was a disappointment, it was at least a paying disappointment.

Connie didn't flinch, when she saw Jamieson picking his way through his English breakfast. She came and sat opposite him. He looked up, and indicated the travel bag on the carpet.

– I put a few things together for you. In case you didn't intend making it out to the cottage.

– It's best I don't.

He understood, and apologised for the fact that he probably hadn't packed as neatly as she would have liked. Men seemed to be lacking something as a species where packing was concerned, didn't they? Maybe there was a packing hormone involved.

She wasn't amused. It was all very clever of him to have traced her, and he was making it very civilised. But did he have to order himself such a large breakfast? It looked like he'd got stuck into the self-service breakfast bar, as if he intended to stock up for a siege.

Well if he could be so insensitive, so could she. So she took the croissant back, and helped herself to the dishes on the hot plate. Double egg, double sausage, double bacon, hash browns and onion rings. It looked revolting, and smelt worse, but if he could calmly chomp his way through it, in one of the emotional troughs of his life—she could hack that too.

They sat chewing in silence. Connie torn between misery and surges of excitement at the size of what she was about to do. Jamieson putting the brave face on, but scared stiff that Arnie wasn't doing his bit. The first part of the idea that had struck him the day before had worked. Jardner had traced Connie to her hotel. Now it depended on Arnie coming up trumps.

Connie asked how he'd found her. He indicated Jardner, sat in the foyer, pretending to read a paper. Clocking everything, but looking as if he was spelling out the words of the tabloid.

– That's your private eye. He called after you left the second time. I took advantage.

Connie advised him to forget any idea of using Jardner Security and Investigations International on the planning scam. That was her baby, and nobody else should be allowed to hold it.

Jamieson nodded agreement, and asked her if she wanted more hash browns. Another tray of them had just been slid on to the hot plate.

She didn't want more hash browns. What she wanted was for him to grab her arms, shake her around a little and tell her she was getting on that plane over his dead body. And to ram the point home, to take her there and then on the breakfast bar tables. But even as she thought it, she knew that she'd throw him away if he laid so much as a finger on her. That demon of contradiction was working overtime.

Could he come to the airport with her? He wasn't thinking of doing anything operatic, or UnEnglish. No leaping through the plate glass of the observation deck, and running along after her plane, waving his arms. No last-minute whinging on the way there. No setting his trousers on fire or trying to impress her with comedy juggling routines.

She wouldn't agree to it. Too risky, again. Besides, someone was going to be accompanying her to the place, apart from Georgiou.

– Nesta? He guessed.

She nodded. So now he knew for sure that Hector had been put up to it by his step-daughter. That didn't make him feel any better about Hector. It only made him feel worse about Nesta. He'd done his best to stay clear of the revolving blades of this family row. But they'd pulled him in. Despite himself, he got to figure in their trench warfare. As a victim.

– Decided what you're going to do? She asked, as they prepared to say goodbye in the foyer. The car would be calling for her any minute now. Still he hadn't lost his control, or made a scene. – You're doing a good job at the House of Bea. But is it really you?

He nodded, meaning it. Despite what Hector had told him, he wanted to stick to it.

– You're hooked, my God. Connie shook her head. – The fashion business has got to you, too. I told you it was an addiction.

Put like that, he had to agree. He was beginning to understand why the Arnies and the Hectors stayed in the business, even when it was clear they were all-time, international-class losers. Because every minute of every day you were seeing the stuff of your business. People wearing clothes. Every stitch of which they had made a conscious or unconscious decision to buy. They disguised themselves, or they advertised themselves through what they wore. And the feeling that you were in business to out guess and second guess them, was compulsive.

He'd fallen in love with the pirate life, like he'd fallen in love with Connie, the pirate queen. And wasn't giving either of them up easily.

Nesta waited until she saw the final embrace between them through the smoked glass swing doors of the hotel. As great as was the temptation to walk in and break up the gum-sucking, she knew she was playing with dynamite. There was no telling, but that the slightest wrong move might unscramble everything. She was walking on eggs with the unpredictable Connie until the plane rotated off the ground.

Georgiou, in the car alongside her, didn't see the farewell between the two of them. Too busy looking at the pretty pale English girls on the pavement and street. Such a pity to be going back without having at least one of them in their natural habitat. There had been a score or so, since Connie left. But after a while they all turned into the same topless windsurfer or pedalo-pusher. And he was genuinely curious about what they were like back home, in this dismal, cold, wet country. Which did, however, have the advantage that there seemed to be lots of money around. And so many pale English girls.

He snapped his attention back to Connie as she appeared at the car door, bag in hand. And gave her a welcome that almost made up for the night they hadn't spent together. Connie pressed against him all the way to the airport, ignoring Nesta's triumphant checking look in the rear view mirror from time to time. Nesta thought she had won. But Connie had been playing for a different prize.

Losing was winning if losing meant getting your fella back and heading out of good old, dead old, damp old England.

Not even those lingering doubts remained. She was fireproof, even if, as she rightly suspected, Jamieson was racing to the airport for one last try.

Fifteen

The confessional urge hit Arnie at the most unexpected time. Like the lack of any sense of good timing, his sudden overwhelming desire to grab hold of you and tell you exactly what he'd try to do across you in business or personal life had its charms. It also got him from time to time into serious trouble. There ought to be treatment available. Or maybe you could insure against it?

He usually got the urge out of a blue sky. Like that morning, when he'd done exactly what Jamieson asked him to do. Pulled it off. Found Kyprianou opening up one of his discount warehouses fifty miles away, passed on the message, reported by phone to Jamieson, and driven back, before breakfast, to the stall.

Babs was used to him getting up in the early hours to get a delivery, or follow up a hunch about what was about to break all sales records that week. Saw the note on the toaster, and drove the van to the market herself. Dressed the stall, and cupped her hands on a cracked mug of tea waiting for the first customer. Or any customer.

By the time Arnie showed, she had sold three pairs of cords, a pair of the previous year's leg warmers, and exchanged a pair of Taiwanese jeans with a faulty zipper.

– I told the Ferrari salesmen maybe next month. Where have you been?

It was a fact that Arnie had told himself all the way back down the motorway that the last thing it would be wise for him to do, would be to level with his girl. Whatever Jamieson was up to was intended to stop Connie getting on the plane that day. And he knew that what Babs wanted second only to him completely giving up the booze, was for Connie to head back to the Med.

So, naturally, he told her what he'd done.

Why? For the simplest and most universal of reasons. Profit. Jamieson had put the proposition to him, promising him not only first refusal on the House of Bea seconds but discount prices on top-of-the-range numbers. It was plain that Jamieson was doing this off his own bat, without authorisation from Hector or Bea. But Jamieson was a power in the firm now. He'd cut himself a slice. And if he said he could fiddle the books to get Arnie good gear at reduced rate Arnie wanted as much as the van could hold.

He believed Jamieson, because Jamieson was desperate. The cleft stick that was attached to Arnie's thumb was that Jamieson was desperate because he wanted to keep Connie in the UK. And Babs was equally determined that she should leave.

If that had been all there was to it, he might have come down in favour of Babs's view of things. But there was a bonus in what Jamieson had suggested. Which was that this way offered a chance for him to ingratiate himself with Kyprianou. Finally smooth over any difficulties the bouncing cheques had caused. There was no guarantee that Kyprianou would jump at the chance. But they were in with a shout, a very definite shout.

He told her what he'd done.

Babs had no time to work him over for it just then. That could wait, until she'd warned Nesta.

Only Nesta wasn't in. Dev was in. The blonde assistant with the teeth brace hadn't showed that morning, so he was consoling himself by looking through Nesta's private papers. You never knew. If things went even sourer between them, it would be nice to know that she had a few bodies buried somewhere in her files. But she was too canny for that. He'd drawn a blank.

Dev was therefore in an even worse mood than he'd been when Nesta had walked out, leaving him in charge. He looked at Bea from the other side of the desk, over the top of his crocodiles. Which he'd made Nesta buy for him, so that every time he looked at them, he'd be reminded of her.

Babs's edginess made him think straight away that granny might be up on the roof.

– Can I help?

Babs doubted it. He hardly inspired confidence, even though it was the boss's chair he was lounging in. But it looked as if she'd no option.

– There he is. I said he'd try to cut you off at the pass. Nesta had seen Jamieson first, waiting by the boarding gate.

Half of Connie hoped that he was still going to play the civilised gent, and the other half that he was finally going to crack. The latter looked doomed to disappointment, as Jamieson walked amiably over to them. Could he carry Connie's case to the gate, when the call came? He promised to behave himself. Wouldn't run off with it, or anything childish like that. And was this Georgiou? Could he shake hands? Show there was nothing personal between the two men? And then buy them all a drink?

Nesta was nervous, but there was no good reason after check-in not to let him stand a round. But she was sticking to St. Clements, and with bitter lemon at that. No chances. Not within a half hour of success.

Conversation was stilted. Could hardly be anything else in all the circumstances. It just wasn't possible that they'd be chatting away like old pals beside the noisy party group who took up the rest of the bar, gathered to see a honeymoon couple off. Not even though this was a sort of honeymoon as well, wasn't it? A return engagement of a honeymoon. Connie and her man flying off to a new life in the sun.

Nesta knew that Georgiou wouldn't be content to stay in the village, reunited with his bluebird of happiness. Not even now it had flown up his nose. She saw that he couldn't even keep his eyes off the girls in the bar at this most solemn of moments. He'd be pestering Connie to bring him back, even before the undercarriage had locked the other side. But even if he kept her away for a matter of weeks, that was enough time to work on Bea.

She watched Jamieson carefully, as she sipped her soft drink. And no less warily eyed Connie and the Greek. Increasingly confident with each boarding announcement bringing the Olympic Airways flight nearer that she was going to pull it off.

Jamieson couldn't get up to much sitting on the bar stool before her very eyes. And hadn't she left the airport phone number with Dev, with instructions to bell her if it looked like Jamieson had sent granny up on the roof elsewhere?

– I need her now. I need to speak to her now. Babs was insistent. That insistence flushed her cheeks, and Dev told her how much more attractive that made her. – If such a thing were possible.

– Cut the shit. The girl showed for a moment that she'd once had to handle tougher opposition than Dev. The little mystery picked up off the lay-by had known a world where a girl had to take care of herself.

Dev was sure Nesta had left a phone number. Properly reproved for bringing a wrong note into the unexpected meeting, he started to search for it. Couldn't find it anywhere. He was positive that Nesta had left at least one number to be belled urgently if anyone turned up like this. Especially anyone from the family. But he couldn't find the scrap of paper, even though he turned the desk upside down.

Not surprising, as he'd palmed it into his slacks pocket as soon as the girl asked.

Maybe if Babs filled him in on what was so urgent, that might trigger something?

She hesitated.

– Jamieson sent Arnie to make a deal with Kyprianou concerning the other Greek.

It was important that Nesta be alerted something was up. Didn't he see that?

Dev saw that. And screwed the scrap of paper into an even tighter little ball. This meant a lot to Babs. That was plain. Maybe he could get that number. But there was a price for everything. She ought to know that, having worked on the barrows with Arnie. What was she willing to offer to get the information?

He wasn't talking cash.

She caught his glance at the spiral staircase that led to the private quarters.

Jamieson wasn't going to make any last-ditch attempt to haul her off by force, Connie concluded. Not sure whether that disappointed her or not. He was going to do the British thing, the prickish thing. Stand by and let her be whisked from under his nose by someone ten years younger, and obviously a heart-breaker. Couldn't he see she was aware she was doing the wrong thing? That she regretted that sudden decision to walk out, as soon as she made it?

But again, wearily, she knew as she finished her flat white wine, that the one thing guaranteed to make her get on the plane was any attempt to keep her off it. Or even an attempt to make her see reason. He was in the wrong world. He wouldn't be able to handle this. Because it meant fighting dirty, fighting clever, and he didn't seem capable of either. Hector was right about him. He needed a boss to kick him around. Not a self-starter. Not someone who should be signed up on a pirate ship at all.

When both lights started flashing she would walk between the two men in her life to the gate. Nesta behind her, no doubt, making sure. And that would be that. She'd be jumping out of the window with a fella yet again.

And even if she was getting too old for this sort of thing, she'd do it. Because Jamieson had run out of his drink, and small talk. And Georgiou was about to come out of the gents' toilet.

Come to think of it, he'd been in that toilet quite some time. Maybe he was playing with the flush and the taps. As fascinated and impressed by British plumbing as she had been fascinated and appalled by the Greek version when she first went to live there.

Nesta was stabbed by the same thought at the same time.

Their eyes locked, and then, as one, went to Jamieson. He was staring ahead at the bar shelf mirror. In which, a good five minutes ago, he had watched Georgiou leave the gents with two of Kyprianou's cousins on each side. Talking as persuasively to him as they had obviously talked to him in the gents. Outlining the advantages of working for such a wheel as Kyprianou.

Something in his expression, though he tried to keep it blank, must have been a giveaway. Suddenly he was alone at the bar, and Nesta and Connie were shouldering their way through the noisy honeymoon crowd.

He sat on, feeling no elation. How could he feel that? It had been a dirty trick and the only person to do well out of the deal he'd fixed would be Georgiou himself, given the keys to the promised land. By Kyprianou, who had to have come off next best, because he'd been presented free of charge with someone who would graft until his buns broke. Not because he was a natural born grafter. But because if ever he showed signs of slowing down, Kyprianou would shop him to the immigration police.

Connie came back without Nesta.

Nesta had gone straight to her car when she realised she'd missed him. She had no idea as yet exactly what Jamieson had fixed, but she knew there was no point hanging round. Even though it did mean that Jamieson and Connie were stranded at the airport without a car.

Connie perched on the bar stool and silently took the large brandy he'd ordered for her. Wryly, she noted it was a Metaxa.

– Sorry, was all Jamieson had to say. But you had to say sorry now and again, if you were living out a love story.

They sat until the plane she should have been on had lifted over their heads. And then until the honeymooners party had congaed to the Benidorm plane. And then until the barman coughed, and they realised the lights were off, and the bar stools piled around them.

And spent the night in the nearest hotel to the airport.

And she only cried a little bit. And slapped him hard the once.

Sixteen

A chestnut in the knitwear business goes something like this. There's a manufacturer whose quality control is on the floor so much that one shirt interlocks several hundred dozen of blue sleeves onto red fronts and backs by mistake. Or any other colour the teller hits upon. The point being that nobody notices, even when the goods are packed and sent off to the customer. When the owner of the factory finds out he's on the point of firing everybody in sight. Just then the customer turns up. The owner is about to apologise by offering to rip his own throat out, if that'll help. But the customer says—I want ten thousand dozen of those sweaters with the contrast sleeves. I've never seen a line shift so fast. Congratulations.

Most people have at one time claimed to know the person that story is told about. Quite a few even claim to be that person. Hector could have put in a bid to have figured, except that in his case the customer would probably have accepted his suggestion that he rip his throat out. It had to be no ordinary unlucky star that Hector had been born under, so far as business was concerned. The ten thousand mouldering hot pants in that Leicester warehouse said that.

Quality control was something they would have to get a hold of, if they were going into High St. lines seriously. Hector was deputed to get a grip well before Connie succeeded in swinging those planning consents. He grumbled about it, but Bea swung the hammer, and he gave in.

– But I'm not doing it the straightforward way, he warned, still smarting at the way he'd been spoken to in the meeting that discussed the matter. – You don't get results with the girls by bullying and chivvying.

What you needed was a programme. The business magazines he subscribed to all said that. You have to have an innovative in-house programme. Something designed to alter and upgrade employees' perception of the workplace. Or something like that. The name of the game was corporate identity. And having been directed to crack the problem, he would take it away and sweat on it.

Connie was sweating on something, too. Physically as she fought to keep the momentum of production going in the fire-damaged factory, invoking the Dunkirk spirit in the girls. Mentally as Jardner picked up the threads of the investigation she had set under way. The investigator hadn't taken much coaxing before saying yes to the job. Not the way Connie had crossed her legs all the way up to her thighs, in the raw silk number she had worn to his poky office above the Chinese restaurant.

A waiting game for her.

You would have thought that Dev would have been sweating more than anyone. Especially once he knew for sure that Babs was like that with Nesta, and sooner or later his part in the debacle over the Greek would come to light. But it wasn't as if he'd put the bolt in Nesta's neck just because, in a sudden moment, he wanted to put something else into Babs. No. That little betrayal of the woman who'd picked him up when he had nothing had been a long time coming. Now he was free, and enjoying that freedom. And before he even had time to regret what he'd done, and calculate the cost of that freedom, came the offer of a job. From a most unexpected source.

Arnie sweated. He'd put his neck on the block with Babs over the Kyprianou affair, and was due to collect. But all he got off Jamieson was a forearm smash. Delivered with all the icy control of the organisation man. But the effect the same as if he'd struck out wildly in a bar-room rough-house.

– You call that quality gear? Arnie protested, when Jamieson indicated what he could load in his van.

– These are tats. They're not even good enough to be seconds.

– Take them or leave them, Jamieson faced him head on. – And it's cash down.

– You said deferred terms. You said the usual discount, but six months to pay, if I set up Georgiou for you.

– You did, and I'm grateful. But what you got out of it was making your peace with Kyprianou.

Which was true, and he was grateful, but he couldn't dress the barrow with thanks, could he? What was the reason for the switch, he wanted to know? Why the sudden blast from the freezer set at quick-chill?

– It's just not good business to do business with someone like you, Arnie.

– That's supposed to be an explanation? Arnie really could not believe this. After the deal with the man, he'd confidently expected to get along even better with him. Which, for Arnie, read be able to take advantage. Now he was walking into a brick wall.

– You were talking about family, Jamieson reminded him. – You made me realise I'd not been thinking family. Not thinking the House of Bea. Listen. I've fought too hard, risked too much trying to keep her. I can't afford to get my loyalties mixed up. So I don't do favours any more for anyone outside family and the firm. You don't get favours from now on, Arnie. You don't get air to breathe from now on, so far as I'm concerned.

So Arnie was sweating. For his own back, for a way to keep up the rent on that barrow. But mainly to one day put that knife in Jamieson's shoulders, just as how he had so neatly planted him.

Bea floated above it all. Not a trace of sweat on her upper lip. Or damp patch under the arm of the black jersey. Things had never looked so good for a long time. The insurance cheque was in, Connie was working on the planning side, Hector had promised to get his finger out on quality control. There seemed, so far as she knew, only to be sweetness and light in family affairs.

There was even the bonus that Nesta had packed it in with her coloured boyfriend. Not that Bea, god forbid, had a colour thing. Not in this business, where appetites seemed to be greater than in, say, the hardware business. But people talked. And Nesta had flaunted her good fortune. That diamond stud in his ear, say. Those tight white slacks that he could hardly bend in.

But he'd been a looker. No doubt about that. She could well understand Nesta falling. Take thirty years off her age, and say she hadn't yet met the love of her life, Hector, and she could almost see herself falling for him. Just as well he'd gone to ground, and wasn't even caddying for her daughter on their weekly round any more.

And out of the blue, it suddenly looked as if the thing she almost wanted more than anything else was due to come about. Nesta and Connie were about to make their peace.

Nesta made the move. When she turned up at the office that

afternoon, Connie was wary. Especially because she looked so bad. Nesta had been reaching for the make-up box even before she was out of her maternity cot. Now it looked as if she hadn't even washed her hair for days. She normally dressed to make every shot count, but today looked as if she'd walked into her wardrobe at one end, and came out the other, wearing whatever had fallen off the racks on to her.

– Another declaration of war? Connie had asked, after clearing the office, and hanging the Bugger Off sign on the door.

Nesta took her time replying. Another departure for her shoot-from-the-hip step-sister.

– Am I slowing down? she asked, and she wasn't particularly asking Connie. – Or is it that running your own show gets that much tougher every year, month, week and day? You look around you. Every new tower block seems to be VAT or Inland Revenue, or local government. Or somebody working out ways to load even more on your grafting back. I've enough to cope with, without carrying on a war with you and your fella. I've got a business that needs more looking after than a sick kid, and I'm spending my time and brain juice working out ways to do you two down. Or worrying what you might be up to, out in the woods, to do me down.

She offered a deal. If Connie accepted she was never going to get any of the shops back, Nesta would leave her and Jamieson alone. Accept she was back in good old, wet old, boring old England for good.

– Sisters again? Connie asked, and got a nod. She'd heard that Dev had done a bunk. Could Nesta's new spirit of reasonableness be down to that?

– I miss him. Nesta said simply. – He's done me in, but I miss the little rat.

Which was the first human note sounded between the two of them for so long as they could remember.

– I don't want this war either, Connie didn't linger on Dev. Didn't she have her scars from the little rat as well? – But what are the chances of peace breaking out? How can I be sure you're sincere?

Nesta wrong footed her. As completely as Connie had fazed her, when she first called on her after getting back. That time Nesta had fired off all her rockets, exploded all her landmines, and they'd just clanged off her sides.

– It was you turned me on to the business in the first place, Nesta said, not even looking at her. As if hearing what she was saying for the first time – That's true. Even before you brought me in as a Number Two.

She paused, then started again, as if getting more and more interested in something she had barely considered before.

– I was an awkward kid. Buck teeth, bad skin, specs like bottle ends. You know every good-looking girl totes her plain friend around with her? The plain girls used to toss up for me, whenever they drew a date. I was no looker, kid. I was the definition of dog. I scored once. Nearly. There was a fella called Charley Middleton. I'll never forget the bastard's name.

Nor would Connie her trainee dentist. It was uncomfortable, and almost dangerously touching to listen to this honesty. It strummed a chord with her, too.

– Charley Middleton was no looker either. And did he have a skin condition that made him look as if his dad used his face to chop sticks on. But, as I had a clock stuck on me that made me look as if I played back-stop for the darts team, who was complaining? I was even prepared to overlook his peculiar itch.

He'd stood her up. She was kicked into touch on her first real date. Stood on the pavement outside the Gaumont so long she was afraid they'd have to drill her five inch heels out.

– When you arrived in my life, with the way you dressed, and the way you talked about clothes, I saw the light. I knew I'd nothing else going for me, except what I wore. I saw this ugly duckling was going to have to sprout brilliant feathers, if it was going to dazzle the world.

There was silence between them, when she finished. Then Connie cleared her throat.

– Well who says God doesn't have a sense of humour? She fixes it that it's me who gets you hooked on fashion, and it ends up with you pinching all my shops off me.

Connie had been touched, but sure as hell she wasn't going to show it. She wanted some details of the future Nesta foresaw for them. Would it be all girls together? Sitting up until all hours, giggling about fellas, and saying would you, if he really pushed you to say yes? That sort of smothering sisterdom?

Which wasn't what Nesta had in mind. All she intended was that they ignore each other. That would seem to be the perfect relationship between them. Icy silence. But with no fear that the other was out there, prowling and plotting.

The idea being, Connie wanted to make sure she had this all locked up, that bygones would be bygones, and their personal affairs not allowed to get in the way of their business?

That sort of thing, Nesta agreed.

– Not getting lines crossed? Not looking at the other's every move and being suspicious about it? Thinking it's a way to do a sister down?

Exactly that sort of thing.

In that case, Connie would shake on the deal. And spit on her palm like a gypsy, to clinch it. And as a first test, Nesta ought to meet her new sales rep. And she stuck her head round the corner and whistled up Dev.

– You can't have agreed to it. I don't believe you agreed to it, Hector confronted Bea, once he'd got the news of the new appointment.

Bea lifted one black, angular shoulder.

– He knows the business. He was a designer, taught at fashion school. Then did a spell in retail with Nesta.

Bea wasn't revealing, even to Hector, her own doubts on taking Dev on. Connie had presented her with the fait accompli. By which time Nesta had stormed out of the building, nearly knocking her own mother flat on the way. But he was a charmer. And it was nice to have something in crutch-hugging slacks around the place. The fellas all had skirt to look at. Why shouldn't the girls catch a little trouser now and then?

– He's a danger. Hector asserted flatly. He should know. – A moral danger.

Bea wryly inquired since when had part of quality control been to superintend the morals of their staff, but he shrugged it off.

– We've all heard the stories about what he got up to when he was on the road for Nesta. The trouble she had with him. Keeping his hands off the Manageresses and the buyers. Slipping lengths to little slips of a thing of shop girls. And here you are, giving him a car, and an expense account, plus carte blanche to roger his way through the retail knitwear business in the country.

It was like setting loose a sexual highwayman, operating in the firm's name, and he wanted no part of it. Bea stopped him leaving and asked him to think about what he'd just said. Nesta had had no professional use for his bedroom talents. But surely what the House of Bea needed most from now on was a first-lead sales who could batter his way into bedrooms, if not boardrooms?

– You mean we hire him for exactly the reasons that Nesta fired him?

Bea nodded, watching the penny drop. Wasn't that very Connie? And how could she have said no?

Jamieson also saw at once how very Connie it was. The professional side of him agreed wholeheartedly with the new signing. The personal side flashed red. Connie and Dev was the return of a theme. Dev was the guy who had so nearly done for her eight years ago. And he still wasn't sure of all the details of their relationship while she was suckering the design school drawings out of him.

But he was stuck with it.

And sweating.

He'd have sweated even more if he'd known that Arnie was serious about getting even. This was a grudge Arnie couldn't wash away in a thousand boozy nights. Or forget in playing his expert games with Babs. What hurt as much as the rejection, was that it came from someone who Arnie thought he had all worked out. His vanity was hurt, as much as his pocket.

Looking for allies, the natural was Nesta. As always, his timing could have been better, because he hit her while she was still smarting at Babs having failed to get warning through. As well as at the sight of Dev with his feet tucked happily under a desk in the House of Bea.

His shoulders were down, as he stood in front of Nesta. The fight was gone. For the first time he was beginning to doubt that God put him on the earth to shift fashion. This was a large admission for Arnie. Even in the blackest days, he'd been able to console himself with the thought that he had a gift. That one day he'd make that golden deal.

But now—

– Shifting schmutter's gone off me, or I've gone off it. Or something. I don't get the kick anymore. And I owe people right and left. And is it what I want to do for the rest of my life—standing out in the rain measuring inside legs?

He had a prospect. A very definite prospect of making money, that was nothing to do with fashion. That would free him from the House of Bea, and mean that if Nesta wanted ever to use him to sort out Connie and her fella, he'd not have any business complications.

– It's a donut-making machine. You must have seen them. You put the gunge in one end, and the donut comes out the other. You put it in a van and follow the markets, fetes and carnivals. It sells itself.

Nesta had never seen him as a caterer, she had to admit. Having failed to dominate the retail knitwear business, Arnie had now been called to the food trade, had he? If he wanted cash to set himself up, why didn't he go to Hector? They'd always been pals. Put a few bodies under ground, without their respective women knowing.

– Hector never takes my calls any more.

Nesta could guess why. Even a little scrubber like Lisa came pricey. Running two households seemed, by some mathematical freak, to triple the living expenses at the very least.

– Babs helped you. He played his trump card. – She came here to warn you what Connie's fella was up to with Kyprianou.

– She helped me? Nesta's eyebrow lifted a fraction. Always a dangerous sign. The stiller she went, the deadlier she was. – Is this a new usage of the word help?

– She tried to help you. Tried to get that message to you.

– And ended up being shafted by Dev.

He coloured. That wasn't true. The proof that she hadn't was that Dev hadn't given her the number. But didn't he know what a rat the little rat was? Wasn't he perfectly capable of taking her and not paying up?

Whichever way it was, whatever had occurred between them, Arnie could never set his mind at rest about it. And she certainly had had no favours done her.

How could Arnie help her in her war with Connie, which was now to the death? You didn't sign up losers, did you?

Arnie could have backed the van through her plate glass display window. Could have dropped his petrol can into the bins at the back of her shop, and torched it. Could have done a dozen things that would put the same sort of stripe in Nesta, as she had so much enjoyed putting in him.

But he didn't. His shoulders were down, and he was so lost he didn't know what business he should be in anymore. He went back to Babs waiting in the van, and said he'd take up her offer.

If she could raise the money they needed to get out of the knitwear, and all its business and personal complications, he wasn't going to ask for details. If she told him she could do the impossible, and be back in a couple of days with the cash, go ahead. There was nowhere else to turn to even though the pain he got every time she caught a south-bound lorry from that lay-by would be worse than ever. Because how does a girl who looked like Babs get that sort of money in two straight days?

– I've a bank account. It's something I've put away, against the day.

Against the day when, after all his turnings and twistings, Arnie had to face the fact he was bust. And touch up his girl for the very petrol to put in his van.

But how did she get the stash to put in her account in the first place? That was the question he didn't want to ask. And she wasn't volunteering anything.

He drove her to the lay-by, and watched her through the headlight murk and lorry spray, as she thumbed. Just the once. And stood back to take her pick from the vehicles involved in the pile up.

Through all this Jardner worked stolidly. Chasing up the files Connie chased, fingering the minutes she'd rubbed her eyeballs raw on. And then doing some legwork. Using muscles he thought they'd taken off him when he turned in his warrant and his little black notebook. Getting into the rhythm and the swing of things again. Turning up the collar and beating the pavement with the feet.

And enjoyed it. Even the bits where you hung around in the outside office, waiting for someone to say they weren't prepared to see you. Even the bits where you leant against a lamp post, scraping dogmuck off the size fifteens, as you waited for someone to show. Who you had known for the past wet half-hour had sneaked out the back way, as soon as his secretary said you'd called again.

He enjoyed it because it wasn't like the million matrimonials which had filled his time since leaving the force. Because it was more like policework, with all its routines, disappointments, sudden flashes of insight, and then the painful realisations that your two and two didn't add up to four after all.

Like police work, it ended every night with a few well-deserved beers in the bar, or feet-up on the office desk. Not rapping with your pals, true, because this was loners' work now. But reviewing the day's legwork, and musing out a plan for the next.

Jardner liked a little smoke with his little drink.

Nothing over the top. He didn't want to see the filing cabinets revolve, or feel he was talking to the Buddha. He liked a quiet evening roll-up.

The night the roof fell in he'd been quietly rolling one, while smoking the previous, when the police arrived. In the person of the meanest-faced DS from his old nick, and a couple of sour-looking DC's. Who, by the way they kicked his feet off the desktop and started knocking the furniture over, appeared not to be calling round to talk about old times.

Seventeen

Connie stood bail. Personally, not as representative of the House of Bea, even though that was strictly speaking who Jardner had been working for at the time he was turned over.

On the way from the police station, after Connie and Jamieson had sorted out the formalities for him, he surprised them by asking if they believed in reincarnation.

– Reincarnation. The eternal circle, birth and rebirth, and all that Eastern crap? That the wheel revolves, and we're paying off in this existence, what wrongs we did in a previous?

If there was anything in that at all, he reckoned he must really have done something brutal last time in to bat. To have drawn Connie in his life this time round.

– I knew you were going to be trouble, when I saw how you sat in that raw silk dress you nearly weren't wearing.

– And there I sat, admiring those broad black shoulders in that tight leather jacket, thinking I was hiring a pro, Connie came back. – And all the time I'd walked into a dope fiend's den.

Jardner took it on the chin.

– I like a little smoke. Who says I can't have a little smoke in the privacy of my own office?

– The Lord Chief Justice? For a start?

– You know what I mean, he insisted. – What's happening to this country? They even took away my window box.

Which probably happened to be stuffed so full of marijuana that it would put the Columbian mafia out of business, hazarded Connie. Grim, but with the suspicion that she was amused. That amusement, if it was there, went when he told her about the videos. As a favour to a good friend whose name and address he didn't know, he'd stored a couple of videos. A couple? Well, twenty-five, all in their original boxes. With the labels snipped off.

– I'm the sort of guy, he tried to clarify his temporary possession of the items – someone comes to me and says, you being in the security business, where better to store certain high value items—

– And a fence, Connie was scandalised. – I've hired a junkie and a fence.

But that hadn't been the end of it. For after the office had been turned over, they gave their attention to his car, parked outside. Minus tax and MOT, but plus bald tyres and defective brakes. That set of charges should have been a technicality, he'd tried to joke with them – because he was disqualified from driving, anyway.

They hadn't laughed. But had checked, on getting to the station. True enough, he was disqualified. The ploy hadn't worked any better than had the joke.

The office had certainly been paid a visit by beefy men with toe-caps to their shoes. That was plain. And there was no way that Jardner was going to pick up the bill. Because he had only been busted because of what he was doing for Connie.

Jamieson argued, but then realised that Connie was saying nothing.

– It's possible, she shrugged. – You have been chasing up important people.

Jardner grinned. A grin that cost him something. A grin that said he was well ahead of the game she'd been playing, at last. And despite himself admired how she'd set him up.

– You meant for me to get a visit like that. You only hired me because you wanted to stir things up.

– Perish the thought, Connie tried to dismiss it. Not the strongest of denials.

– You hired a black face, knowing I'd be about as discreet as a flashing disco light, asking questions about the council.

Connie composed a face of injured innocence, and Jamieson realised he'd only make a fool of himself by arguing further. With that familiar sinking feeling he realised Connie's move had been a knight's one. Not for her the straightforward rush at a problem. The side-step, and then the strike, was getting to be more and more the style.

It was true. Jardner had sussed her, but too late to avoid being seated under the fifteen-ton weight when it fell on his head. She had nothing at all to go on, on those four names she'd taken from the files. Only her intuition that as they appeared so regularly in the council minutes, and in the town's public affairs, one of them had to be up to something. For why else lose all your leisure time to public affairs? Not to mention the risks of sacrificing your marriage, and probably worse, your digestion?

Jardner had rushed about the corridors of power and influence like a puppy-dog on speed, drawing even more attention to himself than a white investigator would have done. And someone had bitten. Behind one of those locked doors, at one of those blank windows, someone had noted. And done something about it.

No way could it be coincidence, she insisted to Jamieson on the ride back to the cottage, after Jardner had itemised the likely out-of-pocket expenses the bust would cost him. True, the guy who'd twisted someone's tail had got bitten. But also true, he'd been paid. With a clear conscience she could push everything else off the desk, and wait for the follow-up.

The moment of elation suddenly punctured. Her shoulders went as low as Arnie's were, that day. Jamieson spotted it. Worried about it.

– It suddenly hit me. It's always going to be like this. Bluff and lies, and little wars. People hurt, and some of them nice people. Always knowing you should hate yourself for what you have to do just to stay alive.

– Look at me, he commanded her. – Those are the values. The ones you taught me. We're stuck with them, like we're stuck with each other.

She nodded. Those were the values. And Hector's daughter, and Bea's step-daughter, and the pillar of the House of Bea believed in them more than anyone.

The shoulders went up, and she got ready for the call. Whenever it was due.

It was sooner than she expected. A couple of days spent checking up on the names Jardner had most recently called on. Then an invitation to drop by on the Employer's Federation offices, for a chat. Nothing formal. But could she come in person? And because this was a small town, like the knitwear was a small industry – without telling anyone what appointment she was keeping?

The bosses' trade union was something Hector and Bea never had much time for. Their natural antipathy to any sort of trade combination kept them at arm's length. Pure untrammelled competition was the God they worshipped. Connie had been meaning to mend fences but things had piled up. Now she was walking to the shabby door of the resurrected Edwardian villa, as guest. Maybe threat, as well. Or perhaps target. She wouldn't know until she got through that door, down the dank corridor, and into the room where Borridge sat.

Borridge was a legend in the town and the business. He was only the secretary to the Federation, and not a very well paid one at that. But over the years he had come to know every secret, personal or commercial. That was one of the things which had made Hector and Bea edgy about getting too closely involved with the organisation. Their second God was commercial confidence. Not for them the quiet word in Borridge's ear when bad news came their way about someone else in the knitwear. But equally, not for them the returning phone call when something that might be to their advantage came up. They didn't put their elbow on the mantelpiece in Borridge's ramshackle office enough to make their mark. And consequently lost out on the many little packets of assistance which the Federation in general, and Borridge in particular, were able to dole out.

Not to say that Borridge was anything other than a disappointed man. At the end of the day he was the association's hired hand, who could be dismissed at any time, if he stopped being of value to the members. If it hadn't been for the accident which had blinded him in the fifties, he too might have had the factory he only needed to walk in on two days a week, the hunting commitment, the big house in the heartland of this richest of shires, and the light plane.

As it was, he sat every day in the same swivel chair, listening to the feet on the gravel outside, or to the complaining phone. Always polite in response, always with time for a word or two. Always ready with a suggestion for a fix, or a little murder. Knowing he wasn't paid half what he was worth. Knowing that at the end of it, there wouldn't even be a pension that would enable him to pay for his housekeeper.

Borridge was looking for an opening. A way to secure his own future, after he had worked so hard, and so silently, to secure that of others. Every time he heard a new voice he wondered if this was the opportunity he'd been waiting for. Connie's straightforward, not to say knee-in-the-crutch approach struck, from the outset, a note he was interested in.

– I had someone do a job. Name of Jardner. I gave him a list of names. He thought he'd check here, as most things in this town have something to do with the knitwear, at some point.

She paused, watching him start the pipe routine, that was as much a giveaway with fellas, as the handbag routine was with women.

– The fella said you listened to him, sucking on that pipe like it was some fat blonde's titty. You said you couldn't help.

But two days later had come the raid on Jardner's office. Followed by the suggestion that she drop by. To be told, no doubt, to call off her dogs. Or else the House of Bea would run into more trouble with the planning people, and anyone else the important men who ran the town could throw at them.

His play. She'd thrown her bricks at his windows, and it was up to him to respond. He decided she'd best understand if he threw a brick straight back.

– You didn't find anything in those newspaper files. You don't have anything on anybody.

Was this meant to be news? She admitted it. Without qualification or stalling. She knew better than to snow someone like the blind man sat opposite her. The whole point was that someone had his tail twisted. Someone had bitten. It didn't matter if she never came within a mile of finding out why. Was she crusading against corruption in local government? Was she hell. She was hoping to get cut into it.

Borridge discounted the force of her attack. The method was one he knew well, and could deal with better. His disability meant that he could sit through something like this, missing out all the body language and concentrate not on the words, but the way they were said. He ran the tape through his fingers, and listened to those telltale pauses which gave the game away. The inconsistencies which added up to bullshit in content, even though the presentation was intimidating.

He had to admit he couldn't accuse Connie of faking. This wasn't an act. The House of Bea was being run by someone with razor tips to her high-heels. He knew the job he'd been given of scaring her off was going to be more difficult even than he'd had intimation of, when he heard her determined feet on the path outside.

Well, no one could say he hadn't given warning. He had argued, politely but firmly, that the problem be allowed to drift away like smoke. That no action be taken against the investigator, not even at third or fourth hand. No word to be passed down the line, no mutter to run from ear to ear wherever the powerful in the town met. The golf and country club, the committee rooms, the robing chambers, the factory forecourts, the freemason's lodges and the well-stocked bars in large houses behind ten foot privet.

And when his advice had been ignored, he had insisted—insisted this time, that no further action be taken, even after Connie had started asking questions again. Without any clue to what she was after, or who had been wincing because of that twisted tail. And he had been ordered, ordered this time, to get her in and lean on her.

This wasn't a lady to be leant on. He knew that already. But even though a reference back was already forming in his mind, he had to try. If only for form's sake.

– I hear you've done great things for the House of Bea since you've come back. The change of tack was sudden as was the new tone in the voice. Reflective, musing. Concealing the claw about to strike. – What a shame it would be, if things were to come crashing down, through the same ambition which had raised them up.

Connie, too, shifted a little. There were times to swing the big hammer, and other times to suggest you were prepared to deal. If the price was right.

– I'm not looking to eat anything bigger than my head, she assured him. – I don't want to blow the whistle on anyone.

How could she? She believed in the values, didn't she? She wanted to join the club, not blow it up.

And she liked the thought of developing a professional relationship with the Federation. Or, more precisely, with Borridge, because what she heard told her that he was the Federation. She liked the thought of being able to pick up the phone and pass the goodies on to someone. Who would know what to do with them – and in return help her out.

He said how kind she was to venture so, and she picked up on the slightly off-the-wall phrasing he slipped into when he was being careful to give nothing away. Especially not his own quickening interest in someone.

– You do talk nice, she sighed. – I suppose it's having to be so polite to all those important people who pay your wages here.

The fencing was over. They had both, in their own way, prepared the ground for a return visit. Now to the purpose of this one. Which suddenly wasn't for her to get the spike in her neck. But to hammer in one of her own.

– We get to level the site, and put twenty thousand square feet on it. With no fuss about road access, noise levels, or the fact it's slap in the middle of a residential zone. If they want a few trees and flower beds chucked in, to keep the natives happy, we can hack that. So long as we can keep it cheap. But we don't settle for anything less than that square footage.

Failing getting it, and getting it with the minimum of aggravation and delay, she would cause the maximum of aggravation to whoever had suggested Borridge have this word with her.

Borridge nodded, and put an incoming call on hold. Message received, if not appreciated. He would get back to the person he represented in this matter. In the meantime, he knew she'd excuse him. The phones never stopped. There was always someone wanting advice or assistance.

– If I ever got either off you – I'd take it, – Connie assured him, turning at the door. – Only a mug would turn it down.

And left. Knowing she was all tee'd up for that second visit.

Which would have been a good note to have ended the day on. But the afternoon board meeting was compulsory, since Jamieson was running the formal side of things. And at this particular meeting Hector would be delivering the goods on quality control.

His solution to the problem of giving the House of Bea's staff a share in the company was a mucky calendar, with the firm's name across the top.

Hector explained the mechanics, after attempting to dispose of the mucky epithet.

– It's an art calendar. It's very progressive thinking. You've heard of the Pirelli? They're collectors' items.

He had taken great pains to make sure he was dealing with a reputable company, who did calendars for all the names. None of which he could remember off-hand. But they would know them as soon as they heard them. The girls weren't chosen in particular for this calendar, but their photos taken from an agent's stock. Then printed off, as if they were House of Bea specials.

– The idea being that our girls associate the company with glamour, with allure, with success—

– Tits and bums? Bea wasn't convinced.

– Knitwear's about sex, as much as any other of clothing is, Connie chimed in on her father's side. – Whether a mucky calendar is worth the five grand he asked for is something else.

Hector waxed indignant. It was not a mucky calendar, no more than the Naked Maja was a dirty snapshot. What else could have carried their subliminal message of sexual success? Fishing boats in a Cornish harbour at sunset? Dusk falling on the Cotswolds?

The point was that clothes advertising had to push a very simple message. That the lady who slipped their gear on in the morning, would have some hairy hand rip it off her back, come night. That was putting it crudely, and there were different emphases to be struck in different market sectors. But in the main, their company profile had to carry the whiff of dangerous sex, heightened by romance.

Bea didn't see it herself. But Hector did take all these magazines. And just so long as he hadn't been at the photo calls in person, helping out with a touch of baby-oil here, a rub of blusher there, she would wear it. Even if it did come expensive at five grand.

– Connie's moving us into High St. outlets, he pointed out, wanting to steer the spotlight away from that five grand figure. Two and a half of which headed towards Lisa, who was learning her way around the better stores in town, making up for lost time. – You have to face up to the fact that we're in the ring with the big girls now.

The show of hands was stayed by Connie. She was taking a professional and female interest in the girls. This wasn't a major contribution to the art of the photographer, but it wasn't tat. And there was something to be said for Hector's argument. Nothing that helped with quality control, of course. That was basically the hard and unwelcome slog of chasing up the girls. Wearily, she supposed that would fall on her, like so much else.

How nice to be able to do this for a living. Strip off for the cold eye of the camera, pretending it was for the hot red eye of the fellas it was intended for. On garage, shop, office and factory wall. How nice to be able to fall back on the basics. To make your money out of the body you'd been born with, honestly, just be exhibiting it. Selling it in one clean operation, rather than spacing out its attractions, selling little bits of it off to the highest bidder. Which was so often what romance, and usually always marriage, was.

How nice to be arctic Miss January.

How devastating to be wicked Miss August.

And if she wanted to know what Miss December felt like, all she had to do was drive down to Arnie's stall.

For Babs was Miss December.

Which made it all fall into place, of course. Arnie could see that, when the calendar was spread in front of him. Courtesy of Dev, still smarting from his rejection in Nesta's office. It hurt even more that he knew he'd been rejected by someone who'd been in the skin game as a professional.

The London trips, the bank book, the things about the Babs she'd been before that she wouldn't talk about. All fitted. All he wasn't clear of was his reaction. What should he do, when the girl came home? Assuming she did. That the latest pick-up from that South-bound lay-by hadn't been the last?

If Arnie had stuck to his instincts, it might have turned out all right. If he'd met her with a clip round the ear, and a fist held under her nose saying on no account was she to turn another trick like that, it could have been Darby and Joan. But a lifetime's failing in business had made him suspicious of first reactions, and he'd believed too long in the commercial virtues of disguise and deceit.

Maybe if it hadn't been so plain that this was a turning point in their affairs? That this was a bridge, and a house fire, and a ticking bomb? Then he might have won out through the famous Arnie cool, that slow charm based on lethargy and a deep-down belief that nothing mattered in the end. But ever since Connie had come back, he knew every decision he made this side of forty would be a major one. And Arnie had a sort of stage fright about his own life now.

He'd have asked Connie's advice, but that meant going through Jamieson. And the only way he wanted to deal with him now was through a medium. Besides, all the miles he'd put on the clock with his ex stood in the way of him asking intimate advice.

Bea was hard to get hold of these days, enjoying herself playing the new role of coming woman in the knitwear, instead of has-been. Four marriages proves you've either learnt it all, or still learnt nothing, and he could never be sure which.

The only other woman he could turn to, to help him X-ray his own woman's likely reactions, was Nesta. Normally he would have considered that prospect for the space of a little more than half a second before giving it a comprehensive no. In present chewed-up circumstances, he decided to give it a shake. The post-Dev Nesta was rumoured to be a different woman. People did change, Arnie seriously believed. On no evidence, it's true. But he believed.

– What do you do when she comes back? Nesta gimletted the barman from fifteen feet, and ordered Tequila Smash. Double Tequila, dry ginger, one chunky glass rammed down hard on the bar-top. Drunk while still exploding in the glass, like a nuclear fruit salts. Guaranteed to put a smile on a dead rhino, the minute it hits the nervous system.

Nesta was different. Shaded under the eyes. Dressed so-so, rather than oh-yes.

– That depends what sort of girl she is. Does she have fantasies of being chased through beech woods in a long white dress? Or is she one of the girls?

Nesta's guess was that she was one of the girls. That the very last thing she would respond favourably to was the old-fashioned approach, the macho style which Arnie felt instinctively. The smack round the ear might work with nine out of ten, but he had to remember Babs was one of her own. Because of her looks, and because of how she'd been exploited through them.

– I could be wrong, Nesta allowed just the smallest of pauses, to point how major a leap of the imagination would be required to accept that. – I've only spent twenty years or so selling women's clothes, that doesn't say I know anything about them. Again that pause. – But it's your decision, in the finish. I can't guess her for you.

Which was what he wanted her to do.

– How am I qualified to give out advice to the lovelorn, when my guy's just walked out on me? Nesta looked and sounded impatient, as she nodded the barman for two more of the same. – I am really not qualified, picking up the pieces of my own thing, to talk about yours. If you feel threatened, tell her to knock it off, and keep your fingers crossed. She'll either take it on the chin, or jump into a passing truck. Either way, your worries are over.

Arnie was moved to say it wasn't a case of his feeling threatened. A lot of fellas might feel threatened by their girls doing this, but not him. He'd been around. He had the scar tissue to prove he'd been around. His worry wasn't feeling threatened, but how he should play his discovery of her secret.

– I can't just ignore it. The family are going to make sure that she knows I know.

All he was asking for was advice. Judgement. For another woman to narrow her eyes, and make a better-educated guess than he could. A lot depended on it. So much that he was prepared to choke on his own natural reaction, and do whatever would most likely keep the girl with him. Because if he lost her, he'd be in the same boat as Nesta, now that Dev was gone.

Put like that, what could an ex-step-sister-in-law do, but put him straight? Make her educated guess, and tell him what he had to do was take it on the chin. Nod the level head, forget the old-fashioned virtues. Go along with her stripping for strangers, making love to those hot red eyes.

Tough to swallow, running dead against the grain of what he wanted to do. But advice that he had to stick to, now he'd bent his neck to someone and asked their best opinion. Nesta did know women. She had been selling women, ever since Connie took her on as Number Two. She had every qualification.

So Arnie put his fourth Tequila Smash away, and got ready for Babs's return. Not pleased about what he was going to have to do, but confident about the final rightness of it. Nesta was qualified. Better qualified than he knew. Someone else had been gulping Tequila Smash with her.

Babs wanted advice too. Advice as to how Arnie would react, and what difference the calendar pic would make to their two-hander. And as part of their little chat on a cocktail banquette, she'd had to tell Nesta what she'd really wanted. Which were of course the old-fashioned, the lacey things. She did want to be chased through beech woods in a long white dress. She wanted that band of gold, and Mendelssohn, and all the trimmings. And if Arnie turned round and denied her them, if he was going to turn out to be yet another of the guys who saw her as a body first, a pay-day second, and a person long way third, she didn't know what she'd do.

– Catch that truck back to the Smoke? Nesta had hazarded, pushing another chunky glass at her, along the beaten copper of the tarty little table.

Babs hadn't answered. But her look had said it all.

So when Arnie walked out, his knees a little loose from all the liquid cactus in them, Nesta couldn't help but feel a girlish interest in how it would all come out, when he and Babs next met.

Eighteen

Connie didn't have to justify using Jardner to Jamieson or anyone else. The Board had delegated to her the job of swinging the planning permissions, and to Jamieson the job of getting the accounts in order. He had no right even to lift a quizzical eyebrow, when Connie started making confidential phone calls. But he was only human. Jardner did roll a powerful pair of shoulders under that tight fitting black leather.

Knowing that, Connie risked none of the misunderstandings that were about to happen between Babs and Arnie. She made it clear that Jardner was being used for his skills, not his looks.

– Like you've been hired for your bookkeeping whizz. She brushed him a kiss as she slipped past. On her way out of the office with the bulky brown package containing the amendments to the architect's drawings of the new factory.

Both pros came up trumps in their own specialities. Jamieson by burrowing deeper and deeper into the accounts until he had the proof that Hector was running a girl on the firm's books. Jardner by dropping the package off with Borridge, and nailing Crawder when he came to collect.

– Crawder?

Bea winced at the name. The Crawders were everything the House of Bea could be someday. Like five hundred years away, because it seemed that was how long they'd been in the business. The business of owning, and running things, as well as the everyday business of making knitwear.

The stakes were getting higher, if Crawder was involved. So Bea hung her angular head even deeper into her turkey neck, and hung the Wake Me Up When It's Over sign on her office door. There was no question of keeping Hector up to date with this one. The yellow streaks would have spread each side of his back and met in the middle of his chest.

– Crawder?

The gent in the tweeds didn't even flick his eyes towards Connie as she approached him in the Lace Museum. His idea of a venue, not hers.

– Mr. Crawder?

He must have liked that better, for he allowed a couple of inches travel of his head, above the much-washed classic Vyella country gentleman's shirt. Then he removed his look from her, and implied his interest went with it. For when he spoke, it was nodding in the direction of the glass cabinet, in front of which they stood.

It had taken Connie all the five minutes she had been searching for him to get her eyes to adjust to the dim light in the cramped insides of the Museum. Necessary to protect the delicate, expensive and rare fabrics on display here, hugged up close against the walls of Nottingham Castle. Effective, in how it emphasised the clandestine nature of their meeting. With Connie, again, threat or target.

– All down to soap, you know, the entire industry. Crawder was almost conversational, as he moved them to another display case, further away from the curator on the desk. – The necklines started plunging in the late fifteenth century, because they found how to make better quality soaps. The lower the neckline, the more lace was needed. In the end they came up with a machine. Just down the road from here. In Calverton. Did you know that?

– I never did the history of fashion. I've been too busy selling it.

If Connie thought that was an effective return of service she was put right on his reply.

– My family's a part of that history. My great-grandfather peddled lace and other odds and ends. Then he bought a stocking frame, and cashed in on how fast Birmingham was growing.

Fascinating, nodded Connie, wondering how to take the initiative.

– There are two others on the Board beside myself with a direct line to great-grandfather Crawder. We're old money, you see. There's a lot of old money in knitwear. But every generation has known how to get its hands oily, has got down on the floor, has been able to fix a bust machine. We're practical men. We're not content with owning things. We like to run them, too.

She picked that up, leaving until later to decide if she loved or hated that easy assurance which his possession of old money gave him.

– You like running things like the planning sub-committees?

He wasn't to be railroaded.

– Every so often new money comes along. Or someone who would like to be new money. Don't get me wrong. I'm not against it. It keeps the old money sharp and bright.

– Great-grandad must have been new money once. Crawder nodded, accepting. – And I bet he was a right bastard.

A pause, then the acceptance. The old money weighing up an unexpected quality in the new. And then hitting a new line of attack itself.

– I know the name of your tinshack firm, of course. But refresh me on who you are.

Connie did so. The etiquette of the moment asked for it.

– Hector? The Hot Pant King?

So the story had even reached the hang-outs of the heavy mob? Hector was a joke not only in barrooms, but baronial halls? Connie made a note that it was one more stripe she had to get paid back off the establishment.

– And you? He asked, swivelling another look at her, as they passed up the case of lace bobbins.

– I'm just Connie, who believes in the values.

– Which are?

– All the ones your great-grandad would have recognised and approved of. The ones that sticking to makes new money into old money.

– Being?

– If we're only here to look after the others, what the hell are the others doing here? And rather than figuring that one out, the wise get on with looking after number one.

He liked that. From the point of view of politics, and how you run your life.

– Are you a wrecker? he surprised her with that one. But he had to be sure.

– I want to join the club, not burn it down.

He liked that even better. But wasn't that an unfortunate choice of phrase, considering what he knew about the loss by fire of the listed building. So convenient, for the House of Bea.

– I could have cried, Connie said simply. Leaving him to decide for himself what that meant. Whether she had cried with happiness, relief or what.

Outside, Jamieson fretted whether or not he should buy a ticket and go in. Rain was dripping down the back of his neck, and he knew he had a duty to be with Connie. Because he'd been asking questions about Crawder, and knew the roughness of the people she was playing against. Who weren't rough in the way Kyprianou was, but whose contacts could do with a phone call what the Greek couldn't with baseball bats.

He was held back by that gambling piratical streak which he hadn't known was in him. Not until he started in the knitwear, and felt that daily excitement. There was just a chance she could pull it off, and he was enough of a fashion pro by now to know that that's not enough. It has to be pulled off with style.

Creasing the man she was in there with now, was sky high style.

– Borridge told me not to have that black detective warned off. He said let it be, you'd go away.

Why hadn't he taken the best advice in the business, she asked? Was it his arrogance or his carelessness?

That he didn't like, but rode it well.

– Curiosity. Would you settle for that?

– Or maybe you just love a row?

That he did like. There was a lot to be said for not only never ducking a fight, but looking out for one. One you could win, of course. It kept the muscles and the footwork in trim.

– How do you know you can win this one? And don't tell me just because you're old money, and you've been doing in the likes of me ever since great-grandad.

He answered obliquely, pausing in front of a model of an early machine frame. Did she know that he was a collector? He collected early machine lace, and stocking frames. Bloody expensive, even for old money. But if you had the collecting thing, there was nothing you could do about it, could you?

– Do you collect? He watched her reflection in the glass, and she knew how important a moment this was.

– Only scars, and what I think I'm due.

She didn't get away with it. He kept his eyes on her, and this time took her in from heels to hairpiece.

– You might say I'm an obsessive, once I decide I'm going to collect something. Silly, isn't it? A chip of an ice-cold smile here, that could have turned you blue as gun metal. – A man works long and hard at his own business, then works harder, and plays dirtier, in his hobby. For his collection.

She kept his eyes locked in the glass of the case.

– And the having's not all that important, is it? It's the getting that counts.

He disagreed, but not profoundly. There were the pleasures of having, he thought. And then, as if on another subject, told her how well she wore the Italian dress.

Still she held his eye, though aware that someone else was several display cases away.

– How much do you want in? Crawder asked, his hand starting to twitch the buttons of his tweed greatcoat.

– A lot.

– How bad? He let the hand rest for a moment on his lapel, and it was a workman's hand, an engineer's hand, the hand of someone who could do a day's work, or bust a chin. This was old money that hadn't forgotten its roots.

– Just bad. That shivery sexy little word bad, that's all.

– All down to them inventing soap, you know. After they'd invented soap, they all sat around with nothing to do, because they thought everything had been invented.

Connie was bright, as she walked back to the car with Jamieson. Too bright. Brittle bright.

– Then someone had the idea of inventing lace, and here we are. Or something like that. I've seen more lace than I ever thought there was in the world, and more than I ever wanted to see. I could tell you things about the history of textiles in the East Midlands which could make your hair curl.

And while she'd been doing the round of the museum with her expert guide, she had made the deal.

– No strings?

Jamieson pulled her to him, avoiding the spray from a passing artic. Connie would never use subways or underpasses when there was a chance of getting killed by the traffic on a main road. Preferably one with a solid great metal barrier down the middle.

– None.

Except that if this thing was to get much further, she'd have to share her panties with him. And not on alternate days, either.

Jamieson read it right.

Nearly made the mistake that Arnie was about to, and choked back what he really thought. This was a pirate crew he'd signed with. But even pirates give in to unprofessional, unpiratical outbursts of sincere feeling now and again.

– You're not even going to think about it, he warned her. – Not for the good of the firm, not for you and me in the long term. You're not even to think about stringing him along.

He knew all about Connie being an all-the-way person, about her being prepared to pay any price to get her spoon in the gravy right up to her elbows. But he wasn't prepared to have her do this.

– I know how much the rebuilding means to you, but I'm not hanging you on the meatrack for the Crawders or anyone. And if you say you're going to hang yourself there I'm leaving. Even though I've no job and no home to go to. Because I love you. And I'm daft enough about you, to stop you doing the thing only you would be brave enough to do.

And it wasn't necessary, anyway. Because if Crawder was in the market for a girl, he could fix him with one.

– Hector's. I know who she is.

– Perm any ten from fifteen. Or whatever those boring no-hopers who filled the football pools in every Thursday do, Connie suggested. – Bea knows what a sexual hooligan he is. So long as he doesn't do it on the desk on her blotter.

– He's set this one up. As Jamieson prepared to take her through the paperwork which proved it, he checked. This was hardly something to relate to the only daughter of the man involved. Even if it did offer a chance of getting her off the hook.

Connie guessed what he was thinking. And loved him for it the more, even though it made no difference.

– I've known him longer than you, and lived with this all my life. It doesn't hurt anymore. If it ever did. Don't forget wanting to beat up all the fellas and screw all the birds is a family trait, not just a personal itch.

When it came down to it, the moral equation was simple.

Bea loved Hector, Hector loved Bea. Currently Hector was up to his tricks with Lisa. But a girl like Lisa and a fella like Crawder looked more natural and was a damn sight more convenient just now than Crawder and Connie.

– He's never seen her. He's never likely to, in the normal way of things, Jamieson didn't want to make protest, but felt he had to. No point getting carried away by the beautiful intricacies of one's own low-down cunning. – We can't just post her to him, with no stamped addressed envelope enclosed.

Connie took his point. But there had to be a way. She knew there would be a way. Because God wouldn't have thrown up the girl's name at that precise moment, unless He meant them to use it in any way they could.

Would she?

Jamieson squeaked lucky on that one. Tossed the coin, watched it catch the light, and guessed right. It helped that he was in love with the woman he was dealing with—but so was Arnie, and he got it wrong.

He was in the bar, and sticking to iced water, when she showed. He'd been drinking what unkindly friends insisted on referring to as Arnie's Eskimo Piss for three straight days, waiting for the girl. And when she showed, he knew. She'd seen the calendar. Someone had nobbled her already. Family, probably. Or Dev. One of the exes.

And if she hadn't seen it thanks to family, she would have been in the bar only long enough to walk to the servery before she clocked. Because there she was, in pride of place, over the optics. Given better billing than the yellowed postcards and signs that informed that a request for credit often lead to a smack in the mouth.

Arnie was going to tough this out.

– Don't say a word until I've said my piece. He slid a stool towards her. Deliberately not moving from under the calendar twelve by ten. Not asking himself what that tightening of the mouth when she'd seen it meant.

Luckily the bar comics and smart-arses were not yet piled in, so he had a clear run at this. No competition from the yahoos who normally crowded the place, once the stalls were stripped, and another day's buying and selling over.

– That bird up there wearing nothing but the pink leg warmers is nothing to do with you, or me. That's not the Babs you are, not the Babs I know and want.

So far, so good. She was waiting for his play, knowing as well as he how important that he get it right.

– So the best of luck to that Babs there, he nodded at the calendar.

– Anytime she needs to get that South-bound truck, that's all right by me.

Still no reaction from her. The big eyes searched his.

Now she knew.

Ever since she'd known she would have to face this moment she'd been dreading it. Scared that he would get it wrong. Prove that she'd been wrong all the time. About him, and him and her.

The only reason she'd levelled with Nesta was hoping that his ex-relative would blab, let something slip, give him a pointer. Just in case he was going to react like he was reacting.

She didn't even hear, as he made the rest of his little speech. Watched the eyes plead with hers, his mouth make the shapes that made the sounds.

Arnie was just another punter, after all. When it came down to it any professed outrage at his girl stripping for the still or video eye was more than outweighed by the advantages in it for him. In his pocket, especially. It had looked as if she'd made a safe haven, after everything that had put those marks around her eyes, marks it took a woman to see. And now Arnie was putting himself through those same hoops all the other fellas in her life had. Preparatory to putting her through them, too.

Arnie was her dad pushing her bedsheets down in the early morning, hoarse with lust and shame. Her first boyfriend, panting his lies as he pushed himself into her against the bare brick of the council flats wall. All the fellas after that, blasting their bad breath at her, as they grappled somewhere below.

Arnie was all them, and worse. She'd thought there was a future here. In him she'd found someone who wouldn't want to move on from enjoying her for himself, to packaging her for other men at so much per pound.

You never could tell. Except that everyone of them were lice.

So Babs excused herself halfway through his self-justification for making her keep on doing it, and went to the ladies'. Only she turned right instead of left in the corridor to it, and on to the street. And across the market, and out the other side, before he'd have a chance to follow.

Babs got that south-bound truck again, and gave herself to the trucker in a soiling fifteen minutes at the far side of a service station. Said nothing all the way through, and nothing after. Sat, when it was through. And she threw the key away on where she'd locked the years with Arnie, looking straight ahead.

Southbound.

Back to the Babs she used to be.

And if it took all the money she earned turned into stuff she shot in her arm, or put up her nose, to keep that Babs, she was ready for it. Not welcoming it, but accepting.

Time for Jardner to get his, Connie reckoned. Unaware that the other side of town Arnie was getting it, too.

Years back, she might have enjoyed stringing the private investigator along, and watching what it did to Jamieson out of the corner of her eye. Not now. Too many miles on the clock, too many hard lessons paid for. Jardner would have to be bounced.

– I don't bounce easy, he told her, over the meal that she was paying for. – You picked me up, you had the police walk all over me. I'm interested in how the planning department scam is going to work out for you.

– Taken care of, Connie assured him, dipping into the wonton. Jardner was persona at the restaurant below the office again. Her severance terms had been generous.

– But what if I get curious? he asked, giving her six inches of smile. – What if I find myself short of a few bob, and nobody walks into my office wearing legs all the way to her navel?

That was going to be taken care of too, she assured him. She didn't like loose ends. Especially hungry ones, who could talk themselves into thinking they had a grudge against an ex-employer.

– Take this.

This was a list of names and phone numbers, in her own hand.

– There are a lot of lonely high-heeled women in this business. They need looks and muscle. Chasing bad debts, pirating designs. This is a business full of small-time crooks trying to be big-time crooks. Run by women, more than most.

Given those shoulders in that black leather, Jardner should be able to parlay a smooth phone manner into paying work. And once his name got known inside the industry, there was nowhere it couldn't take him.

But she hoped he'd remember who gave him his start, when he was cruising at the wheel of some widow-woman's Roller.

He bought it.

He and Connie were quits.

C.—10

– All the same, he folded the sheet of paper into his pocket. You did make my eyeballs sweat when you walked my way.

– I'm not going to tell you what it did to my knees when you walked mine. She told him the truth. Holding his gaze for a count of three, as it flicked a suggestion to her. Involving his office upstairs, and the evening ahead.

Once she might have picked up that suggestion. On the principle of why merely complicate your life when you can, with a bit of effort, make it totally unmanageable? But this Connie was learning, and changing. So turned down the chance of feeling that pleasant shock of cold leather on bare-skin, on the sag-springed four-seater settee in the private eye's office.

And never looked back when she hit the street.

Arnie did climb strange stairs that evening. After it hit him that Babs wasn't coming out of the ladies' toilet that night or any other night, he'd drunk a little, and bit his lip a little, and wished he could grab the clock on the barroom wall and wrestle it back two hours. And this time when Babs arrived, he'd play it exactly how he felt.

Too late. That golden sale was eluding him in real life, like it was in business. The barrow was piled with tats, and so was his love life.

The inspiration to call on Nesta was sudden. He had a brief flare of suspicion that somehow he'd been nobbled by that uglier of the sisters. Then it died again, dampened by the weight of his misery. Too often he had blamed others for failings in himself. This time he wasn't going to look round for scapegoats. For how could Nesta gain by queering things between himself and Babs? When he broke the news, confused now as to what he was doing, in her office, there was no accusation there.

She said nothing, but made drinks. Something she'd done many times before for him. In that office, too. Juicing him up, waiting for one of the girls she'd pimped for him. For the best of motives, of course. What was a step-sister there for, if not to keep the step-sister's man happy when the step-sister was on the road so much?

One thing she'd never done was go up those spiral stairs with him herself. Out of self-preservation, not wanting to risk introducing the personal and vulnerable note. But also because, face it, Arnie had the pick of the bunch, and where did Nesta rate, against them?

Never done it until this evening.

Never sat with him, listening to his story, and making all the right noises. Never let him wind down, while filling him with drinks. Never float the idea of a sweet revenge, in a sympathetic bed.

Never got him up there, and having got him there, never went for a fella quite so hard. So hard it scared him as much as it at first flattered him. And then he went for her, with his second wind. Soiling himself with her, just as Babs was with her trucker a hundred miles away.

Another pair of lovers were in bed that night. With each other, this time. Hector and Lisa, eating black olives from salad nicoise. The girl was coming on. Supper no longer meant automatic fish and chips, with a curry take-away for high and holy days.

– White or red? she asked now. He'd educated her off the rosé, and that sparkling Italian wine that tasted like alcoholic coke.

The girl was learning what fork to eat her soup with, and Hector was apprehensive, as well as pleased. Her growing sophistication in taste and dress was all down to him, of course. He could take the credit. But there was no gainsaying that tug of jealousy, every time she had to cry off a meeting with him. She was entitled to nights in on her own, of course. And nights out on her own. There had to be some air in their relationship, Hector was too old a hand not to appreciate that.

Equally, he was human. If this bust, there could never be anything like it again. He wouldn't have the stomach. He hadn't intended to fall in love with the girl, any more than he had intended to set her up with the little flat and the car. But he was an all-the-way person, like his daughter.

He ate the olives, and drank the wine, unthinking that a larger and more unstoppable event than even love was about to run him down.

Nineteen

Dev was finding it difficult to sell one of those Rolls Royce widows, whom Connie had indicated the existence of to Jardner. Mrs. Adamson looked as if no jury could acquit her, should the deaths of her three husbands ever come to court. She kept a grip as tight as a nun's kneecaps on her order book.

The new chief drummer for the House of Bea had turned every trick in the salesman's book without getting the nod from that formidable face, frozen as the sheet ice of the pole. He'd tried to sell her on quality, price and delivery. With charm, enthusiasm, and outright sex appeal. She'd resisted every tactic, and not dented the crusted pancake on her witch's face.

As a last throw he'd decided to give her the less-than-grand tour of the premises, including the walk-round the mock-up of the new factory. Whose detailed planning permissions were even now been processed, he could assure her.

– It looks a horror story, he admitted, surveying the rain-sodden remains. – But when this is complete there will be twenty thousand square feet of prime industrial site, turning out prime quality knitwear, priced so sharply you could cut yourself.

The concept was what mattered. The design philosophy behind the look and the cut. Without that, you were just talking dish rags. Dev could speak with confidence on that, because hadn't he taught the theory and the philosophy at college?

Things were changing with Dev. The same way they had changed with Jamieson. No matter how much you went into the selling end of the fashion business thinking it was beneath you, or a stop-gap job, something happened. One morning you woke up and found you couldn't wait to get out there, making the pitch. Jamieson was getting the kick in the back room. And Dev was getting it even worse, because he was on the road, hacking his way through the underbrush of buyers, buyers' assistants, managers and owners.

He thought, much to his surprise, that he could take or leave the creative side, if an offer came his way again. He still had a sneaking feeling that no other designer in Europe, let alone the UK, knew their business as well as he. But he was at peace, even with that knowledge, for the first time in years. Connie had given him the break and he appreciated, again for the first time, what a good chooser of people she was. In professional life, if not in the personal. She had built the chain of shops that Nesta now bestrode on a dozen shrewd personnel decisions, and it looked as if that sure touch hadn't deserted her.

Of course, he still itched to get her to bed, but it wasn't because of the hands-off she'd given him after the art school business. Out of gratitude. He sincerely believed that the greatest gift any woman could give herself was an evening in the sheets with him. Jealousy of Jamieson didn't come into it. That was plainly a love job. He'd service Connie at what he had the testimonials to show he was best at. And then hand her back to her steady fella, for the steady, dating sort of sex.

All heart, was Dev these days.

Except to Mrs. Adamson, this morning. Mrs. Adamson who seemed waterproof to a depth of several thousand feet against salesmen in general, and Dev in particular. This was going to have to be chalked up as a loss, by the look of it. And Dev was starting to enjoy that sniff of success.

– Thank you for allowing me to show you around the factory, he decided to cut this short. – Here's my card and home phone number where you can get me twenty four hours a day. Thank you for calling, and if you have any other questions please ask.

– Just the one. Mrs. Adamson turned the key in the door with that soundless click that suggested bank vaults and deposit boxes. – Have you ever done it in a Roller?

Watching the startled but quickly recovered Head of Sales drive off with the bejewelled *grande dame* of the Lincolnshire madam-shop chain, Connie grinned. Staff selection, eh? Fitting the right face, and other bits, to the right job.

And Dev wasn't just a sound business choice. Allowing him to get his self-respect back meant that there was one less prowling out there in the woods, looking for her blood. Another way in which she had to acknowledge she had changed was in not wanting to drag her beaten enemies behind her galloping hooves. Or rear bumper and registration plate.

This was less fun, but more sense. And with Crawder likely to be a threat if she handled him wrong, she was happy to trade the one for the other. Especially as only this morning Crawder's office had asked her personally to call round.

– I'm sending you, she told Jamieson, called away from his de-bugging of the new computerised stock control system. – He won't like it, but I'm seeing someone.

That someone was Lisa, stood before her suddenly, the door crashed shut behind her. This wasn't a girl who hung around on her entrances, obviously. Though when she saw that Bea wasn't to be found in the office, the wide shoulders relaxed a fraction. The eyes were still watchful under a better-than-average attempt to get an East Midlands hairstyle to look like a West End salon one.

– Breathe out. Drop the shoulders, and the boobs. You're not up before the Governor for setting fire to A-Wing.

Connie offered her a cigarette from Bea's rumpled packet on the desk. She always left them behind when she went golfing with Nesta. A nod in the direction of giving them up, just as the round of the greens was a nod in the direction of defying the years.

– I don't.

– You used to.

That was true, Lisa admitted, automatically pulling her hand the other way round so that the nicotine stains she hadn't been yet able to pumy-stone away didn't show.

– I chucked it.

– Like you chucked dressing on staff discount?

No answer, except a self-conscious check of what she was wearing, against what Connie was wearing. Connie was hands-down winner, but the gap between them wasn't as large as it would have been before Hector took her in hand.

Connie understood.

– A girl has enough of picking her way through seconds? Like she has enough of catching the corporation bus to work every morning? And out of nowhere treats herself to a nice little car with a sun-roof.

Connie had done her homework. Lisa's shoulders lifted again, in self defence.

– Won the snowball at the bingo, did you? Twenty times on the trot? Or is it a rich uncle job?

Whatever, it was nothing to do with Connie, and Lisa was losing piece-work money stood there.

Connie told her not to get her wrong. She liked people who had it in them to change. People who suddenly turned round, shrugged off the Old Me, and went for a New Me. She'd done it herself.

It so happened that Lisa's change in lifestyle was coinciding with one in the firm. There was a new House of Bea in the making, and there were going to be openings in it for girls who could measure up. Lisa could head back to her machine, and pick up where she'd left off. Or listen in. And maybe hear something to her advantage.

– What openings? she'd decided to bite.

Connie held the moment, surveying her. Ordered her to turn. Checked her legs and backside. Told her to sit, and stand again. Put the coat on that was hanging on the rack. Take it off. And put it on and take it off again. But this time with style. Letting Connie hear all the s's as she slid out of it.

This was a job interview and an audition. Lisa had to pretend Connie was a fella. Sweaty, hairy, with eyes like a boiled lobster's that had been up and down her from the moment she walked through the office door. Pretend Connie's hands were twitching like an octopus at stud. Pretend she was every fella who ran his eyes up and down a female rep in the fashion business.

She wasn't looking for the tart in Lisa. She was looking for the woman who could take that treatment, and still keep the most important thing in mind. That she was representing not herself, but the House of Bea.

Could she do that? Or was she content with a lifetime on piece-work? With the occasional gloss of a cut-price sugar daddy who would drop her the minute he put her in the club?

– Sell me class, Connie insisted. – Even though I'm every Jack the Lad in every office in his flash suit that stinks under the armpits, wiggling his toes in the sweat that's run off his feet and into his nylon socks. Aren't fellas terrible? They just don't bother.

Or else pretend she was selling some old smoothie, who'd been around for a bit, turned every trick, bullied his way into it, or paid for it. Some old smoothie sitting behind the king-size desk, under the ten-foot square portrait of the right old bugger who founded the firm he ran. Some old smoothie ripe for the taking, because he thought he'd done and seen it all.

Like Crawder, she could have added. Except that Lisa wouldn't have known the name. Like Crawder, who at that very minute was leaning on Jamieson. Refusing to handle things through third parties. Demanding that next time there was business to be done, Connie did it herself. In that Italian number, for preference, that she was wearing when he ran his tape up and down her in the image on the Lace Museum display case.

Lisa got her breath back. Fought for some control. A job interview with Connie could be as unusual and bruising as one with Nesta.

– What's the job? Selling?

More like sales promoting than sales closing, Connie said. The job would be wearing House of Bea lines, and looking good in it. Girls who looked like Lisa were far too useful to waste on selling jobs. There were fellas hanging out of the Job Centre doors you could get for that.

– Promotions girl? Lisa had never seen herself doing a job like that. That was the sort of job girls from private houses got. Who had solicitors for boyfriends, who drove red sports cars. Who did that sort of job only to meet fellas who owned shops and businesses, and drove even bigger red sports cars, and had yachts.

– Not promotions girl if by that you mean some brainless blonde with the name of a fag painted on her car, and likely as not stamped on her fanny. Not some failed tart of an actress or model whose face is falling in faster than her arches.

The House of Bea meant to be serious contenders, so they needed girls who knew the business from the footplate of a sewing machine up.

Lisa said she'd think about it. But inside, as she left the office, she knew she'd signed. And Connie did, too. All she had to do now was break the news to Hector that a new post was being created specially for his girl, and at a salary to match her responsibilities.

She didn't expect any problems from him. Nor when she would suggest that Lisa took a week at a health and beauty farm to have those small-town corners chipped off her. To get her skin fed, and her hair fixed. To attend to all those things you could only start on if you had a week in the country, away from real life. A whole week giving in to the worship of every cranny and pore of your own body.

Hector would ride that one. Especially as his girl was going to be made even tastier, courtesy of the firm. There would be problems later, when he discovered that her job was to go-between Connie and Crawder, for Hector would know that man's reputation as a collector. But even that could be ridden. It would only be when Crawder made her the same offer, or better, than he had half-made Connie, that the problems would start.

She'd hack that when she came to it.

The problems of bringing up your parents, she shook her head, looking up as Arnie hit the office.

One damn thing after another.

You tie up two loose ends, like Dev and Crawder—and another bursts into the happy home, bringing the reminder that he could still be a problem, if he put his mind to it.

And Arnie, sure enough, was bringing a problem. But not, for once, anything that guile, cunning and speed of gut reaction could do anything about.

Bea had collapsed after the fifteenth that morning.

Did Connie want to say goodbye?

Hector was shaken, but handling it. He stood by the fire doors, getting a breath of air. Shocked, but capable. He'd been shot head first into sudden brick walls before in his life.

Sudden serious illness was one he hadn't needed to deal with before, but he guessed it was only like a variation on a business upset. People got sick like firms got sick. They were going along full steam one minute, the next the shutters were up while things were put right. Sooner or later you opened up for business again. What had happened to Bea, he vaguely assumed, looking for a landmark to keep in sight of, was something like that.

Odd, but he'd been talking about pattern and shape and meaning with her only the other day. When she'd been musing on the figures the younger ones kept turning on the ice. Prompted by the discovery that Arnie was now where Dev had been.

Unusual for Bea to lift her head any length of time from the desk, or bridge table, to comment on the larger forces at work in the universe. The cosmic had always seemed to her the least important scale to think in. Not that she had had any intimation of the aneurism that had exploded in the left side of her head on the green three hours ago. Just one of those coincidences. One day you allow yourself to muse over coffee on the ultimate meaning of it all—the next day you find yourself in a position to give first-hand answers.

– She got sick, and none of us noticed, he nodded at the peck on the cheek from the flushed and out-of-breath Connie. – Can you believe she's in there? British made, is Bea. She can't be.

– Crafty old cow, Connie tried to rally him. – She always did play things close to her chest.

Nesta came through the doors, her face drawn. There were high spots of red on her cheeks, and she looked angry. And was. Because all she knew how to cope with was anger. That was the only interior resource she had. Even at a time like this.

– You can clear off. And him. She indicated Arnie, and Jamieson, who had got the news on his return to the factory, and put his foot down.

– No fellas. What are fellas good for at a time like this, but standing on one leg looking dead embarrassed? Pretending to have a fag, and wishing it were over?

Connie nodded to Jamieson, who made to say something in sympathy to Nesta, but thought better of it. Arnie watched him go, and then made off with as much dignity as he could scrape together.

– Couldn't we suspend hostilities, just for today, an already weary Hector asked.

But Nesta only had one speed, and that was fast forward. Connie had a nerve to even think of taking Jamieson away from the office. Someone had to be minding the store. The store that very shortly would be part-owned by herself.

– I'd not been thinking about that side of things, Connie admitted. Biting her lip, determined not to help her sister make a scene. Especially not by the intensive care fire doors.

– Pull the other, its got bells and tassles on, was Nesta's instant comeback. – You dropped everything and ran, looking for a hint from behind the oxygen mask there'd be even more coming your way.

Connie was suddenly tired, too. Tired of the row Nesta seemed almost crazily insistent on. Tired of the day ahead, even before it started. Knowing the dull long hours, nursing the nagging aches of anxiety and suspense, and almost worse, raw-edged boredom ahead. Sat in that antiseptic corridor. Or by the bedside.

She pushed past, and if Nesta had tried to stop her she believed she would have been willing to strike her. Just as she would have been prepared to do so in the hotel foyer that morning she found that Georgiou had been hijacked.

But there were gaps even in Nesta's chain underwear. The flamethrower got heavy in even her hands from time to time. She stood aside, and Connie went through.

– I resent this. I want you to know I resent this.

Bea was shaded, and at peace. Her strong features, a miniature in ivory, never more shown to best advantage. Not even the technology of the major road works the hospital was trying to perform on her detracted from her chin-first glare.

Then she had the same thought that Nesta had, clutching Connie's hand with the one of hers that wasn't plumbed in to several thousand pounds worth of tubing and electronics.

– Who's looking after the shop? We'd got that rush on with the roll necks.

– My fella's there, taking care of business, as per.

– He could have the makings, Bea moved her weight, careful not to disturb the pipework. – When you first showed up with him in that single-vent suit that made his bum stick out, I gave it a fortnight. Maybe you've finally got the hang of picking them.

– Like you, with Hector?

Conversation had never seemed so easy between them. Connie realised she was still holding the hand, and felt closer to this woman than she ever had.

– He's a right old villain, your dad. But he never was a bastard. And I could write the spotter's guide to them.

Connie said she'd been told not to stay too long.

– Because goodbyes are supposed to upset you? Bea grinned a grin well-known in the business. – In my life the goodbyes have been far and away the best bits.

That sort of whispered instruction at the ward door was just a ramp by the doctors and nurses to stop them being upstaged. Like fashion people, medicals were even bigger hams than show-business people. They wanted Bea to turn her head to the wall like a sick cat. They liked the glamorous bits like running up the ward and thumping you on the chest.

– But I'm a fashion person, and I'm a show person, so nobody's going to steal my lamps.

Fashion, the selling of it, the wearing of it, was all performance. Connie instinctively knew that, had been born knowing it. Like her.

– Why do you think I always wore the black? I hate black. I always hated black. But everyone in the business knew I wore black. They might hate me for an old cow, but by Christ they remembered the old cow.

Which brought her on to something else. Connie was to hold Nesta and Hector to what they had already promised. That when she went, she wanted it to be with show. Didn't want to be tastefully slipped into a corporation bin-sack at the crematorium, with a half dozen people stood by on a wet Tuesday. Wanted many people trampling the flower beds. Plus the biggest, showiest headstone they were still allowed to erect. Not for Bea an apologetic little cross with her initials and dates, that said she was sorry for taking up all that valuable mortuary space. Something that would smack the buggers in the eye was what she wanted. A stone that would drag anyone across the grass to read who she was, and what she'd been, even if they were only using the cemetery as a shortcut across the back of the gasworks.

– And the hell with it being vulgar. The more vulgar the better, so long as they notice.

Afterwards, Nesta and Hector were to be held to putting on a do at the factory. The house wouldn't be big enough to hold everyone she'd known and offended in town, who would want to come to make sure she was finally out of their hair. It was to be a big spread, for all comers, and they were to float her out of their lives on malt scotch and pink champagne. She'd already earmarked a budget for it.

One more thing.

– You're not to waste the chance to sell the new House of Bea. You'll never get so many important people under one roof again. Do it for me. Hit them with the new lines while they're still filling their handkerchiefs with fake grief, and wondering whether to go for the smoked salmon or the quail's eggs.

Connie promised.

– I'll hold you to it, Bea warned. – I'll be floating overhead, making sure you do.

In return for those promises, Bea would have liked to be able to say she was cutting Connie, post mortem, into an even bigger share of the firm. But blood told, in the finish. Nesta would cop for all Bea's share.

– Sorry, kid. I know how hard you and your fella have worked. But that's capitalism for you.

Connie didn't even want to talk about it. Not out of disappointment, but because what time they had left between them was too precious to be used in talking business.

Bea winced. No time was wasted talking business. That had been a fundamental of faith with her for all her years. Was she trying to bring about a deathbed conversion?

One last thing.

One thing that made Connie wonder how much Bea was clued to.

– Find him a bird. Not someone my age, that'll mean he has to go through all this bedside business again. A young girl, someone to put the lead back in his pencil. With a place of her own. He's getting too old for quickies in hatchbacks.

The girl would be on the make, for why else would she settle for a well-worn face like Hector's. But what was the harm in that? At least it wouldn't end up a love job, because Hector was too old for them. Too vulnerable.

Connie searched for evidence that Bea was telling her she knew all about Hector and Lisa. Been keeping it under her hat. Been as canny a wise old cow as she looked. Didn't find it. Bea would be going out in the dark about her final and most complete betrayal.

– You're not giving this job to Nesta? she rallied, twisting a smile and a protest together.

– Can you ask your own daughter to do a thing like that?

– But you can ask your step-daughter?

Maybe she was right. Out of the two of them, it was Connie who more naturally had the instincts of a dockside madam. And she could be sure that in the old warrior's eyes, now misted with sudden pain, that would be a shining quality. Because they were fashion people, all the way through, and to sell fashion you had to have access to all those darker secrets of how women worked.

And one very last, one genuinely final thing. And perhaps the most important. Could Connie try to make her peace, sooner or later, with her step-sister?

It was a toughie to ask, and she should blush to ask it from the fortress of a sickbed—but the question had to be put. Could Connie try, even though Bea had been there in the office, when Nesta had said no. Could she? She didn't have to say she would—just that one day, she maybe could.

She got a nod.

Not a grudging one. But not a hopeful one.

Connie didn't hang around the hospital while the dying went on. To do so would have meant rowing with Nesta, and she had a promise made. And if Bea was serious, which she plainly was, about fixing her wake as a fashion show, there were invitations to write, and arrangements to be made. Throwing herself into those, she kept in touch with the reports from the hospital as that little indomitable black figure said its goodbyes and ran out of steam.

In between the frantic moments, chasing up people who Bea would have known years back in the business, and the unpleasant moments, like haggling with the band she wanted to play through the send-off, were the quiet moments. When she sat, slumped, staring out of the window at the yard which had circumscribed Bea's life.

She suddenly knew why she never wanted kids, in one of those moments. Trying to figure if there was any meaning to all the years Bea had spent grafting down these narrow streets. Because when you had kids, at some point life plays a nasty on you. A confuser. It starts out with the darling little bundle of dribble and wind being a part of your history. Then at some point you suddenly realise you're only part of what the chapter's all about. Then suddenly, without noticing how you've got there, you find you're just a footnote to someone else's.

Connie wasn't having that.

Not having any sly bundle of pink-cheeked innocence turning round and sticking the blade between her shoulders.

Besides, there was a business to run.

True, very shortly, with Bea dead, it looked like she'd be running it for step-sister. The grooming of Lisa, the plans for the rebuilding of the professional reputation of the firm, as well as its physical plant, would be lining someone else's pocket.

But businesses had lives of their own that sucked you in, and refused to let you go. They were like love affairs in that. Trains you could not conceive you had a possibility of getting off, once they were rolling. Let alone a right. Companies may have been in lawyers' terms legal fictions, but they had personalities of their own. And demanded their dues off you. Just like people.

Like the woman who died, without too much difficulty, with Hector on one side, and Nesta the other. Blood one side, love the other. And genuine hurt and regret on both.

Bea never was one to hang around at parties she wasn't enjoying. She'd stopped enjoying this one, much.

Twenty

– She did nothing mean.

Hector leant forward on the rail. Chewing on his bottom lip, eyes fixed on a spot above the heads in the packed cemetery chapel. So strictly multi-denominational that you could have buried a man from Mars in it without giving religious offence.

He was trying to frame it exactly right. To say, for once, everything he meant to say, and nothing more. Not trimming a few pence off the truth, or adding to it. The genuine and simple thing. To sit with the genuine and simple grief he had been, despite himself, surprised at feeling since Bea had left the party. Quietly. But leaving a sort of silence after.

– If she was buying she'd argue for a day and a night to get another ha'pence off a dozen. Then she'd ask for a ha'pence off a dozen dozens. And then a ha'pence off a dozen gross. But never meanly. Always with the unspoken understanding that this was business, and the usual rules don't apply. And all of us here, I think, understand that. Because we're her sort of people. Business. Backbone.

The mourners gave a collective nod at that. They understood.

– She had a tongue on her. Me of all of you, maybe, felt its edge. But she was born a flyweight, in figure. When you're a flyweight, you count on speed of punch and footwork. She had both, and I should know.

And indeed he should, the Hot Pant King, making a speech no one there thought he had in him.

– But she was never cruel. She could hurt, often she meant to hurt, but sometimes, in business you have to hurt. Because no one does any favours for the small businessman or woman.

Another heart-felt collective nod, dipping mink-trimmed hats, and handsome foreheads with three-months-worth-a-year of genuine Bahamas or Mediterranean or both, tan.

– After she'd bawl a girl out on the shop floor, there'd be the arm round the shoulder, the mug of tea, the afternoon off. And like as not, an extra something in the packet that payday, and no hard feelings.

A nod, this time from those of the staff in the front of the chapel, given the afternoon off for this farewell.

Not as heart-felt or self-congratulatory as the other ones, but definite, all the same.

– Always the Boss. Always Madam Bea to the girls, and the girls always Miss to her. Never any doubt that she had money in the firm, and they only put their time in. No mistaking that she was the Bea in the House of Bea, and will still be there in the New House of Bea.

He searched for more, wanting to pin down that elusive, that very Bea quality he wanted to share with all here who'd known her. To hate her, or admire her.

– One of the old school. First there in the morning, and last to leave at night. And always dressed in a way that said—give me respect. I respect you, for what you are, whatever that is. So respect me, too. I don't pretend we are the same. There is a gap. I will not cross it, I will not let you cross it either. Not in my time, on my shop floor. British made, was Bea. Never the bully, but always the Boss.

Which she was. And unmistakable in the part she'd carved for herself. Unmistakable, searching through seconds on market stalls, looking out for what was selling and what wasn't selling out there on the street. Unmistakable pumping the buyers among them full of their own particular poison for some clue as to what they were looking for, for the season after the season after next. Unmistakable Bea bending the dyer's ear because a batch was off colour by the faintest shading.

Sharp, and busy, and looking for an angle, but never mean or cruel, and always the Boss.

And beautiful.

To him, beautiful.

And he missed her.

And after the song played, as they filed out after their last respects, he was asking them back to the factory. Not for himself. But because she had asked to see them one last time.

And he sat by himself, as Sarah Vaughan and Billy Eckstine sang 'Passing Strangers' to the line of backs filing into the sharp and blue skyed morning.

When he could decently do so, he excused himself from the party, which was every bit as vulgar, glitzy and successful a thrash as Bea had known it would be. You could never supply too much free food and booze to a crowd of fashion people. Or find a reason for throwing a party that they'd find too vulgar.

It was a wow and a hit and a smash, and the pity was that you could hardly say to your host – Let's do this again sometime.

Hector decided to party-poop shortly after the first glass was dropped, and it was plain that the order book was filling fast. The New House of Bea was well and truly launched on a tide of malt scotch and pink champagne. Plus a lot of leg, from the girls of the model agency Connie had hired to drape around the walls and the more influential of the male guests.

He paused for a moment in the yard jammed with Rollers and Mercs and the classier sort of Jag. He said his goodbye in his heart and, dues paid, headed back to Lisa. It had all fallen in place. He grieved for Bea, but her timing was spot on. He'd meet his girl now with no fake mourning bands showing. Bea was one for the library shelves, his future was with Lisa. That slim-hipped girl who was proving so hungry for the better things. In the sheets, and outside them.

No more reserve or deception between them. A new cleanness about their relationship. Nothing underhanded, or stained.

But when he walked through the door of the flat, carrying the red roses he'd swapped for the lilies, she was packed and ready to go.

– Sorry. The word seemed even smaller and more useless than usual, as she faced him. Bags full, wardrobe and drawers emptied. – I was going to leave a note. Don't read this wrong. It's not another fella. It's a job. I'm going to be mixing with different people, so I need somewhere nice to take them back to. Not just to screw. It's that sort of job.

He fought his breath into his throat. This couldn't be happening. The timing was too cruel.

– You've got a place of your own here.

– It's not the same.

– Because the old fool, the daft old sod who set you up might walk in any minute?

She closed her eyes, as if in pain. She hadn't wanted it to be like this. Knew how much it was going to hurt him. Tried not to be around to see that hurt.

– It would have been easier if I could just have left a note.

– In that handwriting of yours? That educationally subnormal handwriting that's all you had to show for six years at the local comprehensive?

This wasn't going to get him anywhere, he knew. In the morning hours when he'd thought how he would handle the moment when she did walk out on him, he'd promised himself it wasn't going to be like this. He'd let her go with dignity. Not play the old sod going down with desperation.

– There are things you have to let go of, you told me that. She kept her patience. – I'm going to be mixing with different people. So some of the ones I've known before have got to go.

– You can't afford me? I'm too cheap, too old? Is it because I'm too old? There must be another fella. Some stud with ten thick inches and pills like cricket balls?

– No. She was hurt again, and showed it. Hurt for herself, but also hurt for him. In her morning hours, when she'd known the day would come when she'd move on from the guy who had given her the chance to break free, she hadn't wanted to have to plug him like this between the eyes. Or legs. It was the job. Didn't he see that? She'd been offered a job that would give her a chance to make the break final. Because she knew, as Hector never could, how steep was the slope she was only just starting to climb. And how jagged the rocks were at the bottom if she ever now lost her grip.

How could Hector know her terror at having to go back down those council streets he'd pulled her out of? She could guess what her life would be like if she lost her nerve now. If Hector ever tired of her, as his legendary track record so very strongly suggested, she would end up imprisoned in one of those tower blocks that fringed the town. Married to a guy called Eric; in the club after their three-day honeymoon in Skeggy; breeding more little Erics every eighteen months on the dot until her womb caved in; bent over the same machine down there on the floor, in pink acrylic, with a fag in her gob and a spreading backside. With only the memory of the girl she'd been, and the chance her good legs and better shoulders had given her.

She was walking. Hector was getting bounced, and she couldn't tell him what the job was that would turn the next key in the door for her. Sworn to secrecy. Given her word.

– As a tart and a whore and a little bitch who owes me everything, even the high heels she's walking out on me in? The word of that?

She might have cried, being shouted at like that if she'd been the Lisa she was before. This new Lisa didn't cry. Took it on that lovely chin, and held his gaze.

– I love you. Doesn't that make a difference?

It didn't. And he knew it was time to stop protesting. He'd do anything to make her stay, if there was a chance she might. But he knew the girl well enough by now to know that level gaze meant she had clamped tight on her decision. Never had he wanted her more. Never had he so needed that body and that company. He considered pushing her into the bedroom, and taking her. Making another corny old male move, to go with all the others he'd pulled since finding her stood there, bags packed. You never think you'll handle it that way yourself. You always think you'll be different, and carry it off with a Gallic shrug. But always, he knew with angry finality, you made that old fool of yourself.

– Take the job. Clear off. I'll keep the flat on, if you ever need a place again.

– It's finished. Her turn to reach for the corny, the well-used. But at a time like this, you had to use the words men and women had found for these moments going back to the first couple ever to have a bust-up and a falling-out.

A rebel part of her said screw him now. Push him into the bedroom, and give him something to remember you by. Because she too ached in a sudden way for that now familiar, expert body. No matter that he was that much older. He'd been hers, and she'd been his and she did owe. But she feared he would misread even such a final slicing of the knot. See it as a weakness. Her foot and toehold slipping on that smooth rock face, she was now determined to make her way to the top of.

– I've got a job waiting. And a taxi, to pick up my gear. I shan't need the place again.

She moved to the door, and nearly got it in the face. Connie apologised, out of breath from taking the stairs two at a time to collect her. Because Connie looked after her investments. If she hadn't taken care of them so well, Hector might have had no idea.

Connie realised something was wrong, in Lisa's face. Turning around, she saw Hector stood, a moment away from the realisation that his own daughter had somehow, incomprehensibly, unbelievably been behind this betrayal, and leant back against the door, winded.

There was only one word for such a moment's misfortune.

– Shit.

So Hector went into his weeks of hibernation, or shell-shock, or whatever it should have been called. Pulled the door closed on Connie and Lisa, and the rest of the world. The big world, and the small world of the New House of Bea. Mourned for Bea, and mourned for what could have been between himself and Lisa. Missed the larger and the smaller events of the next month, which decided so many of their futures.

Missed, for one, the endless squabbles about what right Nesta had, in advance of the legal handover of power and money, to sit in on Board meetings, and poke her nose into the day to day running of the firm.

Missed the row about who was going to sit in the place Bea had sat (a win for Connie) and the row about the colour ranges for next season (a win for Nesta).

Sat in his room, always with a growth of beard showing, and let the business, and the lives of those involved in it, run on without him.

Missed what should have been the biggest triumph for Connie yet, the news that Crawder had railroaded the planning permissions through, and there was now no stopping them.

– You did it. Jamieson clinked crystal against crystal and sipped. There were a lot of champagne empties stacked up in the yard of the House of Bea these days. It was almost the firm's tipple, the champagne break taking the place of the tea break.

I did it, Connie echoed, waiting for the sense of triumph that should have come with the words. But didn't.

– Celebration? Jamieson suggested. – Candlelight glittering on silver and gold somewhere? A weekend in Paris, without having to check out a collection?

She moved her head. Puzzled. And he noted her lack of enthusiasm, alarmed. Was there something she was keeping back? Perhaps it wasn't the final okay?

– It's final, all right. As final as the fact Crawder's screwing Lisa until his eyes pop, by all accounts.

What was wrong was inside her. She felt she had unwrapped the Christmas paper, only to find a great big ball of nothing inside.

– That's Connie for you.

Hector wasn't used to visitors, in his self-imposed retirement. Wasn't interested, any more. Which explained the fact he hadn't tidied up the litter in the flat, which had so shocked Jamieson when he arrived. He'd been expecting something less than the usual chipper Hector who ran up clothes bills to rival many a woman's. But the unshaven, blinking reality, with stained shirt, and nails to match the griminess of his cuffs, took him aback.

He'd come to pass on the good news about the planning permission okay, and to see if Hector had any thoughts on what builders to use. It had soon been plain that Hector only wanted to dwell on the grudges he had against the world in general, and his two daughters in particular.

Jamieson had edged the subject away from that, on to how Connie was missing her dad's friendly advice in the office, and then on to a more personal matter. Why was she going round like a spring had broken inside? He hadn't meant to bare his soul to the old man, but he found himself talking on. Into areas that were more personal than business. Except that, in this world, the two cut across and interfered with each other at every turn.

– That's Connie all over. The wet red eye held Jamieson fast. – That's why you ought to cover your backside.

All her life Connie had been a wrecker. Look what she'd done to her own dad. What drove her, and this was her father speaking who should know if anyone did, was the desire to smash up the happy home. Look at her track record. She'd had a great marriage going with Arnie, but she walked away from him to concentrate on the boutique business. Marriage smash. No sooner had she lost him than she let the business go. Business smash. She'd shacked up with the Greek, only to walk out on him, when all he'd done was play around with a couple of young girls. Love smash. Now she was back, and had got the knitwear business at her feet, she would find a way to wreck things for herself in that, too. Commercial and personal smash. And who would be part of the pile-up? Jamieson.

– Cover your backside, Hector advised, sucking teeth that hadn't seen a brush for days. – You've dumped your wife and your job for her. If she gets out of the business and clears off back to the Med,

C.—11

how long do you think Nesta will let you stay on there? And then what do you do?

– You think she might do that? Jamieson rotated the teacup, trying to find a clean corner to sip from. She might throw everything over?

The proof wasn't there already? asked Hector. Hadn't she told him, in so many words, it wasn't the having which drove her, so much as the getting?

– Find yourself a back way out. Hector watched him gingerly press his lips to the dirty cup of lukewarm tea. – You need a job. Like somebody else knew she needed one.

Jamieson didn't get much more after that, for Hector turned his eye in on himself and his own woes again, and let Jamieson see himself out, and back to his own affairs.

A back way out. An escape chute, should Connie not snap out of it. Up to now he'd been ready to put off a decision, put Connie's behaviour down to a natural after-reaction to what had taken place since she'd got back. The fight to get into the business, in the first place, the even tougher fight to stay there once she was in. The little wars, and the big decisions. Most hurtfully of all, the death of Bea, and the shaking-up of the boardroom.

He'd assumed Connie was going to come off the ropes, ready to mix it with Nesta and the rest of the world in a few days, or weeks. He'd been prepared to give her the benefit of the doubt for a month or two. But if she was never going to come off the ropes, except to slip out from under them one day he wasn't looking . . .? If she would do what she had so plainly done so often in the past, and give in to that sudden urge to run . . .? Where was he, in that situation? Bejasused, screwed and fucked, was the answer. And an ex-forty-thousand-pounds-a-year man couldn't be expected to take that lying down.

He worked out a c.v. one afternoon, when things were slack, and he was left alone in the office, surrounded by the tidy files, and the humming hardware of the computerised accounting system. The system of his invention that was still being debugged, but which was weekly making him more and more just a book-keeper.

There was no ulterior motive to his writing up his career details. No intention of posting it off. He was curious to see how it read, what it would add up to, in an employer's eyes. And it didn't look too bad, when it was finished and neatly typed.

His business school qualification led neatly to his work with Kellard Bower and Comer, and his rise to the potential number two slot. And his mid-career break into a fashion house could be written up in such a way that it looked deliberate. A serious career person's decision to see small business in practice, to flex the entrepreneurial wings in a world he had no background in.

Having typed up such a document, it seemed careless to leave it in the drawer, where it could be found by someone who might get the wrong idea. And maybe he was fooling himself that it looked as good as he thought? Maybe it wouldn't hold an employer's attention for one moment?

The only way to test that was to pass it round a few—not, be it severely understood, because he was taking Hector's advice and looking for a job. But because he wanted to prove he still could get one, if things did turn sour in the New House of Bea.

He sent a copy off to each of the six most important firms of executive head-hunters, and put out of his mind that he'd done it. After all, it wasn't as if he expected any job application forms to come winging their way back by next post. An acknowledgement, and a bland note that they would keep his details for future reference: that was all he expected. All he wanted, in fact.

The new accounting and stock control system started getting even more glitched up, in the next few days, as successive parts came on stream, so he genuinely gave no thought to the bread he'd cast on the waters. Didn't rush to open the first of the envelopes in reply. Hardly bothered to re-read that one, and the four that quickly followed, thanking him for his interest, and saying they would keep his details on file.

And certainly never felt low at the implications that this was an overcrowded job market already, and no one was scanning the horizon eagerly, waiting for him to turn up.

The sixth reply was pay-dirt. They were interested. They had a client who was in the market for someone with his particular skills and background. Could he name a week he'd be in London for a preliminary chat?

He wouldn't go, of course. It was enough that they were interested. That is, he wouldn't go with the intention of saying yes. Having got the interview, it would be churlish to refuse to attend. Cowardly, too. Indicating he still had doubts that he could take the big world on again.

He'd go to the interview, without telling Connie, and talk his way into the offer of a job. Then come back, compose his rejection of it, and sit back knowing he was still worth hiring. Still without telling Connie. But having assured himself there was a back way out, as Hector recommended, if she cut and ran.

So he didn't tell Connie. But the word processor did.

– Damn this machine, Connie had sworn, punching the keyboard for the tenth time, in an attempt to get it to show the current stock situation on the yarn. For the tenth time it didn't push that material on to the screen, but it did flash up something else. The letter of application which Jamieson had typed up and forgotten to wipe.

If Connie had the sudden sharp smell of betrayal in her nose, Dev was twitching his, ever now on the lookout for it. Nesta had sworn to get him out of the Sales job he had so securely got a hold of, and was running with Arnie now, who also had a grudge against him.

As Connie watched Jamieson, and waited for his move, Dev watched Nesta. He was wise to do so.

– You owe him, too, urged Nesta, for the twentieth time. – He threw that calendar in your face.

– I didn't sign up for a Holy War as your Number Two, Arnie replied as always. It was her gut that was griping, not his. Arnie had so many people put stripes in him that it had long since ceased to hurt.

But what did hurt was her constant nagging. One day he knew he would snap under that, and do something about Dev, if only to shut her up. For the moment he was content to enjoy the benefits of being the latest in the line of Nesta's kept men. While keeping one lazy eye half open, looking for a way to put that stripe into Dev, when the day came, with minimum risk to himself.

All of which Dev guessed, knowing the family better than any outsider ever had. Making sure he did his six days a week, and more, with total dedication, flair, and, most unusual for him—honesty too. There was no way he could be fired on business grounds, and he would make sure no personal or sexual involvement gave the ugly sister and her fancy man the loophole they'd be looking for.

Which made it all the tougher that when he was framed, it was Connie who found him with the smoking gun in his hand. The woman who'd given him the chance. The woman he'd been determined to convince that he could go straight.

Twenty-one

– I wouldn't say this place is a mess, dad, but you feel you want to wipe your feet before going on to the pavement again.

She tried the gag, but didn't get a twitch of a response from the thin lips, the sunken eyes glowering out from that unhealthy, pallid skin. Hector was looking like something left out for the dustmen, something they'd probably throw back.

– You'd get talked about on personal hygiene grounds in a camel-drivers' brothel, she tried again. The frontal approach, with gag. Hoping to jar him out of that hand-dog sullenness.

Nothing. Hector's defences against the outside world were complete. Day by day he had sunk deeper and deeper into a depression that now threatened to get clinical. Connie was calling every couple of days, with a change of clothing, and the offer of a shave. He wasn't taking.

Bad enough to have Jamieson up to something behind her back without Hector doing an impression of a late-night documentary about the lower depths. Those grainy black and white films that won awards at Yugoslavian festivals.

She was getting worried. The time wasn't far off when someone was going to have to take some tough decisions. Like whether or not to get a doctor to see her father. And not an ear-nose-and-throat man, either. A trick cyclist was very definitely on the cards, and she didn't want the expense of that, any more than the stigma.

Was it Bea? Had that been the trigger more than the leaving of Lisa, who was now at the stage of being moved into a large apartment of her own, and being recognised officially as Number One Girl?

She accepted that it wasn't. Bea's death had affected her more than anyone else including him. Even more than Nesta, she would guess. And that wasn't just because it had come at a time when Connie was about to crest the wave she'd been whipping up for herself ever since her return.

Hector's trouble had to be put down to it being a love-job. And for that, there was no cure except time. And, if Hector refused to let the Great Healer fix things for him, then maybe twenty thousand volts in the side of the head, at a discreet clinic somewhere.

Came a ring at the bell, just when she was deciding that was enough Flo Nightingale for one day. Hector made for the door first, but hung back before he got there. Those feet on the treads weren't Lisa's. When the door swung open it was Jamieson stood there.

– Had to see you, he took the room in at a glance. Things hadn't got any better since his visit. He was talking to Connie, and if he had anything to say to Hector would have had to say it through the slammed-shut bedroom door.

He was off to London. Straight away.

– The job offer?

He took that in his stride. So many people in this business seemed to subscribe to spy-in-the-sky satellite intelligence services. They knew what hand you were going to lift before you thought your brain had shaped the impulses.

– The job offer, he agreed.

– The one you went for behind my back?

He checked the bedroom door, and dropped his voice. Explained, reasonable and patient, what he'd been up to. That at each step along the way he'd wondered if he should tell her. That he'd put that moment off, egging himself on to the next part of the challenge. One thing he'd found he couldn't do. Go to the job interview without coming clean.

She was relieved, but tried hard not to show it.

– You didn't trust me?

– It wasn't that, he insisted, and it really wasn't. It was just that for the moment he wanted to live some time on his own account. Not cut her out, but withdraw. Prove that he could make it on his own, if ever he had to again.

– Prove I haven't cut your balls off?

Jamieson sighed, and checked the time. The business day was going to be fraught enough, without a full-scale up-and-downer with Connie, whose temper hadn't been improved by her visit to her father's squalid den.

– Sorry, Connie apologised. – But I've been waiting for you to explain about that letter. Tell me about the job.

He told her on the way down the stairs, after she'd made sure that Hector hadn't cut his throat and was dribbling his life's blood away on the bed. Which was another nagger of a possibility they all had to live with, now he'd turned recluse.

– It's not a job offer, just the shot at an interview.

He explained how the head-hunting system worked, at his executive level. Someone out there was looking for management talent with his particular blend of experiences. The client wasn't allowed to know his name, which was kept separate from his c.v., retyped by the firm themselves. That way embarrassment to the itchy exec was minimised, and it also meant that sly employers couldn't con their senior staff into giving their career game-plans and dissatisfactions away.

He didn't know who he was going to meet this afternoon, in the plush offices, near the sweaty, packed square mile of the city. There was no guarantee he'd get over the hurdle of the interview. And if he didn't do that, the client would be informed that they'd had a wasted journey to town.

– The client will be there? Even though there's no guarantee you'll be good enough?

He nodded. The client was in a hurry and had business in town that day anyway, which was why the appointment had been rushed through. It should have been a week later. By which time he would surely have told her all.

– So you're taking your bags with you? In case you get offered? You'll be walking out straight away?

He sighed, and checked his watch again. This busy bus route was no place to have this sort of talk. Much better if he'd levelled in bed one night, or defused the danger of his misunderstanding over breakfast.

– I'm not taking the job, even if they offer it.

He thought he'd made that plain.

He had, said Connie, but he had to be working to a different definition of the words than she'd come up against, until then.

The row was short, sharp, and nasty. He went off for his train with bile in his throat, knowing he'd mishandled things from that first poisonous meeting with Hector. She feeling she ought to be relieved that things were out in the open, but annoyed that her cowardice had stopped her clearing it up sooner.

You had to see his point of view, after all. Anger had so much given way to relief and regret by the time she got back to the factory, that she could admit that. What she ought to do was get the next train to London, and cheer her man on. If she arranged for the afternoon's meeting with the architect to be moved to later in the week, she could get to the firm, whose address she could get from Yellow Pages at King's Cross, in time to send him into the meeting with her blessing. Or at the very least, give him a big smacking, congratulatory kiss, when he came out.

For he'd get the job. There was no doubt about that. She was an old hand at spotting two-legged talent herself. And Jamieson was at his best in those boardroom one-to-ones.

Dev was in the yard, kicking the tyres of his estate car, in frustration. He was due out on his weekly sweep, but the innate malice of the internal combustion engine had done for him. The back was loaded with a dozen boxes of samples, all ticketed and marked, and it looked like he was stuck until the garage could send someone round.

– Bloody thing. About as useless as that stock control computer.

He kicked a tyre again, risking terminal shock to his lizard skin shoes. Although the breakdown wasn't his fault, it was just the sort of incident Nesta could use against him. Right now it was plainly not his fault that the selling side was well and truly stalled for a couple of hours, or maybe twenty-four. But days after, a clever way of presenting the facts at a board meeting could suggest he made a mountain out of something much less than that, and was malingering the sales graph line into the floor.

– Take my car. Connie had the obvious solution. She could get a cab to the station. Who knew? She could talk Jamieson into staying in London for the night. They could see a show, have that expensive meal, mend fences across crisp white sheets in a four-star hotel, with a view of the park or the river. Get to know each other again, without that sniff of suspicion.

She'd even help Dev shift the boxes into her boot. When that was jammed full, there should be room for the rest in the back, and in the spare seat in front. This would be one trip where Dev couldn't pick up any little mysteries, to demonstrate the remarkable tilting mechanism of the near-side seat.

– Perish the thought with Nesta breathing down my neck, Dev grinned, opening the big rear door for the transfer. – I do my trip, make my pitch, then it's back to my modest hotel room with a quiet book and my travelling iron.

Connie took the sheet off the dash, ready to count the boxes in. As they piled them into every possible space they chatted like old friends, rather than old lovers. There was something very pleasing in being come to rest, after that storm of passion. Desire had gone, but still left a warmness that maybe no other relationship but the sexual one could give quite so richly.

They talked about the new lines, and about Nesta's growing influence in the boardroom, and Connie's determination to stick at her promises to Bea (that presence again), and had the boxes shifted, and tallied off before they knew.

One box left.

Connie frowned and checked the manifest. All accounted for. She looked at Dev, who looked at the box, and then back at her.

In that moment Dev lost his job, and Connie whatever remaining faith she had in people's decency.

Jamieson had a good steak on the train, and made sure it was well digested. A rumbling stomach isn't a good interview technique. Likewise, he limited himself to two coffees after the meal. You didn't want to give the impression that you were a urinary tract problem, even if you were just going to the interview for the hell of it.

It was in his mind to phone Connie, and ask her to come and spend the night in London with him, letting the business go hang for once. He promised he'd do that after the interview, if all worked out right. If they offered him the job, which he was going to turn down as politely as he could, once he'd got it.

He wouldn't even see the client. Just to make sure he didn't commit himself across a legal line, he'd make an excuse, and ask to be given time to make his mind up. They couldn't fail but be impressed by that. Over-eagerness could be a crippler in a sharp career plan. You had to know when to lower the temperature, when to be the first person to break off the smile and the small talk, and suggest you ran your own life as toughly as you ran whatever business would be lucky enough to get you.

No seeing the client.

He was only proving he was good enough to be *asked* to see the client.

– A franchise operation. The chief head-hunter, in his tribal pinstripe, Harvie and Hudson bengal stripe shirt and bookbinder finish brogues, got crisply to the point.

– Our client is a retail fashion house, which is looking for expansion. They have a manufacturing arm, and a proven track record. Franchising is a way for them to grow, without getting buried by the banks, or trying to get a public quotation.

The principle of franchising in its business format was quite straightforward. Jamieson, being an ear-to-the-ground exec, would probably know the outlines. Pinstripe would run through them, if only to give a chance for the head-hunters' witch doctor, with his psychology degrees, to eyeball him as he listened.

– Our client will offer a way into retail fashion for prospective franchisees who don't have enough capital or experience to start from scratch. They'll be offered a chance to kick off as big or little a business as they think they can hack. Our client supplies all the stock, gets them a deal on all fittings and advertising materials, advises on planning and property matters, and helps with a publicity launch. They sell our client's line of fashion either in complete High St. shop units of their own, or as concessionaires of a larger store.

Jamieson was familiar with the storyboard being outlined to him. He'd been aware that there had been an increasing trend in small business towards the franchising concept. Some years back it had got badly tainted by the pyramid-selling scams, but the reputable firms were now in an ethical organisation, and anxious to clean up the image.

There would still be sharks in the water, but he assumed this respectable firm wouldn't have got involved in the search for people like himself, if there was anything bent in the deal.

One thing puzzled him. Why had he been chosen to get this far? He'd never worked in a franchise operation before.

– It's a growing market, there aren't enough experienced pros to go round, Pinstripe explained. And had Junior Pinstripe at the far end of the table, who hadn't said a word up to now, take up the storyline.

– You've got a first class business background, in finance and efficiency. Recently you've been working in the manufacturing side of knitwear, and with some success. You've got the virtues of still being fresh, but with a track record behind you. Our client liked the profile.

– And what would my profile be doing, and at what salary or financial participation level? Jamieson asked. Adding, faintly, to himself, that this was only a hypothetical question, because he wasn't after the job.

– You'd be chief executive, in charge of the franchise launch, and thereafter heading-up the on-going development. You'd have complete say as to how to get the thing off the ground, and thereafter as to how to keep the momentum going. Subject only to agreement on the overall approach with the client. Who has said they're prepared to give whoever gets the job the freedom they need to prove themselves in it.

This sounded good. This sounded, in fact, the sort of job that cropped up every ten years in your career, if then. A keen exec, just rounding the dangerous forties, could establish himself for good, if he made a success of it.

Jamieson, again the forty-thousand-a-year man, who plotted his career once week by week on a wall-chart, ran it through. Get the business on its feet in a year, allow two years to prove he'd got the right formula, make a bid for some sort of equity participation, so that he was talking capital appreciation now and not just salary, and walk out if that wasn't forthcoming. Walk out with solid track record and career points, into management at senior exec, and junior board room level.

And it was exactly the sort of thing his particular combination of talents and qualities and appetites were suited to.

Such a pity he was only playing at this interview. Such a shame that he wouldn't even be prepared to meet the waiting client, should he get the offer . . .

Connie sat up late. Waiting for the London train. Somehow she hadn't the energy to take the train herself. It wasn't that the scene with Dev had taken so much out of her, in itself. He'd denied he'd been flogging stuff for other houses, lining his own pocket, using the New House of Bea as cover. She'd pointed, mutely at the evidence. He'd sworn this had to be a fit-up by Arnie, working for Nesta. She'd looked tired and sad, and indicated where the door to the yard was, out of which she expected him to walk. In those elegant, slight shoes.

What sapped her strength was the fact of the betrayal. That here was Dev, who had everything to gain by playing it straight and fair with her, getting up to a cheap and easily-rumbled stunt like that. Across her. Of all people. The person who'd brought him into the firm, in the teeth of all opposition, and kept him there until he started proving he could hack it.

Now this. He'd thrown it all over for a twopenny-halfpenny scam, that wouldn't have made him as much as he could fiddle in the normal course of events on his petrol money. She'd read another fella wrong, just as she'd read Jamieson wrong. And that could be the first sign that her touch had gone for good. Because selling fashion takes knowing people.

She sat late, waiting for her man. Knowing he'd come back to the factory when he got off the train, because she had business on. The endless paper and pocket calculator work with the rogues who'd been tendered to build the thing, now that she'd disposed of the rogues who had made the building possible.

When he showed, it was with Nesta.

Nesta who hung in the background, pretending to look over some figures pinned to the corkboard. Despite the tide of computerisation and word processing, it was still only possible to keep up to date with the state of play by using caveman technology, and writing things in very large letters, on the walls.

– Did it go well?

He nodded.

– Thanks for bringing Nesta in, but I've already eaten supper.

He smiled quickly, and looked at Nesta, and then back at her.

– We shared a train. That is, we came down on the same Inter-City. Or up, or sideways, or whatever the direction was.

She nodded. How very cosy that must have been for both of them. But she always understood that British Rail made her step-sister travel first class. Even better than first class. In the guard's van, behind the wire mesh.

Nesta acknowledged the gag, and moved a little closer. Connie was intrigued. Could this day hold any more surprises?

– Don't tell me you two have been having it off all this time? That really would make my day, following on having to fire that little rat Dev.

She watched sharply, for any reaction from Nesta. Nesta who had so conveniently been in London today, so couldn't have planted Dev, as Dev had claimed. Arnie could have done it, of course. But she didn't like to think of the implication that Nesta had Arnie so well wrapped-up now that he'd stoop to something like that.

Nesta didn't twitch. Either her hands were clean of a frame-up, or there was something else going on that took mental precedence just now.

– You shared a train? That all?

– Nesta was in London, too, Jamieson offered.

– Auditioning for the London Dungeon? Again? How many times do they have to tell you you'd scare off the curators, let alone the kids.

All light banter. All good sisterly to-and-fro. Nothing that broke her promise to Bea at least to make the effort to get on with her step-sister.

– Not just in London. In the city. More than that. In the same office block I went for the interview in. Nesta's been the client whose job I've been trying for.

Only he hadn't been trying. Not really trying for the job. This had to be kept straight. He'd sworn to it and protested it before, but that had to be kept in sight. He'd only agreed to see the client because, after all, the client had taken the trouble to go along that day, expecting to okay the appointment, if the interview panel had okayed Jamieson himself.

Which they had.

But he'd not known it was Nesta the other side of the door. No more than she had known it was him.

– Lying bitch, was the first thing it came to mind for Connie to call her. – You've been working on this from the day you set eyes on my fella.

Nesta wrinkled her nose.

– I'm not here for a fight. I just want to know what we're going to do about this.

– Do about it? Connie was puzzled. – You've been scheming to get my fella, and you ask me what I'm going to do about it? I'm going to fight for him. What the hell else am I going to do about it?

Nesta kept her temper. She had sort of guessed this was going to be difficult.

– Get it straight from the top: I have not been trying to poach him off you.

– Liar, snorted Connie, raring for the fight.

– I'm not lying. Nesta fought down her temper again. It would be easy to walk out now, and break all negotiations off, but she had a pitch to make. One on which a lot depended.

Jamieson came to her aid. He'd had an edgy day, only that steak to eat hours back, and he genuinely believed that Nesta had been as surprised as him that he'd walked through the door. Connie was being unreasonable. Granted, she might have had a tough day with Dev, and every cause to be unreasonable, but it could get on his nerves.

– It makes sense. What Nesta is suggesting makes sense. I've seen the figures.

Connie was lost again. She didn't know about the franchise. They had to talk her through it, as she sat mutinous, but quiet. And she would have been the first to admit it made a lot of sense, if the personal factors hadn't kept getting in the way.

Nesta had had a stroke of near genius. She had seen that even the relaunched New House of Bea would still be a tiddler—if business conditions didn't change while the rebuilding was taking place, making the commercial logic of the expansion less secure anyway.

Now they had a manufacturing and a retail interest, with her shops, they could get outside punters to finance their expansion. The punter would be able to scratch that itch of getting into business on his or her own account, at different levels of investment—and the New House of Bea would grow as fast as it recruited the punters. Who would get all their start-up stock from them, be bound to buy in-house by legal contract, and pay over a percentage on the gross.

– The gross, Nesta pointed out, impatient. – Think of that. Not ten percent after sales, tax and financing. On the nose. Out of the till, even before the buggers have started paying anyone else their wages, or sorting out their loan charges.

Connie liked the sound of that. Through her personal grievance against this sudden, unlikely, suggested collaboration, the word gross rang like a clean trumpet note. Such a nice word, when you were on the right side of the ledger with it. Such a satisfactory word, a word you liked rolling in your mouth, and hissing the promise of the ending of.

There was a word to set against that.

– Loyalty.

Jamieson's loyalty to her. Her loyalty to the memory of Bea.

– No problems. No contradictions, both Nesta and Jamieson jostled to answer that one.

Jamieson's very success in the office was making him redundant. The New House of Bea owed him some loyalty for all his hard work—what better way to repay it than by setting him to work even harder in organising the franchise operation? And so for the memory of Bea—what better way to serve that ghostly black presence than by seizing this chance to really put the firm on the map?

– It's sure-fire, Jamieson assured her. He'd seen the figures. He'd checked the trading projections. If Connie came in with him and Nesta, Bea could rest in peace, knowing the firm was on the up. On a scale that she could only have dreamt of.

– I can only see one reason why you won't come in with us, Nesta said, sly. – Because you hadn't dreamt it up yourself in the first place.

– Us? she came back sharply, eyes on Jamieson. – It's definite? You'll go in, even if I say no?

He opened his mouth and closed it. Did the impression of an expiring goldfish two more times, and finally went and stood looking down at the yard, shadowed and grim.

– I need the job. I need the challenge.

Then he said it. The phrase she'd thrown at him and apologised for. The phrase that had been rattling around all that day, as he got nearer and nearer the moment of decision, as to whether he was just playing at job hunting, or serious.

– I need to prove to myself you haven't cut my balls off.

Connie asked for time. This was a toughie. This was a possible fracture point, where the personal and the business both vectored in.

There were business reasons for saying yes to the deal. Nesta had come up with something that made commercial sense, and which also gave her something to get her teeth into, while the grinding out of the rebuilding details took place. It made personal sense, in that she had promised Bea she would do her best to hack along with Nesta. Who knew, but the excitement of a new business launch might not bring them close together again? The way it had been, when she'd brought her step-sister in as her number two, only to be filleted by her.

This time she'd be coming in as the Number Two, because it was Nesta who had the shops, in addition to her share of the manufacturing arm. Who knew, again, but this time there might not be a neat reversal possible? That she could find a way to screw Nesta out of shops, and the New House of Bea, and her split of the franchise operation?

A tall order, but it was ambition on that scale which attracted Connie. This was something worth being fucked-up by Georgiou for. For nothing less than this was her return worthwhile.

That wasn't just her own opinion. It was Borridge's too.

The blind man had taken on something of the role of a father confessor to her, which was convenient in the continuing absence of her father himself. Borridge padded across with her cup of tea, not spilling a drop, and gave his considered opinion. Connie was looking for something bigger than that back street factory slum. That accounted for her dissatisfaction, and for her feeling of emptiness when the news about Crawder's final assent to the planning scam came through.

– When you heard that, you realised inside you were stuck with having to build the bloody thing. Those endless rows with the architects and the builders. And after it, the endless grind of working in it for year after year. Turning yourself into another Bea.

Connie made to protest, then realised he had again put his finger on the part that hurt, and pressed in his nail. Yes, she was still knocked sideways by the older woman's death. A person who had been more than her real mother to her, because Connie had blotted out all thinking of her real mother. But not because her memory of Bea was unadulterated worship. There were things in Bea she wouldn't want to copy—and one of them was being stuck down those mean red-brick streets until her looks went, starting with her skin and hair.

That factory had been a sort of living death for Bea for too many years. Connie wasn't going to have that happen to her.

Was she?

Borridge posed the question.

Was she just another small businesswoman, one of those hard-working high-heeled women, who would forever be busy in the same small circles? Or did she really have what he had suspected was in her, the day she had walked into his office, ready to take on the world?

– Count me in. Connie made the call short. No point dwelling on the fact that she had been out-talked. – But take warning. We're going into this bare-arsed, intending to make a million out of the punters out there.

– She's in? Arnie didn't have to ask. He knew from the look on Nesta's face that she'd got the result.

– She's in, as solid as Dev is out, Nesta nodded, and rolled back across the bed to him. She slid down him, hands and mouth working. As he stretched, eyes closed, ready to do battle with her triumphant malice, to best her body for the third and final time that evening, she asked him a favour. More than the ones he was being cajoled into doing her already.

– Tell me how you fixed Dev again. And tell it slow.

Twenty-two

Dev had been a big fan of Hector's. Recognised many of his own qualities in the older man. Admired his hell-for-leather style with life, cars and women. So what if he risked being made to look a fool, carrying on the way he did at his age? What counted was that he hadn't let the bastards grind him down, in a long and colourful and scandalous career. If Dev was still toppling the birds at his age, he'd be more than thankful.

So Dev took it almost harder than anyone, when he learned that Hector had slammed the door on the world. Especially when he heard the whisper that it was all to do with a woman. His own dismissal from the firm had eaten into much of his interest and time, but when he got unscrambled, paid him a call.

True, he hoped against hope that the senior board member would believe that he hadn't been doing a foreigner on the New House of Bea's time and money. But he was realistic to guess that the power in the firm lay securely with Nesta now, and Hector would be unlikely to risk a knock-down and drag-out fight with her.

Mainly this would be a social visit. One young rogue dropping in on an old one, for old time's sake. Risking a peep ahead into the future, to see what lay in store, perhaps for himself.

Things were stirring in Hector's mind, too. An idea that self-pity was all right, in its way, but it did get pretty boring after a while. A self-awareness that if he didn't pull out of this nose-dive pretty soon, he might never be able to get a firm enough grip on the rudder, ever, and that would be a pity. Because there were plenty more screwable women and girls out there. And though he would never find what he had with Bea and Lisa in any combination, the fun would be in the trying to.

Wouldn't Bea have wanted it that way? He'd paid her back every penny for his serial betrayals of her, in his exile in Lisa's flat. Wouldn't she now want to cheer him on, as he started biting chunks out of the world and female flesh again?

And he never felt right, unshaven. He'd always been one of those men whose day has to start with the scrape of steel on skin.

He started off with the razor, then put on his clothes in order, attacked the inner man by eating regularly and properly for the first time since he'd slammed the door behind him, topped it all off with three new suits and a blow-wave, and felt ready to face the world.

But needed a challenge. A final shove or kick to send him out of the door, and down the steps, feeling that there was a job of work waiting for him. And the nearer it came to sorting out the personal as well as the business, the more good it would do him.

Dev supplied it, with one word.

– Franchise.

Hector frowned. Franchise was something you came across in catering, or petrol. It certainly wasn't any way to build a fashion chain.

– I've got eyes and ears in the firm. Dev offered, thinking of the interlocker he was seeing on a trial basis, view sex. She wasn't a looker, but she was a gossiper. – The three of them are spending more time on getting the franchise operation off the ground than fixing the rebuilding.

That was an exaggeration, because Connie was splitting her work day evenly between the two. But the sense was true, in that, as ever, the newer of the prospects was the one that most fired her.

– Franchise is a con, Hector protested. – It's pyramid selling.

Dev explained the safeguards now in operation since the time when so many people had lost so much money in the pyramid scams. The franchise deal that Jamieson was devising was above board. True, sheer enthusiasm for the deal might perhaps lead them to sell it a little too heavily, but that could hardly be called fraud, could it?

Hector wasn't convinced. He might have had yellow streaks down his back, that had showed so livid in the Kyprianou business, but he had a basic moral sense as well. Reserved strictly for his business life, and not his personal. But it was there all the same. There were values, and he wasn't going to have any firm of which he was a senior partner waltz across the line, into outright fraud. Even if they did dress it up as excessive enthusiasm for spreading a good deal around the deserving. .

His jacket was on, and his Crombie followed.

Hector was in business again.

– I won't start by saying good afternoon ladies and gentlemen, nice to see you. I'm going to start by saying good afternoon mugs, because that's what every one of you is. And I'm not pleased to see you, because I don't like to think I'm having to go into business with mugs.

Connie let that sink in, and waited for the audience in the motel convention room to settle again. There were forty or so prospective punters out there, lured by the mailing shots, and the classified ads which Jamieson had been responsible for devising and targeting. Aided always by Connie, urging him to make them less subtle, more blatant in their promise that fashion franchise could make their fortunes, for little investment and less work.

On the platform, beside and behind her, Jamieson and Nesta stirred uneasily. Connie hadn't let them have a preview of her presentation. All she'd said was that she should be allowed to handle it in her own way, and if her reading of the psychology of the prospective franchisee was wrong, they could beat her over the head. From then on she'd stick to licking stamps for the mailing shot envelopes.

– I say you're mugs, because you're working for somebody else at the moment, otherwise you wouldn't be here. And anybody who works for somebody else is a mug. Because all you need to get into fashion is a couple of hundred. If you've fifty thousand, we can show you how to double that. But if you've just got two hundred, we can get you a start. And one day, we guarantee you'll be on fifty thousand too.

The punters were hooked, and Jamieson and Nesta relaxed. Connie had, as so often, gone for the shock opener, and was about to follow it up with the sweet talk.

– Do you know how big a business fashion is? Have you ever stood on a busy High Street or shopping precinct on a Saturday afternoon, and watched those people fight their way into the shops, to throw money at the assistants? Did you ever wish you could find a way to get a toehold in that business, without having to worry about borrowing over your ears from the banks, or having to find good premises with no experience? Did you ever think you had the judgement to guess what people would be wearing this time next year? And make a killing? Or if you don't know or care about that, have you never thought it would be nice to have someone make that sort of decision for you, so that you just stood behind the till, collecting the lolly?

She was beginning to roll now, fixing one, and then another of the oddly assorted group of people who had already paid out ten pounds for the privilege of having a sherry on the house, and being exposed to this presentation. Connie had stuck out for charging an admission, and won. People never appreciated something they hadn't paid for. And once people had proved they were daft enough to part with ten hard-earned green ones to be talked-at in a grotty motel bar, they'd proved they were worth taking for much much more.

Moving off the platform, she tackled the first row, head on.

– Tell me you're a mug, she demanded of a gentleman in a turban, whose sari-clad wife nervously tugged at his elbow, as Connie bore in. – Tell me that you've kept your eyes and ears open in the England of the Eighties, and never realised that this was the time to get into business for yourself?

Wasn't it all so obvious, she wanted to know? How come no one had the vision or guts to go into business on their own account before they'd seen her advert? That they'd been prepared to wage-slave for some fat-bellied employer, who only turned up at the office from the golf course, or his mistress's water bed, in order to raid the till? How come they'd not noticed that the one booming business left in UK Limited was fashion? Because people always needed clothes, even in a so-called depression, and clothes were still one of the few things we did best?

There was a murmur of protest, from someone in the back row, who did work for himself, in a garage. He'd not come here to be insulted on his lack of work ethic. The moment could have been a nasty one, and not just because he looked the type who wouldn't be too embarrassed to ask for his tenner admission back.

But Connie turned the moment quickly.

– This is the sort of person we're looking for. She clapped a hand on his back, and nudged just close enough so that he could feel her body against him. That kept him quiet for a breath or two. Unfair tactics, but the future of the business depended on this presentation being a success.

– This is the sort of person you could be. Tough, independent, street-wise. Someone who sees a commercial opening, and goes for it with both hands. Probably drives a Jag, has matching sheepskins for himself, wife and the kids, and lives in a five-bedroomed house with a paddock. Am I right?

The garageman wasn't likely to say no to that inflation of his somewhat precarious lifestyle, and sat down mutely. Connie passed on, the moment of danger over. The people she was interested in were the ones who just sat there, looking worried. They were itching to part with their hard-put-together capital, and all they needed was to be told that was the clever thing to do.

Afterwards, doing the post-mortem with Borridge, who'd asked to be kept informed, she put her finger on what exactly had made her pitch so blazingly successful.

– I said to myself: anyone who walked through that door and parted with a tenner was looking for something for nothing and deserved all they got. They read those ads, and decided life after all did offer a way to get on without effort. All they had to do was buy a share in a franchise, let us do all the work, and sit back while the money rolled in.

So she'd mentally said, Right you miserable bastards, you're begging to be plucked. So she was going to make sure they got plucked.

A blind man (excusing herself for the reference) could have seen how rigged the franchise business was for the organiser of the franchise. If they were daft enough to ignore the warning signs, and be conned by her sales approach, well and good. She was taking their money out of their hot sweaty little hands before they could fall among bigger thieves, who'd strip them of everything.

Not that this was anything other than a respectable business opportunity, of course. The fact that it was being sold so hard didn't mean that it wasn't all perfectly legit, and the ideal way for the small punter to turn himself into a fashion retailer overnight.

– Not that anyone can succeed in fashion without lifting a finger, she warned them, circling behind them, totally in control. That was what they were being promised, of course, but people swallowed the bigger lies more easily than little ones.

– And not everyone is going to be allowed to take up a franchise who wants it. Even if they have the cash in hand. Another lie, just as big. The original idea had been that they'd go for the big investor, who'd be tempted into spending the sort of money they'd plunged in buying and shopfitting the show outlet Nesta had designed. Connie had convinced them that there were lots of penny packets of savings out there, from redundancy and bingo winnings, for example.

Going bare-arsed to make a success of this deal, meant being prepared to grab percentages of those small investments.

– You'd take somebody's hand off at the wrist, if you saw a pound note in it, wouldn't you? Jamieson had said, one night, after an unusually bruising session with the copy on the mail shot.

– Too true. And I take that as a compliment, she'd responded. After all, it was Nesta and Jamieson who had talked her into this. And the values said that once you were in, you had to go flat out.

Before she got half-way through the routine she'd worked out, she knew she had them. It was a worrying and a sexy feeling at the same time. Crawder must feel like this, she suddenly thought, when he was involved in the more political side of his life. It was power. It was talking a bunch of people who should have known better, into a deal that only just added up, in the bits where it wasn't exactly bent.

Sexy.

Dangerous.

A sort of striptease, where the roles were reversed. She was persuading the audience to take off all their clothes, to reveal their primal urges of greed. And when they were stripped and naked, she would screw them, by taking their good money off them.

Which happened.

Out of the forty who showed for the presentation, ten came forward as definite prospects, who couldn't wait to plunge. Another ten said they'd be maybes, if they had more time to think about it, and five left their names, saying they might be in touch.

Even with a wastage and think-again and think-better-of-it factor, they knew they had the makings of a roaring success. If they repeated these results up and down the country, they'd be challenging the major retailers in the foreseeable future.

– It's an idea whose time has come, Nesta urged, flushed with success. Her baby had turned out to be a real red-cheeked bouncer.

– Unstoppable, Jamieson allowed himself an unprofessional, unexecutive bunching of his fist, as if he'd scored a goal. – The way they fought to get a brochure with an application form.

– And every one a mug, Connie stayed cold, after the heat of the event itself. – We don't forget that. We never listen to the crap we tell them, or we're sunk. Remember that.

As she turned, wanting to get the sour taste of her success out of her mouth, she saw Hector watching her across the cheaply decorated room. It had been passably glitzy in the black-out while the presentation took place—now with the curtains back, and the ash-trays full, it looked like a ballroom after the band had gone.

Hector had seen and heard it all. She knew that straight away. Expected him to come across and row. Was ready to fight her corner, even though she still wasn't finding the satisfaction she had thought she would in this hard sell. Because the franchise was a way of keeping her promise to Bea, as well as keeping close to her man.

Hector stepped back through the door, and disappeared.

He'd seen enough. He'd put a stop to this somehow, for the memory of Bea, and because he genuinely did believe in the values.

But this was a Hector who had been through the fire, and come out tougher, and wiser. No taking the three of them head-on. He'd wait his moment, and forge his silver bullet. And with one shot get Nesta, Connie, and Jamieson plug through the forehead.

Back at the shops, Nesta's favourite management tool was still the flame thrower. The trouble with a flame thrower is that sometimes the wind changes, and the wielder of it gets their hair burned off. Something like that happened just when they were about to hit the road to take the now tried-and-tested sales pitch to all the little people out there.

She'd never exactly felt that a week in which no one got bawled-out or fired was a week wasted, but things did get rather operatic at times in the chain. More so these days, when her attention was mostly elsewhere, and even more than the usual shouting-out and table-thumping was necessary to keep the girls in order.

In many respects Nesta was a good employer, but her staff had to understand she could only function in an atmosphere of perpetual turmoil, crisis and civil war.

It was her misfortune that she hadn't made this clear to her new window dresser, who took the abuse Nesta left for her on a cassette tape personally, and not as just another blowing off of steam.

The girl would have left, angry and tearful, without any further fuss, had not Dev walked through the door the moment she was putting her coat on.

They'd bumped into each other before. Dev explained he was looking for Arnie, for he had something to give him, before he noticed how upset the girl was. She explained all, and found Dev a sympathetic listener. It was Dev who put the idea of some sort of revenge into her mind. Before then she'd been prepared to take it on the chin, but the sheer inventiveness of Dev's suggestions appealed to her straight away.

For starters they swept everything off Nesta's large desk, and made slow love on it; and then the girl worked in the show window behind a white-out, helped by Dev, who was most inventive for his suggestions as to what compromising positions the models could be set up in. What they did was guaranteed to draw the biggest crowd to the shop front in its history. Which it did, along with four police, who failed to have the nuisance immediately put a stop to. Mainly because Dev and the window dresser had filled the locks with quick-setting cement.

The girl was quits. How could she thank Dev, save in exactly the same way as on Nesta's desk, now of happier memory.

Dev made the date, but assured her that he was well content. He'd taken a souvenir, in the shape of the entire contents of Nesta's most confidential files. His intention was the crude, mean and unsubtle one of making official life difficult for her. But something in red ink on one of them caught his eye, as he prepared to dump them in a chance dustbin on the way home.

Dev wasn't a figures man, but Hector was. Maybe he'd be interested in seeing just how healthy the business was that Nesta had conned off Connie all those years before? Red was a very intriguing colour to find in Nesta's shop accounts.

Unaware that her shop was staging a pornographic window display, Nesta was attending the final briefing before herself, Connie and Jamieson went over the top. And that expression could be understood in a couple of different ways.

After Jamieson had talked them through their sales-packs, and made sure everyone knew what conference venues they were hitting, and in what order, Connie rose to give her final few words.

– The wise man in the baggy trousers and the stovepipe hat said, Never give a sucker an even break. In my book, that was being far too generous to the suckers.

She held their eyes. Nesta's narrowed and excited, Jamieson's equally so. She had their attention. The same shiver that had gone through her when she realised she was selling the punters at that first seminar grabbed her, shook her up, then let her go.

– We're after the little fish, as well as the big fish. It doesn't matter if they have to borrow up to and over their ears to put a quarter

C.—12

deposit down on the franchise. We're giving them the chance to be that most wonderful and special of all God's creatures—the small businessman. These are the Eighties. The small businessman is king. Everybody says so. Successful small businesses are the only way this bankrupt country is going to pull itself out of the brown stuff. A nation composed of small businessmen taking in each other's washing is the magic cure for unemployment, regional economic black spots, and piles. The politicians tell us so, so it must be true, mustn't it. What we're doing is cramming that ethic down the punters' throats, and if it costs them an arm and a leg, it's cheap at the price.

She was going to send them off with what was the firm's unofficial motto ringing in their ears.

– Go out and screw the bastards.

And they would have done, had not Hector burst through the door, followed much more quietly by Dev.

The welcome-backs died in their throats as Hector silently cleared a space in the middle of the table. He took a contemptuous look at the six colour graphics in the glossy brochures which had cost a small fortune, and knocked them on to the floor.

He spread Nesta's accounts in front of them.

– Anyone ever stop to think why Nesta was so keen to get the franchise racket going?

No one had. Nesta opened her mouth, but said nothing.

– That's the answer, Hector indicated the papers, over which he had worked since Dev, on the off-chance, had brought them to him. – She's gone bust. She's only kept the shops going by robbing the factory blind. Now she's emptied the cupboard here, as well.

And there was something he had to add, as a by-the-way.

– It's nice to be back.

Twenty-three

The heavy irony, the really heavy irony, the thing which dropped with such a weight on Jamieson's toes, was that it had been the computerisation of the accounts and stock control which had made it possible for Nesta to get her hands on the loot from the factory.

That had been chortlingly plain to Hector, the minute he'd started working his way through the papers. The old-fashioned way, with pen and paper, and a large pot of black coffee to hand.

Hadn't he complained right from the start about Jamieson being allowed to whizz-kid the office procedures? Hadn't the old methods been good enough for long enough for himself and Bea? The previous routines may have meant that now and again something could be slipped through the books, for example, the rent of a girlfriend's flat. But no way could depredations on the scale Nesta had been responsible for have passed unnoticed.

It had been made easy for her, of course, because Connie's attention was taken up with the hundred-and-one things to do with the planning and building problems. But the main culprit was Jamieson, and the fact that the system was still nowhere near working properly.

– It's still being debugged, Jamieson protested, knowing as he said it how weak it sounded.

– You've so many bugs in that thing you ought to call in the public health, retorted Hector. From day one he had had a down on those humming, clattering, busybody machines. Sweet to find they were incompetent, on top of everything else.

No one had thought to ask Nesta to deny the accusation. Jamieson and Connie were both expecting her to summon up her strength, and blast Hector out of the water. It couldn't be true. She might have dipped into what were properly New House of Bea funds, to tide herself over a sticky retail week. But wholesale misappropriation? On a scale that threatened the very existence of the factory?

Impossible.

But she didn't deny it.

– Sorry.

That weedy little word again, that was even weedier when set against the scale of what she'd done.

– It's true?

They got a nod, and in the silence following the devastation implied in that single gesture there was a sound almost like a sob. From Nesta. A sob of relief. A confessional hint. Then it all came out, in a scalding rush.

It wasn't Nesta's fault, of course. The process of decay had started when Connie had broken her word and returned. Despite herself, Nesta had found she was drawn more and more into the family rows that the return entailed. No matter that most of them were unnecessary and the others imaginary. The point was that she couldn't keep an eye on business while worrying that Connie was out there prowling in the woods. Hadn't she said so in so many words, when she'd come to make her peace?

– Then you found Dev was here, and it started again, Connie pointed out. There had been a truce on the table, and it had been Nesta who walked out.

Whatever way it had been, Nesta shrugged that off, the important thing was that week by week the returns from her shops were getting less. She couldn't devote the hundred-and-ten percent to them she normally did. They knew how it was—or should do. A sort of dry rot set in, that galloped into every wall and ceiling. You no sooner got one patch put right, than fungus started sprouting out of another.

Then there had been the blow of her mother's death, which whatever they might think, had set her back on her heels. As was only natural, even if you were a hard case like Nesta, who was supposed to have been born wearing a sneer and boxing gloves. The fact that she now had an extra source of cash only dawned on her after the successful funeral splash. When she started she was only lifting petty cash, to pay the phone bill and so on at the shops. When she realised the accounts were in such a mess, and that Connie had her work cut out on the rebuilding, she'd started to lift her sights.

After all, this was her money, sloshing around the now-successful factory. Or would be, when all the legal and financial ramifications were sorted out. She could repay then, and no one would be any the wiser.

But her bad run in the shops had continued, and she'd needed something to plug the holes in the factory accounts, which had grown alarmingly large.

– That's why you went for the franchise?

Nesta nodded, heavily. It hadn't been a stroke of genius after all. More one of desperation.

– Let me get this straight, Connie was tight-lipped, but breathing hard. – You robbed the factory to pay for the shops. Then you intended suckering us into the franchise business to pay for that?

Nesta wouldn't have put it in exactly those words, but that was the general idea.

By now Jamieson had got some figures together, from the computer and from the manual records. It looked bad. In the past couple of weeks he'd given less and less attention to the books, concerned with the launch of the new scam. A couple of weeks is a long time in accounting, especially when there is an embezzler loose around the place. There was a multiplier factor involved, that accelerated the rate at which the roof started falling in. They were now in the area where the multiplier took over.

– But we're not going bust. It's not as bad as that, is it? Connie tried to keep the hard edge to her voice. She didn't want to sound pleading.

Jamieson lifted his shoulders, and looked helplessly at Nesta. The figures were in such a mess, there was no way he could tell without her help.

Nesta lifted her shoulders too.

– We might technically be trading while insolvent. There's a pile of papers in that desk. Things I haven't looked at.

Connie got to the drawer at the same time as did Jamieson. Two minutes frantic envelope ripping and speed reading convinced them her guess was spot on. They were headed for liquidation by the next pay-day, unless their long lost uncles from Venus arrived, all at the same time, and all having struck it big, in the Venusian goldfields.

Dev passed round the drinks. Sympathetically, but with the light of triumph in his eyes, and his walk. All that was missing to make his pleasure complete was Arnie. It hadn't hit him yet that his very success meant the end of the line. He'd been responsible for proving the existence of the very scam which meant there was no job to go back to. No matter how clever he'd shown himself to be, or how much Hector owed him now, there were no prospects at the New House of Bea, because now there was no New House of Bea.

How could there be? They'd be lucky to scramble out of fraud charges for illegal and reckless trading.

Then he realised that Connie had That Look again. The one that usually spelt trouble, or Idea, or more often, both at the same time.

– Where's the problem? she asked, suddenly getting even Nesta's attention.

The room was very still. You had to listen very hard to hear the beating of the wings of what would rescue them.

– All it means is that we go after the punters with the franchise that much harder. And we reshape the split from the profits.

Her eye was on Nesta, and it bored like steel.

– We can talk about the exact carve-up later. For now you just have to nod your head.

And nod it Nesta did. Knowing the nod said she'd lost. Connie had got what she came back for. The deal would be that Connie got the shops back, and Nesta stayed on, if she could stomach it, as Number Two. The factory would be run Connie's way, and Nesta's share would very much be the minor one. She'd have a cut of the franchise, because it had been her idea, after all, whatever the crooked roots of it. But even more than how it had been up to now, Connie would run the show, lead the band, and play all the instruments.

Now, of all times, she should feel she'd pulled off everything she'd come back to do.

But before she could work out if that was the feeling she had, Hector coughed, and explained why it just wasn't going to be so.

– Values, he paused after the word. – You've all paid lip service to them. No one's actually believed in them. When I've said we should stand by them, no matter where it lands us, you've thrown orange peel at me. Now I'm telling you those values are real to me, if not to you. And I'm sticking by them.

– Which means? Jamieson was in first, suddenly aware of more danger.

– Which means I draw the line at this franchise ramp. I may be a bloody old fool, who's rogered his way round this business far too long, but I've been a principled bloody old fool, in my twisted way. You may all laugh at me behind my back, or to my face, for those hot pants I thought I had a corner in, back when. But that was a commercial deal. That was the entrepreneur making an honest mistake.

Where was this getting them? Nesta wanted to know. She was impatient to get on with it. No sense hanging around, crying over spilt milk, even her own. She'd pulled a stunt and come a cropper. Connie had come out on top for now. She wanted to get the show on the road, so that she could start scheming how to turn the tables again.

Wasn't that how it was always going to be? Her and Connie, matched fairly in a lifetime ding-dong and Battle Royal? For the moment Connie was on the up. Give her a couple of weeks, and she'd be plotting her way back as top dog.

– It's getting you nowhere, was Hector's reply. – It means you're at the end of the line. I'd rather have the New House of Bea go bust, than save it by conning those poor bastards out there.

And he did mean it, on principle. It wasn't just that he would be ashamed or afraid to have his name linked with something that shaved the legal line so closely.

– We're fashion people. Born and bred to it. To selling clothes, and making them. Not to crack-brained con-men schemes that'll probably blow up in your faces inside a month, anyway.

Hector had been through the fire. Those weeks spent as a hermit, grieving for the two women who, in their contrasting ways, had meant so much to him, had changed him for good. Nothing would matter ever again quite so much as once it had, in business, or in the personal life.

They argued and they pleaded, and they threatened and they scolded, but he just sat there, and took it all. He'd no idea what they could do now, to save the bacon. He was giving up bacon, and it looked as if they would have to, as well.

Hector couldn't be talked out of his decision to plunge for those hot pants all those summers ago. Now he couldn't be shaken from this resolve, perverse though it was, in the eyes of what was going to happen if he didn't budge.

Nesta gave up first.

Slammed the door so that the hinges started. She felt the way she had the moment she realised Jamieson had snatched Connie and Georgiou away from the very steps of the plane. So near, only to be cheated again. This time by her old fool of a step-father.

And what was this phone-call from the owner of the shop next door to her, complaining about her unfair methods of drawing Sales crowds to her obscene window display?

Jamieson retired next, knowing how ugly it was going to get, as Connie wriggled every way to get inside her father's guard. It had been a hard slog, getting the promotion ready on the franchise. And bitter to have the chance snatched away to prove himself worthy of forty thousand a year plus. But he did need to get his head down for a straight twelve undisturbed hours.

And when he woke, who knew, but Connie might have worked the old magic on her dad?

Connie suddenly realised there was no chance of that. Long after even Dev had gone. Dev, who had hung on, waiting for his chance to make his apologies to Connie. He had never intended that she should be brought down alongside Nesta. Cruel irony indeed, that it should have worked out like that.

Her shoulders went down, when she was about to start fighting really dirty, and ask what he thought Bea would have made of him?

And which of the two of them had the best right to guess what she would have thought? Who had been closer than the guy who had slept with her?

– I gave up on it.

It was the next day, and Connie was with her father confessor again, that wise if somewhat grubby and carpet-slippered old owl Borridge. Boridge with the sharp ears, and ever questioning expression. Borridge who knew where all the bodies were buried, and who kept a file in his head of every foolishness anyone in the business had ever been responsible for.

– I was going to ram his old sod's head through the door until he agreed to let us work the franchise number. Even a scaled-down version. Then I thought, sod it. Let it go.

Because it was then, as she faced the full and clear realisation as to how huge a wreck of hopes this was, that she felt what she'd been waiting for. That moment of triumph, that moment of release. She had realised she had nothing left, and that was freedom.

– I'm free of everything. Responsibility for the factory, for the lives and futures of the people who worked in it. From now on they can sort their own lives out. I'm off.

He wanted to know what she meant by that.

– You could keep working away at Hector. Grind him down.

She shook her head. She'd fought long and hard to reach this moment of inner peace and content.

– It's back on the speedbird for Jamieson and me. Greece again. Or Timbuktu, or wherever. We're going to tidy up the odds and ends, so that it doesn't look as if we're just cutting and running. Then it's the first plane out, anywhere where the sky is blue, and the water cool.

It was going to be just like Jamieson had asked for, those months before, in that sudden hotel bedroom, when their love story had started. They were going to jump out of the window together, holding hands.

– You're a grafter, Borridge protested. He had a lot invested in Connie, he had plans. Their futures were linked, he knew it. She couldn't just walk out on him.

– I used to be a grafter, just like Bea was. And look what happened to her?

– She had a good innings, she wasn't complaining as they wheeled her out.

Wasn't she? Connie wanted to know. Underneath, wasn't Bea complaining bitterly, screaming with her mouth tight shut, at the waste of it all?

Borridge said not. Because Bea believed in the values, just as Hector, in his cack-handed way, believed in them as well. And the values went through Connie too, like a name through a stick of rock.

He asked for time to see if he could mount some sort of rescue package, patch something together. She shook her head. That Look fixed to her face with vanadium steel bolts. He begged her to call in at least once more, for old times' sake, to say goodbye, and she promised that. The least she could do. Shame that they had never been able to really test their odd partnership, find out if their complementary qualities had a more important use in the business than just putting another planning committee fiddle through.

– One day, again, who knows? The chip of a smile from Borridge, as he held his thin hand out for her to take by the fingers.

– I know, Connie assured him. – Wherever we end up, this time I'm staying there.

No matter what other ideas he had.

Arnie had missed the shoot-out in the factory, when Hector had left his hermit's cell to lay waste so many carefully sorted plans. He'd got it in the neck for not being on the premises when the window dresser had left in such defiant style. Not his fault for not being there, of course, but that sort of excuse had never cut much ice with Nesta.

Halfway through the ledger-throwing, Arnie had suddenly wondered what the hell he was doing, taking all this? He could always live in the back of the van, if he walked out. There were always ways in which someone who had cut his teeth on street trading could make a crust. In the Smoke, perhaps. And who knew, but that he mightn't be able to find Babs again?

That's what he'd do, he decided, not bothering to duck as a large ashtray came flying his way, missing him by a couple of inches. He'd take off, and look for Babs. And this time he'd do what he'd wanted to do the moment he heard about the way she'd been making the money. Grab her by the shoulders, shake her around, and make it very plain that from now on she only slipped her zips for him, and no one else.

There was no telling what sort of shape she'd be in, of course, especially if she'd gone back to her old friends down South. She'd been in a bad way the time he'd picked her up two years before. Having failed to make the break, she might have thrown herself back into that scene with redoubled desperation. That was his fault, and he'd take her back, whatever the intervening weeks had done to her face, or how many needle marks they had put in her arm.

– Bye. And good luck with the court case, he said, as he slipped out of the door, Nesta about to reach for the twin of the ashtray, which had made such a satisfactory dent in the plaster of the wall behind his head.

He'd look out for news of how she got on. It wasn't every day you had to answer an obscenity charge based on a window display, after all.

There was someone he had to see, before he headed South, with quickening excitement and determination, after his girl. Who was still his girl, no matter what company of thieves and rogues she was keeping now.

Not Connie, not Hector. They were family, and Arnie felt for the first time he was really free of them. He had a new life to make, after he had patched it up with his girl. There was another family to start thinking of.

Dev watched him warily, as he moved across the bar towards him. No hero, he wondered if he could get a quick jab to the eye before Arnie could react, and then leg it out through the gents. He owed Arnie, didn't he?

– You certainly do, Arnie sighed, taking the drink which Dev in his discretion had decided to fetch him instead of a punch. – It was me who rigged the stuff in your car. Nesta kept nagging me to get even with you, for her sake as well as my own. I was going to wait until you were on the road, then phone in, shopping you.

– Tell me something new, said Dev. But it was a relief to know that his enemies were exactly who he had guessed. That there were others he didn't know, he'd picked up along the way.

– I'm leaving town, that's new, Arnie offered. – And if I ever come back, it'll be with Babs on my arm. For good. Wed, with a mortgage and the makings of four kids.

Dev wished him well. Meant it. It sounded like hell to him—saving the fact that the girl would be Babs, who he had a lot of time for—but if that was Arnie's choice, he wished him the best.

– You?

Dev set his drink down. He wished he knew what the best for him would be. He was still hooked on the idea of getting back into fashion—this time where he belonged, at the design end. He'd seen enough of sales, and the executive life. He realised now he was never going to make an international name. Probably not even a national one. But he'd be content to have a quiet, unspectacular career, in a small house, designing whatever was thrown at him. Even if it was the pink acrylic for the old bat trudging around the supermarket with a fag in her gob and her stockings round her ankles.

He paused. There was something he could maybe do for Arnie that would help him on his way. He excused himself, leaving Arnie sat there, wondering if this was some sort of gag. Or if Dev was at that moment taking a knife to the tyres of his van.

Dev came back, having been to the flat he now shared, two streets away. He had a parcel in his hand. He seemed awkward about it.

– It's a video cassette. I was watching it with a girl I know the other night. About ten minutes in I saw a familiar face.

And more than face.

Arnie took it on the chin. He'd guessed that Babs might be turning a few tricks for the hand-held video.

– I don't know whether it could be of use, but you could check back from the distributor to whoever made it.

Arnie took it.

– Ta.

A hell of a way to start your quest for the woman you had decided was going to settle down in some sort of suburbia with you, and bear your kids. But it had always been a love-job between himself and Babs. And love-jobs always kept you turning unexpected corners.

Dev watched him go, and then turned back to his drink.

Should he develop a booze problem? That would be expensive, but he was, after all, shacked-up with the window dresser now, and she very obligingly left her handbag lying around most nights.

At least it would be something to do, while his looks ran out.

Jamieson was leery of calling on Borridge with Connie. The man had been of use strictly during the negotiations over the planning business only. He'd always felt uneasy about him, even when they were depending on him. His involvement seemed to go beyond the immediate and the business.

– I promised. Once we knew the date we were off, I said we'd say goodbye.

He still wasn't convinced. It was his feeling that they should get out now, before the brown stuff really hit the air circulation equipment. Leave Nesta to deal with the complications of the impending bankruptcy, and get their toes in the water, a thousand miles away.

That feeling was reinforced when Borridge said he had a rescue deal.

– I didn't ask for one, Connie warned. But she was intrigued. Only on the level of human interest. Only because the speculation as to what might have happened would be something to fill the long days, as she lay on the beach with her man.

Borridge wouldn't go into the details of the exact financial arrangements, because they were still being worked out. But in outline Crawder would pick up the factory, and the shops, and put someone in to run them. He wouldn't go near the franchise deal with a stainless-steel bargepole tipped with asbestos. But at least Nesta wouldn't have to show up in the court, and Connie and Hector wouldn't have the stigma of compulsory liquidation against them.

– It wouldn't matter a damn to me, Connie retorted. – I'm out of business for good. Christ knows how we'll make a living out there, but we'll manage.

And Jamieson gave her hand a squeeze. That was the sort of bridge-burning talk he wanted to hear.

– That's what you say now, Borridge retorted. – But think it over.

– You'd get trapped, Jamieson urged. – You'd start talking about the ins and outs of the deal, and before you knew it, you'd get interested again.

Connie had enough self-knowledge to be aware of that danger. It was tempting to think that she could go into negotiation with Crawder, hoping to come out of it with those shops, as her price for signing her share of the factory away. But that was the slippy slope, to getting involved over her head in business again.

No. She was a retired exec, a small businesswoman who had walked out, for good.

– You could maybe talk him into giving you the shops, Borridge suggested. There it was, laid out naked. The suggestion that Borridge had read her well enough to know this would be the one to change her mind.

Only it didn't.

– Mr. Crawder only wants the factory. He could be persuaded to put you into retail again. That's where your heart is.

And that would mean that he himself would be adding another careful piece to his empire. As well as being owed by even more people in the business. More bodies buried where only he knew, apart from the person who had wielded the spade.

– No.

That was the final and definite no.

Nesta had already had a call from Crawder's office. She was waiting at the factory when Hector got there. The last girl had been paid off the previous week. They'd just managed to scrape up enough for the pay packets. Now was the calm before the legal storm. She had no real hope that anything could be pulled out of the wreck, but Crawder's name was enough to bring her running, high-heels clacking across the cobbles of the yard.

– There's a deal, Hector apprised her. Hector was ahead of the game. The approach to him had come very early on.

– Crawder will take the factory off our hands, and settle the debts.

But he wants you out.

That was fair enough. Nesta was used to brutal news by now. It had been coming thick and fast, since the day Hector had spoiled the franchise launch. That multiplier factor in operation.

So long as she managed to wriggle out of the twisted metal with a clean sheet, she didn't care. There were always openings for someone like her in the big world of fashion. Even if it did mean flogging yourself ten hours a day, six days a week, the way she'd flogged the Miss Greers of the business.

– And you? she asked, attention elsewhere. As a matter of form. – What happens to you?

– He stays on, Crawder was at the top of the stairs. The man jangled his own keys to the place now. – I need someone who knows how this slum fits together to make knitwear. Someone who can keep on top of the rebuilding.

Who better than Hector? The fact that he had once made a disastrous deal on hot pants shouldn't for life disqualify him from opportunity, should it?

He'd be working directly to the new management, of course. The person that Crawder was putting in over his head, to really run things. Hector would advise, counsel, warn. He would buckle down and do all the things he should be good at, having spent so many years in the firm. But real power would lie elsewhere.

– With who, exactly? Nesta wanted to know. As she also wanted to know why it should be assumed that Hector would do the buckling down required, flogging himself as an executive, without any perquisites of ownership.

When the new management stepped out of the office, behind Crawder, she had her answer.

Lisa looked a million.

– Her?

Connie stopped short in the doorway to the empty shopfloor. The light was on in the office, and she could hear the murmur of a tough discussion.

At that moment the door opened, and in the spill of light, she saw the girl. The girl she'd invented. The little thing she'd taken off the machine on the shopfloor, and carved afresh. The girl whose walk and looks she had fixed, in order that she should get out from under Crawder. And now the girl who looked every inch the steely businesswoman, whom Borridge and Crawder were putting in charge of the factory.

Crawder came through, and looked down at Connie. His hand was very casually on that firm backside of Lisa. Connie knew in an instant, as surely as she had smelt it, that this was a love-job. She had been devastatingly right. Crawder was head-over-heels with Lisa, and would have done anything to keep her.

Even put her in over Hector, in the seat where Bea had sat for so long.

It was blindingly clear to Connie, in that snapshot image of Crawder and his girl.

The Crawders of this world didn't need back-street factories like the New House of Bea because they were a threat to them, or because they needed cheap expansion. The Crawders could afford to add the cost of the acquisition to any one of a dozen balance sheets, in order to keep their women. This factory, in which Bea had slaved, in which she herself had worn out shoe-leather and stomach lining ever since her return, could be handed across to a bit of management stuff, like a cheap piece of jewellery.

Great for Hector, of course. It had all suddenly panned out right for him. He could spend his days in the company of the girl, his previous involvement with her known only to a few of them, of which Crawder wasn't one. That would give him a hold on her that he could parlay into something more. Probably not the taking up of their sexual relationship again, that would be expecting and risking too much. But he could certainly use it to lean on the girl, to let him live something of his freewheeling life again, while he was supposed to be grafting for Crawder.

Great for Nesta, because it meant she got out from under the results of her own fraud.

Not so great for Connie, however, because she had nothing. And even though she knew that was the exact sum total of all she wanted—she was annoyed.

Not annoyed—furious.

– The sweat that's wringing down these walls, that Bea and me put in here, she stood inches from Crawder's nose, shaking with anger. Anger at her own stupidity. Anger at how she'd been used. Not just by Crawder, but by the system.

– We spend all our lives grafting away, trying to make a living, and all the time you people could snuff us out, just like that. You can buy and sell us without even having to check the figures, because you're old money, and you got here first. Great grandad, that ripe old bastard, put the roots down, and what chance do we ever have of catching up?

The whole thing was a ramp. All that talk about the virtues of being a small businesswoman, grafting for yourself, was so much hot air. The truth was that no one had it worse than the girl who tried to hack it for herself. There was no one on her side, despite the politicians' ranting. She'd been vaguely aware of the con trick they were pulling, as she grafted. But it needed this moment to crystallise it for her.

Good luck to Lisa, she said. No one should get her wrong and think she was attacking the girl. And she was hardly attacking Crawder personally, either. It was the system, if you could call the ragbag collection of cause and effect that.

She saw it frozen frame, with total clarity, in that image of Crawder, his hand now on the girl's handsome and confident shoulder.

He could give the girl the factory, and the lives in it, as casually as he might have given her a box of chocolates. Lisa had decided, and good luck to her, that it was time to put the screws on her fella, now that it was turning on to what hadn't been contracted for—a love-job. And Crawder, urged by Borridge, had come up with the solution to her dissatisfaction.

A nice ending for Lisa, of course. Or rather, a nice conclusion to the first part of her story. For there was no doubt that a girl who had shown her qualities was going to go far. Very far indeed. Her learning curve was wicked, and as soon as even bigger fish than the provincial Crawder swam into her view, she'd be snapping at their tails.

How nice to be coming back to the factory the next Monday it opened, not on the machine, but sat where Bea had sat. Where Connie had sat, but could sit no longer.

It wasn't sour grapes, nor even a feeling that she could have been the one on Crawder's arm at that moment.

It was rage.

And she gave Crawder the full force of it, hanging the consequences.

For she was on the next plane out, after all.

Twenty-four

Borridge wanted to say something.

Much as he was unused to public speaking, to talking to more than one person at a time, and then usually behind his hand, he thought he should tidy up some details.

The first was one for Mr. Crawder to agree to, or not. He seemed to have found himself in a position of go-between the various parties here, and reluctant, as they would understand him to be, to appear to be interfering, he felt he had to honour the obligation.

– Mr. Hector feels he shan't be able to come in, unless he gets approval for an in-house designer.

Connie looked sharply at Hector. Her father was showing unsuspected mettle, in trying to make conditions to Crawder, especially at a time like this.

Dev was equally surprised when he heard his name. But Hector owed it to him that he had finally left that room. Crawder lifted his shoulders. The name meant nothing to him. If Lisa agreed that they needed, on Hector's advice, a proper designer, so be it. It could only add a fleabite to the firm's wages bill, and he had promised her six months' free hand in running the business. That is, she had made him promise that she should be allowed to show what she could do for the first six months. And that determined line to her mouth said there was no chance of her failing.

She looked at Dev, and nodded.

Dev tried very hard not to catch Nesta's eye. He had an idea it wouldn't be a pleasant experience. His triumph was too narrowly achieved to risk upsetting even someone so apparently floored as Nesta.

The second was to dispose once and for all of exactly what Nesta's position was. Borridge had suggested to Mr. Crawder that it would be better all round if Nesta's removal from the scene was geographical, as well as commercial.

As part of the price for being bailed out, she would be required to sign a covenant that she wouldn't have any part in anything to do with the fashion business, retail or manufactory, in fifty miles. And everyone involved would be that much happier if she made it further still.

– You understand why? Borridge asked, in his soft voice that defused the implications for her. That no one could trust her to take her enforced retirement lying down, or assume that her gratitude would prevent her from trying to get her own back.

– What am I supposed to do? She wanted to know. – I don't know anything but fashion.

– Like to borrow an *A to Z* of London or Aberdeen, sister dear? Connie asked with a sweet smile.

And wiped it when it was her turn to figure in Borridge's tidying-up of the remaining loose ends.

– Miss Connie comes to work for Crawder plc.

She could still have her holiday with Jamieson. Could still catch that silver bird, and paddle her toes in the Med. But Borridge had plans for her, and so did Crawder.

– I said no to you weeks back, Connie snapped, when the door closed on the top of them. – Isn't Lisa enough?

– She's enough and more than enough, Crawder acknowledged. I don't want your body, not this time. I want what you showed just then, on the floor, when you called me out.

– You want your own back, Connie snapped again. The sooner the throat of this deal was cut, the better. – You know I suckered you back then, so you want to sucker me too. You'll give me a pointless job, just to show you've got a hold over me. Then, when you get tired, you'll kick me out.

– I meant what I said that time, about old money needing the new money to keep it bright and sharp. I thought you had the makings of a career bigger than the House of Bea, from the start. Borridge feels it too.

– Look at my track record, she suggested. This was one job interview she didn't want to pass. – What have I done since I got back but screw up?

He disagreed.

– But in the end it was a screw-up, she insisted. – Okay, I might have turned ten drachmas into a third of the firm, and been all set to make an even bigger killing on the franchise deal. But it didn't come off. And that's me all over. I get so far, and then I come to a dead stop.

– Think why, he urged. – Think why you've always done that.

It was obvious to her why. There was a flaw in her or her stars somewhere. In business, and in her love life, it seemed no sooner had she reached a point of perfect balance than she screwed it up. Or caused it to be screwed up. She gave in to the sudden impulsive moment, and went lurching off, after what was worst for her.

Take the business with Georgiou, for example. The way she'd taken one look at him and been prepared to risk all. And that hadn't been particularly for love, or even lust. It was that self-destruct button that she seemed unable to keep her finger off.

Jamieson was at the foot of the stairs, pointing at his watch.

There was no way she was going to miss this flight.

– Think really why you've done that in the past, Crawder closed in, between her and the pane in the office door. – It's because you've known inside what a pointless treadmill you've been on. You knew there was a bigger world to be taken on, but your entire energies were taken up going round and round in the same small circles, with no-hopes like Dev and Arnie. Even like Hector and Nesta.

Didn't she see what Crawder and Borridge had seen in her? That her future was in the big world, working for a company like his?

– Flying a desk? After I've been used to carrying the weight of the entire business on my shoulders? Checking in at half eight every morning? Catchng the Zurich shuttle like my fella used to do?

Exactly that.

And in the 'losers' category, in case she had any misconceptions, Crawder was including Jamieson. He was another no-hoper she had to leave behind.

That was plainly preposterous.

Leave behind the man she'd hi-jacked at the airport, and then grown to love? Not in the frantic, gut-turning way she'd grown to love the Greek. But in a domestic, slowing-down way. Could she consider for a moment dumping him after all they'd been through? With Kyprianou? The fire? The sweaty business on the planning scam?

The man had left his wife for her. His wife, and his house with the storm porch, and the filing system he'd built up to help his career into the Number Two in Europe slot.

– That's what he'll always be, Crawder was the other side of her now, shepherding her away from the door. – You don't see that?

He's a Number Two, born and reared, and you are one of those rare things—a Number One.

Supposing, just supposing she was stupid enough to take the challenge and walk out on her man? Her man who was on the stairs, waiting for her, calling up to her—?

What would Jamieson do, if she walked?

How could he put the pieces back together?

Crawder indicated Nesta, furiously chewing her nails in the far corner, waiting for the word from Connie, that the deal was fixed in all its details.

– There's someone who could give him a shot as a Number Two. And wouldn't there be a sort of shape to that?

Connie opened her mouth, then closed it.

If Nesta bagged Jamieson, then she would have won, wouldn't she? The game would have been all for nothing. But would it be so straightforward? Wasn't there another way of looking at it? Couldn't it be suggested that while Connie had Jamieson in tow, she was never going to steam ahead, at full speed on her own account?

A man did hold you back. They were useful on those long cold nights, and for helping a girl over temporary embarrassments, like arriving in England with nothing to show but ten foreign coins of small denomination.

Nesta and Jamieson?

That was a twist to the pattern that she had never thought of.

That one would have been beyond Bea, as well, sharp as her stepmother had been in noticing the shifting alliances and fallings-out.

Maybe she could get the best of both worlds—? Take the job with Crawder plc, and keep Jamieson with her?

Even as she said it, she knew how hopeless a relationship that would be. The more important a desk Connie would be flying the less private life she would have. Jamieson would be seen at weekends, and on days off, and in between the poison would start to work at him. She'd seen so many marriages break up in the fast stream, and had no wish for that energy-sapping complication, spread over many weary months or years.

Jamieson was at the window.

Determined to break the door down if he had to.

Her decision was clear.

Going through that door meant flying out with him, and all that entailed. Time on the beach. Time to relax, and expand, and find out more about each other. The things they hadn't time to learn in the hurly burly of business.

Time, maybe, to find they could only have a relationship in the gaps of a business life.

Time, maybe, to get bored with and used to each other. Time for her to regret that she'd twice turned Crawder down, and that was twice more than most people got in a lifetime in the business.

But to turn from that door, and shape a yes to Crawder meant working for somebody else. Meant starting a whole new style of warfare, sharpening new weapons, proving herself from scratch. Sure, it would be a high-gloss lifestyle, she knew enough about the big-scale business to know that. There would be the limos to the airport, and the first-class recliners, and the best hotels. There would be important people to meet, and toughies to solve, and she would have to think fast on her feet, and maybe on her back too.

But would it be worth it, at the price of her fella?

Her fella who was stood there, his mouth open, pleading through the glass for her to open up, and leave with him. With Nesta, in the background, eyeing him as if measuring him for something. Like another nibble at the franchise scam, perhaps?

Would Bea have thought it worth the price?

That was the question to ask.

Would the woman who had founded the business, had fought so hard for it, and who had mercifully not been around when it finally folded due to her own daughter's shenanigans, have said go for it?

Connie went for the back door, and up the fire ladder to the roof. It was a moist Midland day, with a curtain of mist that looked as if it would never have the energy to clear itself up. Up on the roof that gave such a good view of all the other roofs. Over the street that gave a view of nothing but other streets of the same size, and the same pointlessness.

Given a chance, would Bea have stayed here? Or would she have taken a cool look at Hector on the one hand, and the golden key dangled by Crawder on the other, and gone for gold?

She was quits with the dead woman. Performed every act of remembrance and duty she had promised her. It hadn't been her fault that it had come to nothing, in the end. Nesta had to shoulder that one.

Suddenly she knew very clearly what Bea would have done. As always Bea would have tried to get the best of both worlds. As she had when she'd turned a blind eye to her suspicions about Hector's philanderings, knowing she had to share him to keep him. As she had when she had conflicting loyalties as between her natural and her step-daughter. Playing the one off against the other, for the benefit of the business.

Bea would have used that female wit, intelligence and cunning that was far superior to any of the men's: Crawder, Hector, Jamieson, all busy thinking in straight lines, from A to B.

Bea would have had that luxury of a walking away with Jamieson. The days on the beach, the nights making love until she felt relaxed as a cat, and just as dangerous. Then, early one morning, while the poor bastard slept off his Domestica headache, she would have risen early, padded across the marble floor, dressed quietly, and taken the taxi to the airport—a taxi she'd booked the night before.

And once back in England, where there was still the money to be made, still the values to be lived to, she would have gone knocking on Crawder's door. Taken up that job offer. Moved behind that desk. And lived a life that didn't need a fella in it, to make sense.

That's what Bea would have done.

– I thought . . .

Jamieson stopped. Didn't want to say what he had thought, seeing Connie leave the office and Crawder by the back door.

Connie shouldered her travel bag. The one she'd had on her arm the first time he'd seen her.

– Let's make that flight.

They had half an hour.

But before they left, she wanted to have a quick word in the still-waiting Crawder's ear.